Contents

THE
UNACCEPTABLE
FACE

To Joan – my biggest fan.
With Love
Brian Jackson
October '19

BRIAN JACKSON

1

THE UNACCEPTABLE FACE

Copyright © Brian Jackson 2012 (revised 2019)

The Unacceptable Face

PART 1 – 1984

Chapter 1 - The river of time

The house on the corner is silent. For most of the day it has remained bereft of sound and from the loneliness of her armchair in the bay window Helen Allenby watches disconsolately as the late afternoon sun briefly glimmers through the trees rising high on the hillside beyond the houses opposite and the February sky begins to fade through shades of green to darkness, a portent of another freezing night. There had been music playing earlier– scenes and arias from Madame Butterfly – a brief stab at normality but that had long finished; now once more the house is silent.

Tuesday and still no word. Not from Eric, the police, Eric's work; his father. On the point of ringing the police again Helen had faltered, imagining the facetious comments her enquiry would provoke at the station; "Bloody woman's lost her husband and hadn't a clue what he was up to. Must be something up with her. He'll be off with a bit of skirt..." and her fragile self-esteem wouldn't allow that. So Helen sits and waits; for news; for developments; for Eric to come blithely through the door, for normality to return. And later they will make love with passion and an intensity that twenty-five years of marriage could not diminish for, she reassured herself, they were lovers and none of the trials of life could shake that. 'So why this?' she asks herself bitterly, 'How do I come to be sitting here, lonely and distraught at the waning of a cold February afternoon? How could he? How could he?'

Beauchief – 'Beautiful Headland' the Normans had christened the distant wooded hillside centuries before when Sheffield was a mere hamlet and in summer the woods are gloriously lush and alive with birdsong. Now the hill is become a brooding silhouette, dark against the winter sky and as daylight fades a memory rises in Helen's mind and she sees, not the hard outline of Beauchief but the looming mass of an Alpine mountain rising in the darkness. Oh! - that wonderful holiday; their anniversary present to each other. The long drive down the Romantikstrasse, Salzburg, the lakes, moonlight... And in her mind the opening chords of The Alpine

Symphony rise just as the mountain had risen before them in the dawn. Where had they first heard it? Ah yes… There was the sleepy Italian quayside, Punta Sabbioni, a backwater on the lagoon where they had browsed at the battered souvenir stalls, smelling the drifting aroma of coffee and sharing a love of Italy…

The ferry, when it came, took them first to the Lido. Villas set amongst pines in the quiet of the noonday heat retaining an air of Edwardian timelessness, parasols, muslin and malacca canes, as though the journey was deliberately contrived to take them back along the river of time to enter a golden romantic age. The Lido being left at the gateway to the twentieth century they sailed on to enter the seventeenth, past the suspicious water-level eyes of gun ports in the forts emblazoned with the proud lion of St. Mark until they were admitted to the sanctuary of the inner lagoon. The skyline of Venice was instantly familiar and with sunlight sparkling on the water the wooden piles marking the channel formed a guard of honour as they sailed on towards the Palace, the Campanile, the bustle of merchants on the quay, gondolas and the Santa Maria della Salute gleaming in welcome.

They had discovered Venice for themselves. Not amongst a gaggle of tourists, desperately craning in crowded alleys for the guide's raised umbrella but as independent travellers, returning to their hotel tired and exultant. And after dinner, with the sounds of pleasure seekers coming to them from the street below the open window of their room they made love, greedily as though for the first time, each caress made to please the other; long, prolonged, exhausting, then strolled in contentment amongst the cafés with knowledge on their faces and sipped wine whilst the world passed them by. The culmination of their holiday was a return to Venice for oh, what glorious chance, they happened upon La Fenice, once the premier opera house in Europe, marvellously resplendent in green and gold. They took a box, the music of 'Ein Alpensymphonie' flowed over them and with it echoing in their minds once again they consummated their love affair with Italy, with mountains and lakes and above all, Venice…

The doorbell was ringing! Helen started from her reverie, stiff and cramped from sitting too long by the window and went reluctantly to the door, rapidly drawing her composure about her. Frost was already sparkling on the roofs and Jill Morgan, her young neighbour was standing in the sickly yellow glow of the street lamp.

"Oh hello Jill." Helen forced a smile.

"Hope I'm not disturbing you Helen. I wondered if you were alright; whether you'd heard anything."

"Not yet. As a matter of fact I was just dozing."

"Oh I'm sorry Helen. I… I…"

"No it's alright Jill," Helen said, "Come in. I'm just going to make myself a cup of tea. You don't mind kitchen company do you?"

"Well, if you're sure. I shan't stay long, Peter'll be home soon; I've got to get his tea ready." She watched Helen fiddling with the ignition on the hob. Helen, well-groomed as always with her auburn hair falling in soft waves; wearing a sweater over her blouse and a flattering russet skirt but already there was a desolate air about her and the muscles at the corners of Helen's mouth, normally so ready to lift in a smile were sagging. So soon, so quickly. "Can I do anything?" Jill offered.

"No thanks Jill I'm alright. Thanks." Helen bustled with cups and saucers then took a jug from the cupboard and filled it with milk.

"Is there anything you want?"

"No," Helen replied. She turned to the window and glanced out but the garden was hidden in darkness then, quietly, "Well… you know." She pulled the blind down and turned to Jill with a half smile. "Let's have that cup of tea shall we."

They made small talk but it was chatter for chatter's sake. Jill told Helen about the changes at Peter's firm but Helen couldn't respond. At last Jill rose to leave.

"I almost forgot to ask you Helen. Why don't you come round and join us for tea."

"Oh that's good of you Jill but I won't if you don't mind."

"I wish you would," Jill pleaded. "I mean, it'd be a bit of company. You look worn out."

"No," Helen insisted, "I'm fine really."

"Oh well," Jill said, "I'd better go." She hunched her shoulders in the doorway and drew her collar close. "That wind's freezing. Are you sure you won't come?"

"No really. I'd better be here. Just in case. Thanks Jill."

Helen closed the door and retreated inside. She washed and dried the cups and saucers and carefully replaced them on the dresser. Then, in the glow of firelight with the curtains open to the darkness, she resumed her vigil in the armchair by the window...

Wednesday morning. Helen stirred in the chair and blinked, reluctant to emerge from her fitful slumber. The central heating was off and she was cold; her stomach sour with anxiety. She desperately wanted to sleep, endlessly, in a bed beneath the covers then wake and find everything normal again; the table laid with gleaming cutlery, the bustle of breakfast and the house bright with chatter, light and anticipation. But the world she had taken for granted had gone and once again her mind was drifting. Another image arose. Scotland - mist upon the water, sunset gleaming behind the ruined palace, she and Eric in a landscape, the hero and heroine of their own story. "Oh Eric I'm so happy. Thank you for bringing me here." The preparations for the house; a bare plot of earth, the walls rising, the roof, a garden, sunshine, laughter upon the echo, betrayal...

She was slipping away into memory again but the memories were beginning to give rise to an uneasy sense of guilt. But for what? Helen forced herself to get up, determined to banish the insistent, unbidden thoughts as she prepared to face the day. Breakfast was coffee and buttered toast then she brushed her hair and put on a little make-up. The look of care remained, the heaviness around her mouth, the tired eyes. But, Helen told herself, she did feel better.

She checked her watch; five past ten and the day's activity already over.

She willed the 'phone to ring and stood in the angle of the bedroom window gazing down at the road. What would she normally have been doing? Ironing? She recoiled at the idea. Surely the police would telephone. Oh why hadn't she thought to ask...? The milk was still on the doorstep; she hadn't brought it in. Or had she? Perhaps she should change the bed. But it hadn't been used and she couldn't bear the thought of disturbing its pristine neatness. Helen glanced through the window but the road was empty and she turned and threw the bedcovers back violently. There, now it didn't look so neat and smug! But its disarray mocked her and she hated the bed for the untidiness she had imposed on it. Now she would have to demean herself to make it. She reached down to the sheets but withdrew her hand and pressed it to her temple. What is going on? Will someone please tell me? Why won't somebody tell me...

"What is going on!!"

The unexpected sound of her own voice gave Helen a start but the house remained silent. She drew the sheets deftly over the bed and smoothed them down then glanced at herself in the dressing table mirror and went downstairs...

Lunch, a frugal affair was barely over when the doorbell rang. A young policewoman was on the doorstep. Helen took a sharp intake of breath, afraid of the words she might hear but the policewoman gave Helen a look of encouragement. "PC Hammond," she said. "We spoke on the...?"

"Oh yes. Yes, please, come in."

"Thank you." She followed Helen inside and looked round. A comfortable lounge with tasteful prints arranged upon a wall. Mrs. Allenby, well groomed, mid forties, running a home in which friends would be plentiful and welcome. "I'm sorry to have to trouble you Mrs. Allenby. I'd just like to go over things again, make sure we've got everything covered." She pulled out her notebook. "Then I can get out of your way. I mean... You know what I mean."

Helen gestured to the vacant settee.

"Now... May I call you Helen? Do you mind? Now you said Eric didn't usually leave on a Sunday. It wasn't usual."

"That's right."

"But on this occasion he did."

"Yes."

"And he was going to Manchester."

Was it really necessary to go over everything again, repeating things? Helen wished they would leave her alone. "Yes. Well Salford actually?"

"So this meeting was in Salford and Eric was going to be away - how long…?"

"Just 'til Monday. He's com… was coming back Monday evening…" Helen's voice trailed off.

"So he was planning on just being away for the day?"

"Yes! I've said! The meeting was on Monday then he was coming back. He had an appointment on Tuesday. Yesterday. He was coming back."

"Do you know who the appointment was with?" Julie persisted.

"A customer. A big customer he'd just got; a big contract," Helen answered.

"Do you know who this customer was?"

Helen raised her head assertively. "I don't really know a lot about it. Something Textiles," she replied. "Something to do with textiles. They had this new resin for making fabrics. Or something." She felt such a fool; she knew so little. "John would know," she continued lamely. "John James. His boss. They were having this sales meeting," she cried in exasperation. "The sales group. Then Eric was going to see this textile firm."

"Have you got John James's number?"

Helen rose; Julie heard her searching the drawer in the telephone table in the hall then Helen returned with two sheets of typewritten paper stapled together.

"Here's the company list… names and addresses. That's John James' home number there."

Julie wrote the number down then handed the list back. "I wouldn't worry too much Helen… Mrs. Allenby. These sort of cases crop up every day. We get them all the time. At the end of it there's usually a perfectly logical explanation." Julie gave her a smile. "Now I'd better be getting back to the station."

Helen escorted Julie to the front door. The panda car was parked against the verge; Julie's intercom crackled, she lowered her head to her shoulder to take the call and Helen closed the door against the cold. What she needed now was a warm drink and a quiet sit down. Perhaps there was something on the radio; a play or... She felt a headache coming on and went to the kitchen cupboard for the paracetamol. Had she made the bed? For the life of her she couldn't remember and as Helen returned along the hall to the stairs she saw a shadow against the frosted glass doorpanel. She ran to open it but there was no-one; beyond the garden the road was empty and the small hope died. She hadn't really thought...

The bed was made and Helen recalled with a sense of foolishness her earlier fit of protest. She sat on the edge of the bed with an irresistible desire to weep but tears wouldn't come. Overwhelmingly tired she pulled the counterpane aside, kicked her shoes off and laid her head on the pillow. Almost before she had pulled the cover around her Helen was asleep.

Chapter 2 - The Snake

The comfortable suburbs rising west of the city end abruptly and give way to farmland. Beyond Ringinglow and Dore the neat houses and bungalows yield to old stone farms and cottages set in the plateau of moors that begin at Fox House. This is the gateway to the Peak District, Britain's first National Park, a weekend escape from the industry which had made Sheffield grow from a hamlet to the great city which it is today. From Fox House, identified by the moorland inn which bears the name, the road winds past Toad's Mouth, an outcrop of gritstone rock resembling the head of a great toad overhanging a bend, to The Surprise, a sudden drop at the edge of the escarpment and the unsuspecting motorist is met with the wonderful panorama of Hope Valley with the villages of Hathersage, Edale, Castleton and Hope itself stretching away to the high Pennines on the distant skyline. The valley is green and fertile, threaded by the River Derwent and dotted with tourist landmarks like Peveril Castle, a Norman stronghold perched above a cavern; ancient Blue John mines, one of the few places in the world where this unique blue and purple veined rocky flourspar is mined and crafted into ornaments and objets d'art; and the grave of Little John, legendary friend and lieutenant of Robin Hood. In summer the tourists come to wander and picnic, to relax and enjoy themselves. But beyond the valley the moors rising in the west are less accessible unless you are equipped for fell walking and the sudden changes of weather which high altitudes can bring about.

There are two routes across the Pennines from Sheffield to the west unless you take the long route north to Leeds and cross them by the motorway. There is Woodhead, the preferred route for the streams of lorries using it. And then there is The Snake. But whichever route you choose, in winter the Pennines demand that you treat them with respect.

The sun had been dazzlingly bright all morning and as it traversed the valley the frost melted away before it. But high on the Pennines, even under the full glare of the sun, the temperature

13

remained well below freezing. The frost persisted and the heather moors remained white, with dead bracken frozen in crystal shapes and each blade of coarse grass brittle with ice. A straggle of moorland sheep huddled in the lee of a remnant of drystone wall to escape the cold but on top of the moor everything was hanging still and desolate.

The road climbing The Snake from the valley was almost deserted; a lorry toiling laboriously up the long drag and behind it a police car. Rounding a bend a stretch of clear road presented itself and the police Rover surged forward and passed it. The officers were nearing the end of their patrol and for Sergeant Ward it couldn't come too soon. His constable had been sniffling alongside him all morning brewing up a real stinking cold. The car heater was turned full on and Ward knew that if he didn't get out of the car soon he was going to catch it too! If he hadn't caught it already!

Now they were clearing the pine plantations; two more bends would see them emerging at the top then the long descent to Glossop, turn round and home. Sergeant Ward grunted to his constable and pointed. Ahead of them a car was parked close against the parapet of a small stone bridge below which a culvert channelled the mountain stream beneath the road. Normally the stream would be pouring in torrents into the ravine; now only the merest trickle dripped from the funnel of ice at the mouth of the culvert. Ward eased the Rover onto the patch of rough ground behind the parked car.

"Well, go on then. Go and take a look." It would be a relief to have Harris and his snotty nose out of the car for a bit.

Harris stepped out reluctantly and approached the car. It was glistening with frost, so thickly encrusted that its number plate was illegible. He bent and scraped at it then consulted a list of numbers on the clipboard he was carrying. "This is it sarge," he called.

Ward stirred and climbed with resignation from the Rover. "We'd better have a closer look at it then hadn't we!" The cold hit him with an intensity that stung his nose and ears. "Christ!" He drew his overcoat rapidly about him. "Better leave 'engine running."

Harris was trying the car's doors. "Locked," he reported.

14

"Well get 'scraper; have a look inside." Ward rubbed his gloved hands against the ice on the window and gave the driver's door a tug. It remained secure. "Come on then get a move on." He took the scraper from the constable and set to work on the windscreen. A fine dust of ice covered his gloves, getting into his cuffs. He stopped and peered through the small patch he had cleared. "Can't see a bloody thing!" He gave the scraper back to Harris. "Here get that side window cleared. Christ its bloody cold." He peered dismissively at the interior again. "Nothing!" Ward grunted. "Not a bloody thing."

"There's some papers and files looks like. On the back seat," Harris said. "And a briefcase." He continued staring intently.

"What's up?" Ward grunted impatiently. "What else you seen?"

"Nothing much." Harris remained focussed. "There's a little notebook; beside the front seat. Could be an address book."

Ward approached and shook his head dismissively. "Don't think so. There's a name on the cover, a title or something." He twisted his head round to try and read the words. "No. Can't make it out." He stepped back and stood surveying the empty landscape with the road winding back down the ravine. The lorry was just hauling into sight, the haze of its exhaust hanging in the air. Above him the road disappeared behind the final shoulder of the hill half a mile ahead to the summit. Across the road the moor fell vertical to the shadowy floor of the ravine where not even the thin wind ventured from the open moor above. Ward turned to his constable. "Any keys?"

Harris bent and peered beneath the steering column. "No; nothing. Must have taken 'em with him."

"H'm." Ward surveyed the scene once more. "Better report it then. No sign of damage?"

They circled the car. Nothing, only the crystal rime of frost over everything. Harris headed back to the warmth of the Rover.

"Where you going then?"

Harris sniffled. "I were just…"

"Better have a look round."

Harris looked at his sergeant. "What for?"

"Him," Ward replied. "What's his name… Allenby."

"Nay, come on sarge."

"Won't be far away will he?" Ward looked up the road leading to the summit. "Look where we are. Middle of bloody nowhere. Next stops 'bloody sky. Can't have gone far; nowhere to go!"

Harris pressed his sodden handkerchief against his nose. It was starting to become sore and he wanted to get back inside where it was warm and cosy. "Perhaps he went for a piss."

Ward was scornful. "What, and locked 'car up? Frightened somebody were going to pinch it? One of 'passers-by?"

"Well I don't bleeding know do I?" Harris replied resentfully. "Christ its bitter."

Ward searched for inspiration. He didn't want to be back up here again. Not this side of winter anyway. He crossed the road to the rail guarding the ravine.

"Perhaps he fell over 'edge."

"What, down there?" Harris could see which way his sergeant's mind was working.

"Better have a look." Ward peered down into the ravine.

"Bloody hell sarge I'm frozen already. I'm not going down there."

"Come on," Ward insisted. "Bit of exercise'll do you good. Can't be far away. You take 100 yards down 'road – I'll go up."

They examined the ravine, peering into the depths, looking for signs, anything which would reveal if someone had fallen, scrambled, slithered from the road above. But there was no sign of anything. Nothing had disturbed the even pattern of frost lying over everything.

"Better report it then." Ward led the way back to the car and paused with his hand on the door. "But where the hell's he got to? I mean, where can you go?" He gestured helplessly. "Look at it."

"Perhaps he met a bird and decided to stay on," Harris offered and climbed inside. "God, that's better."

Ward took his seat beside him. "Wouldn't meet a bird out here though would he. Not this time of year anyway. Alright in summer but not much fun this time of year."

"Might." The constable reached over to the back seat for the flask. The smell of hot coffee filled the car as he removed the stopper.

"Nay, come on," Ward retorted. "If you were meeting a bird you'd meet in town. Wouldn't you? You wouldn't leave your car up here. Would you? Eh! Now would you?" He reached for coffee. "Christ we're steaming up."

"Don't open your window," Harris cried, "Put 'blower on."

Ward grimaced. "No bloody sugar in it. Again!"

"Well why don't you bring your own then!"

Ward settled back in his seat. "Better call in and tell 'em we've found it."

Chapter 3 - White lies and deceptions

Helen woke as though rising from the depths of the ocean, emerging from darkness into a world of sound and consciousness. The sleep had done her good and she savoured the warmth of the bed then reality swept over her and she was seized with guilt. She rose and washed her face and prepared to face the evening.

The telephone rang. Helen gave herself a final inspection in the mirror, pursing her lips in critical approval and crossed to the phone standing on the bedside table amongst the clutter of Eric's pen, his small notepad and spare glasses, and raised the handset from its cradle.

"Hi Hel. Are we still alright for Sunday?" It was Rita, speaking with her usual lack of preamble. Helen pictured her friend. Misfortune seemed to have added to Rita's character, leaving her just the right side of a size fourteen and with an attractively underplayed worldliness. Helen pictured Rita at home immersed in the chaos and bric-a-brac that always seemed to surround her. Rita's blonde hair would be pulled up on top of her head and gripped in an outrageous plastic clip and she would look wonderful, bouyant and attractive. "…should have phoned before," she heard Rita say, "but you know what it's like. I've been so busy; time's flown. I don't know where it went. It was Susan who reminded me; we're all looking forward to it."

Helen tried to concentrate on Rita's chatter and felt a pang of guilt. Though she had been Rita's confidante throughout Rita's troubled relationships she hadn't confided Eric's absence to her. What to say now? Surely he won't be gone another night, then who need know? Helen's mouth opened, seeking a response and suddenly she was seized with a surge of unreasonable irritation. How could Rita ring her about pleasure at a time like this? Surely Rita must sense something was wrong. They spoke to each other most days; how could she be so uncaring? But even as she was thinking these thoughts Helen knew she was being unfair and trying to remember the original question she replied, "I think so. Yes."

"You alright Hel?"

"Migraine," Helen lied. "I was… I was just sleeping."

"Ahh." Rita's voice dropped in sympathy. "Have you had the lights?"

"I've taken some paracetomol. I was trying to sleep it off."

"Sorry love; sorry to have disturbed you. I'll give you a ring tomorrow." An afterthought. "Is Eric alright?"

Did Rita know something? Why doesn't she just come out and say it? Helen's mind became confusion. "Sorry Reet. He's… I'll… I'll have to go."

"Alright love."

The phone immediately rang again; a man's voice, vaguely familiar, asking for her by name. Helen couldn't place him and it gave rise to further unease. "Yes?" she answered cautiously.

"John James," the voice said.

"Oh John, yes," Helen replied, flustered, "I'm sorry… just for the moment I didn't… Yes, John. Of course." She had never met the man but she had a mental picture of someone younger, full of ideas and on his way. The Christmas card he'd sent still rankled and Helen did her best to be polite. "I was just in the middle of doing something," she lied.

"I'm sorry. If it's not convenient…"

"No, no," Helen protested, her mind racing, wondering what to say. He had telephoned her on Monday morning saying Eric had failed to arrive at the hotel and on the spur of the moment, knowing nothing, she had said Eric was ill in bed. She had lied for him and that had been the start of it.

"Is there any news of Eric?" James was saying, "I've had the police on," and Helen's heart sank. "They were asking if Eric had been at the hotel. Whether he'd arrived then left. Stuff like that."

"I'm sorry John. When you phoned on Monday I didn't know," Helen replied simply.

"I wish you'd told me. We might have been able…" The voice paused and changed. "Are you alright Helen? I mean, is there anything…?"

"I didn't know what to say to you."

"We haven't had time to get to know each other properly. When Eric's back we'll make some arrangements. Dinner together. I'll get Monica to come along. Perhaps we could do a show."

Helen hesitated, that unnerving sense of guilt rising again. "What are they saying? Eric's colleagues. What are they saying about him?"

"They don't know anything. I told them what you told me." Accusation crept into his voice. "I wouldn't have known anything either Helen if the police hadn't called me."

"What are you going to tell them?"

"What do you want me to say?"

"I'd rather you didn't say anything. Not for the moment. Not until…"

"Alright. But you will tell me won't you, as soon as… when Eric gets back."

Helen drew herself erect. "Yes, of course. Did the police… have any ideas?"

"They were just asking about the meeting, travel arrangements." He paused then added, "Is there anything you need?"

"No," Helen replied.

"You will let me know?"

"Yes."

"Yes – right. I'll call you again. Unless you…"

With relief Helen heard the front doorbell. "There's someone here. I must go."

"Yes. Of course."

Helen replaced the handset, checking herself again in the mirror as she went downstairs and opened the door to Julie Hammond. "Oh, hello," she said, hope and anxiety in equal measure flowing through her. "Please, come in."

Julie followed Helen in and took a position before the fireplace. "We've just had a message Mrs. Allenby. We've found your husband's car."

Helen seemed to grow in stature; she became suffused with energy, more erect. "Oh what a relief. Oh, you don't know what a relief that is." Helen cupped her hands over her mouth, shaking her head and screwed her eyes closed. "Oh," she sighed at last, "such things come into your head. You've no idea." She went to the window, glanced briefly outside then turned to Julie. "Thank you. Thanks for letting me know. Oh what a relief. How is he? Is he alright?"

Julie sought to give reassurance. "We don't know. Not yet."

"But you said... you said you'd found him."

"No I'm sorry Mrs. Allenby, we..."

"You just said you'd found him!" Helen protested wildly. "You said you've found him."

"No Mrs. Allenby. We've found Eric's – Mr. Allenby's car."

"His car?" Helen's face clouded in bewilderment and she sank into the chair by the window.

"Mrs. Allenby," Julie said earnestly, "Helen. We've found Mr. Allenby's car. Locked up and parked - safe and sound. I just came to let you know. We think he's probably... gone somewhere."

Helen scanned Julie's face, searching for deceit. "There hasn't been an accident has there? Tell me. Please, you must tell me."

"No," Julie replied, relieved she could answer with truth, "There hasn't been an accident."

Helen searched Julie's face again. "You would tell me? You're sure?"

"Of course. Of course I would Helen."

Helen's body sagged with relief. "I could do with a cup of tea."

"So could I. Come on, show me where the things are. I'll help you to make it."

They sat and Helen rested her elbows on the kitchen table and pressed her fingers against her temple, speaking softly as though to herself. "There was to be a dinner in the evening. For all of them. Eric didn't want to go and I resented it too. Breaking into the weekend like that. But he had to go." Helen paused. "It was expected." She raised her head with an expression of earnest appeal. "I mean, it's a good company, don't get me wrong. It's just that... Four o'clock he went. He should have been there by six." She appealed to Julie. "Shouldn't he?"

21

"Six thirty latest," Julie replied and added, probing gently, "Did you go out at all?

"When?"

"Sunday evening."

"No. Why?" Helen resented the question.

"I just thought Mr. Allenby might have phoned while you were out."

"No," Helen replied and then, more vehemently, "Anyway even if I had he'd have telephoned later. Or left a message."

Julie pressed ahead. "What about Monday?"

"Monday? No, I've told you. I haven't heard from Eric at all."

"And you didn't go out?"

"Well yes. Monday morning. I was out for some of the morning. Just for an hour." There was something else, something behind the officer's gentle probing. Helen hesitated then said, "He wouldn't have called then, would he? He was supposed to be in a meeting. That's what he'd gone for."

"Perhaps in his coffee break?"

"No!" Helen cried. "I've told you. He'd have called in the evening. But he didn't! He didn't... Not at all. Not Sunday or Monday or..."

"How do you know if you were out?" Julie persisted.

"Because John James called! His bloody boss called! That's why."

Julie regarded Helen in brief silence and replied carefully, "I'm sorry Helen. I just wanted to be sure. I spoke to Mr. James. He said you told him Mr. Allenby was ill. That he was here. At home."

There was conflict in Helen's eyes. "I didn't know then. Eric hadn't called me. But I wasn't worried. Then John James called and... and I just wanted to cover up for him."

"Cover up?"

"He's been under pressure. He doesn't like John James. Not like his previous boss. I didn't want him to get into trouble. So I said he was ill."

"Where did you think Mr. Allenby was?"

22

"I don't know." Helen's head was spinning and she began pacing the kitchen. "I don't know. Anywhere! In a hotel! In another town! I wish I knew!"

"I'm sorry Helen. But… we need to be sure." Helen stood gazing through the kitchen window and Julie changed her tone. "Come on," the young policewoman coaxed her. "Come and sit down. Was Eric alright when he left?"

Helen turned sharply. "How do you mean?"

"You hadn't been arguing… or anything?"

"No!" Helen cried indignantly. "What are you suggesting?"

"I'm not suggesting anything. I just wondered, was he alright? He wasn't acting strangely? Any differently?"

"No," Helen protested. "Look – officer! We are happily married! I don't know what is in your mind but we are perfectly happy. We have been… for so many… twenty years... longer... since before…" Her voice tailed off and tears began streaming down her cheeks. "I don't know… where he…" She couldn't form the words; Julie fished out a handkerchief and Helen wiped her eyes. "I'm sorry," she mumbled, "I'm just so worried."

"I know," Julie said. "You might feel a bit better for that."

Helen gave Julie a wan smile. "I didn't mean to be disrespectful."

"Will you be alright? Would you like me to fetch a neighbour to sit with you?"

"No!" An afterthought, "Thank you."

Julie began to gather the cups but Helen said, "No. Leave them." She couldn't have a stranger handling her things. "It'll give me something to do. Occupy my mind a bit," she concluded flatly.

Julie took a long look at Helen. "Well, if you're sure."

Helen drew herself upright and dabbed her eyes and forced a false smile. Julie smiled in return. "And if there's any more news…" She gave Helen a quizzical look; there was something else, a sudden preoccupation that Julie couldn't pinpoint. "What is it?" she asked.

"It's his father," Helen said unexpectedly, "He doesn't know yet. I mean…" She heaved a sigh. "I haven't had a chance to tell him."

"But there's nothing to tell is there. Why not wait a bit longer?"

"We never got on. But… he ought to know." Helen flared again, "Why should I have all the worry? He ought to know…"

"Do you want me to wait while you phone him?"

"No," Helen said, "I've got to go. To tell him myself. In person."

"Are you sure?"

"I've got to tell him," Helen insisted. "It'll be alright won't it? It won't matter will it?"

"If you really think you ought to."

"Yes I do."

Julie bowed to the inevitable. "Of course." She gave Helen a final reassuring nod and left.

Chapter 4 – Paterfamilias

The house was at the end of a row of Victorian terraces with double bay windows at the front with the door between them and a tiny concreted area, a low wall, and artificial shrubs in plastic tubs. Nothing had changed and Helen heard the distant sound of forge hammers rising from the industry in the valley below. The door opened and George Allenby looked at her with surprise. His rounded shoulders reduced his height from the six feet he had been in his prime but his face was remarkably unlined and, Helen noted, even in his seventies he still dyed the grey out of his hair. She gave a weak smile of greeting.

"Hello dad."

"Oh," he said. "Helen." There was reproach in his voice; it was seven months since Helen and Eric's last visit. "You'd better come in. Shut door. It's cold." He returned to the living room and sat before the gas fire rubbing his blue-veined hands. "Where's our Eric? Parking?"

Helen sidestepped the question and looked about the room. "You've been decorating again."

"It wanted doing," he replied shortly. "Some paint I had left over from work. Been lying around in the cellar. It wanted using. I like green. Cream and green." Helen sat on the settee before the fire and warmed herself. So many times she had heard the litany. Somewhere in his past Eric's father had lived in a home decorated in cream and green, a home where he had been happy. She heard his continuing self-justification. "I don't know why. They go together perfect. You can't get anything better," he insisted, "always looks clean. I've always liked it. You haven't been up for a bit. Come and see my bathroom. Come and see how I've done it. It's lovely..." He hauled himself from his chair and went out to the small lobby inside the front door and began to climb the stairs. "Come on, I've had a new stair rail fitted. Much easier having two."

Helen sighed and followed him up to the chill bathroom. The doorframe and bathroom cupboard were an appalling shade of pink.

The pink bath panel was quilted plastic and on the wall above the bath was a pink plastic splashback with moulded shelves.

"I got it from the market," Eric's father preened. "They go well together don't they? It sets it off." He gestured at the clutter of tubes and plastic mugs. "And I can keep all me bits and pieces on the shelves without 'em getting wet."

Helen followed his gesture. "Yes," she said.

"Only cheap but it makes it look really nice," he repeated with self-congratulatory emphasis, "Makes it look good! Really good! I painted the cupboards up to match. Only took me a day. What d'you think?"

Helen wished she were somewhere else. It was a mistake and she wished she had listened to the policewoman. "Nice," she said.

"Do you like it?" he insisted.

"Yes," Helen said flatly, "It's lovely."

"Where's our Eric? You haven't been up for ages." The voice held accusation again. "You ought to come up a bit more. People notice, you know." He led the way grumbling down the stairs as he made the slow descent into the warmth. "He doesn't come up as often as he should. When was the last time you came up?"

"Dad…"

"Well you've got to be fair about things. I know!" He leaned over the fire, rubbing his hands, "Him over the road, his family's always in and out. I should have had more family." He turned and regarded her malevolently. "And I would have done if things had been different. Instead of having only one." Helen tried again but he overrode her. "D'you know what I'd have liked? What I'd have really liked? Lots of grandchildren climbing up on my knee." He gestured at the window again. "He does. Over there. And people notice these things."

Helen suppressed a sigh and patted the arm of his chair. "Here dad, sit down. I'll put the kettle on."

She went into the kitchen and heard him calling, "There isn't any trouble is there? Where's our Eric?"

Helen closed her eyes and bit her lip. "I'll tell you in a minute," she replied unsteadily.

"Eh?"

"In a minute." She drew two or three deep breaths. "When I've made the tea."

The kitchen was cold and she shivered. It was a mistake! He wasn't here. It had been a wild hope; she couldn't think why she had ever thought it likely but what else was there to think? Well he had to be somewhere. Why not here, seeking some sort of refuge with his father? Why not? Now she was here Helen knew why not; she had known the instant she entered the house.

"Bring some biscuits," the cry came from the living room. "In the cupboard over your head."

Helen reached for the tin and placed a few damp biscuits on a plate.

"You haven't had a row have you?" Unmistakable satisfaction in his voice. "Is that it? There's something isn't there? You've had a row. You've never come up here on your own. I can't remember the last time you came up with our Eric. I only see him once in a blue moon."

Helen was close to exasperation. "Where's the caddy?"

"In the cupboard. Do you want me to...?"

"No! I'll get it."

She made the tea while the voice of accusation continued. "It'd have to be something wouldn't it! I don't know what's wrong. I only ask you to come up and see me sometimes. Our George never comes. Me own brother! If I didn't make the effort I shouldn't see 'em from one year-end to the next. Can you manage in there? Don't fill the kettle right up; it'll never boil."

Helen carried the tray through and set it down on the hearth.

"Just let it mash," she said. "Have you had anything to eat?"

"I had some pork pie for me dinner," he replied with satisfaction. "There's some left if you want it. Do you want a piece?"

"No thanks," Helen replied and added hastily, "Do you want me to get you anything?"

George Allenby shook his head and Helen poured the tea while his small snake eyes watched her from the smooth contours of his face. His stare made Helen uncomfortable; it always had. Helen averted her face and pretended to be admiring the newly decorated room.

"You've split up haven't you? And he won't come and tell me himself. That's it isn't it?"

"No I..." She hesitated.

"I knew it," he cried. "It's in your face! In the eyes. You can tell. Always look at the eyes; they're the mirror of the soul. You can't hide it in your eyes. It always shows." He paused, waiting for Helen to respond.

"Can't I come and see you now without there's something going on?" She spoke unsteadily. He regarded her carefully over the rim of his cup and Helen made an excuse. "I'll just go and see if I turned the kettle off. I can't remember if ..." She escaped into the kitchen, trying to regain her composure then returned to the sitting room. "Anyway," she said with an attempt at brightness, "how have you been?"

"I'm alright," he replied. "Have to be." The criticism continued unabated. "I'm not daft you know. You think I don't notice things. I can see more than you can tell; do you think I don't know? I've never understood why you never bother to come up and see me. Like a normal family."

Helen gave reconciliation a final chance. "Well I'm here to see you now dad. Come on, don't keep going on."

But it was no use. Although George Allenby allowed himself to be mollified there was an unbridgeable gulf between them. It had been built and widened every year since Helen and Eric had announced their engagement under his disapproving gaze. And for no reason that Helen could find. She had never sought to distance Eric from his father; George Allenby had done that with his icy disapproval. And so this visit failed too under the strain of Helen's deception and the old man's suspicious perception. Helen finished her tea hurriedly.

"Are you having some more?" he demanded. "There's plenty."

"No dad, I've drunk more tea..." Helen checked herself and continued quickly, "I've got to get my bus; I daren't miss it."

"Well if you're going... Leave them," he ordered as Helen bent to carry the teapot and cups away and she heard her own words echoed. "I'll do 'em. Give me something to do. It gets lonely. You need something to pass the time..."

Chapter 5 - The masquerade

Once more the short afternoon closed and the sickly glow of the street lamps accentuated the darkness outside. Helen was listening to Jill and trying to resist her young neighbours' earnest invitation.

"I'm doing some chops for Peter. It's not very special but…"

"I won't if you don't mind."

"I wish you would Helen. It'd be a bit of company. You look worn out."

"Yes," Helen conceded. "It's the waiting." She began moving aimlessly about the kitchen. "It's ever so good of you Jill. It's just the police; they promise to let you know; and then you don't hear anything from them." She forced a smile of reassurance. "I might do a bit of bacon and an egg later."

"You will let me know won't you Helen."

"The moment I hear anything."

The doorbell rang and Jill followed Helen to the front door. It was a police sergeant with Julie Hammond at his shoulder.

"Oh," Helen said with a fleeting smile of recognition.

"I wonder if I might step inside a moment," the sergeant said.

Jill said, "It's alright Helen. Let me know if there's anything you need."

As Helen led the sergeant toward the lounge he gave Julie an imperceptible nod and she placed a restraining hand on Jill's arm before following him. Helen was in full flow, "…and I didn't know where his car was. I forgot to ask and nobody told me. I didn't like to ask then. You feel such a fool." She stopped as Julie entered.

"You know Constable Hammond of course Mrs. Allenby. I'm Sergeant Ward. Would you mind sitting down please." Helen sat; he took a chair opposite and marshalled his thoughts. An aeon of time descended between them. "Mrs. Allenby," he began. His voice was grave, clear and respectful. Helen adopted a hopeful look to sweep away the doubts hovering about her, giving nods of understanding, a nod punctuating each measured word. "We have found your husband Mrs. Allenby."

Found? Helen's brain shrieked. Say what you have come to say, say it quickly.

"I'm afraid he's..." Sergeant Ward watched Helen carefully. "I'm sorry to tell you... Eric is dead."

Helen sat immobile, unreality all about her in the distant room; artificial light, faces watching. She couldn't understand her incomprehension; she could not understand why her mind was debating logic. All she wanted was to hear his words again so she could deny them. The face before her cleared into focus and she heard the sergeant's voice, close, concerned and appealing trying to reach her.

"Mrs. Allenby. Are you alright Mrs. Allenby?"

As he spoke a sound rose, breaking from Helen in a long wail of grief and falling on them with despair, "Noooo!!!"

Julie Hammond crouched at Helen's knees. "Helen. I'm so very sorry." She looked across at the sergeant but Jill was already in the room. Convulsed by sobs Helen gulped for air until the sobs were broken by another rising cry of grief, "No... no... no..."

Jill put her arms about her. "Oh Helen, Helen. It's alright. Let it come, let it all come," and Jill's encouraging words drove the tears from Helen; she looked up at Jill as though recognising her for the first time and turned from Jill to Sergeant Ward.

"I want to see him." Her voice broken, almost inaudible.

"Please Mrs. Allenby..."

"Where is he?" Stronger, more insistent. "I want to see him."

Ward tried to give reassurance. "I'm very sorry to have to break it to you like this."

"I want to see him," Helen repeated. Her voice was low but determined and she sat motionless, searching in the weave of the carpet for some meaning to emerge, something in its pattern to explain the events unfolding about her. "You told me you'd found the car. That it was safe."

"It was," Ward said quietly, "We won't know anything more until..." He paused, the image of the abandoned car up on that lonely road vivid in his mind. He hoped she wouldn't press him to elaborate further, "...until after the post mortem. There'll probably need to be an inquest."

Helen began weeping softly.

"Is there anyone you'd like us to call for you?" Jill asked. "Your mum? Eric's...?"

Helen shook her head. "Not yet. Sorry; I'm..." She braced herself. "Could you let Rita know..."

It didn't look like Eric. Here was something masquerading as if to say, 'I've come in his place, a substitute for the man you used to love.' Helen felt the hot surge of tears, not for herself but for Eric, for everything he had been. Where was the smile, the energy? Where was the man? Where was love? What happened to the love he gave me? Where has it gone? I feel nothing now. This cannot love or have hopes or dream and aspire, or excite me and embrace me. This is not what I knew and she spoke gentle, inaudible words, "I'm sorry Eric. So sorry," and turned away. "It doesn't look like..." she murmured and saw their sharp quizzical glance. "No, I'm alright. Really, I'm alright. It's just that... he doesn't look like... I'm sorry, yes it's... Eric."

Back at home with Rita and her mother she began the unending calls. She knew she would have to tell them and the visits would begin. No! No! Not today. Let me just get through another day. And she replaced the handset

"Do you want me to call?"

Helen looked at Rita; their eyes remained locked. "Alright," Helen sighed, "you're right."

The call to George Allenby was difficult and prolonged. Helen found herself apologising defensively against the old man's resentful accusations until Rita took the telephone from her, added her condolences to Helen's and ended the call. In the evening Jill came and joined them and they sat in silences until the time came for them to leave.

"Thanks Jill. I'll be alright now. Really mum I will. Promise."

"I'll look in again tomorrow Helen."

"Yes. Thanks Rita. You've been a brick."

"No more than Jill." They exchanged a wistful smile. "Now you're sure?"

"Yes."

"Goodnight then."

Goodnight! Such a strange, inappropriate word. The night was filled with images tumbling incoherently together; silent figures confronting one another, the mute reaching out of hands, twin pinpoints of light like red eyes receding in the darkness, winking and winking again until they slowly disappeared; and a blank expressionless face...

Saturday dawned with snow; not the blizzard that was piling in drifts on the High Peak but a thin, swirling, miserable sleet gusting out of the laden sky. Helen stared through the bedroom window towards the high moors beyond the swirling flakes, then she turned away and tears were rimming her eyes.

Chapter 6 – Immolation

Within the chapel Helen presented a picture of quiet dignity. She would not entertain them with a harrowing display of emotion; her tears, shed in private, were for herself alone, to quench the anger hidden beneath the sorrow. She felt the eyes of the mourners on her and as the curtain parted she made an involuntary movement of almost imperceptible subtlety, as though the coffin bearing Eric away would draw her with it, then lowered her head and sat bowed, alone amongst the overflowing pews. Afterwards in the cold corridor lined with flowers and supported by Rita and her mother Helen stood while they filed past, each one pausing as if making an act of loyalty to a matriarch with a murmur and deferential touch of sympathy, and each receiving a wan smile of silent appreciation before they were discreetly ushered out to the purring black limousines.

They were grateful for the meal. Eating enabled them to shed the sombre mood of restraint and conversation began to flow around the room. As Helen rose from her seat expectant faces turned to her and George Allenby banged his spoon on the table and scratched his neck in embarrassment. There were so many people and Helen felt light-headed. "Excuse me," she began. "Ladies and… Could I…?" She reached for her glass of mineral water as calls for silence hushed the room. "Thank you. I would just like to… to thank you all. It's… I was going to say it's so nice to see you… I don't mean that. I'm sure you know what I mean. Our friends; Eric's friends; the family." Her gaze rested on John James and Reeder. "Eric's colleagues from work." She raised her head with determination. "Thank you for coming. I wish we could all have met… Not like this but…" Helen's control began to fail; she searched for a handkerchief; in the embarrassed silence there was a single attempt at applause but Helen remained standing. It was time for reconciliation and again her eyes swept the room. "This is a sad time for all of us," she continued. "I don't think I shall ever get over it. But I ask you to commiserate with me for dad, Eric's father." She looked down at George Allenby.

"It is a terrible thing for a parent to bury a child." George Allenby's hand reached out to Helen's and he muttered something with his head lowered, gently nodding amongst low murmurs of approval. Helen hesitated, other memories engulfed her and she sat down.

Uncle Tom, wearing a black silk armband over the sleeve of his ancient suit rose from his seat. He had been a schoolmaster until his retirement; known to stop and raise his hat in the street at any passing funeral and he regarded himself as the guardian of tradition.

"My dear friends," he began in his high, precise voice and the assembly fell into attentive silence. "I call you all friends although there are some here that I have not met before. We meet today as one, in friendship, to honour the passing of Eric from amongst us and to pay our respects to his memory. Helen your tears and distress on this occasion..." The orator droned on. "...the loss of Eric is deeply felt... honoured, yes honoured by all who knew him... in the operatic society... faces here today well known on the stages of this city... a thorough professional... always be relied on... honoured by all who knew him... our sympathy must go to Eric's widow..." At the word 'widow' Helen averted her face and Rita glared at Uncle Tom. With open-mouthed realisation Uncle Tom hastened to his peroration. "And now would you all charge your glasses" - a bustle of activity - "and join me in drinking to the memory of our dear departed friend, colleague, husband, Eric."

They raised their glasses then the chatter of relief was stilled as another figure rose to speak.

"Who's that?" Rita whispered. The new speaker was standing between Reeder and Uncle Tom, now sitting with his head lowered in an attitude of meditation.

"John James," Helen murmured. "Eric's boss."

James inclined his head to Helen. "I couldn't hope to follow, with any adequacy, the tribute which has gone before. But I am here today with my colleague Mr. Reeder on behalf of Eric's many friends and colleagues at work. And really, all I would like to say is how sadly Eric will be missed by all of us at International. Eric had a first class career with us and we have been prematurely robbed of his wise counsel. Thank you." With another inclination to Helen he resumed his seat.

Now the guests began to rise from their places, moving and regrouping to exchange memories with those they would not see again until the next funeral brought them together. Two elderly aunts approached, Uncle Tom's wife Hilda and Great Aunt Freda, heavily wrinkled with deep creases in her leathery face. Aunt Hilda took Helen's hand and squeezed it with heartfelt sincerity. "Wasn't that nice Helen; that young man speaking up for Eric like that."

Great Aunt Freda pushed herself forward. "Is he from Eric's work?"

"It's Eric's boss Aunty Freda."

"They must have thought a lot about Eric," the old lady replied. "Who's the other one?"

Helen saw Reeder glancing at his watch. "Oh, that's Mr. Reeder. He's from Eric's work as well."

"They thought a lot about him you know," Hilda said earnestly and Helen gave the two old ladies a wan smile and bit her lip as another elderly member of the family approached, her face set in a mask of sympathy.

Rita appeared at her side, "You okay love?" and Helen detached herself with relief from the group assembling round her.

"Thanks Rita. They're er…"

"I know love. It won't be long. Be a good job when today's over."

Helen gestured toward Reeder and John James, standing apart and engaged in discreet discussion. "I'm going to have to see them. Come with me will you…"

As Helen approached them John James stepped forward but Helen forestalled him. "Excuse me John," and turned her attention to Reeder. "I suppose I should thank you for coming Mr. Reeder. Do you always do this or was Eric special?" Helen met Reeder's eyes steadily. "Only it's so… so…"

John James tried to retake the initiative. "I'm so sorry Helen. We'll all miss him."

Without turning to face him she said, "Well, you said such nice things about him. It's nice to know Eric was so well thought of."

Reeder took Helen's hand in a practised grasp of sincerity. "I'm sorry we never had the opportunity to get to know each other better Mrs. Allenby. It's too late now of course. I echo everything John said. Eric is going to be missed."

"Really!" Helen replied.

Reeder gave a benevolent nod. "And you'll be well looked after Mrs. Allenby. That's one thing about a company like International, we do try to look after our people."

Helen braced herself. This wasn't the right place or time but she owed it to Eric; if she didn't say it now the moment would be lost and there would never be another. "You shit!" Her quiet words spoken with unexpected venom took Rita by surprise but Reeder didn't flinch. "You hypocrite," Helen hissed. "Why didn't you value him when he was alive? You bastard, I wish he'd never met you, you bastard."

Reeder returned Helen's look with an unresponsive gaze and then George Allenby arrived, deferential in the presence of the two company men. "I'm off Helen. I don't want to get back too late. Goodbye Mr...?"

"Let me introduce you," Helen said disdainfully. "Mr. James, Eric's boss and Mr. Reeder, his boss." She gestured. "This is Eric's father."

"Very pleased to meet you," George Allenby said.

Reeder shook George Appleby's hand. "I wish it could have been in happier circumstances. Your son was a great asset to the business."

"Yes." George Allenby smiled sadly. "He was so well thought of by everybody."

"Well goodbye Mr. Allenby. Mrs. Allenby." Reeder offered his hand. "We must be off too. Business waits for no man I'm afraid."

"If you'll excuse me," Helen said icily, ignoring his hand as she turned on her heel, "I have friends to talk to..."

"What was that all about?" Rita asked as they walked away.

Helen replied softly, "Nobody else heard did they?"

"No," Rita replied and Helen sighed.

"We'd better mingle..." She hesitated. "Look... Reet... I wonder... can you come over tomorrow? Would you mind? I need... There's some things I need to talk about."

Chapter 7 - A séance

Helen threw her dark clothes off with relief. The brief confrontation combined with the kind, sympathetic tactfulness of the afternoon had denied her any peace of mind and her eyes were drawn to Eric's photograph beside the bed. It gave her his smile and a longing rose inside her and she set music playing - Rachmaninov, a hymn of love - while she ran a scented bath and immersed herself deep in the embracing foam, and gave herself to her memories. As the music of the piano ended it was replaced by a long forgotten song rising into her mind from God knows where, the dusky voice of Johnny Mathis – 'A certain smile' - and a pang of memory as sharp as an arrow shot through her; she was nineteen again and a bittersweet smile turned the corners of Helen's mouth. There was Eric, waiting for her on the corner by the shoe shop opposite the Town Hall as she stepped down from the tram in her new, tightly belted white gaberdine mac. He was wearing that white sports jacket and his face lit in delight as he swaggered towards her. "You look wonderful."

"Thank you kind sir." She kissed him lightly and lowered her head. "You don't think I've overdone it do you?"

"Not a bit," he smiled as he took her hand. "You look like a film star."

Their favourite café was The Sidewalk in a narrow lane near the cathedral with a basement lounge dominated by the huge golden head of a Pharoah. They ordered Danish open sandwiches and then, unable to contain her excitement Helen produced a carefully folded copy of the morning paper.

"It's just off Ecclesall Road," she declared. "A house!"

"A house," Eric echoed.

"I telephoned this lunchtime. Part furnished £11 per calendar month plus 7/6 per week for cooker. I had to be quick. We've got an interview with the agent tomorrow morning."

"A house," Eric repeated earnestly. "Now we'll be able to get married…"

Later, in the corner by the nurse's hostel they kissed their lingering goodnight deep in the shadow of the trees. Eric so ardent and reluctant to release her; driven by all the desire of youth he sighed in ecstasy as he reached down to raise her skirt and Helen, sharing his desire consoled him with her kisses and frustrated by the imminent curfew she smoothed down her skirt and pulled her coat about her. "I must go," she murmured as she gave him a gentle parting kiss, a token to carry him home. "I'll be late if I don't go now." And aching with frustration Eric watched her as she disappeared into the darkness with the promise of her parting whisper echoing in his ears, "Tomorrow…"

Tomorrow! Helen emerged from her reverie. Rita was coming tomorrow! The bathwater had grown cool and she shivered as she stepped out, seeking comfort in the soft folds of her robe.

She turned the television on and sipped a glass of the deep red wine of Italy and sitting there she thanked God they had been spared the gift of prophecy. Images flickered across the screen and the bland sound of laughter filled the silence and her mind wandered to Eric's father across the city, sitting in embittered loneliness, listening to the same laughter with the same indifference and Helen knew, without regret, that she would never see George Allenby again.

A blustery wind was massing clouds high over the distant moors as Helen woke and prepared to face the day. She dressed carefully and sighed before the mirror and wound the lipstick back into its case.

Rita arrived at eleven, gave Helen a hug and thrust a box of chocolates in Helen's hands. "I was going to bring flowers but you've seen enough flowers. You alright?"

"Yes." Helen gestured with the box. "I've got a pot of coffee on. We'll have a fuddle."

Rita settled herself in deep cushions on the settee and Helen brought the coffee in.

"I wish you had told me Hel." Rita spoke gently and without accusation. "You know you could have. Any time."

"I wanted to. That day you phoned I wished I had. That day when… But – oh I don't know – I just wanted time to think and then Jill kept popping in and then the police…"

"I'd have been the same."

Helen returned Rita's commiserating smile. "You've had more than your share Reet. I should have told you. But you keep thinking 'this isn't real' and you don't like to make a fuss… You hope it'll be nothing…" She paused and took refuge in practicality. "They're sending me Eric's pension details. Then there's the life insurance." She broke off and sighed. "Trouble is I don't know if I want to start making decisions. Not yet." She shook her head and lowered her eyes. "You know Reet, we had the perfect marriage."

"I know. I always envied you."

"Oh Rita, I didn't mean…"

"No but it's true. Oh and we were all so young and full of love." Rita crooned softly, "'We were so young and full of love...' You know it's a funny thing Hel, everybody said it was me and Rob who'd got it made at first. Nobody gave you and Eric more than a couple of years."

"Eric was the original angry young man. He used to have terrible moods."

Rita said reflectively, "I didn't know how you put up with it. Rob was never like that."

Helen pushed down the plunger and poured coffee. "Have you heard from the kids?"

"Not for a week or two. Haven't heard from Antony for about two months."

"Ah well. Look," Helen continued, trying to brighten the conversation, "I'm going to make us some lunch later. There's plenty of cheese. And eggs. Or I could open one of those risottos."

"Don't mind," Rita replied. "I'll go and fetch us a bottle of wine."

"No I've got some… anyway…"

"You said there was something you wanted to talk about."

Helen gazed at the fire with concentration, marshalling her thoughts. Finally she said, "You know - they don't know how he died."

"I thought it was... the cold. Up there." Rita paused uncertain, watching her friend carefully.

"No I don't mean that. But..." Helen's brow furrowed. "How could it be 'Misadventure'! What's 'misadventure'? what does that mean? I mean, whatever made him go up... there's nothing up there!" she cried desperately. "Something must have taken him up there."

"At least it wasn't violent Hel."

"No but..." Helen raised her eyes imploringly, "You would tell me if there's anything I need to know..."

"Helen!" Rita was shocked at Helen's words. "You're not suggesting me and...?"

"Oh no!" Helen threw herself onto her knees in front of Rita. "No! No! I didn't mean that," she cried. "Oh Rita, not that! I didn't mean you. The words came out wrong."

"It's alright." Rita took Helen's hands and drew her up onto the seat alongside her. "There was nobody. I'm sure. You needn't worry yourself about that. Believe me, I know."

She averted her eyes and a silence grew around them and Helen rose and as she poured more coffee for them she watched Rita struggling with something. Twice Rita opened her mouth to speak then hesitated. Helen waited. Finally Rita spoke, measuring her words carefully. "He didn't... you know... didn't leave a note or anything?" She immediately tried to smother back the words. "I mean, you know... give any sign... any indication?" She saw the look on Helen's face. "I'm sorry, it just came out wrong. It wasn't...? But... Could it have been su...?" Rita couldn't say the word, couldn't give expression to the thought troubling her and Helen turned from her, seeking and failing to find words of denial. "Sorry Hel. I shouldn't have... I'm sorry..." Rita's words trailed off in silence. "I'm sorry."

Helen replied, speaking softly, her face averted from Rita's earnestly imploring eyes. "No... it's alright Reet I would have known. I should have known! But we were… Well you saw us that weekend. You know there wasn't; you'd have seen something. You know there was nothing… nothing like that. You needn't have asked, you'd have known! I'd have known!"

"I'm sorry Hel. I shouldn't have…"

"No." Helen's voice was heavy, infinitely sad. "Nobody knew. That's what's so cruel."

They sat in silence with their coffee. Finally Rita took Helen's hand and squeezed it gently.

Helen gave Rita a small, reluctant smile of appreciation. "But there must have been something mustn't there? Don't you think? Something else Reet. You don't think it could have been the baby do you?"

"But that was years ago!" Rita protested.

"I thought I made him happy…"

"You did Helen, you did. You were the perfect couple."

Helen smiled wanly at Rita's words. "My mother just keeps saying 'You'll soon get over it; I had to when your father died,' things like that."

"She means well."

"It doesn't help much…"

Lunch over they sat before the fire with Rita's chocolates and their afternoon was peppered with reminiscence. Helen told Rita how 'A Certain Smile' had returned to her from nowhere, which prompted Rita to recall 'The Twelfth of Never,' a prelude to memories of how they used to be, helped by sudden spurts of, 'Do you remember…?' and 'I wonder what they're doing now?' The grey afternoon wore on and warmed by wine and friendship they returned to the springtime of their youth.

"Eric always had ambition." Helen smiled at the recollection of summer evenings gazing with envy at suburban houses and Eric's stern resolve to escape his father's life. The drudgery of his working day in the factory was stultifying and Eric had tried night school to gain qualifications; ONC, HNC, perhaps even MIMechE. Left to pursue his own ambitions he might have succeeded but lacking any qualifications himself George Allenby goaded Eric to study and imposed a watchful discipline on his son. But his intervention robbed Eric of motivation and a silence grew between them.

"And then Eric met me," Helen continued, "a student nurse of seventeen."

George Allenby regarded Eric's obsessive love for Helen with the suspicion of a man who was afraid of sex and the power it exerted. For Eric was his bastard and George Allenby was determined that his shame would not be repeated by his son. But Eric would insist on seeing this girl...!

Helen paused in her recollection and poured more wine. "For some reason he blamed me," she said. "He blamed me for the breakdown in his relationship with Eric. But it had failed long before I met him. If we hadn't met I don't know what might have happened to him..."

"That was the big difference between them." Rita's voice was gentle and sympathetic. "Rob loved his work. He loved the railway, he'd joined straight from school as a cleaner. All he ever wanted was to be an engine driver." She grinned in self-deprecation and shook her head slowly. "I don't know what I saw in him. But it was different then." She gave Helen a smile of forgiveness. "I remember you said I was daft even to consider him." Helen raised a hand in protest but Rita insisted, "You had ambition and dreams too. Oh yes you did Hel. You know you had. That's why you and Eric were such a match." Rita's eyes took on a faraway look. "But he was such a devil-may-care charmer."

"Not Eric, not in those days."

"No." Rita smiled in recollection of their first date, "Not Eric; Rob..."

They had gone to the pictures; Rob slid his arm across her seat and inclined his head against hers in the darkness and after the film he said, "You haven't got to be in early or anything have you?"

"I can't be ever so late," Rita answered cautiously. "They have a curfew; we have to be in by eleven."

"In where?"

"I'm a student nurse at the Royal. I live at the nurse's home." And Rita told him about the accommodation she shared with Helen and the fun they had visiting each other's rooms, exchanging stories about boyfriends...

"I remember you coming back to Ranfall after that first date," Helen said. "Your eyes were shining."

"He walked me right up to the gate." Rita smiled in recollection. "It was all dark and lonely. Anyway, he'd been ever so good all evening." Helen laughed knowingly and Rita paused at the memory of the first touch of his hand on her breast, unfastening her blouse so lightly beneath her coat. "But I didn't let him go too far." Her smile softened into pity. "I can forgive him now..."

Helen roused herself from the comfortable lethargy their reminiscences had induced. "I'll put some more coffee on. Unless you'd rather...?"

"No, coffee's fine. Do you want a hand?"

Helen shook her head, a forlorn expression of preoccupation on her face. Until then her memories had been a composite picture, like standing on a high promontory surveying a distant landscape with everything in view but nothing clearly seen except a few defining landmarks. Now other images were flooding into her mind. It was like cruising along a much loved but neglected river, approaching each bend with the anticipation of what was beyond. Forgotten memories were returning with startling, unnerving clarity. Only now Helen wasn't sure if she wanted them.

45

Part 2 – 1962

YOUTH

Chapter 8 - A chorus of approval

At twenty, having defied his father and married Helen, Eric abandoned his apprenticeship and was soundly berated by his father for a fool. Eric ignored him. He had dreams to fulfil and he answered a small ad in the evening paper and became a door-to-door salesman, operating from an office on a dingy brown landing above a ladies outfitter near the town hall, selling vacuum cleaners. There was no salary but what looked like a generous rate of commission. Eric looked at the projected figures and with Helen's nervous support set out on his journey of world conquest. But selling vacuum cleaners 'on the knocker' was an apprenticeship of a different kind and Friday lunchtime in the third week saw Eric sitting in the lounge bar of the Brown Bear, just around a corner from the office, on the threshold of disillusion and nursing a half of bitter that Alfred had treated him to in a rare moment of generosity.

Alfred, in his late thirties, was one of the longest serving members of the team. He had the florid, chameleon features of a salesman with an expression of worldliness that could descend into lines of worry or just as easily crease in folds of laughter after a good week on the road. It was a face lived in beyond Alfred's years and seeing Eric's subdued air as he emerged from his weekly review with Monty, Alfred had felt uncharacteristic pity for the earnest young man and invited Eric to join him for a drink. Eric had been reluctant but Alfred recognised the well-known signs and insisted. Not many rookies managed to make a living. "Come on," Alfred said, "I'll buy you one. Had four good closes this week." They found a seat in the corner beneath the window. "Smoke?"

"No, here." Eric hurriedly fished in his pocket for his Park Drives. It was the least he could do. "Here, have one of mine."

They lit up and took a long drag together.

"How's it going then?" Alfred was in reflective mood. He sat back comfortably and reached out with yellow nicotine stained fingers for his glass.

"Didn't do anything this week. Had a sale last week though," Eric added disingenuously. "And the week before that."

But Alfred knew. The first week's sale hadn't been Eric's at all. Monty had taken Eric on a previously arranged appointment to show him how it was done and credited the sale to him, '…just to get you started,' he'd said generously. The agent always did that with the new boys.

"No money then?" Alfred said.

"No." Eric sipped his beer carefully, shamed by Alfred's insight.

"You want to get out of this." Alfred spoke simply and without reproach. "Get into real selling."

"I thought this was real selling," Eric replied, pulling at his cigarette.

Alfred leaned forward. "You don't want to finish up like me."

Eric looked at Alfred in surprise. "I don't know about that. You don't seem to be doing so bad. You said you'd had four closes this week."

Alfred's face lit in a grin of pleasure, "They were good 'uns too. One with no PX and two of the others straight against the allowance."

Eric tried to hide his envy. The straight sale alone with no part exchange would have netted Alfred £9 commission. With one of those a week he and Helen would be made. And Alfred's other two sales within the set part exchange rates would be worth £5 each as well. "Why wouldn't I want to finish up like you?" Eric said. "I'd be laughing!"

"You ought to get into repping."

Eric squeezed his cigarette out and returned the stub to the packet for later. "Yes, well…" he said.

"Not like this," Alfred continued. "This is done for, on the knocker. You want to get a real job. Salary, expenses. A car."

"Yes, well," Eric repeated, "that's why I took this job. As a stepping stone."

"Forget it. This'll get you nowhere."

"But look at the commission you made this week," Eric protested.

"It's feast and famine." Alfred ruminated briefly, "This week was good. It's not always like this…"

"Don't I know it!"

"…and there's too many weeks when you're paying back what you've over-allowed on the PX just to get the sale. So even a good week doesn't always leave you with good money."

Eric said nothing. It was as though Alfred could see straight through him, and for the first time he noticed the cuffs on Alfred's jacket were beginning to fray above the wristwatch on his left wrist. They felt a sudden draught and looked up; Dave was in the doorway; he gave a gesture of acknowledgement and crossed to the bar.

"Who else is coming?" Alfred called.

"Andy's out," Dave announced. "Monty's given him the push. Nobody's surprised. Poor sod. He came out of the office and started to cry." Alfred's eyes rested briefly on Eric; he raised an eyebrow then Dave came across and cadged a cigarette from Eric. "There'd been some talk about going to Retford. I don't know now though. Apparently there were some hard things said the other side of that door." He blew smoke into the air between them. "It's left a cloud hanging over everybody, him going off like that."

"What did he say?" Alfred asked.

"I don't know; I missed it. I were downstairs," Dave replied nonchalantly, "Somebody said they heard him call Monty a twat. Well he wouldn't like that would he? It's his own bloody fault." Dave took a swig of beer. "The others are coming across in a bit. I expect they'll tell you."

Suddenly Eric could see it; Andy approaching middle-age, humiliated and desperate while Monty raised his voice to make sure his colleagues listening beyond the door heard everything. Then Andy emerging shamefaced, trying to conjure up the smile of bravado while his erstwhile colleagues distanced themselves from the taint of failure until Andy's eyes met Len's cold stare. Len, the first to speak, a swaggering thug built like a middleweight boxer in a tailored suit, his hair greased into a 'Tony Curtis', "It's your own fault. Should have kept your fucking mouth shut."

49

Andy's smile stillborn as he mumbles, "He won't pay me. I've no money."

"It's your own bleeding fault then. You should have sold more fucking cleaners."

They had seen it all before, these survivors. When a man failed as Andy had failed, Monty would always be sure to take the opportunity to brand the man publicly. Then Andy began to cry and they moved uneasily like a herd sensing a dangerous scent in the wind until Dave, arriving at the head of the stairs called, "I'm going to 'The Bear'. Anybody coming?" Then the square, thickset figure of Monty appearing in the office doorway, crooking his finger. "Len," the professional smile, "Are you coming in son." And seeing Andy the smile drops from his face, "You still here? What you waiting around here for?" as he puts a familiar arm on Len's shoulder and steers him through the door. Now the humiliation of Andy is complete and he sidles past them to the stairs and is never seen again...

Eric was determined it wasn't going to happen to him. "You think Retford'll be off this afternoon then?" he asked, looking from Dave to Alfred.

"Should think so," Alfred replied shortly.

Dave nodded agreement. "'Others'll be over in a bit. Monty won't want to hang about. He's got his figures for this week and he's had his fun."

It was going to develop into a session and with a sudden misgiving Eric was conscious of the precious little money in his pocket. He supped up quickly, thanked Alfred and left before the others began to arrive.

Helen was pleasantly surprised to find Eric at home when she returned from work. "Oh, hello," she said. Ten o'clock was his usual time. "I thought you were going to Retford."

"Finished early," Eric replied.

With sudden apprehension she said, "You've not been...?

"They got rid of one of the salesmen today," Eric said. "Retford got cancelled."

"I'll put the kettle on." Helen went out to the kitchen then paused; it was ages since they had been to The Sidewalk. "Do you fancy going out for tea then?"

Eric made no reply.

"Didn't you hear me?" she said, "We could go out for tea if you like."

Eric shook his head sullenly and with dismay Helen saw the onset of one of Eric's bouts of moodiness.

"Did you get any money?" she asked carefully.

"No!" Eric replied bitterly. "I told you yesterday. I didn't get any commission."

Helen's mood of expectation evaporated. "Well it's a pity you had to cancel Retford then. We can't live on nothing."

"I didn't cancel it!" Eric mumbled.

"I'm going to get changed."

She went upstairs leaving him gnawing his fingers in anxiety. How could he tell her there'd be no money next week either? It was awful. Last week's sale, that he'd been so pleased to tell Alfred about should have resulted in commission but the old biddy had been better than Eric and insisted on him vacuuming the stairs and the landing carpet as well. 'It's not been done for ages and it'll show if you don't. Only with my back...' she'd crowed from the gloom at the bottom of the stairwell. Eric completed the demo then dug in for the sale with Monty's mantra pounding in his head, 'Get the sale, you must get the sale.' It was one of Monty's favourite themes at his pep talks. 'Get the sale; that'll lead to the next one. Get the selling habit. Never mind the commission; that'll come if you get the sales. Get sales you'll make lots of money.' Eric had looked with dismay at the decrepit old Hoover she fetched out from the dirty cupboard under the stairs. 'Get the sale; get the sale.' In desperation Eric capitulated; he over-allowed on the part exchange and walked from the house with the contagious old machine at arms length. They laughed when he returned to the van and told them. Now he owed the company money and they knew. They all lived off the legends they told of the commissions they made but in reality their own buy-back deals decimated their earnings. What hurt Eric most was deceiving Helen to hide his failure. What he couldn't admit was that he was deceiving himself as well...

Helen returned and Eric heard the rattle of cups in the kitchen.

"We'll be alright," he said bravely as she entered with the tray, "It's coming, I know it will."

"We can't carry on like this Eric," Helen said firmly. "Not knowing if you are going to get paid or not."

"I know we can't," Eric protested desperately.

"Rent's due next week!"

"I know it is."

"Where are we going to get it from? I try to be careful..."

"Helen please! I do know."

"...then there's the gas."

Eric turned in exasperation. "Can't we get him to wait a bit? Just for a week?"

"Don't get angry with me Eric. It's not my fault."

"I'm not getting bloody angry! I didn't say it was your fault! I do what I can. I can't make 'em buy the blessed sweepers!"

"Well that's what you're supposed to do!" Helen cried desperately.

Her words fell like a stone between them.

"You just don't understand," Eric mumbled.

"You'll have to get another job. Something that pays regular wages."

"But this will," he protested, "Don't you see, once it starts. Once the sales begin to mount up."

"When Eric? When's it going to start?"

"Give it another week," he pleaded. "Just another week. Some of the fellows are making a good living. They wouldn't do it otherwise would they?"

Against such an irrefutable argument Helen was silent and Eric was silent too. In his three weeks in the job the only sale that had made him any commission had been an act of charity; the cleaner his father bought from him.

The following week Eric gave in. Helen was relieved but Eric found himself back on a capstan lathe turning drill sleeves in endless quantities. He looked at the men on the lathes around him, trapped within the confines of their limited aspirations, gratefully excited by their brown payday envelopes. 'This is not my life,' Eric protested to himself and he spun the lathe turret angrily and rammed the drill against the steel sleeve in the chuck. The drill broke and Eric cursed. "These fucking drills are no fucking good," he railed. "They ought to give us decent tools! No wonder I can't make any bonus here!" And the men around him 'tut-tutted' and lowered their faces. He didn't fit in and they thought him a snob.

"Why don't you come and join the operatic society?" Helen suggested, "Now you're not out on the road 'till all hours. They're crying out for young men." Eric grunted. He didn't want to be a 'young man'. He was a married man, to be taken seriously. His failure weighed heavily and he didn't want their condescension. Helen bit her lip; there was no talking to him sometimes. "Would you like a cup of tea? I'll make you one if you like."

"Not bothered."

Helen left him to his mood. Eric watched her getting ready to go and wished he had been kinder but he didn't feel like being kind. He felt left out and unworthy.

His sense of isolation grew as show week loomed into view.

"Will you get your own tea?" Helen said, "Only I'll have to be at the theatre for six."

"You're going early aren't you?" Eric responded morosely.

"I've got to give myself time to make up and get changed. I daren't leave it until the last minute. You know that Eric."

"I expect I'll get something," he sighed petulantly. A thought struck him. "What about you? What are you having?"

"I'll get something. But you'll want more than a sandwich won't you."

"Oh do as you like."

Once again Helen bit her lip. She prepared a meal and left it for Eric to warm up. "I'll make you one for every night if you like," she said and watched as Eric examined it in silence. "Well it's there if you want it. Anyway I'm going; I've got to go."

By the second evening of the show Eric relented and told her not to bother preparing him anything for the rest of the week. "I can get something for myself," he said, slinging his knapsack onto the kitchen table.

"Are you sure?" Helen replied.

"I'll come round to the Montgomery and collect you later. Save your mum and dad bringing you home."

Helen gave him a kiss of forgiveness. "You can come backstage and watch it from the wings if you like."

"Are you sure they wouldn't mind?"

"Course not. We could collect some fish and chips later for supper. Anyway, come on, I've got to get going or I'll be late."

He hesitated. "But - I'm not changed or anything."

"It doesn't matter. You'll be in the wings anyway. It's dark in the wings. Nobody'll see you."

The light on the stage was radiant beyond anything Eric had experienced, its intensity accentuated by the gloom backstage. He seemed to be in everybody's way; wherever he placed himself there was always somebody brushing him aside with a fixed look of concentration until their cue sent them striding into the light. The stage manager was particularly impatient of him.

"Look," he said in exasperation as Eric sidled away from the chorus of Jolly Jack Tars assembling in a line alongside him in the wings, "why don't you go out into the hall and watch it from the back?"

"Can't I help?" Eric whispered.

"No – just keep out of the bloody way." He tapped the leading sailor's arm, "Now, now, go on!" he exhorted and the men stumbled into step and marched briskly onto the stage. The Professional Bridesmaids giggled coyly at the approaching men and Richard launched into his song. Eric couldn't take his eyes off Helen. Her dress was ornamented with rosebuds; she had a garland in her hair and he thought she had never looked more beautiful. She was smiling flirtatiously at an approaching sailor, he put his arms around her waist and Eric seethed with jealousy.

At the interval Eric took a discrete position opposite the ladies dressing room and was largely ignored. Everyone seemed to be in a rush to change their costumes or crowding round the refreshment table for tea. He was torn between a fervent desire to belong and resentment at his exclusion. To his relief Helen emerged holding a cup of tea carefully before her.

"Are you alright?" she asked in an excited, breathless voice. "Have you had a drink?"

"I thought it was just for the cast."

"Don't be silly. There's enough for everybody. Come on." She led the way through the melee to the tea urn. "Cup of tea please Madge."

The elderly lady looked up at Eric. "Oh I'm sorry love. Didn't you get one?"

"This is Eric," Helen said and Madge's face lit in a welcoming smile.

"So this is him is it. Sugar?" Madge passed Eric a spoon. "We've heard a lot about you from Helen's mother." She smiled archly at Helen. "Have you had anything to eat yet?"

"He's come straight from work?" Helen said. "We're getting some chips afterwards."

"Fancy coming out without any tea poor lamb," Madge said. "I've only got biscuits I'm afraid. Here," she passed Helen two or three extra, "give him these. They'll help a bit."

Helen gave Eric the biscuits and they moved away. "She's ever so good is Madge. She and my mother are ever such good friends. They've been members since – oh I don't know, for as long as I can remember." She acknowledged a cry and the girls beckoning from the dressing room. "I can't be long. I've got to get ready for the second half." She looked at him coyly. "The girls think you're smashing."

Eric squirmed at the compliment. "I feel as though I'm in the way."

"No you're not. Why?"

"Him with his arm round you," he muttered sulkily. "And you, lapping it up and enjoying it."

"Oh Eric," Helen protested. "It's nothing like that. It's just acting that's all. We've got to look as though we're pleased to see the sailors."

Eric looked at the animated group round them. "I don't feel as though I belong." He was a commoner at court. He knew what his father would have said, 'A lot of pansies,' followed by nervous laughter disguising his own sense of inferiority and Eric watched as members of the orchestra in black tie and dinner jackets began making their way through the crowd and the stage manager appeared at the end of the passage calling, "Five minutes. Five more minutes."

"You'll have to get back I expect," Eric said quietly. "You'd better go."

"Will you be alright? Are you coming up to watch it from the side again."

"Expect so," he replied.

"You could be helping with the scenery."

"They won't let me."

A chorus of voices from the dressing-room called Helen's name and he saw Rita in the same frilled petticoat with roses in her hair, her voluptuous figure made more desirable by her discreet décolletage, peering round the doorway, beckoning.

"I'm coming," Helen called; the girls lingered briefly, Rita bobbed a mock curtsey and they retreated, laughing. "I'm sorry Eric. I'll have to go. I'll see you later. Oh look, here's my mum."

Helen's mother was approaching from the principal dressing room, a diminutive figure in the severe black of a Victorian dame. She was carrying an empty teacup. "Hello Eric," she called, her voice carrying along the corridor. "Now I hope you're enjoying it. Are you in the wings?"

"Yes," Eric replied.

"I thought I saw you there earlier." She continued her stately progress past him. "Here you are Madge. Lovely cup of tea."

"Thank you Alice. I hear the first act went well. Is your voice alright now?"

"Oh yes. Thanks Madge. That lemon and honey works wonders you know."

"I'm so glad. We were all really worried." Madge took the cup and said, just loud enough for the others to hear, "We can't have the society's leading contralto losing her voice show week."

Helen's mother smiled and turned to leave. "Excuse me Eric; I've got to get ready for my scene with Despard." And she retreated back along the passage to her domain.

Helen gave Eric a light kiss on the cheek. "I'll see you down here later," and she dashed off to the dressing room leaving Eric in the fast dispersing crowd.

The show ended to prolonged applause with Eric joining in from the wings. He was totally captivated by the theatre; not just the old building with its corridors and the secret world of backstage; he wanted to be out there, under the lights and bathing in approval. The cast made their way down to the dressing rooms in an ecstasy of mutual congratulation and Eric found himself once more in an island of solitude. A small elderly man, formally dressed in a black tie with a neatly trimmed moustache began moving among them, bestowing and receiving praise. Eric became conscious of being under scrutiny; he turned and saw Rose Maybud, in conversation with other members of the cast surveying him across their shoulders. Her gaze was direct; Eric smiled then Alice Crawford appeared at his side. "Isn't Helen out yet?" she asked.

"Haven't seen her," Eric replied.

"She won't be long. Well Eric, did you enjoy it?"

Eric's response was cut off by the arrival of the dapper little man in the dinner suit. "Alice, you were wonderful." He took Alice's hand in his and lifted it to his lips. "I saw d'Oyly Carte's Mad Margaret some years ago; you were much better."

Alice beamed with satisfaction. "Thankfully I got my voice back in time."

"We were all very worried you might not be able to go on. Wonderful, wonderful. And who is this?"

"Oh I'm sorry Max. This is my son in law – Eric - Helen's husband. Eric, this is our producer Max Grey."

Max took Eric's hand in a firm grip. "Are you coming to join us then?"

"I don't know," Eric replied self-consciously. "I'm not sure I can sing."

"We're always on the lookout for young men aren't we Max," Alice said.

Max turned to her. "You'll have to see if you can't get him to our next rehearsal. Lovely; lovely performance Alice. You are coming back later aren't you?"

"Yes," she replied, "Frank should be here for me any time now."

Max moved on, shaking hands and beaming at the cast.

Helen emerged from the dressing room with a small suitcase; Alice Crawford smiled benevolently at her and Rita came and joined them.

"Well," Rita said in mock accusation to Eric, "did you enjoy it then after all that?"

"Yes," Eric replied with spontaneous enthusiasm. "It was great."

"Oh I'm so glad." The voice at Eric's shoulder was unexpectedly light and clear. Eric turned and saw Rose Maybud smiling at him. "I thought you must be Eric." She was pretty, with a smiling mouth and dancing brown eyes. She turned to Helen. "Is he coming to join us?"

"If I can persuade him to," Helen replied. "Eric, this is Marlene – Rose Maybud."

"Oh you must come and join us," Marlene said and Eric felt the warmth of her approval. "Do you sing?"

"I'm not sure," Eric replied modestly.

"It doesn't matter. We haven't got enough good looking men to go round have we?" and Marlene received nods of laughing agreement.

"Oh Rob's here," Rita cried. "Got to go."

Rob, dark haired with handsome, regular features was standing at the exit door.

"Going for a drink?" Rob mouthed the words at Eric. "Just got time." He gestured to his wristwatch.

"What d'you think?" Eric looked at Helen. "Shall we?"

58

"You've not had anything to eat yet," Helen protested.

"Don't worry. We'll get some chips on the way home."

"Are you coming Marlene?" Helen asked but Marlene shook her head.

"Got to wait for Jim. I expect he'll be ages yet." She made a good-natured moue towards the men's dressing room and the sounds of a chorus bellowing within. "But we will get together."

"See you mum." Helen gave her mother a kiss. "You were terrific."

"Goodnight love." Alice Crawford returned her daughter's kiss, "And you were very good too." She bestowed a bright red lipstick mark on Eric's cheek. "Goodnight Eric. Don't forget," she called after them, "we've got another show tomorrow night."

Chapter 9 - The mushroom

Eric paused, tie in hand, and watched as Helen reached for the dress draped across the bed, a figure hugging sheath in fine white wool with a high roll collar. She raised her arms like a figure in a seraglio, holding the dress high above her head, careful not to disturb her carefully arranged hair. Eric was transfixed by the unconscious eroticism of Helen's pose and he pulled her down onto the bed.

"They'll be here soon," she protested playfully. "We haven't time. I've just done my hair." She succumbed briefly to his kiss. "Later," she said and drew away but the simple word held a world of provocation. They were interrupted by the sound of knocking at the door.

"That'll be them," Helen cried. She gave a final critical look at her makeup and ran downstairs.

Rob entered and went through to the sitting room but Rita detained Helen in the kitchen, biting her lip to contain her excitement and said, "We're going to get engaged."

Helen gave a cry of joy and clapped her hands. "When?"

"Probably Christmas. Nobody else knows yet; we haven't said anything."

"Oh Rita! I'm so glad. Can I tell Eric?"

"Of course you can."

Helen glanced down at Rita and whispered, "You're not...?"

"Course I'm not," Rita said, adding coyly, "It's not as though we haven't..." The rest was smothered in giggles, quickly suppressed as Rob appeared in the doorway.

"Isn't he ready yet?" A flicker of realisation. "Oh she's not told you...?" Suddenly Rob was tongue-tied with embarrassment. "I told you not to say anything," he protested. "Not yet!"

"She's my friend," Rita riposted gleefully. "Why shouldn't I tell her?"

Rob coloured under Helen's knowing smile, Rita kissed him lightly on the cheek and Rob retreated into the sitting room leaving Helen and Rita laughing at his embarrassment.

Eric came down the stairs, paused briefly in the kitchen and went into the sitting room.

"What's up with them two?" he said.

Rob assumed a casual pose in front of the fireplace and began preening his sleek dark hair before the mirror. "It's Rita," he replied. "Can't keep her mouth shut."

"Why what's up?" Eric asked.

"She wants us to get engaged."

"When?"

"Christmas, she says."

"That's months away."

"You know what women are like." Rob gave a final tweak to the high quiff above his brow.

"He's told you then!" Rita was framed in the doorway with Helen close behind.

"Yes," Eric enthused. "It's great."

Rob put his arms around Rita's shoulder. "Why shouldn't I tell him darling? It's not a secret any more is it?" He began singing 'Once I had a secret love' and gave her a kiss.

"See," Helen beamed, "they're made for each other. Anyway, are we going?"

"He only wants to go and see it because it's been banned," Rita said in a voice of censure.

"It's not a sex film you know," Helen said. "It's a serious film dealing with serious issues. Everybody should be able to see it instead of banning it."

"What's it about?" Rob asked.

"What do you think it's about?" Rita said impatiently. "It's a war film." She put her hands on her hips and struck an attitude. "It's called 'The War Game'. Get it?"

"Who's in it?"

"Well nobody's in it!" Rita cried in exasperation. "It's been banned from television. It's not a real film!"

Rob capitulated. "Alright then. I just hope it's worth seeing."

They joined the small queue in the foyer, a mixture of earnest students in college scarves and duffel coats and a smattering of well dressed people with a vague sense of unease about 'the issues.' They left the cinema far from reassured by the obligatory atomic explosion with the billowing mushroom cloud soaring above a desolate landscape and scenes of casualties being stretchered into ambulances while society descended into lawlessness. But the image that affected Helen above all others was of an unprotected child running out into a garden...

"Everybody should be made to see it," she said reflectively as the audience dispersed around them into the night.

"Bit serious wasn't it," Rob muttered.

"Well of course it's serious," Rita responded. "Did you think it wasn't going to be?"

"Well I said it was serious didn't I." Rob checked his watch. "We can still get a drink if we get a move on."

"Why can't people just get on together? Why do there have to be wars?" Helen protested in a voice bitter with the despair of idealism. "There's so much good in the world but we go to such lengths to kill and destroy."

They made their way beneath cold yellow pools of sodium light through deserted streets, past the blank bright windows of silent shops, their footsteps loud upon the pavement.

"You'd think there'd be more going on wouldn't you; a city this size," Eric said mournfully and as they passed the Town Hall Eric took Helen's hand and squeezed it. "They'd all go running into their bunkers," he said with a glance up at the building. "They'd just leave the rest of us to it." The emptiness of the street reflected the desolation of the film. "There'd be nowhere for us to go. Even the café's are shut. Look at it."

"Come on Eric," Rita said. "Let's not get miserable."

"I wish we'd never gone to see it now," Helen said, then she added with resolution, "I mean, everybody should go to see it. Especially the people at the top." She shared Eric's sense of hopelessness, a deep and profound anxiety feeding an unquantifiable fear. "They'd be alright," she concluded bitterly, "but what can we do? Where can we go? If it happens?"

"You shouldn't worry so much," Rob said as they reached the pub. "It's never going to happen."

"You don't know!" Helen protested.

Rob pushed his way through the pub door and Eric let Rob buy the drinks. After all, he was the one that could afford new suits. Behind him Helen and Rita were deep in conversation.

"I started to read '1984'," Rita said, "but I gave it up. It was too depressing."

"What's it about?" Eric asked.

"Science fiction," Rob said with a smirk.

Rita ignored Rob's scepticism. "It's more than that. It's about the future. They're always at war and they have these rallies to cheer the leader on – Big Brother. And there's a screen in every home and instead of you watching the television, the television watches you."

"Did you ever read 'Brave New World'?" Helen asked.

Rita shook her head. "After '1984' I decided not to bother."

"That's what you were reading when we first met," Eric put in. "You enjoyed it."

"It's a lot more optimistic. And," Helen added, "it's very sexy." Her expression darkened again as the shadow of the film came back over her. "Although… in its way I suppose that was about manipulating people too. Only they didn't know they were being manipulated. They were conditioned before they were born. I suppose that's just the same really," she concluded sadly.

"You read some funny things," Rob said, and took a deep pull at his drink. "Come on, we might just manage another before 'time'." He went to the bar draining his glass as he went.

Rita said, "There was this slogan, 'Big Brother is watching you'."

"I don't think they had any slogans in 'Brave New World'," Helen said. "They didn't worship God though. God didn't exist; instead of 'our Lord' they prayed to 'our Ford.' It's quite witty really."

"What would the slogan be in our world?" Eric mused. "It'd have to be something innocent with a mushroom in it."

"I heard a story about a mushroom," Rob said, returning with his drink. "How do you grow mushrooms?"

"Don't know," Eric said, glad of a diversion.

"Keep 'em in the dark and shovel shit on 'em."

Eric joined Rob's laughter but Helen looked at Rob, her innate innocence offended. "I don't like that word."

"What word?" Rob asked disingenuously.

"What you said. I don't like it."

Rob jabbed Eric in the ribs. "D'you get it? Shovel…"

"It's not all that funny," Rita said sharply.

"No but it's what you were all talking about."

"No we weren't," Helen said.

"Yes you were," Rob replied with unexpected insight. "Politics. You let 'em tell you anything, you believe anything." Further argument was interrupted by the clang of the bell and the landlord calling, 'Time.' Rob made vast inroads into the contents of his glass and peering over the rim he saw Rita eyeing him quizzically. "Oh forget it," he said, and he drained his glass and they left.

They parted under the varnished wooden tramstops at the Peace Gardens.

"I'm glad they've decided to get engaged," Helen said, waving back down to Rita as their tram glided away

Eric lit a cigarette. "I wish I were making his money. I could have gone on the railway." The shadows of the film began to gather about him and another morning was looming, another day of discontent at the lathe.

"Never mind," Helen said, "we've got our own little bed to go home to. We can snuggle up together." The scent of perfume still hovered about her and Eric pictured Helen as he had seen her earlier. A tingle of expectancy arose in his thighs as the tram jolted beneath him. "What are you thinking?" Helen whispered.

"Nothing," he said but now the tram was almost at their stop and Eric squeezed his knees together desperately in embarrassment. "Come on," he said quickly and turned for the stairs.

In the darkness of the street Helen took his hand and began tripping in small steps beside him, drawing Eric along in play and singing in a breathless whisper, "Hot chocolate, drinking chocolate; hot chocolate, drinking chocolate..." in soft imitation of the advert until they reached the haven of their home. In the bedroom Eric watched her as she undressed. She held up her nightie, "Shall I put this on?" but she needed no answer and clambered in beside him. He began to caress her and Helen murmured reflectively, "I hate to think of things like that going on in the world."

"Shhh. Don't worry," he murmured, "It's alright." Helen sighed and closed her eyes, a small shudder suddenly ran through her and she let passion sweep the world's cares away into the darkness.

Chapter 10 - A misconception

It was Frank Crawford who proposed a solution to Helen's problem. Her father was painstaking with detail and known to send drawings back to young draughtsmen qualified with ONC and HNC for revision with the comment that 'a bit more experience on the bench wouldn't do these college lads any harm.' And although he couldn't understand Eric's rejection of the craft - for engineering had always brought a kind of happiness to Frank - he remembered his own youthful discontents and recognised the pressures upon the young man who had married his daughter. And so, being a practical man, Frank proposed a solution. And then, being a wise man, he sat quietly while his wife broached it to Helen. It was done casually, during tea one Wednesday evening.

"We've been thinking," Alice said, "about doing some alterations to the house."

"What sort of alterations?" Helen asked.

"Well, it's a bit big for us now isn't it Frank. We're thinking of converting it into flats."

"Flats?" Helen echoed in dismay. The house was a detached Edwardian villa on a quiet avenue and Helen had happy memories of childhood there. Flats! It was a desecration! "You're not taking in students are you? You wouldn't like that. You wouldn't be able to call the place your own. They'd ruin it if you took students in," Helen protested. "You know what they're like."

"We weren't thinking of students," Frank put in mildly.

"Oh," Helen said, piqued, "what then?"

"Well…" Alice glanced at Frank and received a bland look of approval. "We were thinking of you."

"Us?" Helen and Eric exchanged glances. "But we've got our own place."

Eric was equally incredulous. "Why would you want to alter it? It's a lovely house."

"It's getting a bit big for just me and your father," Alice smiled innocently. "And we don't want to move, not at our time of life. But there's plenty of room so why not make good use of it."

"You'd have to pay rent of course," Frank added.

"Oh but nothing like you're paying now," Alice added quickly.

Eric assumed a serious air. "Yes, well, we'd have to think about it wouldn't we Hel."

"Yes," Helen said, already thinking very hard indeed.

George Allenby listened to his son with rising suspicion. "What do you want to do that for?"

"Well dad it'll be a bit cheaper."

"You've got your own house. You don't want to go living in rooms."

"We won't be in rooms. It's going to be made into proper flats."

"Oh aye." His father's voice was heavy with sarcasm. "And whose idea was this?"

Eric tried to shut it out. It was envy. And jealousy too; his father was jealous of Helen's parents and now his son was going to compound the felony by going to live with them.

"We're not going to live with them," Eric protested. "We'll have our own place; it's going to be a self contained flat." But whatever he did, Eric knew it wouldn't be right and he sighed and willed the visit to end.

As Spring blossomed into summer Helen watched her father's progress with appreciation and adoring looks and by the end of June the division of the house was complete. Eric insisted on the downstairs rooms and Helen got her mother to agree. "You won't want to hear us crashing about upstairs," she said persuasively.

"That's alright," Alice replied, "As long as your father can get to his cellar."

They decorated the lounge in abstract patterns of grey and white and coloured the bedroom ceiling deep blue scattered with silver stars and locked the door of their house for the last time. "It was our first little home," Helen said wistfully as they walked away.

Meanwhile summer continued hot and they entertained Rita and Rob to salad tea on Sundays and on the moors the bracken dried to tinder and they thought the summer would never end...

It was a warm Sunday evening in September. Rita and Rob were giggling together on the settee but the entertainment was beginning to wear thin and now they were whispering!

"Whatever's up with you two!" Eric demanded in exasperation.

Rita looked at Rob with a coquettish smile. "You're blushing," she cried with delight.

"No I'm not," Rob said, red faced. "Come on then, are we going?"

"About time," Eric said.

Helen turned from the mirror with a flourish. "Will I do then?"

"Course you will." Rob put his arm through Helen's and marched her out into the hall. "You'll do anytime."

Eric locked the door, Helen paired off with Rita and Eric hung back with Rob, admiring the girls. He wouldn't have argued the point but he reckoned he'd got the better of the two. Rita might have full breasts but Helen's waist was slimmer. Not that there was all that much to choose between them, Eric thought with satisfaction, but if you were going go be critical...

"I didn't want to say anything in there," Rob confided closely, "in case Helen's mother came in. You know what they're like." Eric's attention was still on the girls' hips moving provocatively ahead of them. "Only we've decided to get married," Rob said casually.

"Thought you were getting engaged at Christmas?" Then as realisation dawned Eric turned to Rob with a sly smile. "You've not...?"

"She's only got herself bleeding pregnant hasn't she!" Rob said without malice.

"Blimey." Eric slowed his pace. "When?"

"Well, we've only just found out haven't we," Rob said.

"Does her parents know?"

"Went fucking crackers didn't they." Rob spoke without rancour. "Should have seen her mother's face. Wanted to know if I was going

68

to do the right thing. Well we'd already said we were getting engaged hadn't we! There were no need for it." He paused then added. "Her father didn't have much to say. She said it all for him." Rob raised his gaze to Rita. "She's as happy as Larry!"

Eric looked with renewed interest at the girls. "So what are you going to do then?" he asked.

"I've just told you. We're getting married."

Rita and Helen were also deep in conversation.

"Are you going to wear white?" Helen asked and Rita pursed her lips.

"Mum doesn't want me to. She says she'll die of shame if I get married in white. She doesn't want me to be married in church either." Rita tossed her head defiantly. "She's so old fashioned. Nobody worries about that anymore. I don't want a register office wedding."

"I'm sorry Rita." A thought struck Helen. "You'll still want me as a bridesmaid won't you?"

"Of course I will, silly."

Rita's mother felt her daughter's disgrace profoundly and in the grey silence of early morning she lay fretful and sleepless, asking herself how she was going to cope with 'him' and a baby. She and daddy had wanted so much more for their daughter and the prospect of sharing her home filled her with trepidation. The house was big enough; a pre-war white stucco semi in a pleasant avenue overlooking the park with access to the tennis courts and the boating lake with the woods that camouflaged the railway line rising in a picturesque backdrop. It was only after much heart-searching and with the example of Helen's parents before them that they made two rooms available at the back of the house. But the arrangement was so different to the one Frank and Alice had made for Helen.

"And then," Rita's mother thought venomously, "there's him, working shifts, coming and going at all hours in his dirty greasy overalls, whistling down the road on his bike." She tried to hide her feelings but a brave face is not brave at all and her mask of disapproval confronted Rita daily and she steadfastly refused to let

Rob move in. "Not until you are married," she said. "I don't care what he's done. Not until then. And that'll be soon enough."

Now the distant sound of the trains became a source of irritation. Each day Rob let Rita know which service he was on and Rita listened for it with such expectancy that her mother left the room in exasperation. But whether she willed herself to ignore it or not, she couldn't help hearing the blast of the whistle from his train echoing up the avenue, Rob's peurile reminder of her daughter's disgrace, a serenade to his beloved sending Rita into raptures and causing her mother to turn from her in disgust. That her daughter, her beautiful Rita should come to this!

The wedding took place on one of the last sunny days of the Indian summer with everyone conscious of the sense of shame simmering beneath the bright festivities. The chapel was a compromise and Rita had compromised too, wearing a stylish tailored suit with a corsage instead of a bouquet. The reception was held at Rita's parent's house, Rob and Rita's new home and on everyone's faces there were smiles of benevolence.

"It's not the start we would have wished for our Rita," her father said bravely, "but if they love each other, well, there's no reason why they shouldn't make a go of it." He looked down at his daughter and her groom. "And you can rest assured that your mother and I will continue to do all we can for you and," a slight hesitation as his glance strayed from Rita to Rob, "and your new family." Then an afterthought, instantly regretted, "When it arrives." He raised his glass in a toast of harmony and reconciliation, drank it quickly and sat down.

There was no honeymoon. "You'll need every penny you can scrape together," Rita's mother admonished them and when the weekend was over Rob cycled off happily to work and Rita listened to her mother's advice and the sound of Rob's train passing through the woods.

Helen and Eric came for tea.

"You've given it to us often enough," Rita said. "It's our turn now. You'll be our first guests."

70

Rita's mother answered the front door. "You know where they are," she said, indicating the room along the hall. "And how are you two keeping?"

"Oh we're fine thank you," Eric replied cheerfully, "Aren't we Hel?"

Rita's mother closed the front door behind them, muttered a non-committal, "Yes well," under her breath and called, "Rita - Helen's here," and returned to her lounge. She could never forgive Rita's husband - she couldn't bring herself to refer to him by name - for stealing Rita's future. Oh the plans she and daddy had dreamed of. Now she couldn't look at Helen without being reminded of her loss. And Helen asked herself as she had so many times, 'Why does she blame me? What could I have done?'

Rob emerged and scowled along the empty hall. "It's alright," Eric said, "She's gone in."

They left the disapproving sanctity of the hall and Helen gave a cry of delight. The table was set with salad, pork pie, a jug of celery, dainty bread and butter and Rita's new tea service with blue roses around the rim. The centrepiece was a small vase of flowers.

Rita entered with the matching teapot and placed it carefully on the table. "Hi Helen," she said happily, and looked at them again. "What's up with you two? Won the pools?"

"No," Helen beamed, "We're just pleased to be here that's all. Your table looks lovely Reet."

"Yes it looks nice doesn't it," Rob said proudly.

"We can sit straight down if you like." Rita hesitated self-consciously. "Oh well, just sit where you like. I'll have this chair; it's easier for me to get to the door."

The meal began and Helen said, "Your mother didn't seem very cheerful just now."

"She's never bloody cheerful," Rob scoffed.

Rita looked up sharply. "That's not fair Rob. You've got to give her a chance. She's made a home for us."

"Very nice," Eric said diplomatically.

"Been nicer if we could have had the place decorated. God, look at it."

"Oh I don't know Rob," Helen protested, gazing round. The pale green paper was embossed with gold roses. "It's nice. Well it's better than Eric's dad's anyway." Eric let her remark pass and Rob reached for more pork pie. "Anyway, guess what?" Helen steered the conversation to less contentious waters. "Eric's got an interview for a job."

"Great," Rob cried. "What as?"

Eric preened. "It's a firm selling fire extinguishers. Stuff like that."

"Oh good luck," Rita said. "You deserve it."

Rob wasn't a man to be cowed by disapproval and the relationship between him and Rita's mother degenerated from mutual dislike to intolerance.

"I can't do with this," Rita said, torn between loyalty to Rob and defence of her mother. "I've never had any upset with my mother before."

Rob was unmoved. "Well why doesn't she leave us alone in our own place then?"

"Because it's still their home, that's why."

"Yes, that's the problem isn't it!" he sneered. "Well it's not what the arrangement was supposed to be. This is our place! That's what they said. I wouldn't have agreed to come if I'd have known."

"Why don't we get our own place then?" Rita countered.

"Well if you're so bloody clever you try! I've got to go in a minute. Is me snap ready?"

"It's in the kitchen."

"Go and get it for me will you. I don't want to bump into her again."

Rita hauled herself reluctantly from the chair and moved slowly to the door. Rob followed her, glanced along the hall to see that 'she' wasn't there, collected his railway cap and jacket from the hallstand and returned to the sitting room. Rita found him checking his pockets for the greasy pack of playing cards he always carried with him. She handed Rob the knapsack and said softly, "I wish you wouldn't."

"Now what?"

"I wish you wouldn't play cards. You know you can't afford it."

"Who says I can't? Anyway what do you know?"

"You play for money. You told me yourself."

"Its only coppers."

"That's not what you said the other week. There was nearly eleven pounds you said."

"Well there you are then," he replied triumphantly. "If I keep winning like that we'll soon be able to move out of here then won't we. Anyway duck," Rob softened his tone. "I've got to go. I'll see you in the morning."

Rita sighed. "Alright love. Take care." She kissed him at the door and sighed again as she watched him cycle away.

Chapter 11 – Natividad

Alice's ritual for visiting Helen followed a set pattern. First a knock on the door, then she waited outside in the hall until her call of, 'Can I come in?' was answered. So when Helen looked up she was surprised to find Alice already in their room. Eric, drawing the curtains against the dark October evening, turned at the interruption. Alice had a wild, distracted air and her eyes swept the room. "Have you had your telly on?"

"Mum, what's up? It's not my dad is it?"

"Put it on quick!" then before Eric could switch the set on, "No, come upstairs, ours is on."

"What is it mum, what is it?"

"There's missiles in Cuba," Alice announced melodramatically.

Eric searched for a non sequitur of his own like, 'There's bananas in…' but Alice forestalled him. "The Russians are putting rockets in Cuba. They're aimed at America!"

A confusion of fears rushed into Helen's mind and images from the film arose; wailing sirens, the roar of rockets. "Oh my God!" Her anxieties were becoming real and she rushed upstairs after her mother. Frank was sitting before the set in deep concentration. He turned gravely to face them and Helen crouched beside him, staring at the screen.

"Kennedy's given a warning to the Russians," her father said gently. He sighed, a deep, melancholy sound. "Cuba's only ninety miles from America." He paused. "They're talking about war."

"Oh God."

"War?" Alice wailed. "I missed that. What does he say?"

"He's going on television. They've just given it out. He's addressing the American people tonight."

They spent the evening listening to endless speculation. News bulletins showing American silos opening and nose cones emerging in arid desert landscapes, each obscene phallus rising, seeking the air as though scenting prey, preparing for the promiscuous ejaculation of fatal radiation across the earth. Strangely there was no panic; that came later when they remembered what followed and what might have been. Tonight there was only the unreality of helpless inevitability and recollections of holding their breath as the following awe-full day unfolded. A hundred American warships converging on Cuba as Russian submarines patrolled the Caribbean and the freighters carrying the missiles approached the island until, oh God! The first Russian ship veered away and the rest followed, retreating into the grey Atlantic and the newsmen, cheated of a great story consoled themselves in guesswork and analysis. But on the ground, in the streets and in the houses in those streets, people gathered and wondered how they had inherited such a world. It wasn't like the end of the War in 1945 with cheering and joy. There was a profound mood of sadness and regret leavening their relief.

"It's an awful world Eric," Helen whispered.

"But it's over now."

"I know, but when you think of what might have…"

"But it didn't happen," Eric insisted. "They saw sense. It doesn't matter who thought they were right or who was wrong. Thank God common sense took over."

"We should never have got into that situation in the first place," Helen wailed, "aiming atomic bombs at one another? Why can't we all live in peace?"

"But we do," Eric insisted.

Helen's sense of hopelessness was prolonged by Eric's failure to get the job he'd been interviewed for and she became reflective.

"I feel sorry for Rita."

"Why?"

"Having that baby. Fancy bringing a baby into a world like this."

"Oh Helen."

The image of the child in the film still haunted her, for as it ran outside its eyes had melted from the heat radiating from the blast. "I wouldn't want to have a child. What future has it got? What future have any of us?"

Helen's melancholy hung over them and in the last week of November Helen said, "Why don't we book a decent holiday? The best holiday we can afford."

"When?"

"Next summer. If we live that long."

"Oh Helen…"

"I mean it. What's the point in not doing things? What's the point in saving? We've got to live life while we can…"

Rita was untroubled by the philosophies that were worrying Helen. She had her baby to look forward to and the new life within her was a reaffirmation of the future. She listened to Helen's worries and humoured her friend and gave a satisfying display of envy when Helen told her of the holiday.

"It sounds great," Rita said, sitting with her hands across her belly. "Still I've got this to look forward to."

So the months passed by and in the first week of March Rita's contractions began and Rob ferried her to hospital in a flurry of solicitous care and gazed rapturously at the red faced, wailing child who was his son. "He's got a good pair of lungs on him," Rob said and Rita smiled, flushed in happy exhaustion.

"He's hardly stopped since he began; not even for his feed."

When Helen saw the child she forgave the world. "Can I hold him?" she asked and Rita reached into the cot and raised the quivering, whimpering infant and tucked the sheet securely round him and offered him to Helen. He shuddered in Helen's arms and renewed his crying while Helen rocked him, lost in motherhood. "There, there, there; it's your Aunty Helen," she whispered, holding him close. The child's head began making involuntary, blind movements against her breast and an expression of divine joy spread over Helen's face and Eric had an unaccountable feeling of embarrassment that was almost sexual in its intensity.

"He's a bit red," he said in an offhanded way and expressed surprise at the frailty of the skinny little arms and marvelled at the perfection of the baby's fingers.

Helen asked, "What name did you decide on in the end?"

"We're calling him Antony," Rob replied proudly.

"Without the 'h'," Rita added.

Chapter 12 – Liebestraume

Eric woke to find the windows of the train misted over with condensation. They were plunging in and out of tunnels and Eric brushed the glass clear with his sleeve and called Helen to the window. Across the valley, through the rain they could see mountains rising sheer into the clouds from the level green pastures of Switzerland and alongside the track a river of milky water, tumbling and racing in foam. They were interrupted in their admiration of the view by activity in the corridor, the compartment door slid open and the conductor collected their pillows and announced that breakfast was being served. They declined and were left alone once more. Eric surveyed the rain with disappointment but Helen reaching for a bag on the rack said, "I expect it's because we're still in the mountains."

"What've we got?" Eric asked. They had budgeted carefully and hadn't allowed for buying meals on the train.

"Not much," Helen said ruefully. "Some chocolate. That's all."

They shared the chocolate watching the view outside.

"You feeling a bit better now?" Helen asked.

Eric nodded. He had set out with romantic notions of exile and as they watched the harbour at Folkestone receding he suffered overwhelming homesickness. At the rail terminal in Boulogne they had milled around the waiting carriages like refugees in the fading light before being directed onto the train amongst strangers. Now Eric smiled and said, "Yes, I'm fine now."

Their fellow travellers returned from their couchettes and breakfast and the train swept into the Simplon tunnel, finally bursting from the mountain into Italian sunshine at Domo d'Ossolla. The transition was amazing; the passengers came to life, craning at the windows as platform vendors began parading along the coaches with carts of fruit and coffee and ice cream and Eric exclaimed delightedly, "There's oranges. Look Hel, oranges growing on the trees."

They supplemented their meagre breakfast with cake and fruit and the Alps receded as the train wound south through tantalising views of Lake Maggiore. Blue water sparkling between discretely hidden villas prompted lively chatter and it seemed impossible they could have maintained their solitary aloofness for so long.

Helen was in conversation with an elderly gentleman travelling alone. "Mr Turner is from Sheffield too," she said, turning to Eric. "He's going to Viareggio the same as us."

Mr. Turner gave Eric a knowing look, "And is this your first time in Italy?" he enquired.

"Yes," Helen replied, "we couldn't afford it before."

"Helen's been to Belgium," Eric said, adding, "That was before we were married."

The weak smile was tinged with doubt; Eric read suspicion in the steady eyes and turned back to the view from the window. 'He doesn't believe me. He doesn't think we're married.' He was saved by the other passengers.

"How long did you say you'd been married...?"

"A year...?"

"And so young...."

"Ah... this will be like your honeymoon won't it...?"

Helen responded happily but as the sun climbed to midday lethargy crept over the train. Dark poplars dotted the landscape; orchards, quiet red farms and towered towns on distant hills, all passed in a sultry haze. At Genoa the bustle of the station brought a brief spell of activity; they stirred and stretched and peered and checked the time and resigned themselves to lethargy again. Then the sea appeared and their spirits lifted and a buzz of anticipation arose.

"Where are you staying?" Mr. Turner asked, prompting an exchange of hotel names.

"We're at Hotel Margherita aren't we Helen," Eric replied with a vague sense of hope.

"Yes," Helen said, "I hope it's nice."

Mr Turner examined his ticket. "I'm there too."

"Oh. That'll be nice," Helen said...

Three days had gone by. They were lazing on the beach but Eric still felt out of place and 'English'. He was determined to go home with a Mediterranean tan but his body remained obstinately pale and he lay spread-eagled on the hotel beach with Helen beside him in a black and white gingham bikini edged with lace. Eric liked the Italians. The proprietor of a small giftshop on the promenade had greeted them with unexpected charm and pointing to Helen said, 'Esposa?' It didn't matter that they had little to spend; he indicated that he would be honoured to help them to find a gift. The trinket they bought was ceremoniously wrapped and tied, the ribbon crimped by his wife and they left to smiles and cries of 'Arrivederci.' It was play acting but accepted as no more than due courtesy by both sides. New perspectives began forming in Eric's mind and he was uplifted by the encounter. He knew the lathe could never satisfy the restlessness within him; he needed to fulfil a deeper urge and he lay dreaming beneath the sun, listening to the ice cream vendors patrolling the beach with their strangely mournful cry of, "Gelati, gelati a' la main…"

Eric's reverie was disturbed by the sound of spoken Italian. He sat up, blinking into the sun. A young Italian of Eric's age, deeply tanned and with a camera slung from his shoulder was beckoning to Helen. He was dressed in faded blue shorts, open necked shirt and sandals, with dark eyes and unruly hair curling about his ears. His voice was soft and pleading like a child's.

Helen turned to Eric. "I think he wants to take a photograph."

Eric dismissed him with a wave. "No money," he said but the Italian would not be denied and he placed his palm across his heart.

"So beautiful." He gestured to Helen. "Filma'star. Please, no monai. Is pleasure."

Helen suppressed a giggle and to Eric's dismay she said, "Oh Eric? He said no money."

Eric felt threatened. In a gentle, inoffensive way the Italian was overcoming Helen's resistance and once again he gestured, inviting Helen to her feet in a voice of innocent pleading and she rose, self-conscious in her bikini. The Italian put his hands to his face, framing Helen with his fingers and thumbs and Eric turned from her.

"Scusi," the Italian said. He began to pose Helen with one hand on her hip and the other behind her head. Then he gently coaxed her leg forward.

"Hey! Hey! What you doing? Eric protested. "Get your hands off her!"

"Scusi." The Italian professed mortification, his hands opened in a gesture of innocence.

"It's alright," Helen said and Eric scowled and rolled over as the Italian gestured toward a clear area of sand beyond the parasols, slowly leading Helen away.

Eric sat up and scanned the beach, looking desperately to left and right. She was so trusting and vulnerable, the Italian had drawn her after him and, fool that he was, he had let her go! Eric stood and took a few steps, craning and trying to see beyond the parasols and saw them in the distance. Helen was posing and preening on the shoreline and the Italian was circling her with the camera. Eric felt a bitter surge of jealousy! What was she doing, posing for him! He was touching her, coaxing her! He'd taken Helen away, now he was seducing her. Eric's mouth set in a snarl of anger and he shouted, "Helen!" The distant figure turned and waved. For God's sake! "Helen!!" Eric raged, uncaring of the attention his fury was attracting. "Helen!!"

She waved again then realisation swept over her. She spoke briefly to the Italian, his hands rose in protest and Helen walked away. Eric felt the Italian's glare of rivalry; saw his arrogant gesture of dismissal. Eric turned and strode back to their sunbeds.

"You shouldn't have gone with him," Eric said. "You knew I didn't like it."

"Oh Eric."

"You shouldn't have let him touch you like that."

"He was only showing me how to stand."

"I'll bet," Eric said sullenly.

"What do you mean?"

"You know what I mean."

"No I don't."

"He was trying to get off with you."

"No he wasn't!" But she knew it was true and it had been risqué and fun letting the Italian pose her.

"Why did you go off down the beach? Where I couldn't see you."

"I didn't…"

"Yes you did!"

"We weren't doing anything; he was just taking pictures."

"I bet he had no film in his camera," Eric muttered.

"You're being silly…"

"Don't call me silly," Eric snarled. "I saw you!"

"He was just a photographer! Anyway," she spoke with disappointment, "I'll never see the pictures now."

"Didn't he give you a card or anything?"

"No."

"See! I told you!"

At length Helen spoke. "He said he liked me," she said softly.

"I'll bet he did," Eric responded peevishly. "Anyway, how do you know what he said?"

"Because he said it while you were here!" Helen riposted. "He said I was like a filmstar."

They entered into a sullen truce and preparing to return to the hotel they surveyed themselves with disappointment. Their white bodies had begun to redden and Eric said, "I don't feel too good."

"What's the matter?" Helen asked.

"I just feel a bit off." The residue of his anger still remained and now he felt uncomfortable under the sun.

Helen said, "Come on. You'll feel better when you've had something to eat. You must be getting hungry."

They finished dressing, packed their towels into the bag and left the beach.

They went down for dinner and tried to ignore the glances of the other guests in the dining room and sat quietly. The room had a decor of modest elegance with a moulded frieze painted ochre,

81

complementing the soft yellow walls. It was brightly lit, the windows over the vine covered courtyard were open and scents from the garden were overlaid with the unmistakable smell of cigars and the discrete aroma of food. But to Helen and Eric the room was hot and oppressive until the occasional breeze stirring the curtains made them shiver. Mr Turner paused en-route to his table, critical about the dangers of the sun and they insisted they'd had a good day on the beach until he left them.

Eric regarded the hors d'oeuvres trolley with misgiving and Helen, smiling valiantly at the cold meats, salami, pasta and fish boldly selected a variety of meats. "No fish," she said to the waiter and turned to Eric. "Try a bit of meat, you might feel better."

Eric made a small selection of salad, the trolley moved on and they picked uncertainly at their food. Helen pushed her plate away. "I'm going back upstairs," she said. "I'm sorry. You stay and finish your meal." But another wave of cold swept over Eric, he shivered and with a wan smile at the blur of faces watching them he followed Helen out.

In the sanctuary of their room they undressed carefully, drawing a single sheet over themselves, sweating and shivering by turn.

"I've got some cream, it might help," Helen volunteered and she squeezed a white trail across Eric's chest. He winced, his skin was a frail tissue over the bright red flesh and although he was shuddering she could feel the heat emanating from his body but when she tried to smooth it over his chest he cried out and rolled away. Helen waited, kneeling and shivering herself but Eric refused her touch.

"Put some on me then," Helen said finally.

Eric sat up, giddy and weak with nausea. "Are you sure?" he asked. Her shoulders were inflamed and the burn on her chest ended in an angry red weal across her breasts. She nodded and Eric cupped her breast and carefully applied the cream. She stiffened and bit her lip; the cream was drawing her skin tighter and tighter and Oh, the stinging! Eric hesitated; she smiled encouragement and said, "Go on, it's alright," and bit her lip again. The same angry burn was across the bikini line of her belly and thighs and Helen braced herself as Eric began to apply more cream.

There came a knock at the door. Helen reached quickly for the sheet, winced and held it aloft to prevent it touching while Eric carefully pulled on his trousers and reached for his shirt. The knock was repeated and a voice, the voice of old Mr. Turner asked, "Are you alright?"

"Yes, yes," Eric replied. He eased the door ajar as Helen scampered into a corner with the sheet around her, whimpering with pain.

"Are you sure you're alright? Shall I come in?" He tried to peer inside.

Eric held the door firmly. "We got a bit sunburned," he said. "We're going to bed."

"Are you alright love?" Mr. Turner called.

"I'll be alright in the morning," Helen replied.

Another glance at Eric. "Well, good evening then."

Eric locked the door. "I think he thinks you need a chaperone. He was trying to look at you."

"Don't be angry with him," Helen replied, creeping back to the bed. "I'm sure he means well."

"Oh yes? And shivering uncontrollably they drew the sheet over them, trying to avoid touching each other.

The night was interrupted by their moans as they turned in slow, restless movements. But as morning approached the fever passed and they fell into exhausted sleep. Eric woke to the sounds of breakfast on the terrace below and lay gazing at Helen, relieved at the feeling of wellbeing. His skin was still delicate to touch but the inflammation had subsided. The sheet accentuated the curves of her body lying naked beneath and Eric felt the tingle of arousal as Helen began to stir.

"Better?" Her voice was languid; she raised her arms and stretched, moving without any sign of discomfort.

"Yes," he said gently, returning Helen's smile.

"And me." She lay against him. "I feel a lot better than I did last night." She drew the sheet back and they examined Helens breasts. She didn't flinch at his touch and he drew her closer. "It's still a bit tender," she said but as Eric withdrew his hand Helen protested, "No

83

it's alright, I didn't mean that," and she replaced his hand on her breast and sighed. In the slow wakefulness of morning there rose within Eric a feeling he had never experienced before. In England there were always nightclothes and blankets, eiderdowns and sheets enfolding them in a cocoon of modesty. But today the morning sun was burning bright against the jalousie, illuminating the room with narrow bars of light and as they lay listening to laughter entering the room with the aroma of fresh coffee from below Eric was aware of a sense of uninhibited freedom. He felt like a libertine; no longer hemmed in by the constricting morality of damp and fickle England he was free to indulge the passion rising between them. "Are you sure you're alright?" he asked.

Helen smiled, "Of course I am," and he drew the sheet away from her and gazed at the beauty of her body, seeing her as he'd dreamed of seeing her in the days of their courtship. Helen lay motionless and watched him and there was the light of expectation in her eyes. This was a moment to savour of itself, not squandered in a reckless desire for sex.

"You know I was jealous of that Italian yesterday," he said. "I could have killed him."

Helen took Eric's hand and drew him forward and placed his hand on her and began moving slowly against him. "It wasn't like that."

"But he didn't think so. I can't stand the thought of anyone else touching you."

"There never will be anyone else touching me Eric. You shouldn't get jealous." Helen hugged him then relaxed her arms. "Oh I'm sorry. I didn't…?"

"No." He pulled her to him again. "It's alright. Just a bit sore. But not like last night."

"There's nobody but you," she said, "You know that. Nobody." She leaned up and kissed him, a long, slow kiss and felt Eric begin pushing against her. "Mmm," she murmured and her eyelids closed and fluttered.

"Are you sure you're alright," he whispered, moving his hands with delicacy over her body.

"Oh yes…"

"He wanted to get a look at you last night."

"Eric, he's just an old man…"

"More like a dirty old man," Eric said.

"He was concerned that's all," Helen protested gently.

"I don't want anybody to see you but me. It's, it's between us. It's intimate, something that you and I share between us." Eric struggled to find the right words to express the sense of ownership he felt. And then he chided himself for using the word ownership, for that wasn't right either. It was an instinct to defend what was his, ordained by God and sanctified by the promises and consent they had given to one another. Other men might desire Helen; he had seen the lust in men's eyes, imagining what she was like, but only Eric had the right to know her intimately, to see her lying unashamed before him as she lay now. "Are you sure you're alright?" he whispered and again she pressed up against him.

"I love you Eric," she said and reaching down she guided him into her, and pushed against him and her lips parted in a sigh.

"I love you," Eric replied, and dismissing the memory of the photographer's glare of frustrated rivalry he began to make love to Helen with uninhibited tenderness and passion…

They took their seats on the homeward train, drinking in the landscape of Lombardy and reliving their memories: Pisa, the basilica and the holy relics; Eric walking round the narrow ledge on the upper parapet of the leaning tower overhanging the roofs of the city below as the wall threatened to push him between the pillars; the bustle of crowds on the long promenade and their final, careful day beneath a parasol on the beach. Once more the Alps rose before them; the sun set over the plain and they passed through Domo d'Ossola in the fading light of evening and left Italy glowing in the remains of the day. Now there was nothing to be seen except the lights of distant villages twinkling in the darkness.

"I'm going to get another job when we get back," Eric said. "I'm going to start looking again."

"Not vacuum cleaners." There was a serious undertone beneath Helen's banter.

"Don't worry. Not this time…"

Home at last.

Alice ran down to greet them with smiles of welcome. "Oh come on," she fussed, "I'll make you both a nice cup of tea. I'll bet you could do with one. You do look brown," and she called down the cellar to announce their arrival to Frank. Eric looked at the unchanged familiarity of their room and succumbed to weariness. He fell into the armchair and heard Alice saying, "Me and your father's had our tea. We weren't sure what time…"

"We had an orange at breakfast and an egg between us," Helen replied and they began to laugh in a burst of emotional relief until they were both laughing uproariously and Alice could only smile in uncomprehending benevolence.

"Well I'd better get you something then," Alice said, "Beans on toast? Would that be alright? Or there's some…"

"Beans on toast!" Eric sobbed with laughter and held out a small handful of coins. "That's all we've got," he spluttered, "Ninepence. You got anything Helen?"

"I think I've got a sixpence somewhere and a few lira left in my purse." Helen wiped the hysterical tears from her eyes and the laughter fell away and she looked up at her mother with a smile of gratitude. "Beans on toast would be lovely mum. Honest." And suddenly they were sober again.

Chapter 13 - Lachrymosae – 1

They had barely finished eating when Rita and Rob arrived.

"They've had a lovely time; they've seen the leaning tower of Pisa," Alice said with a proprietorial air, turning to Helen. "Where else did you go? Did you see Florence?"

"We called but she was out," Eric said facetiously and Rob fell about with laughter.

Helen shook her head. "No mum, we didn't get that far."

Eric said, "We had a scooter and pottered about a bit. Italian drivers are mad."

"I do hope you were careful!" Alice fretted.

"Course we were careful." A smile at Eric. "We were very careful weren't we!"

Eric lifted a mischievous eyebrow and Frank said, "Anyway, we'll go and leave you in peace. I expect we'll hear more about it in due course."

"He can't wait to get back to his cellar," Alice protested. "I don't know what he does down there; we never see anything come out of it." Frank gave a gallant little wave and they departed.

Rob examined their suntans critically. "You didn't have very good weather then."

"Ignore him," Rita said. "Cheeky devil; we're only jealous. Did you have a good time? Looks like you did."

"Oh yes." Helen glanced in Eric's direction and again she smiled, a slow, inward smile. "It was lovely."

Rita punched Rob on the arm. "See! We should go abroad for a holiday."

Rob said, "I'll bet you got tanned on the soles of your feet."

"He might have," Helen replied, examining her makeup at the mirror.

Rita moved alongside Helen. "Did you get your bottom pinched?"

"No but…" Helen told Rita of the photographer and Rita grinned sidelong through the mirror at Eric. "He didn't half get jealous," Helen added, "but he made up for it afterwards."

True to his intentions, Eric began applying for jobs and within three weeks he was successful.

They went round to tell Rita and Rob. "Eric's going to be a salesman," Helen said proudly. "A proper one with a wage. Not like before."

"That's good!" Rita said approvingly. "Well done Eric. What's it selling?"

Eric tried to sound nonchalant. "Kitchen furniture."

"In a shop," Helen said. "The co-op. A real nine-to-five job…."

"I'll be working all day Saturday though," Eric added.

"But he gets Thursday afternoons off instead."

"Nice one Eric." Rob rubbed his thumb and forefingers together. "Plenty of commission eh?"

"Well…"

But Helen was looking steadily at Rita. "Come on Reet, you're dying to tell us something too."

Rita tried to look coy but a smile spread over her face. "I'm pregnant," she said, "I'm going to have another baby."

Helen screamed with delight. "That's wonderful! When?"

"Early spring. Same time as Antony. They'll be able to play and go to school together."

Eric patted Rob's back. "Two celebrations in one day eh?" He drew Rob to one side. "It's a bit soon isn't it?"

"She's alright," Rob smirked, "No trouble. She just catches easy that's all."

Helen gave Eric a playful glance and said, "I'd better be careful. I might get smittled."

"What?"

"You know," Rita said, "catch what I've got."

There is an old wives tale rooted in antiquity that says fertility is born in the air by some natural miasma arising from association with a young, pregnant woman. Perhaps a deep-seated desire for motherhood is at work, an unknown cycle in the rhythm of life, long forgotten but nevertheless still potent, determining the actions of females at some critical moment of fecundity. Whatever it might be, a month after Rita's announcement Helen had news of her own.

"That's wonderful," Rita exclaimed and she held Helen at arm's length. "When?"

"I don't really know for sure. You know what I'm like; I've never been regular. I think its April but they've said it could be the beginning of March."

"That could be before me! Oh come and sit down."

"Anyway we'll know later. They'll have a better idea when it's developed a bit more."

Rita took Helen through to tell her mother but oh, the chill politeness with which Rita's mother received the news and Helen was relieved to leave the smile behind. It was a smile of regret and sadness; no matter how Rita's mother tried to brighten it with words, her smile carried false wishes.

"I'm sorry about my mother," Rita said. "I don't know what to say. She's… she's changed."

It's alright," Helen said. "Don't let it upset you."

Rita said wistfully, "I wish we could get a place of our own."

"Well we shan't be living at Helen's mum's forever," Eric said tactfully. "I mean it's alright but you still feel you're sharing with them."

Rob entered, bringing the scent of aftershave into the room. "Come on then, let's go," he said.

It was an evening for strolling in the park. The air was still, the high summer clouds were flushed pink with approaching sunset and they paused to watch as a train passed, its smoke rising in the trees beyond the stream.

"I'm going to be rostered for London soon," Rob said.

"Really," Eric enthused. It was good to share each other's good fortune.

"It'll mean more money." Rita took Rob's hand. "But you might have to stay away won't you darling."

"Not always," he corrected her.

"You told me it meant staying away." Rita shook her hand free in indignation. "He did," she protested. "You told me you'd have to stay in London."

"It depends; I've told you," Rob replied with calm superiority. "If we're bringing another train back I might have to. Or we might come straight back cushions." He turned to the others with exaggerated patience. "I've explained it all to her already!"

"What's cushions?" Helen asked.

"Third class. In a carriage. Instead of firing."

"Oh. Gentleman's travel." And they laughed at the notion.

"If I get enough London trips I could make enough money to get us out of... there!" Rob spoke with venom, "...and into a place of our own."

"That's my mother's house you're talking about," Rita said. "If it wasn't for my mother we wouldn't have anywhere."

"Could have gone to our place."

"You know we couldn't." Rita had refused to share the tiny house with Rob's mother. "There was no room, you know that. We'd all have been on top of one another."

"You want to look in the paper," Eric said. "That's what we did." He caught Helen's look. "Well Helen got it actually."

"Yes," Rob said, "and you were glad enough to get out of it too."

Helen protested. "It's just that my mum and dad wanted to make better use of their house that's all."

They were approaching the end of the park. Rob said, "The Millhouses?"

"Don't mind," Eric turned to the girls. "Up to you."

"Doesn't matter much to me," Rita said. "I'm not drinking anyway."

"Let's go to the Robin Hood for a change," Helen decided.

"Come on then." Rob broke away, darting around them in high spirits. "Race you to the steps." He punched Eric on the arm and dashed across the field with Eric in pursuit.

"You know we can't run," Rita called, linking arms with Helen. "We've got to look after ourselves now..."

Eric immersed himself in the world of kitchen furniture and an unlikely bond of mutual respect developed between him and the shop manager. Fred Robertson had broken teeth, slicked back hair and incessant dandruff dropping onto the collar of his dark jacket. But he regarded himself as Eric's mentor and Eric discovered selling skills that had been stifled under Monty's rigidly scripted style. Gradually he began to usurp Mrs. Stoakley in the shop hierarchy. Fussy and birdlike in her blue co-op smock, she had been on the staff for years and was silently critical of Fred Robertson. There was a frayed air about him, she regarded him as an upstart and spoke with fond loyalty of his predecessor. "Of course, Mr. Benson was a gentleman," she said primly to Eric. Not that it mattered to Fred Robertson and the atmosphere between Mrs. Stoakley and Eric remained harmonious despite her otherwise disapproving air.

But Helen began to see a difference in Eric. It wasn't that the job offered great prospects; there were enough examples among the docile, prematurely grey, middle-aged staff in the main store across the road to quell any illusions about that. And if selling vacuum cleaners wasn't going to qualify him for the car and expense account, then neither was selling kitchen furniture for the co-op. But it was somehow more respectable and the poor pay was more than offset by the satisfaction he derived. And, Helen reflected, if Eric was happy, then she was happy too.

"Are we seeing Rob and Rita this weekend?" Eric asked. He was standing by the window gazing out at the November gloom.

"I don't think so," Helen said. "Rob's working. I saw Rita this afternoon." Her eyes closed momentarily and she leaned against the table.

"Are you alright Hel?"

"Yes." Helen gave a little cough. "I hate these dark evenings. I'm just a bit worried about Rita that's all."

Eric followed Helen to the kitchen. "What's wrong?" he said, "You're alright aren't you?"

"There's nothing wrong." Helen placed their meal on the table and began picking at it with disinterest.

91

"You sure you're alright Hel?"

"I've lost my appetite a bit. I'm alright really; just a bit tired that's all. No it's just Rita."

"What about Rita?"

Helen pushed her plate away. "Well, she told me this in confidence so don't you go and say anything to Rob."

Eric crossed his hands over his heart. "I won't," he said.

Helen looked at him earnestly. "I mean it."

"Alright," he said.

"Things aren't right between them." She regarded Eric steadily. "They've stopped - you know, making love."

"Expect we'll have to stop sometime."

"It's not that. They stopped doing it months ago. He told her he was afraid of hurting her."

"You sure?" he said. "They were worse than us! Like bloody rabbits." A sudden thought struck him. "You're alright aren't you Hel?"

"Course I am silly."

Eric thought for a moment and said, "How's he managing then?"

"You might just as well ask how Rita's managing," Helen said indignantly.

"I was only... What did Rita say?" he asked at last.

"Well what do you think she said? She's very upset," Helen cried. Rita hadn't set out to confide but she had suddenly opened her heart, and between condemnation of Rob and trying to make Helen understand she had burst into tears of shame. "She says it's no wonder he stays on playing cards after work," Helen concluded. "He doesn't feel as though he belongs there. He says it's like a half-way house. I feel so sorry for her..." Helen rose from the table and sank into an armchair.

Eric looked at Helen with concern. "Are you sure you're alright?"

Helen nodded. "It's been a very emotional day."

Eric returned from work one Saturday evening in mid-December bubbling with satisfaction. "We did over £1600 last week. That's ten percent more than this time last year." He pulled Helen onto his knee. "Anyway, never mind about trade figures; how's your figure?"

"I'm fine, just a bit tired and getting bigger." Helen placed his hand on her belly and kissed him. "Rob's had a bit of bad news though. He's had his bike pinched."

"Oh!" Eric exclaimed in surprise. "When?"

"It was stolen from work on Tuesday." Helen sighed. "As if she hadn't got enough to worry about."

Eric stifled a grunt of incredulity. He knew the layout of the depot from his trainspotting days; the cycle rack was inaccessible except from the loco-shed. "How can he have it pinched? The bike racks are behind the firehouse."

"Well," Helen said with resignation, "it's gone anyway."

"What's he going to do then?"

"He's got to go on the bus. It'll make it awkward when he's got an early start."

"Does he know who took it?"

"Rita never said. We'll go up and see them tomorrow shall we? Rita could do with a bit of cheering up."

She was interrupted by her mother calling from the hall. "Can we come in?" Alice Crawford peeped round the door.

"We were just going to have our tea," Helen said. "Eric was late tonight."

"Oh I'm sorry love. We'll come back later."

Helen gestured to a chair. "It's alright, so long as you don't mind watching us."

"A pity about you and Rita," Alice said. A look of misgiving crossed Helen's face. "Oklahoma!" Alice continued, "The next show. Marlene's got the lead but there's a lovely part for one of you. Ado Annie! Now neither of you can go for it. They've asked me to think about Aunt Ella." She paused. "I don't think I'll bother."

"She's too old," Frank said, unexpectedly appearing at the door.

"Oh she's not," Helen protested. "Don't say that dad!"

"Not me!" Alice protested with a withering look at Frank. "Aunt Ella. The character! I'm not old enough to start playing parts like that. Yet!" She turned to Eric, "What about you? Are you going to be in our next show? Don't you fancy being a cowboy? All those young chorus girls too," she added, twinkling mischievously.

"Mother!" Helen said; but her outrage was seasoned with amusement.

Sunday was miserable and overcast with cold rain turning to sleet. A dark afternoon of endless boredom. Rita greeted them with relief when they arrived. "Come in and get warm. Rob's not on until five."

"Hiya mate!" Rob looked up from playing 'patience' at the table with Antony's pram beside his chair. "Fancy a game?"

"We're not going to play cards are we?" Helen protested.

"No we are not." Rita's reply was emphatic. "Come on, let's have your coat."

They gathered round the fire. Rob continued turning the cards and Helen said, "I've got a contracted pelvis. I'm to try and keep the baby small."

"How are you supposed to do that?" Rita exclaimed. "Starve yourself? Start smoking?"

Rob looked up with surprise. "You've not starting smoking have you?"

"No, silly. We were just talking about the baby." Rita turned her attention back to Helen and they began comparing notes.

Within the pram Antony began to stir and whimper and Rob absent-mindedly rocked it, his attention still on the cards. Surrounded by boredom Eric said, "We had a bit of a laugh over at the Arcade this week. One of the junior's went to the Town Hall for a Cock Licence."

"What's one of them?" Rob asked idly, looking for a way to release a red king.

"They've got this new kid over at the main store; he's just turned sixteen." Eric grinned, "Somebody told him he'd need a Cock Licence now he was old enough to start putting it about."

"He didn't believe 'em did he?" Rob chuckled.

"He wasn't sure. He came over to us on Wednesday and asked if it was true."

"What did you tell him?"

"Well we told him it was didn't we. Robertson says, 'You should have had a letter about it from the town hall'. So he asks if I'd got one. I told him I didn't need it now I'm married."

"Oh you rotten things," Helen said with a smile of sympathy. "Poor lad."

"You'd better get your Cock Licence renewed!" Rita said, looking directly at Rob. Her words produced a sudden silence and Eric caught a warning glance from Helen. Tread warily, her eyes reminded him.

"He didn't actually go did he? To the Town Hall?" Helen asked quickly.

Eric picked up Helen's cue. "Well, the lad says, 'They don't really call it a cock licence do they?' and Robertson says, 'Its real name is a C.O.C. licence.' So the kid says, like he thought he had us, 'Alright then, what does C.O.C. stand for?' and Robertson, quick as a flash says 'Consummation of Carnality'."

"He didn't really believe…?" Helen asked incredulously.

"He came in Friday afternoon and played bloody hell with me and Robertson. He'd been to the Town Hall in his dinner hour and asked 'em where he could get a cock licence. Silly bugger gave 'em his name and they gave him a blank look."

Helen shook her head. "Poor kid," she said. "You should be ashamed of yourself."

Eric laughed. "You should have seen his face. It was all over the co-op."

Antony's whimpers became more insistent and Rita sighed, "I'm going to make Antony's feed. D'you fancy some ham and pork pie for tea?"

"We haven't come for tea Reet," Helen protested.

"Oh come on," Rita said. "It's not much. I've got a tin of pears. Rob's got to go later. Have some tea with us then you can help me to get Antony ready for bed."

"Well if you're sure…" Helen followed Rita into the kitchen.

Eric turned to Rob. "Sorry to hear about your bike mate. Any idea who took it?"

Rob shook his head. "She keeps on about it. I keep telling her, it's gone so there's no point carrying on." He shrugged and began laying out the cards again.

Eric watched in silence. The girls were still busy in the kitchen and he leaned forward confidentially. "So, what was all that about then?"

"What?"

"Rita. Telling you to get a cock licence." He gave Rob a knowing grin. "Wouldn't have thought you needed one."

"I bloody don't," Rob answered. He picked up the cards and began idly shuffling. "What's she been saying?"

"Who? Rita?" Eric tried to avoid bluster. "Nothing! No it's… its just, what she said, just now."

"That's alright then isn't it!"

So there was something in it after all. Eric took the cards from Rob. "Come on, a quick game of 'Knockout' before they come back."

Rita came in with a cry of exasperation, "Oh don't start playing cards now. I need the table."

"What's the matter?" Helen said, entering with a bowl of salad.

"It's alright," Eric said mildly. "Just passing time."

"It's all he ever thinks about," Rita muttered.

"No it bloody isn't!" Rob snapped and Rita turned abruptly and left the room followed by Helen with a 'you should have known better' look at Eric.

"Sorry mate," Eric said. "What was all that about?"

"Cards! And gambling," Rita cried, reappearing with Helen at her shoulder. "That's what it's all about!"

"Oh shut up will you. You'll have your bloody mother in again."

Rita started to cry and Helen closed the door with a glare at Eric. He held up his hands in protest.

"I'm sorry," Rita snuffled. "It's alright Eric. It's just… it'll be a good job when the baby's come."

Rob jumped up suddenly. "I've had enough! I don't want to hear any more!" He looked at the clock. "I've got to be going soon anyway. I'm going to get changed."

"But your tea's ready!" Rita protested.

"It'll wait! It's only salad!"

"I'm sorry." Rita looked tearfully at Helen. "Fine Sunday tea I'm giving you."

Helen glared at Eric. "It's your fault. It wouldn't have happened if you hadn't started playing with them blessed cards."

"Wasn't me!" Eric protested and he sought protection behind a magazine.

"You wouldn't like it if it was you!" Helen said. "No wonder Rita gets upset. And she mustn't get upset. Not now. It's not good for her."

"Don't blame Eric," Rita said. "It's not his fault. Let's forget about it. Come on, come and sit down. We needn't wait."

Rob returned wearing his suit. He hung the jacket across the back of his chair. "Sorry about that," he said brightly. "Thought of going to work I suppose. We're not always like that are we duck." He gave Rita a kiss and she smiled shamefacedly.

"You don't go firing in your best suit, do you?" Helen asked incredulously.

Rob began to laugh.

"What's up with you?" Eric asked.

"I bet you have a game going in the back of the shop when it's quiet," Rob smirked.

Eric felt Helen's eyes on him and tried to laugh it off. "Bloody don't," he protested. "We don't have time for that," but Rob had already changed tack again.

"Anyway it's London tonight. Then we're bringing a parcels train back at three o'clock."

"So what do you do in the meantime?" Helen asked.

Rob reached across the table and began filling his plate. "Me and my driver'll probably go and have a pint if we can clear the shed in time. Saves sitting around for hours after we've coaled up."

"He goes drinking, don't you!" Rita said accusingly. "That's what the suit's for."

"I wear my overall over it." Rob turned to Eric. "You can't go into a pub in overalls can you?" Again the appeal to complicity and Eric shrugged in mute reply.

"I'll bring the pears in," Rita said. "There's a tin opener in that sideboard drawer Eric."

Rob rose from his seat with a show of gallantry. "You sit there duck. I'll go and fetch 'em."

It was so false and watching him leave the room Eric felt his respect for Rob diminishing but Rita needed their friendship and Helen said, "You need to find somewhere of your own to live."

"We've started looking but it's not easy."

"Is there anything we can do?"

Rita looked steadily at her friend and shook her head.

"He doesn't really go drinking does he?" Eric asked quietly. "Wouldn't have thought they'd let 'em when they've got a train to drive."

"I don't suppose they do let 'em," Rita answered with simple resignation.

Chapter 14 - Lachrymosae – 2

Thursday afternoon. It was Eric's half-day and he was meeting Helen from her ante-natal clinic. She was waiting beneath the statue in the square and as he approached she burst into tears. "I'm sorry. I didn't mean to be like this." She looked about her in embarrassment. "I'm sorry, I don't want to show you up."

Eric held her close, shielding her from the glances of passers by. "You're not showing me up love. What's the matter?"

"It's the hospital. There's a mix up about my dates," Helen sobbed. "They're saying it's my fault. It was awful." Eric led her away to a corner beyond the square and Helen gathered her coat about her and wiped the tears away. "They've been rotten. It was the registrar; she said such horrible things."

"What sort of things?"

"They've not taken any notice of what I told them and they've got my dates wrong. If it goes on too long they say they're going to induce me." Helen's distress was inconceivable and again she dabbed at her eyes. "But it wasn't just that Eric. It's the baby; it's in posterior position."

"What's that?"

"Instead of facing towards my back it's facing forward. It's... back to front in the womb."

Eric became alarmed. "It's not dangerous is it?"

"No, no. It's just not so straightforward. It makes it more awkward."

Eric stayed silent. "No wonder you're upset," he said finally.

"She told me not to be silly; she said I was making too much fuss and in her country women had babies in the fields and thought nothing about it! I didn't take in what she said straight away. And then I didn't want to let it show, to let her see how upset I was. I wouldn't give her the satisfaction..."

"I'm going up to the hospital!"

"No Eric, don't make a fuss."

"They can't talk to you like that Hel!! I won't have you treated like that!"

"Don't," Helen pleaded. "They'll only take it out on me if you make a fuss."

Eric did his best to reassure her and made an appointment with the consultant obstetrician, an immaculately tailored man who regarded them with unyielding condescension. He noted Eric's suppressed anger and sensed Helen's deferential tone of apology. After an unnerving silence he finally spoke:

"What do you want me to do?"

"Well, she shouldn't be talking to women – ladies, the way she spoke to Helen."

"Yes but what do you want me to do?" An eyebrow rose. "Hm?"

"Well…" Suddenly Eric realised his protest was futile. He wanted to say 'sack her' but there was something in the manner of the man before him, a barrier he couldn't cross. "Well what can you do? In cases like this," Eric concluded lamely.

"I can have a word with the obstetric registrar concerned and see if her version of the exchange tallies with your… wife's."

"But, but, you're not saying that…"

"I'm not saying anything. But we only have your wife's version of events don't we."

That was the end of the interview and though Eric attempted to press his point the effort was wasted. "I wish we'd never bothered," he said as they walked down the hospital drive together. "They make you feel so bloody trivial."

In the spring, with her pregnancy reaching its term, Rita had a stroke of good fortune. She found a terraced house to rent in an anonymous back-street in the industrial east of the city. The front door opened directly onto the pavement and the backyard, containing a patch of sour black earth bordered by bricks, was shared with three other houses. Rita surveyed it with all the shining optimism of a bride and forgave the house its cracked plaster and uneven linoleum floor and split skirting boards. She overlooked it's odour, the dirty wallpaper with the marks of absent mirrors and calendars stencilled on the walls and declared it perfect, seeing the rooms as they would be, as Rob and she would make them.

Helen went with her to view it. "Darnall's alright Rita," she said loyally. "And when they come to demolish it you'll get a council house."

The prospect of their leaving brought no comfort to Rita's mother. The distance between her home in the suburbs, overlooked by the woods of Millhouses and Rita's house in the backstreets within earshot of the forges was an unbridgeable gulf and two weeks passed before she could bring herself to go there. She looked at the broken asphalt and the weeds along the wall by the toilets in the yard and heard the dull throb of the steel mills and sighed as she knocked the door. Rita opened it with a cry of pleasure and her mother surveyed her heavily pregnant daughter and forced a smile as she stepped into the kitchen.

"You look well anyway."

The cream enamel sink under the window was on a red and white unit with a plywood door, matched by red-and-white cupboards beside the chimney breast.

"We started on the lounge first."

Lounge! The word was an anachronism. She peeled off her gloves and handed her coat to Rita. "Here, do something with this. I'll make the tea. Where do you keep your things?"

"You'll find cups and tea and sugar in the cupboard; the milk's on the cellar head," Rita called.

Her mother stood at the brink of the stone steps descending into the darkness of the cellar. "Rita, I wonder you don't break your neck. Especially in your condition." She braced herself against the opposite wall and leaned over the chasm to the shelf for the milk.

"It's the coolest place for it," Rita said brightly, determined not to let her mother's disapproval spoil things. She nodded towards the lounge. "Antony's in there. He'll be waking up soon; you can go in and see him if you like. I'll bring the tea through..."

Rita followed her and found her mother bending over the pram. She turned with a vague look of guilt as Rita entered.

"He was awake," she said.

"It's alright mum. He's due a feed anyway."

"Here let me…"

101

"No mum. Sit down. I'm not an invalid." Rita poured the tea and said, "How's daddy?"

"Daddy's the same as always. He'll be glad when you've had this baby. You're not planning on any more after this are you?"

Rita laughed and sat in the armchair beside the hearth. "We didn't plan this one."

"No. And you didn't…" her mother retorted and she bit her lip and glanced at the clock on the mantelpiece.

"It's alright mum. Rob won't be home for hours yet."

"I didn't mean…"

"I know mum." Rita put her cup on the hearth and raised herself from the chair. "Would you like to nurse him while I get his bottle ready?"

"Well… Do you think he'll be alright?"

"Course he will. He might be a bit of a smelly bum though."

She didn't take the child unwillingly only Antony wriggled, it was 'his' child and she held him awkwardly on her lap. Then he stopped struggling, lay still and looked straight up into her eyes, and when Rita returned with Antony's bottle she found her mother weeping.

"Mum. What's wrong? What's the matter? Are you alright?"

"I've got a bit of cold. It makes my eyes run." She gave Antony back to Rita and took a handkerchief from her handbag and dabbed her eyes. "I don't want him to catch anything. I'll have another cup if there is one. When you've finished." The air of strain between them gradually eased until finally she rose to leave. In the kitchen she paused with an embarrassed smile and returned for a final peek at her Antony, gurgling in his pram and at the door she hesitated again. "Are you going to be alright? Is there anything you need?" But again she sought refuge from her feelings. "Daddy told me to ask…"

"Mum…" Rita felt so sorry for her. "We're alright. Honest."

Seventy-two hours later Rita presented her mother with another grandson.

Chapter 15 - In the still of the night

Eric's self-esteem was dented by his attempt to act as Helen's champion. He had been made to look a fool and the reference to her pelvis and the baby's position were causing him anxiety. He wanted to know more about the implications but he couldn't ask in case his fears should come true. Indigestion began to gnaw at him and he was constantly chewing antacid tablets, sometimes up to half a packet a day. He wanted to make their world secure but the world wouldn't take him seriously and she needed him to be strong but he was weak and his anxiety became anger and his anger sought an outlet and Eric hid behind a lie rather than share his real fear, his fear of rejection. He wanted to join the operatic society, he said, but he knew what his father would say and besides he wouldn't know anyone and anyway they wouldn't accept him.

Helen smiled and said, "Yes they would."

"I don't think so," he answered petulantly. "I've seen them, in their fine houses, all dressed up in their dinner jackets. But I could be as good as any of them."

"Oh Eric!" Helen protested, "you're making something out of nothing."

"Am I!" he cried. "What chance have I got?"

"But there's nothing wrong with you. You're good looking and you've got a really good voice if you really let yourself go…" A fit of coughing cut off Helen's words. "Come on Eric, you're making something out of nothing…" But he was damned if he'd be consoled and weary of argument Helen said, "And now you're being childish!"

Her words were lethal and Eric sprang from the chair. "Oh! I'm childish am I? It's a pity we ever got together, you with all your clever friends." His face contorted with rage, "…and your arty family. You don't care," he cried bitterly and as Helen ran from the room, "That's right! Run off," he taunted her. "You know I'm right."

Helen slammed the bedroom door in tears. Why did he get like this? She loved Eric dearly but there was something lurking deep in his personality and this... this... thing was going to spoil it all. Helen curled into a ball with her hands clasped across her belly and hugged herself. The last shreds of light were fading from the sky and she wanted to creep under the covers and wait for Eric to come and comfort her but they were separated by a silence greater than the mere thickness of a wall.

In their sitting room Eric stood consumed with self-pity for being the unreasonable brute that he was, waiting for Helen to come and forgive him. Life wasn't worth living and he wept at his foolishness for casting away the carefully wrought self-image. How could she love him now? Poor weak useless thing that he was! He went to the darkened bedroom and peeped in. Helen was curled asleep on the bed. He crept away and sat alone. He heard a footfall. Helen was in the doorway and an ocean of sorrow stood between them.

"I wasn't asleep." Her eyes were red with tears.

"Helen I'm so sorry. I don't know what to say... I..."

"Oh Eric." There was no judgement in her voice. "Don't you love me any more?"

Her simple words swept all misunderstanding aside. He remembered the advice given at their wedding; 'Never let the sun go down on your wrath.' At the time they had sounded ridiculously pretentious; now he knew what they meant. "Oh Helen, Helen. I love you. I do. I'm so sorry. I do love you. More than anything in the world."

"What is it Eric? What's troubling you?"

"It's just... I wish it was all over."

Helen cradled him in her arms and Oh! The futility of regret...

Eric tried to make amends. They arranged to meet after her next clinic for lunch together but a telephone call from Helen to the shop forestalled him. "They've decided to keep me in," she said. "Can you call home and bring me some nightclothes; you know, my nice dressing gown. A bed jacket; you'll find that in the middle drawer. Oh and some face cream. And a box of tissues..."

"There's nothing wrong is there?"

"No, they're just taking precautions. It's because of my dates."

Eric arrived in the middle of the afternoon. Helen was sitting beside her bed; she greeted him with relief and a furrow of anxiety rose on his brow. "You alright?"

"'Course I am." Helen lowered her voice. "Another week and you'll be a daddy. Perhaps even sooner. Anyway what have you got there?"

He unpacked the clothes and Helen placed them in her bedside cupboard.

"I was going to bring flowers but I wasn't sure..." There were flowers beside most beds and the woman in the bed adjacent to Helen's had three vases full.

"Do you know what I really fancy?" Helen said with a childlike grin. "A carrot."

"A carrot?"

"Yes, you know, like we used to have as kids. A carrot; to chew on."

Eric had heard of women's fads; one of his aunts used to plunge her nose into a soapflake box, emerging after a deep inhalation with a look of ecstasy. "Well if you're sure." They lapsed into small talk and Eric gazed around the ward. "Are they all waiting for their babies to be born?" he whispered,

"Shhh." Helen said. "They'll know you're talking about them." She put on a 'natural' air and spoke softly, "The woman across there – don't look – wearing a blue bedjacket. She's been in for weeks. Her waters broke in the third month. They're afraid of infection now the barrier's gone so she's got to stay in until the baby's born." Eric opened his mouth but Helen continued softly, "She's still got another two months to go."

"Bloody Hell!" Eric turned to the woman in the bed behind him but received a silent stare of inexplicable bitterness. It was time to move to other things. "There's a meeting at the operatic society later this week," he said. "Your mum's asked if I'd like to go with her."

"You ought to Eric. You'd meet more of the people and get to know them..."

The members of the operatic society confirmed 'Carousel' as next season's show and Max Grey congratulated them on a wise choice, "It'll be another money spinner for us." He looked approvingly at Jim, the treasurer, and Jim nodded with satisfaction. Marlene would almost certainly get the part of Julie; it was perfect for her. They broke for refreshments and Alice steered Eric towards a group laughing together. "My son-in-law, Eric," she said. "Malcolm and Jenny, Malcolm's fiancee."

Malcolm was tall with aquiline features and black hair greased in a precise parting. He was not more than two years Eric's senior and he offered his hand with a formal air. "Welcome lad, we could do with a few more like you. I'm fed up having to carry all the men's parts on my own."

Jenny, petite and strikingly pretty, smiled at Eric. "Hello Eric. How's Helen?"

"They've decided to keep her in until the baby's born. Won't be long," he added.

"We heard she'd gone in Alice." The voice, replete with prior knowledge came from one of Alice's friends. "She's alright isn't she?"

"Yes," Alice replied. "They're still not sure exactly when though."

"This is Aunty Sybil," Jenny said.

Sybil said, "Your mother-in-law and I have been friends a long time, haven't we Alice."

"Longer than we care to remember," Alice replied and there was laughter all round.

"Give her our love when you see her," and the conversation turned to Rita's new baby. "You remember when their Antony was first born? He was such a little thing," Sybil continued, "and cry! He never stopped the whole time we were there. Oh but this one's lovely…"

Malcolm and Jenny detached themselves, drawing Eric with them. "Are you going to be in the show?" Jenny asked. Her light soprano voice was as pretty as her looks.

"I don't know. I mean I don't know if I can sing or not."

"I shouldn't worry," Malcolm said with a laugh. "Provided you're a man and you've got two legs... We're going for a drink later, are you coming to join us?"

"I'm not sure. I think I'm getting a lift back with Helen's mum."

"We'll give you a lift back to Alice's, won't we Malcolm."

A voice broke in. "This a new member then?" Eric turned; Jim was at his elbow with Marlene at his side.

"He's not sure if he wants to join us," Malcolm teased playfully.

"Not good enough are we?" Marlene said and they laughed at Eric's discomfiture.

"We're all going up for a drink after," Malcolm said. "You and Marlene coming?"

"Sounds like a jolly good idea." Jim turned to Eric. "Are you putting up for a part?"

"I don't think so," Eric replied but his fears had been dispelled; he was amongst friends.

Eric brought Helen freshly scraped carrots but there was a subdued atmosphere in the ward and the curtains of the bed next to Helen were drawn. "How did you get on last night?" Helen asked.

"Great," Eric said happily. "They were all asking after you."

"I told you." Helen's eyes wrinkled in a smile. She arched her back and Eric eased her into a more comfortable position and pushed pillows behind her. "I wish they'd get a move on," Helen said. "They say I've got at least another week to go."

"Isn't there anything they can do?" Eric gestured helplessly.

"They'll have to induce me." A shadow crossed Eric's face. "It's nothing to worry about. They'll just put me on a drip. Then the hormones will kick in and start me off." She smiled at him. "And then the baby will wake up and be born. He's just being lazy, that's all."

"He?"

"Or she." Helen patted her stomach. "But we want you to get a move on don't we; you can't stay in there forever." A man emerged from behind the curtain surrounding the adjacent bed and Helen's expression changed. The man turned to look back at the woman in the bed, mouthed, 'Goodnight,' and caught Helen's eye. He was not more than thirty but haggard lines of worry added years to his appearance. Helen gave him a wan smile and he hesitated, drawing the curtains closed. "She's asleep," he murmured and left them, looking neither left nor right at the sympathetic eyes that followed him.

"It's awful for them," Helen said softly and Eric saw unexpected tears. "She's having twins but one of her babies is dead. They're keeping her here until she can be delivered."

Eric looked across at the curtain in open-mouthed disbelief and Helen put a warning finger to her lips. "I couldn't tell you while she was awake. It's terrible for her."

Ashamed of his own miserable fears Eric took Helen's hand. "I wish I'd known. I'd have liked to have said something to him."

"What could you possibly say?" Helen murmured.

It was becoming clear that Helen's baby was unwilling to initiate any movement of its own accord and the opinion of the registrar together with the midwives was that Helen had gone long enough. She was well past the date she'd insisted on and their timetable was now looking increasingly unsafe.

"If nothing starts happening today," Helen said, "they're going to induce me tomorrow."

"What'll happen then?" Eric asked, trying to keep his nervousness at bay.

"I'll start to have contractions. And then the baby will be born." Helen made it sound easy and matter-of-fact. "Which it is," she concluded.

Eric rose to leave. "I'll see you tomorrow then," he said as he kissed her.

"If not before," Helen replied and she waved brightly as he turned at the door.

The following evening Eric arrived with flowers. Helen lay with the drip feeding through a cannula taped to the back of her hand. The bed alongside her was empty. "What's happened?" he asked.

108

"They took her away this morning," Helen replied. "They're going to try to induce her."

"How was she?"

Helen closed her eyes then she sighed and roused herself. "Flowers," she said. "Thank you."

"You deserve more than just carrots." He hesitated. "Any sign yet?"

"Nothing so far I'm afraid."

"What if... if nothing happens?"

"They'll try again. They'll probably break my waters to help it on its way." She pushed the leftover carrots from her. "I'd better not have any more of these for now."

They induced Helen again and broke the membranes. Looking at Eric's anxious face she said, "Don't worry. It's got to happen now," and gave him a look of reassurance. "It's alright. They like to let it happen naturally if they can but sometimes they have to use other procedures."

Eric fretted beside her. His eyes wandered to the adjacent bed but it was vacant and he said, "I just wish there was something I could do."

Helen lay calmly and her eyes took on a faraway look. "It'll just take a little bit longer," she said. "By tomorrow I should be on my way."

Tomorrow. Another tomorrow! The following evening Eric was met by a nurse. "Your wife's gone into labour," she said. He looked across at the bed where Helen had lain and his face twitched in relief. "She started at lunchtime."

Eric glanced at his watch, it was seven o'clock. "How much... how long will she be?"

"It won't be easy for her I'm afraid." With barely perceptible hesitation the nurse added, "You can see her if you'd like." Eric followed the nurse along a corridor signposted 'Labour Ward'. "Wait here a moment." He licked his lips in nervous anticipation. He'd laughed at jokes about expectant husbands; the reality wasn't so funny. The nurse returned and said, "Your wife is in a waiting area. Nothing is going to happen for the next few hours. She's resting. It's very exhausting for her. We've given her a sedative; you mustn't disturb her." She led him to a gloomy cul-de-sac off a corridor with a dim blue light in the ceiling to where a trolley was parked in shadow against the wall. "Call me if you want anything," she said and left him.

Eric approached and peered at the unconscious figure beneath the blanket. There were beads of moisture on Helen's brow; her hair was limp and wet. She was moving restlessly, breathing in shallow whimpers of pain. Then the sounds increased; her eyes opened and she stared, unseeing, writhing and arching her back with a cry and crying out again in extremis until the contraction subsided and her eyes closed and she relapsed into troubled sleep once more. Eric wiped her forehead with the edge of the sheet and stood helpless, watching her, his eyes filled with tears. He looked around for help but there was no-one. Helen was seized by another contraction and she arched and shrieked again. Eric wiped Helen's face and leaning over her he began to pray. A group of nurses approached from the light at the far end of the corridor, their bright chatter loud in the silence, then turned into a ward leaving Eric alone with Helen...

Rita opened the door surprised to see Eric standing there. Her face lit in momentary anticipation then she saw the haggard look. "Why Eric, you poor love," she said, "come on in. Whatever's the matter?"

"I've just been to see Helen." There was a sob in his voice.

"How is she? Has she...?"

Rita led him into the sitting room and Eric stood motionless before the mantelpiece, staring down at the hearth. "Is Rob in?" he mumbled.

"You've just missed him. He's only been gone about twenty minutes."

There was a small pile of baby clothes on the old second hand oak sideboard; a tiny blue woollen cardigan and Antony's bib, the one decorated with the kangaroo, on the arm of a fireside chair. Eric began to tell her but the dreadful sounds of Helen's labour filled his mind and his lips moved in silence. Rita took his arm; he allowed

110

himself to be led to a chair and said with a sigh, "She's still in labour."

"When did she start?"

"Lunchtime. About twelve o'clock. It's terrible." Tears streamed onto his cheeks. "She's unconscious… She's having an awful time."

"Women do have an awful time," Rita said. "It's one of the worst things that can happen to a woman. Having a child."

He hesitated and whispered, "I think she's going to die Rita."

"Oh don't say that Eric. Don't say that love. She'll be alright, I know she will."

Eric turned away in despair and Rita tried to comfort him. She made him go to the telephone box in the next street, but all they would say was Helen's labour was continuing and to call back.

"Do you think they'd let me see her?" Rita asked on his return.

"I expect so." He turned to leave and paused at the door. "I'm sorry Rita. I'm so worried."

Rita placed her hand on his shoulder and kissed him, a kiss of comfort for Helen. "Try to sleep Eric," she said. "You look awful."

Chapter 16 - A broken heart

The following morning Eric telephoned again and received the same answer. 'Your wife's still in labour; call back later.' Fred Robertson gave him the day off but Eric declined. "What would I do," he protested, "waiting at home all day?"

"Same as you're doing here," Robertson replied.

Eric buried himself in the showroom until it was time to phone again. 'Your wife's in...' He replaced the receiver in despair and went to the hospital. Helen lay as before and they would only allow a brief visit. "How long?" he asked desperately. "It's been more than a day and a half already."

That evening he sat with Alice, no longer the vivacious woman but a mother reliving memories of her own confinement. But not as long as this one, no not as long as this! Eric fretted the time away, trying not to watch the clock but checking one clock against the other in case the clocks were cheating. What is the time? Will they say the same again and fob me off? Was it too soon to ring again? Eric licked his mouth, raised the handset and dialled.

"She's just come out. You can come and see her any time now."

"And the baby?"

"They're just bringing them down. She should be ready by the time you get here."

She should...? A girl! Eric's relief was inexpressible and he raced upstairs to tell them, anxiety lifting at each step. "It's a girl. A baby girl! I've got to go and see them!"

"D'you think they'll let me see her?" Alice cried. "After all, I'm her mother."

"Ye... er... yes, yes come on...!"

The long corridor overlaid with the smell of disinfectant echoed to the tiny sounds of babies. "Would you mind waiting here please," the nurse said, adding a final admonition, "Only two visitors allowed at a time I'm afraid." She left them and went to an office along the corridor.

"You go first," Frank said to Alice. "I'll wait here."

Eric began pacing. "They'll be getting her ready," Alice said knowingly. "She'll want to look her best for you."

A doctor in a white coat emerged from the office and approached Eric. "You are Helen's husband I take it?"

"I'm Helen's mother," Alice cried eagerly. "And this is my husband. Helen's father."

The doctor saw no point in mincing his words. "Helen has had a very difficult confinement. But she is alright," he added hastily, and Eric sighed with relief. "She is very tired of course. She's sleeping now. But she is alright. Helen is a very strong young woman."

"And the baby?" Eric savoured the word, "Our... daughter?"

A frown creased the doctor's brow. "I'm afraid Helen's baby... your baby, was stillborn."

Alice gave a cry and seized Frank's arm for support.

"But they said," Eric protested desperately, "when I phoned, they said she was being got ready. For us to see her. That's what they said."

The doctor's voice was unyielding. "I don't know who told you that. But they were mistaken. Helen's child was a boy." He paused and studied Eric carefully. "Would you like to see your wife?"

Frank eased Eric forward. "You go first lad. We'll wait here for a minute or two."

The doctor led Eric to the room where Helen lay sleeping. Her breathing rasped in her throat; a voice at Eric's side said, "She'll be much better tomorrow. You'll see a big difference."

Eric nodded silently. In his heart he thanked God but his relief was tempered by guilt. The image of mother and child wouldn't go away; Helen relaxed in serene exhaustion, the child wrapped in her arms, flowers, smiles of joy, congratulations round her bed. He had indulged and nurtured the scene; basking in new fatherhood, claiming pride in his achievement like countless fathers before him. He gazed down at Helen, bitter with regret for all she had endured. For nothing! Nothing!

Alice and Frank came in and they stood like voyeurs round the bed but nothing about Helen changed. Reluctantly they prepared to go, leaving Eric murmuring silent words. 'Goodnight love. Sleep well. Sleep...'

The doctor took them along the corridor to the office. There was a duty to be done. He was satisfied that Helen would be well but the family would have questions and they needed to be reassured. The child had been taken away, he told them. "It's better that the mother doesn't see the child. That would only add to the er, trauma." He spared them the details of the past few hours. Of his shock on arrival in the delivery room, his anger at the panic surrounding the agonised young woman as they grappled with forceps, and the struggle that had taken place. The shamefaced confessions as he tried to sweep their incompetence's aside, the words of accusation mumbled beneath the mask, their answers lost in renewed activity. Was his expertise applied too late? - "Good God! This should have been a Caesarean!" - as he wrestled with her until the wrinkled child emerged into the towels and the forceps were finally put aside as they prepared to cut and bind the cord. The midwife reaching for the baby's ankles to raise him for the slap to shock him into life, the deep indents in the temples where the forceps had compressed the skull, the bruises already beginning to colour. He had shaken his head and around him the exhausted team felt the weight of failure as they gazed at the child with his wet mat of long dark hair and the fingernails already due for trimming, questioning with their eyes and seeing the judgement his own eyes carried. 'We cannot tell to what extent this child is damaged.' The child wasn't breathing, anyone could see that and he turned his attention back to the mother. 'Pray God...'

With the eyes of the family on him he spoke directly to Eric. "The baby was in the posterior position. I think you knew that."

Alice murmured, "Yes, Eric told us."

"Did you know she also had a contracted pelvis?"

Eric said, "Yes." He looked at Alice apologetically. "I'm sorry, I should have said but..." He hadn't understood the implications.

"And of course it was a very big baby. I'm afraid it was the worst possible combination; Helen has had a particularly difficult...

ordeal. Everyone did everything possible. We are all so very, very sorry."

Eric heard Alice's formal, "Thank you doctor," an unnecessary act of deference and he wanted to scream, 'What the fucking hell are you thanking him for?' but his own voice echoed Alice's deferential politeness.

"As for Helen, she's exhausted, as you can imagine. She needs rest now." The doctor gave them a weak smile, careful not to betray his relief. "And all the love you can manage between you."

"Oh she'll get plenty of that won't she Eric."

"Yes," Eric replied sadly.

The following day Helen was awake but the marks of strain were evident in the darkness of her eyes and the unnatural blood red flush that suffused her face. She opened her arms and they hugged in a silence broken only by stifled sobs. Helen raised Eric's face and looked at him, endlessly, wordlessly. Eric looked away, searching for words that had meaning. He wanted to say, 'It's alright,' but it wasn't, and the message in Helen's look was far from clear. There was disappointment. But blame – guilt - regret? Tears began misting his eyes. "Don't Eric," Helen pleaded. "Don't." Her gaze wavered and she turned from him.

"I was with you Hel. I came and saw you. As long as I could. I couldn't do any..." He faltered and hung his head in shame, his words no more than a whisper. "I'm so sorry." Helen's hand rested lightly on his and he grasped it and sobbed convulsively, "I'm so sorry," and felt the pressure of Helen's lips against his unshaven cheek...

Rita arrived with flowers, an expression of sympathy alternating with a brave smile. Eric stood aside and she threw her arms about Helen in a sudden flood of tears. Helen squeezed her eyes closed. "It's alright Reet, really, I'm alright." She looked for Rita's children. "Where's Antony and Raymond?

"Mum's got them," Rita replied. "Rob's on again tonight. She sends her love."

"You could have brought them," Helen said gently.

"I didn't like to…"

"It's alright Reet. Honest. I hope you're going to let me nurse them now and again."

"Oh Helen," Rita protested, "You know…" she broke off, her mouth quivering.

"How long before you come home?" Eric asked.

"A few more days," Helen said. "Nothing to really worry about," she added quickly. "It's just been such a difficult… birth."

"Just as long as you're alright," Eric said, "then we can get you home again."

"I'm just very tired." Helen closed her eyes. "And sore. But it'll get better."

"I don't mean - you know - that," Eric protested. "I meant you. You've no idea…"

"Oh I think I have," Helen interjected softly.

But it was more than a few days before Helen could return home and she told Eric with helpless resignation, "I've got an infection. U.T.I."

"What in the hell is that?"

"Urinary tract. It'll be alright, the antibiotics will sort it out. I'll just have to stay a bit longer."

The days became a week and one week became two until finally… "I was beginning to think I was going to have to stay forever," Helen said as they walked from the ward.

"We're sorry to see you go," the nurse said, "Now you're sure you're alright?"

"I'm fine," Helen smiled at Eric and squeezed his hand. "This is all I want."

That night she lay with Eric and he reached out to embrace her, with tenderness, the way they used to, but at his kiss Helen stiffened with apprehension. "It's alright," he whispered, "There's plenty of time. I didn't mean that."

Helen relaxed and closed her eyes. "I love you," she murmured, "I'll soon be better," and waited for sleep…

116

The first time Rita offered Raymond to Helen he began to cry but Helen coo'd and rocked him and lost herself to the world with the child in her arms until he became calm and Rita said Helen had a mother's touch and instantly regretted it. But Helen appeared not to have heard, and replied to Raymond, "You like your Aunty Helen don't you." She handed him back to Rita and, oh! the ache she felt inside; and no amount of nursing and cuddling could take the ache away and Helen's memories remained, taunting her with humiliation. But confiding in Rita, she received understanding.

Rita was at the sink, sterilising a bottle for Raymond's afternoon feed. "I don't know why they didn't send you to Jessop's in the first place," she said.

Helen, nursing Raymond against her shoulder, replied, "I wish I'd been in Jessop's like you."

"They should never have let you go as long as you did!"

But Helen's commitment to her profession was absolute. "It was all to do with the confusion over my dates," she said but Rita was less forgiving.

"A caesarean would have made it easier."

"I suppose so." Helen swayed gently back and forth while the baby drowsed on her shoulder. Rita was right of course and in the silence of her heart she too cried, 'Why?' For despite her forgiving nature Helen knew she should have been better cared for. Pondering on bitter memories they took Raymond upstairs for his nap. Helen turned the covers back and Rita laid him in and folded the covers over him. Raymond stirred briefly and Helen hushed him. "There, there, shhhh. Sleep tight. Shhhh."

They returned downstairs and Rita filled the kettle at the sink. "We'll have a cup of coffee eh?"

"It's all about natural birth now," Helen mused. "Some women give birth in swimming pools."

Rita said, "I'm not sure I'd want to go in for that."

"She had me doing squats," Helen said unexpectedly.

Rita turned to Helen. "Who did?"

"You know who. It's an awful thing to say but I think she wanted to humiliate me. Do you remember; that day Eric met me; I was upset and we went to see the consultant about her?"

"Oh her."

"Yes her." Helen's expression hardened. "She kept going on about the fuss English women made. After they'd induced me the second time she had me doing squats." Helen fell silent, retreating into the thoughts that were troubling her and the memory brought feelings of shame. "Gripping the bed rail and squatting down as low as I could. Then up and back down again. It was so humiliating," Helen insisted earnestly. "With all the others in the ward looking on! And then I had that infection. She hurt me when she inserted the catheter; she got it wrong and had to do it twice. Anyway I shan't see her again."

The kettle began to boil and Rita made coffee. They carried the mugs into the sitting room and Rita said quietly, "You know Helen, it sounds awful of me to say this, but you were very lucky."

Helen's face remained impassive. "Lucky. Oh yes. Lucky."

"I know what you must be thinking Hel. But when I came to see you that day I…" Rita paused, her lip quivering. "I didn't think I'd ever see you again."

"I didn't even know you'd been. Or Eric."

"I didn't believe Eric at first when he told me. We were all frightened to death for you."

Helen sighed; a distant sound. "They took him away." Her face held a strange, blank expression. "I didn't even see him." She paused. "Eric asked but they said he'd been taken to the mortuary." She looked up at Rita and her eyes were filled with pleading. Rita remained motionless, caught in the moment until eventually Helen sighed. "Anyway…" She turned with a faraway look, speaking with an air of sad resignation, "…at least I'm here."

A smile of understanding flickered briefly about Rita's mouth. "I'll get us lunch while his nibs is asleep," she said. "You can stop can't you?"

Helen nodded. "That'd be nice. What time does Rob get back?"

"About three."

Rita reached for Helen's cup but Helen placed a restraining hand on Rita's arm. "How long did you and Rob wait before you started having sex again?"

Rita gave Helen a knowing look. "Oh you know what Rob's like. You'll be at it again in no time."

Chapter 17 - A den of delights

The society's third annual pea-and-pie supper was held at Marlene and Jim's and everybody turned up for they were rapidly establishing themselves as the nucleus of the society. Jim was treasurer and Marlene was a vivacious hostess and the party was an opportunity to discuss plans for future productions and air ambitions for a part. The May evening was unexpectedly balmy and a cry of greeting arose from a group on the lawn as Helen and Eric appeared walking up the drive. Marlene ran to welcome them and Helen glowed with pleasure. Her dress, pale brown cotton with a high collar over a close fitting bodice and widely flared skirt had been carefully chosen and she heard an impromptu chorus of 'People will say we're in love' greeting them from the open windows. Rita waved from the lounge window and came out to join them.

"Rob's about somewhere," she said and Helen gave Eric a smile of encouragement.

"Go on. You don't want to stay here talking girl's talk do you?"

Eric wandered round into the garden. On the patio Jim was in earnest conversation with Max and he acknowledged Eric with a wave. Jim - expected to make Chief Accountant by the time he was thirty-five. Eric looked around with envy. This is what it's all about, the house at the end of a discrete cul-de-sac, lawns screened by silver birch and shrubs, friendship, influence and a strange thought struck him, something about nemesis.

A distant voice was calling, "What's up? You look like you've lost something." Lost something? Oh yes, I've lost something. And the child too, the thought persisted, accusing him; your child. You can't deny the child. Is he forgotten already? And Helen! Eric turned and saw her with Rita and Jenny amid a circle of girls, laughing, happy and then Malcolm bore down on him.

"You look lost."

Eric cast his thoughts aside with relief. "Well yes actually I was looking for Rob."

"He's in here. Come on."

They strode off toward the house together, the music changed and the girls began singing, 'I feel pretty, oh so pretty,' with Helen amongst them preening and posing as they sang. So vivacious, so desirable and still she flinched from him. Eric waved but it passed unnoticed and he followed Malcolm inside.

Later they queued for supper in Marlene's super modern kitchen and had a few drinks more. Now the singing was over and the sounds of conversation rose from discrete groups enjoying the remnants of the day about the house. Helen was standing with Rita in a recess beside the stairs. "I don't know what to do Reet." Helen glanced round carefully to make sure she wasn't overheard. "It's not that I don't love him, I do. But it's coming between us."

"You are alright?" Rita lowered her eyes over the rim of her drink. "Down there I mean?"

"Yes. It's just..." Helen tried to blame it on 'things.' "It's - fiddling about with those bloody rubber things! I was wondering about having the coil fitted but..." She toyed hesitantly with the cherry on the stick in her Cherry-B and murmured sadly, "We don't do it anymore."

Rita looked carefully at her friend. "I don't know how to say this Hel, but... if he doesn't find it at home..." The unfinished sentence hung in the air between them.

Beyond the door at the end of the hall Helen could see Eric in the kitchen, carefree, happy, laughing uproariously in a group with Rob and Malcolm. "He has pin-up books..." Helen murmured.

"He's not alone," Rita said. "Rob has them. He didn't think I knew. Art photos he calls them."

"What did you say to him?"

"He told me I was a lot better than the girls in the pictures. And then he said they weren't his; he was looking after them for his driver. I ask you."

"But that's what I mean," Helen entreated her. "Why are they so devious about it?"

Rita looked earnestly at Helen. "Why don't you see if the doctor'll put you on the pill?"

"Oh I don't know."

"I don't see why he shouldn't. Not after what you went through. You'll soon be able to get them without prescription."

Helen responded with a sad half smile.

It was almost midnight when the party began to break up. They were given a lift home by Jenny and Malcolm and Eric took it as a further sign of acceptance. "Thanks Malc; thanks Jenny." Eric leaned in through the car window and kissed the cheek Jenny offered. "We'll see you at the weekend then."

Malcolm raised his hand and they drove off. At the corner the little car paused, the signal arm glowed briefly then it disappeared leaving them in silence. Above them in the moonglow the clouds shimmered with light and Eric put his arm round Helen's shoulder but she shrugged him off.

"I saw you looking at her."

The accusation took Eric by surprise. "Who?"

"Who do you think? Jenny." Helen strode indoors, leaving Eric to follow her.

"Don't know what you're talking about?"

Helen turned quickly. "Don't raise your voice, you'll disturb my mum and dad. You've been looking at her all night."

"We were... you were... I was looking at everybody," Eric protested.

"Anyway you won't want a drink will you?" Her voice was sullen.

"No," he replied, suddenly at a loss. "Unless..."

"I wish you'd make your mind up," she riposted cruelly. "You don't have to have one!"

"Well don't bloody bother then!" Eric stalked into the bedroom leaving Helen fighting silent tears. She couldn't bear the way he'd looked at Jenny. He'd been looking at the other girls too; even Rita, and she'd seen the hunger in his eyes. It wasn't fair; she couldn't help it and a tear of self-pity hung on Helen's cheek. She tried to gather her composure and went into the bedroom but Eric was feigning sleep. Helen undressed and slid carefully beside him with a frisson of guilt tempered with relief...

Helen's confession, prompting the advice she'd given her friend lingered with Rita, vaguely troubling her. Rita had never denied Rob. She could have refused him for looking at pictures of naked women but she wanted to keep him, not drive him to seek consolation elsewhere. And that's what Helen was doing! If Helen wasn't careful it would be too late. Anyway Rob always knew how to get round her so why try to deny him? After she'd challenged him over the books he'd pulled her close, gyrating against her groin and she'd pushed him off saying, "You can't get round me like that, you'll wake the kids," but there was a gleam in Rob's eyes, the images from the book were in his mind and Rita's breasts were in his hands. "We'll have to be quiet then won't we," he'd said. "But it's the middle of the afternoon," Rita protested, half-heartedly, "I've got to fetch the washing in…" but her skirt was already above her thighs and he was pressing her down onto the settee…

Rita cut the last of Rob's sandwiches and put them in his snap tin with his mashings of tea and sugar. He was on a late turn again, another London trip, with a white collar and tie underneath his firing jacket. "See you in the morning duck." She kissed him, the dutiful wife, and watched him go. It was bad enough he went dressed up to go out drinking in London. It was bad enough him playing cards and gambling. But no matter, she had never denied Rob and she never would. She would give him whatever he asked. 'If he doesn't get it at home…'

Rita was idly turning the pages of a travel brochure when Helen and Eric arrived the following Saturday evening. "Holiday?" Helen said with interest.

Rita pointed to a picture. "Wales. Look Hel. Right on the beach. What d'you think?"

"Oh yes. It looks great. Look Eric." There were rows of caravans with sand dunes and the sea beyond.

"And there's a station nearby, and a good bus service," Rita continued. "All these places we can go to; Conway. Lanfairpwll…" and they laughed as they tried to pronounce the name.

"Malcolm and Jenny not here yet? Eric asked.

"They won't be long," Rob answered. "I've got some drinks in for the girls."

"They're going out for a drink," Rita said. "We couldn't get a babysitter?"

"Going out! Who's going out?" Helen said.

"Just us," Rob said, "me and Eric and Malcolm."

Helen's look of protest flickered from Eric to Rita and back to Eric again. "Well we can't all go out," Rob continued. "You'll be alright until we come back…"

"I've told him he can't be out all night," Rita said by way of reassurance then the sound of crying came from upstairs and Rob left the room. Eric raised a quizzical eyebrow at Helen. She shook her head at him and bowed to the inevitable.

Malcolm and Jenny arrived and Jenny smiled prettily.

"Like your hair," Rita said and Jenny twirled and glanced at herself in the mirror.

Rob crept back in from upstairs. "They're asleep now." He took his stand beside Malcolm rubbing his hands. "Are we going then? The sooner we go, the earlier we'll be back."

"Well just remember what I said," Rita admonished him as the door closed on them.

"What did she say?" Malcolm asked.

"Nothing," Rob replied. "She's always saying things."

They drove into the city to The Wharncliffe. It was packed and the landlady, resplendent in gold lame was calling over the hubbub into a microphone in her husky, club hostess voice, "Come on boys and girls, let's have your empties back – please!" The glass man pushed his way through carrying towers of empty pint glasses and Malcolm passed their drinks back from the bar over the heads of the crowd. "Never thought you'd get served that quick," Eric said.

It was a den of delights. The atmosphere was heavy with the scent of perfume mingled with sweat and aftershave as a constant stream of girls entered and left in groups, searching for excitement and transient thrills. Malcolm looked round appreciatively, "Not a bad pint either." But for all the glamour and innuendo, the jokes and teasing glances, at the back of Eric's mind was another image; he had a better girl waiting at home.

They returned in a state of glowing euphoria. Eric paused at the door. The beer had gone to his head and he took a breath to steady himself.

"How many have you had?" Rita demanded with a glance at the clock.

"Not many. We've not been out long."

To Eric's relief Helen was smiling. "We have had a lovely time. Rita's been telling us about the holiday she's booked. There's lovely beaches for the kids. She's asked us to go with them. I've said we will. You don't mind do you? We hadn't got anything else planned."

Eric shook his head and sat unsteadily on the settee between Helen and Rita. He turned to Jenny. "What you been doin' then?

Jenny giggled; all three girls giggled. Rita went out to the kitchen and Helen reached for her glass and said, "We've just been talking. That's all."

"Right lads," Rob said cheerfully, "we'll have another beer then shall we?" He followed Rita out and called, "Come on Malcolm, get some glasses. They're in here."

Eric turned to Helen. "Y'alright? Y'sure?"

"Of course I'm alright," Helen replied. "Better than you by the look of it."

"I'm a'right," Eric said. He looked at Jenny. "I'm a'right aren't I?"

"Of course you are Eric," Jenny replied. "What's Rita doing?"

"Making supper," Helen said. "We'd better go and help her." They rose and left Eric gazing after them.

"Beer Eric?" Rob called from the kitchen and Eric tried to refocus his eyes. "Or you can have coffee. Rita's making coffee."

"Coffee." Eric braced himself to rise. "I'll come an' get it." But Jenny arrived to set a small coffee table before the settee and Eric relaxed and sat back, smiling happily, admiring her slim waist and dainty breasts. She bent forward and placed the table in front of him and Eric glimpsed the white of Jenny's thigh above the darkness of her stockings and his imagination conjured the feel of her skin, soft, yielding and warm to his touch. Was she doing it on purpose? She was within reach. He swallowed and Jenny said, "Careful you don't trip over it Eric," and Malcolm came in with his beer. "Don't you have much more Malcolm," Jenny said, "You've got to drive me home remember."

"I'm alright," Malcolm replied.

"Did you say coffee?" Eric looked up; the light in the room was bright. Helen was in the doorway with plates of sandwiches. "Ham and cheese," she said, putting them on the little table.

Eric struggled up from the settee. "... toilet," he mumbled and strode purposefully through the kitchen into the yard. The fresh air cleared his head and he returned to find Rita alone in the kitchen. Even with the kettle in her hand, Rita looked desirable. And she had kissed him. When he needed love Rita had kissed him.

"Ah, here you are Eric," Rita said, "one of these is yours. You can help me to carry them in." She looked at him quizzically. "Are you alright?"

"Yes thanks," he replied. There was laughter in the other room and Eric took the kettle from her. "You are a beautiful woman Rita. Do you know? You are..." He put his hand on Rita's breast. She looked at him with understanding and put her hand over his, pressing it against her. "Helen doesn't love me any more," Eric said gently.

"You shouldn't you know." Rita's voice was low. "They're only through there."

"Rita...?"

"No Eric." She kissed him quickly and lifted his hand away. "Helen loves you more than you can know." She saw tears in Eric's eyes. "And you love her don't you?"

He nodded and snuffled clumsily. "Sorry Rita. But I... I was just going to say I meant it. You are a beautiful woman."

"Not a word," she put a finger to her lips as more laughter came from beyond the door. Eric picked up two cups and she watched as he carried them through. He had imparted a confidence and Rita put it away safely, to reside where it would never be found or referred to.

The following Monday Helen announced, "I've been to see the doctor." She was silhouetted against the window; outside a cool, skittish wind was sending squally clouds across the evening sky with a thin, grey drizzle. A spasm of misgiving ran through Eric.

"Why?" he cried, "What's wrong?"

"There's nothing wrong," Helen said, "only - I'm going on the pill that's all."

Eric shrugged. "I don't know why you're bothering."

"Eric..."

"Well..." He threw himself into a chair.

"Come on Eric. We can't be like this," she pleaded but there was accusation in his eyes.

"It's not me!" he cried miserably and he averted his face from her. "You know it's not me."

Helen remained by the table, trying not to hear his rejection. "I know it's been awkward." She spoke softly, "But I'm trying Eric. I am. Really I am."

He remained silent. What was the point? She'd only push him away again

"Oh come on Eric." Helen went to him and crouching beside his chair she reached up and turned his face to hers, looking earnestly into his eyes. "You do love me don't you?"

Eric sighed. He wanted to say 'Yes' but his eyes betrayed the emptiness in his soul and he couldn't summon the energy to answer her with a lie. He lowered his head and silence descended in the room. Intent upon their sorrows they remained motionless, tension confirming the barrier between them. Helen saw the muscles in Eric's face sagging. "If you don't want me..." she whispered with fearful, simple finality.

"Of course I want you." Eric's whisper followed hers.

"If you don't..." Her voice breaking, "I'll take myself away."

"Helen..."

"I mean it." Her words were a simple affirmation of rejection. "I don't want to stay where I'm not wanted."

Eric's hand stole over the arm of the chair, seeking hers. "I don't want you to go. I love you; don't you know I love you..." Eric turned to her. "Oh Helen. I love you," he whispered, "I love you..." endlessly repeated, desperate for the words to push the bleak memories away. Helen pulled him down to kiss him; his face was wet and the hard carapace of pride that had confirmed them in their isolation melted in tears and Helen sought his lips with her eager mouth, like a newborn demanding the succour of his kiss and Eric felt love rising and flooding through the emptiness of his soul.

"It's alright," she repeated between kisses, "It's going to be alright."

"I don't want to... do anything to hurt you."

"You won't Eric. I'm sorry," she said, "I've been foolish, I know I..."

"No!" he cried, hugging Helen close again. "Not you! It's me! It's me! I should have... I'm sorry. Oh Helen. I'm so sorry..."

"Be careful." This time there was neither fear nor admonition in Helen's whisper. She held Eric close and there was warmth and intimacy in their touching.

"Are you sure you're alright?"

Helen's kiss and the softness of her lips stifled his doubts with passion. Her fears were melting away and now her mind was clear of doubt she wanted to love him, to make love forever.

"Be careful," Helen whispered again. Her hesitancy was not prompted by flight but, "The pill, I've only just..."

"I know."

"It might be better if..."

"I know," Eric repeated and he closed his eyes in rising ecstasy...

Ah, sweet healing passion. Eric lay still, unwilling to disturb her, savouring the wholesome feeling of exhaustion and the closeness of Helen as she slept with her arm across him. She sensed his wakefulness, stirred and slid back into sleep with the faint shadow of the smile still on her mouth. All the world was silent except for the soft breath of Helen. He felt her hair against his face and stared into the darkness. There were strange dancing patterns etched in the blackness. He closed his eyes and the skeins of light were gone. Eric played the game once more, languidly opening his eyes and searching for the patterns in the infinity of his mind but all around was sleep, and he turned and sleep crept over him too...

Chapter 18 - Mona's Isle

Helen resumed work as a technician at the hospital labs. But there would be no more children; Eric was in complete harmony with Helen on that. The trauma of Helen's labour would never leave him; he had almost lost Helen then, and nearly lost her as a consequence too. But slowly the memories began to recede.

Helen and Rita were having lunch together at 'The Shack'; a rendezvous from their courting days where they used to meet for mushrooms on toast and pretend they were living the Bohemian life. "Its aubergines and moussaka now," Helen said wistfully. "Anyway Reet we're really looking forward to going away with you and the kids. I'm going to pop down to C&A for some new holiday things if you fancy coming with me."

Rita flushed with embarrassment and her expression unexpectedly fell. "I've been meaning to tell you. I'm sorry Hel. I don't think we'll be able to come." Helen shot her a glance of disbelief. "I'm sorry Hel. I know its short notice. It's Rob." Rita heaved a sigh. "He's lost his wages. He... he had his wages in his overall pocket and they fell out. It was a big week too; he'd had a few London trips. We were banking on them." She spoke without conviction, imploring Helen to believe her.

"Well somebody will have found them," Helen said.

They paused while the waitress placed their meal on the table. Rita looked through the window at the streams of cars and busy people hurrying by, all intent upon their own life's purpose and she sighed again. "He had them in his pocket on the footplate. They fell out on the track somewhere between here and Manchester."

"Oh Rita." Helen took Rita's hand and squeezed it. "I don't know what to say. Are you sure? I mean, he couldn't have left them in...?"

Rita shook her head. "He took his jacket off for a minute and hung it over the cab window while they were travelling. His wages must have fallen out." Rita raised her eyes to Helen. "He had them in his top pocket." She gave Helen a weak, brave smile. They both knew they didn't really believe what she had been told.

"It might have fallen into the coal or…" Helen began loyally and Rita shook her head forlornly.

"They've gone. Even if somebody found them…" She pushed her plate away; Helen reached for her handbag but Rita forestalled her with a protest and they carefully divided the bill between them.

"I'm alright," Rita said. "But I'm sorry Hel. We'll have to cancel the holiday. I'm sorry."

Eric was less charitable. "He's lost 'em at cards," he said shortly, surprised at Helen's naivety. "He hangs his jacket over the cab rail while the train's going and his wage packet falls out? He's not that daft. Or perhaps he is."

Alice Crawford took a more sympathetic view.

"Oh fancy, what a shame. What are they going to do? With no money? And those babies too."

"Oh they'll manage," Helen insisted. "I offered to help her but she said they'd be okay. It's just – well - they've had to give back word on the holiday and it makes it awkward for us. We might have to cancel as well. Probably lose our deposit."

"Oh surely not," Alice cried. "You need a holiday." She thought for an instant and said, "Me and your dad'll help you."

"Oh mum. We didn't say it for that! We don't need it!"

But Alice Crawford would not be denied and her generosity of heart swept all objections aside, not least Frank's. The following day she came to them with her solution.

"Me and your father'll go with you. We'll have the car so you won't have train fares and we can run about and see different places. It's somewhere we've always wanted to go to ourselves." Against the simple logic and unstoppable enthusiasm of Alice Crawford there was no defence.

Each morning of their holiday began with the frustrating routine of breakfast (Eric noticed that Alice always pronounced it in the biblical sense with emphasis on the first syllable, 'Break-fast'), a

131

slow and unpredictable affair. Alice started well but she fretted and Frank had the unfailing habit of disappearing and nothing Alice said could alter him; he inhabited a world five minutes behind everyone else. Today they had planned to tour the Isle of Anglesey and half the morning was gone already. "I bet you thought we were never coming," Alice cried happily as Frank emerged with a nonchalant grin and Eric folded his chair in silence.

They set off, bumping across the grass in the old grey Vauxhall with the windows open, grateful for the breeze. Puffin Island, its name synonymous with childhood fiction shimmered in a sea unexpectedly shaded with the blues of different currents. Approaching Menai they craned to see who would be the first to glimpse the famous bridge and marvelled in admiration of the white stone towers and the great wrought iron links of the suspension chains.

"We'll get a cup of tea on the other side," Alice decided and Frank drew up in front of a hotel and they climbed out with relief like a band of travellers arriving from the desert and marched into the cool of the entrance.

They were confronted by the maitre d'hotel. "Have you a reservation?"

Vaguely nonplussed Frank said, "Do we need one?"

"We'd just like a pot of tea," Alice said.

"I'm afraid we're fully booked."

"We don't want lunch," Alice persisted, "just a cup of tea."

"I'm afraid we don't do 'cups of tea'. It's lunchtime madam. And this isn't a café."

Alice turned abruptly, speaking in her stage voice, "Come along Frank. A place like this and you can't even get a cup of tea!"

Outside Frank said mildly, "I'll bet we'd have got in if I'd slipped him a fiver."

A mile or so along the road the village sign said 'Llanfair p.g.' but the name was written in full on the station sign. "Take our photo dad," Helen insisted. "We must have a picture of us with it, it's the longest name in Britain." She posed at one end of the sign; Eric leaned up against the other and to their inexplicable delight Frank couldn't get the whole name in without crossing to the opposite platform.

"Shows you how long it is!" Eric called.

They left the station and drove easily in a haze of birdsong with the drone of insects in the hedgerows coming through the open windows, as if they were travelling in a dream. At Rhosneigr they realised how hungry they were.

"Well we're bound to be," Alice said. "We've not had anything since breakfast."

They stepped from the car in the silent village, intruders upon its peace. Along the road a discrete sign, 'The Dolphin Tea Room' caught their eye. "Don't look very open," Eric said.

"They might know somewhere that is," Helen volunteered. "I'll go and ask."

It became one of those memorable events, which are nothing in themselves but in conjunction with the whole assume enormous significance. There was the delightful sense of being strangers in a newly discovered place, heightened by the inherent feeling of goodwill and charm. They consumed mounds of bread and strawberry jam – by common consent the best jam they had ever tasted or ever would taste and tea, endless tea. They demanded more with compliments and praise and despite other excursions; Snowdon, mighty Caernarvon; the majestic cliffs of South Stack and the charm of Trearddur Bay (destined to be endlessly revisited in coming years), the treasured memory, the folklore of their holiday was encapsulated in that simple, magical afternoon tea of bread-and-jam.

"How was it?" Rita asked on their return.

"Oh it was lovely," Helen replied. "I wish you could have been there."

"Maybe next year," Rita said. "How did you get on with your mum and dad?"

Helen laughed. "They drove Eric mad. But we all got along ok. It wasn't the same as if you'd been with us though," Helen added.

"We had a day at Skegness." For Rita, a small consolation prize. "Rob got rail passes. It didn't cost much. It was alright."

"I'm sorry Reet."

Rita managed a smile coupled with a sigh of resignation. "Ah well…"

Eric reflected on the sun filled days of their holiday. There was a yearning in him for mountains. They had seen Snowdon from the island, bathed in evening light, glowing in a delicate blend of pink and mauve. It was a moment of such livid intensity that they stopped in a layby overlooking the bridge, absorbing the images into memory. Now feelings of restlessness and dissatisfaction had been awakened in him again.

"I've been thinking," he said with a dreamy look in his eyes.

"What about?"

"Why don't we go and live on Anglesey."

"Anglesey?"

"Yes. Anglesey," Eric said earnestly. "Why not? We could get work in Holyhead. There's a hospital, there must be. And I'm pretty sure I could get something."

Helen began to be swept along with him. "You really mean it?"

"Of course I do. What do you think?"

"Well I don't know. I mean, I could get a job but where would we live?"

"People do live there."

"What about our friends?"

"They'd come and see us. And we'd make new friends too." Although founded in unreality Eric was suddenly businesslike. "I'll send for the local paper and we can look at the job adverts; see what houses are like. Just think of it Helen, waking up in Trearddur Bay every morning."

Yes, imagine… Helen sought to recapture the feeling that had swept over them at first sight of the serene bay with its rocks and pools. Imagine feeling like that for more than just a day. Imagine it for a month, a year, for a lifetime! It was a vision of what might be. "You know," Helen said, now thoroughly infected with the idea, "if it hadn't been for Rob losing his wages we might never have gone there. We'd have been stuck all week in Conway." She spoke as if the dream was already reality. "Funny how things work out."

"I sometimes wonder," Eric mused. "Do you think there's such a thing as fate?"

Helen thought for a moment. "But if it is fate then there's nothing much you can do about it. You might as well just let fate take over."

"I don't think it's as simple as that," Eric replied carefully. "You've got to make something of your life otherwise what's the point. There'd be no sense of achievement if you just let fate take over. I suppose it's seeing your chances and taking them. I think fate just puts the chances there."

"Well fate didn't do Rob any favours."

"I don't think fate had anything to do with that," Eric said sniffily. "I don't think Rob lost his wages that way."

"How d'you mean?"

"I've told you. I don't think they fell out of his pocket; I think he lost 'em gambling."

"Rita would have said!" Helen protested. "She'd have told me. I'm sure."

"Think about it Hel. First his bike gets pinched, then his wages get lost."

"Well then," Helen concluded, her loyalty to her friend overriding all. "I just feel sorry for Rita that's all. Rob's just had some very bad luck."

"Anyway," Eric roused himself and began searching the sideboard drawer, "we've got some writing paper somewhere. I'm going to write a letter to Holyhead."

135

Chapter 19 – Announcements

They basked in their newly-wrought image of young go-getters. Marlene joked, 'Go west young man,' and Eric stood erect among his peers. They even won the grudging acceptance of Eric's father and the first newspapers from Holyhead were opened with nervous anticipation. Eric learned to drive but that opened up no jobs for him and there were no hospital appointments suitable for Helen and they reported that 'it was early days' and they were 'getting a feel for what was available'. "We're not going to rush or do anything foolish," Helen told her mother and as summer wore into autumn and no opportunities rose to test them they each shared the other's secret relief. It was sufficient to play the game. And meanwhile there was kitchen furniture.

Fred Robertson stood quietly watching Eric in one of the windows amongst a display of tables and chairs and as he re-entered the showroom Fred Robertson said, "What's up? Don't you like it?"

"I've been thinking."

"I know. I've been watching you."

"Come outside a minute will you... Mr. Robertson."

"This sounds serious." He followed Eric onto the pavement, amused at Eric's formality.

Eric gestured at the window. "You see these tables are all different shapes and sizes. It looks a jumble."

"We have to show people the wide range we sell."

"I know. But when they come in to buy they want it to fit into their home. We've got four windows; why don't we create four rooms?"

Fred considered. "But if we did that we'd only be showing one table. At the moment," he gestured at the window, "we've got five in there."

"And we've got another twenty-five in the shop. We can't put them all in the window but we could show people a nicely furnished kitchen."

Fred patrolled along the windows, musing. "We'll set up one of the windows like you suggested and see how it goes."

Eric's room settings were a success and they arranged all the windows with soft lighting and dressed the tables with imitation fruit and cutlery from the main department store. Suddenly people in the street stopped to look instead of merely passing by. Kitchen furniture was beginning to look like interior design.

Saturday night at Rob and Rita's. Rob mixed three Martini Rosso's with lemonade for the girls; passed the drinks round and said casually, "I'm leaving the railway."

Rita added, "We're sick of Rob working shifts. You never know where you are."

"But you love the railway," Helen said in mild surprise. The railway was Rob's life, always had been.

"What are you going to do?" Eric asked.

"I'm going on the milk."

Eric tried to suppress a smirk. "A milkman? Are you serious?"

"Course I'm bloody serious."

"Sorry Rob," Eric said. "I just never thought…"

"Well there you are then!"

"A job with a vehicle thrown in eh?" Malcolm laughed and they all joined in with relief.

"Anyway it's more money," Rita said. "Rob can make commission selling produce besides the milk, can't you darling. You ought to come on it Eric."

"Drinks'd better be on you tonight then," Malcolm said and once more they laughed.

"Anyway," Rob bent over the back of Rita's chair, his eyes lingering in her cleavage as he kissed her, "we're going. Don't have too much will you."

"Cheeky devil," Rita called after him as they departed.

"Are you happy about him leaving the railway," Helen asked when they had gone.

"Oh yes," Rita said. "No more shifts or nights away from home. And I'll be able to rejoin the opera." Her smile concealed a more profound relief; at last he'd be away from the wretched gambling school at the loco shed and they'd be able to do something about the debts accumulating around them.

In the second week of December the operatic society held its annual Christmas dinner-dance. Helen wore a simple black satin dress overlaid with black lace and drop earrings of jet inherited from an aunt. Her hair was piled in a high bouffant and she twirled before Eric. "What do you think?" The alluring perfume of 'Tosca' rising from the daring décolletage filled the room and as she moved her skirt was a swirl of lace over dark stockings. "Will I do?" Eric reached for her but Helen backed away, laughing. "Do you really like it? It's not too much is it? You don't think it makes me look like a tart?" Eric shook his head and she gave him a look of complicity. "I'll let you into a secret. Only you mustn't tell. Promise." He nodded and Helen said, "It's a nightie."

"A nightie," Eric swallowed. "It doesn't look like a nightie."

"You sure?"

"No... you look..." He paused, lost in admiration and caressing her with his eyes...

Kenwood Hall glowed in soft yellow light through the trees as they approached in the damp December mist. They checked Helen's coat into the cloakroom and went through to the lounge-bar.

The lounge was softly lit and they hesitated briefly at the entrance, posing innocently in the doorway to get their bearings. Seen indistinctly in the unaccustomed gloom were groups crowding the bar and jostling in close camaraderie; businessmen, accountants, shop owners, pharmacists, company reps, men Eric took to be the pillars of society in black-tie and dinner jackets. As they entered heads turned and there was a subtle pause in conversation followed by a brief greeting for Eric before their attention was switched to Helen. Eric began to feel out of place in his best suit, fingering his new tie and fighting to suppress resentment at his isolation from the men surrounding her. Seen from the doorway he hadn't recognised them in the low light; now he saw it was the men's chorus, men he was just beginning to get to know. And yet with anyone other than

Helen on his arm he felt he would have been overlooked, relegated to the fringes. 'Yes,' he thought, murmuring his replies to their brief words of welcome, 'for all your dressing up and social pretentions you're all reduced to one common desire, trying to see more of my Helen, trying to imagine what she would be like...' But then a moment of revelation; weren't these the men whose society he aspired to? Wasn't this the world he wanted to be accepted in? Eric smiled gallantly, suppressed a rising sense of jealousy and mouthed brief responses whilst taking consolation in the knowledge that at the end of the evening it was he who was going to be taking Helen home.

He was saved by the arrival of Rob also in a lounge suit and Malcolm in a dinner jacket borrowed from his father. Jenny and Rita joined Helen and shared the flattery being bestowed then dinner was announced and they trooped into the ballroom where the Maitre'd and his team were waiting with smiles to guide them to their table and Eric finally began to relax.

Jenny and Malcolm's announcement was saved for this evening. They waited until coffee was being served then Jenny looked adoringly at Malcolm and said, "We're getting married. We've decided on a date."

There was a whoop of delight and Helen clapped her hands. "When?" she cried.

"Easter," Jenny beamed.

"An Easter wedding. Oh how lovely." Rita kissed her on both cheeks. "Oh I'm so thrilled."

Malcolm rose and headed for the bar. "Come on, we'll get some drinks in while there's a lull."

"And what about bridesmaids?" Helen asked.

"I'm having my two little nieces. And Malcolm's sister." Helen smiled valiantly and tried to pretend she wasn't disappointed and Jenny lowered her voice archly. "I think his dad's going to set him up in his own business. They've been looking at sites. Only don't say I told you," and Rita tried to hide her envy. Rob's wage as a milkman wasn't matching what he'd earned on overnight London trips.

But now the floor had been cleared and the bandleader took up his position onstage and beamed his professional smile, greeting them in the voice he'd cultivated from listening to Edmundo Ros. "… and your first dance is," a pause of anticipation, "a quickstep." He turned and brought the band into play.

It was a night of continuous laughter. Eric lost his self-consciousness and stepped out to waltz with Helen. Then the tempo changed; "A samba," the bandleader announced with a flourish of technicoloured marracas and they jived, to the mild annoyance of the dancers trying to display their technique, and ended the night under the benign gaze of the older members watching the next generation of the society's principals carousing in a growing haze of drink and merriment…

Malcolm and Jenny's wedding took place under Easter skies filled with sleet. Jenny smiled in stubborn defiance of the cold, standing in the porch as the wind tugged at her veil and the shivering guests crowding around her snivelled into their handkerchiefs, willing the photographer to finish. But all was forgiven once they were at the reception. The hotel spread a hot meal and everyone recovered. Jenny remained in her wedding dress until later in the afternoon and then Malcolm made excuses for their departure. "We're just going to put our things together," he announced and they retreated blushing from the room. They returned later to take their leave and Jenny's mother shed soft tears of anxiety at the sight of her daughter in a pale blue woollen suit with a jaunty little feather hat, about to face 'the mysteries' of her wedding night. Malcolm was gallant. "Don't worry about her mum, I'll look after her," then more hugs from Jenny's mother and a special hug for them both from Marlene then they grasped hands and ran the gauntlet of confetti to Malcolm's car.

Jenny laughed with pleasure. "You rotten dogs. Look what you've done." Malcolm attempted to wipe the words 'Learner' and 'Just Married' printed in lipstick from the screen and Jenny pulled the balloons and assorted streamers away. "We're going, we're going," they called, waving from the windows and the returning cries were underscored by the tinkling clatter of cans bouncing along the asphalt behind the car.

Then they piled into two cars and set off in pursuit and found Jenny and Malcolm a hundred yards along the road cleaning red grease off the windscreen. At the sound of horns blaring down on them they jumped back in and Malcolm gunned the engine, throwing the car recklessly into corners until the chase ended with an outraged cyclist shaking a fist as Malcolm narrowly missed him, only to be driven into the kerb again by the two following cars.

"Isn't it romantic," Helen said, watching them drive away into the night. And filled with goodwill and satisfaction they drove back to the party.

Malcolm and Jenny returned with joyfully naïve honeymoon tales. The chambermaid had entered their room, they said, to turn down the bed, and found them already in it, Malcolm muttering some embarrassed inanity about 'having an early start in the morning'. He embellished the story with, "We'd decided to stay up and listen to The Archers before we…' and everybody laughed and Jenny smiled the newlywed bride's smile of pleasure. But her laughter hid secret tears, for despite Malcolm's apparent worldliness, ogling the girls on Saturday nights, Malcolm was a virgin, as innocent as his bride. Perhaps he was too eager and inexperienced a lover to savour the pleasure of foreplay; perhaps the innocence of Jenny's careful upbringing had left her unprepared but their wedding night was a failure. Jenny tried to help him but inhibition barred the way and she cried out in pain as Malcolm tried to penetrate her urethra and a disastrous thought, tarnished with conceit came into Malcolm's mind; 'She's too small for me.' He turned away in frustration, fearful of hurting her and the light of expectation was replaced by the spectre of failure. For three days they denied each other any sexual contact. But on the fourth night in clumsy desperation Malcolm succeeded and Jenny, in tears, finally lost her virginity to him. And so they returned with the blissful tales of honeymoon folklore that was expected of them whilst trying to conceal the emotional barrier which had so cruelly and unexpectedly arisen.

Meanwhile though the dream of Holyhead had long faded the residue of Eric's restlessness remained. "I know we're comfortable here," Eric said, briefly scanning the evening paper, "but we can't live here forever."

Helen picked up the discarded newspaper. "Here's one; four roomed terrace house, two up, two down, outside toilet. Just like Rita's, seven fifteen."

"Seven pounds fifteen shillings a week!" Eric expostulated. "They must be mad!"

"No," Helen corrected him, "Seven hundred and fifteen pounds. To buy." She peered at the small print beneath the ad. "It says mortgage available."

"We'd never get a mortgage," Eric sighed and they resigned themselves to an unending period in the flat.

Chapter 20 - On the threshold

Fred Robertson wasn't the only one watching Eric's progress in the shop. Ted Wainright, a rep for a builder's merchant had noticed Eric too. Ted was middle aged with the same frayed air as Fred Robertson in his well worn fawn slacks and shapeless tweed sports jacket. His relationship with Fred had been good from the start. Neither were high flyers but successful in their modest way and in the two years he'd been calling on Fred the sales of bathroom suites and sanitary-ware had taken a distinct turn upwards.

Over the 'Three Course Business Lunch (3/9d excluding coffee)', approved by his guv'nor and hosted by Ted in the crowded first floor dining room of 'The Canary' Chinese restaurant they were discussing the showroom's success and Fred Robertson was generous in crediting a fair share of it to Eric. "He's a good lad," he concluded. "He just needs encouragement."

"Nothing personal Fred but he's wasted where he is." Ted's guv'nor was always on the lookout for lads with potential.

"Ah, but he doesn't know his own potential see," Fred countered as two bowls of apple pie in Chinese water custard were set before them.

"Coffee?" Ted the gracious host gave the order then returned to the subject of Eric. "Does he drive?"

"Hey," Fred Robertson protested over the rim of his spoon, "keep your eyes off him. I've not done with him yet."

But on the last Friday in June during a lull in the afternoon's trade Fred Robertson sent Mrs. Stoakley to invite Eric into the back office.

"What does he want?" Eric asked but Mrs. Stoakley was uncommunicative. The boy – as she referred to him with her cronies in the head office store across the road – was always privy to Robertson's ideas before her...

The back office was the storeroom with three chairs and a desk where the shop's order book and weekly sales analysis were kept.

One wall was covered with gas fires stacked to the ceiling, the result of an hour's exertion that morning by Robertson and Eric, stacking newly delivered stock but now Fred was at ease with Ted Wainright. He dismissed Mrs. Stoakley and she turned away with disdain at her exclusion as Ted eased his beefy frame comfortably back in his chair. Eric closed the door and leaned against it.

"She alright?" Ted asked and Fred replied with a dismissive smile and Eric tried to convey comfortable nonchalance combined with alertness.

"Do you drive Eric?" Ted asked unexpectedly.

"Yes." Eric gave Fred Robertson a quizzical look but his expression betrayed nothing. "Passed my test first time," he added with satisfaction.

"How's things going here?" Again Ted's question was unexpected. Had it come from Fred then Eric would have answered easily and confidently. But this was from the wrong quarter; it was like being asked to comment on his boss in his boss's presence.

"I think things are going alright," Eric looked at Fred for approval. "We seem to be don't we?" There was no help from Fred beyond a faint smile hidden in his otherwise bland expression and Eric sought to elaborate. "I mean, the gas fires have slowed a bit." Eric hesitated, conscious of the newly arrived stock piled behind him, "But they'll pick up again in the autumn. We're about twelve percent up on last year anyway." He was pleased to be able to quote their performance figures just like that and glad that he'd taken an interest in the shop's progress. His room setting idea was working well; now it looked as though another idea was being worked up and he was going to be part of it. It gave him a glow of pride.

Ted spoke again. "How would you fancy the idea of coming to work for us?"

Eric passed his tongue over his lips and his mind began a furious switch from his previous train of thought. Ted was a rep with a car supplied by the firm. He was already boasting of his next one; the new Anglia with a reverse sloping back window and Eric tried to suppress the seductive thought. But, 'Do you drive?' That had been Ted's first question! And he liked Ted; he was easy going with a repertoire of terrible jokes made more awful by his innate inability to tell a joke at all.

"You mean…? What, you, your firm?"

"Yes. Harker Brothers and Lynley."

"I hadn't thought of it," Eric answered carefully.

"I told you," Fred said with a look of triumph.

"I mean, I like working here with,' he glanced across at Fred, "…everybody."

"We're always on the lookout for good people."

Fred was watching Eric carefully. "Ted and me's been talking about you. He has very properly come to me and asked if he could make this suggestion. I'm not trying to get rid of you Eric. But it's up to you."

"Well I…" Eric floundered, aware that if he wasn't careful the offer – if it was an offer – would be withdrawn. "What would I be doing," he managed to say at last.

"You'd be working for me selling sanitary ware. The kind of things you sell here. Only you'd be selling to the trade; builders and plumbers. You'd be my junior."

Eric was struck by a sudden thought. "Is it commission?"

Ted gave a brief snort of laughter and turned to Fred as if to say 'My turn to say I told you' then he replied, "You'll probably make more than you're making here. Of course you'd have to attend for an interview in Leeds. But if you're interested I'll arrange it."

"Well yes; thank you," Eric replied and his gratitude was tinged with a strange sense of regret.

There was no more to add; Mrs. Stoakley put her head through the door to say there were customers in the shop and Eric returned to the showroom in a state of euphoria. There were customers wandering about the showroom but his mind wouldn't focus on them. Mrs. Stoakley gave him a knowing look but he smiled stupidly and she turned from him to greet the customers at the door.

Helen looked up to see Eric lounging nonchalantly against the kitchen door with a smile like the Mona Lisa, waiting for the moment when he could trust his voice to deliver the news. "What is

145

it? Eric!" Intrigue gave way to impatience. "Tell me, come on, what is it?" A sudden frisson of apprehension flickered. "What is it Eric? Has something happened?" And then she saw his face relax and the smile broadened. "Oh you tease. What is it? What have you got to tell me?"

"I've been offered a job. A reps job." He closed the door behind him and suddenly he couldn't wait to tell her. "You know that rep I've told you about, you know, Ted, he sells us bathroom suites and things, well he's offered me a job with him. Well with his company. I'll have to have an interview of course, a proper interview up in Leeds but Mr. Robertson was there and he said if that's what I want to do..." Eric spread his hands. "And it'll be more money. Well I don't know exactly how much more, not yet but that's what he said." He stopped suddenly and ran his fingers through his hair. "I can't believe it. I'd no idea..."

The interview of course was a success. Jacob Harker had taken over as M.D. when the elder Harker went into semi-retirement and he wanted to make the firm grow. He wanted new blood in the business. He wanted to widen the firm's customer base. He wanted to get more from the salesforce. He wanted...

"I want good people in this Company!"

Eric nodded, conveying eagerness and understanding of what the great man with his energy and ideas was telling him. Jacob Harker was very direct, confident and open. His suit of good West Riding worsted boasted his success. Eric felt shabby in comparison. "Ted tells me you're a good man with potential. Just what we might be looking for. Why do you want to join us?"

Eric was fascinated by Jacob Harker's hair; it was blond, trimmed short and curly. 'Unusual for a Jew,' Ted had said and Eric's eyes continually wandered to it as Harker expounded his ideas and dreams of empire. The suddenness of the question brought Eric's mind back into focus. "I hadn't really thought of it until Ted – Mr. Wainright mentioned it. But then," Eric added hurriedly, "when he began to tell me more about the firm and your plans..." Eric sought to place himself at the centre of those plans, for Harker to see that the man before him was the man he'd been waiting for, "...and my ambitions are to succeed and build a career. I've gone as far as I want to with the co-op. I'm very grateful to them of course…" Is this the man you wanted to see? Would Ted have picked me otherwise? "…looking for the right opportunity with the right company. That's why I was pleased when Ted offered me this chance."

More polite listening, nodding, eagerness until the foregone conclusion could, with great deliberation, be finally arrived at. "What do you earn now?" Eric told him. "I'll pay you £150 a year more than that. When can you start?" Eric told him. "Your title will be Junior Sales Representative. You'll be working with Ted. I think he told you that."

Eric nodded eagerly and blurted out, "Is there a… a car?"

"Not to begin with. You'll be selling to selected customers in Sheffield, plumbers, small builders until you know the business. You won't need a car making calls around the city. Anyway parking's a terrible problem. You'll get a lift with Ted when you come for Saturday's sales meetings."

Sales meetings. Selected customers. Not like being 'on the knocker'. It was a reps job and Alfred's words from the Brown Bear came back to him, 'You want to get out of this. Get into repping.' Well here he was. At last he had crossed the threshold.

Outside Jacob Harker's office, Ted was waiting to drive him home. "Well?" he said disingenuously, "Did you get it?"

Eric nodded happily. "Start two weeks on Monday. Thanks Ted. I'd never thought…"

"I kept telling you didn't I. We're on the lookout for good people. Come on I'll buy you a sandwich."

They drove to a pub on the trading estate and Ted raised a hand in familiar greeting to the barman. "We come here for a sandwich at lunchtime after the Saturday meeting. What're you having? I usually have beef and beetroot with a glass of mild."

"I'll have the same then. Oh – bitter, not mild."

"You're a bitter man are you? Alright then."

Now sitting in the bar with Ted was irksome; Eric wanted to be home to share the news with Helen, Rob, Helen's parents. And his father would have to be told as well... The sandwiches came with a small bowl of sliced onion in vinegar. Eric bit into his sandwich. "Mr Harker didn't mention commission. I suppose I should have asked him."

"I love raw onions," Ted said, inserting them into his sandwich with the beetroot. "You don't want to worry about that yet. You've a lot to learn. You won't be going out on your own for a bit. Not until you're ready. I'll take you round with me."

Eric sought to reassure himself that he was doing the right thing. He hadn't dared to hope there would be a car and Ted's response to his question about commission was disappointing. But the extra three pounds a week would make a lot of difference and besides, he was a rep, and that's what really mattered.

Helen was delighted. "And it's a proper wage?" she asked again as memories of the vacuum cleaners rose in her mind. "Not just..."

"I told you," Eric repeated. "It's £150 more than I'm getting now. And when I do go on commission..." Visions of unlimited comfort and indulgence rose before them. He did the arithmetic again and added a bit to round it up. "Nearly six hundred pounds a year!" He looked at himself in the mirror; white shirt, best suit. "Tell you what Hel, have you got any money? We could go to the Sidewalk. We haven't been there together for ages and then we'll go and tell Rita and Rob."

Walking to Rita's through the terraced industrial streets of Darnall they felt the happiness of contentment. Eric took Helen's hand; it fitted close in his and he became aware of the sensitivity of his palm. "You've got lovely hands," he said. "It's very erotic you know, holding hands."

Helen smiled. Holding hands, erotic? She twined her fingers in his and brushed her hand against his palm and said, "You are a lovely man."

"I wonder how much these are going for," he mused, looking along the rows of old houses, their doors opening directly onto the pavement.

"More than you'd think I expect."

"I'm not serious."

"It would be a start."

"No," he said. "Not here. We want something better than this. Anyway they've no front gardens."

There were nappies strung on a line across the yard and the door opened cautiously on the chain. "Oh, its you," Rita said, "Hang on a minute." The door closed briefly, the chain rattled then Rita threw it open. "Rob," she called, "Helen and Eric's here. Come on through." Antony was scrambling around on the living room floor and Rita began scooping up handfuls of children's clothes and toys. "Here, let's make room for you to sit down. Move up Rob." She brushed herself down, smoothing her hands over her skirt. "I'll just go and make myself presentable."

Rob was nursing Raymond, holding a spoonful of babyfood tantalisingly above the child's expectant face. It kicked and gurgled in his arms and he looked up at Eric. "Weren't expecting you 'till weekend. What's up?"

Helen said, "We'll wait for Rita."

"Oh!" Rob said archly. "Serious stuff eh."

Eric shook his head and took the plunge. "No," he announced, "Just landed a new job that's all. Wondered if you fancied a pint. To celebrate."

Rob's leg began to twitch, a small, nervous tremor. "Can't," he said. "Not yet. Anyway I'm up early in the morning. Can't be out late." He turned his attention back to the baby.

Rita appeared behind them. "There, that's better. Now then. How's he doing Rob? Oh, he's alright now, look at him. So, what's new? Eh?"

Helen shifted uneasily. "We just thought... Well, Eric's got a new job."

"Oh well done Eric," Rita's voice carried a genuine ring of pleasure. "What is it?"

"He's going to be a rep."

Eric smiled modestly and tried not to look too pleased. "I just wondered...if Rob fancied a quick jar. You know, just to celebrate."

"Oh I'm sure..." Rita began but Rob suddenly looked at her.

"You know… I can't," he said.

"You could go later. Couldn't you."

"I've got to be up! You know what time I've got to be up!" A coded dialogue flashed between them and Helen felt tension growing in the room.

"Oh well, stay for a cup of tea anyway." Rita gave Rob a look of disapproval. "Take no notice of him. I'll put the kettle on."

Helen said, "Just a quick drink then," and she followed Rita out to the kitchen.

Rita gave Helen a wry look. "Sorry about that. It's not like us. Well you know it's not. It's just…"

"What is it Reet? What's up?"

Rita went to the cupboard for cups and saucers. "It's nothing Hel. Nothing. You don't want to know."

The knock at the door was loud, sudden.

"I'll get it," Helen said, "It must be your 'at home' night tonight."

Rita turned quickly. "Let Rob go," she cried but she wasn't quick enough; as Helen opened the door a dog with a long black snout and its lip curled back lunged and snarled at her. Helen stepped back with a cry.

The voice from the backyard was coarse, brutal and uncompromising. "Is he in?" Helen was conscious of a bulky figure in dark clothes and a fleshy face with dark glasses then Rob pushed past her.

"It's alright, it's alright," he said as the man hauled back the dog and Rob stepped into the yard and closed the door behind him.

Gasping with shock Helen turned to Rita. Eric was in the living room doorway with Raymond cradled in his arms. "What's going on?" he demanded.

"Oh here Eric, let me take him from you." Rita took the child. "He's not dribbled on you has he?"

"Rita?" Slowly Helen recovered her composure. "Rita… Who was that?"

"Nobody. I'm sorry. You should have let Rob answer the door. I should have…"

"But who is it?" Helen persisted. "And that dog. It scared me I can tell you."

Eric put his arm round Helen's shoulder and she shivered beneath his arm. "What's going on Rita?" he demanded.

Rita avoided their eyes and laid the baby across her shoulder, stroking and patting his back. "It's just somebody Rob has some business with. It's nothing to worry about." Rita sniffled and smiled a brave, wobbly smile. "It's alright. Just... Just don't ask. That's all."

Chapter 21 – Consolations

In the coalfields of South Yorkshire the spinning wheels above the pitheads blur endlessly and in the river valleys the spinning turrets of the lathes are centred on gleaming discs and shafts of steel. But the hum of pithead lifts and the whirring and sawing and grinding of steel, and the rising whine of the electric arc furnaces are dwarfed by the relentless pounding of the forges fed by endless trains of ingots. Ten tons of fine glowing steel in a single block cast at a thousand degrees, the heart of each ingot radiating waves of shimmering heat for days on end as the slow trains trundle carefully through foundry yards, away from the furnaces of the ingots' birth. Two hundred years of industry, secure and indestructible, captured in ingenious crafts honed and developed through generations. A cradle of industry echoing along industrial streets and terraces of back-to-backs and endlessly reassuring toil, destined to continue forever as before…

'Destined to continue forever.' Rita sighs and muses on the reality of her life. She is still in love with Rob, they are affectionate to one another and in all else Rita puts up with – what did she call it? – his 'roguishness', her comfortable euphemism for Rob's 'eye for the girls', and she refuses to allow it is any more than that! Besides there are the children to think of and Rob dotes on the children. But she looks with envy at Malcolm and Jenny, for Malcolm's father has set him up in business and they are doing well. And Jim and Marlene, the leading lights of the operatic society host social evenings and gatherings of friends. Rita looks at them and in a secret corner of her heart Rita is ashamed. She begins to assume a mantle of worldliness, a veneer of sophistication, an emotional carapace behind which to hide, laughing and gay in public while privately she is carried along in Rob's wake on his feckless route to she knows-not-where, ashamed of her inability to influence Rob in the catastrophe looming in their lives. And meanwhile as she tries to deny sordid reality Rita thanks God for friendships, for Helen and Eric in particular, and clings to the consolations of Saturday night.

Who can say from where the idea sprang? Saturday night had continued much as before until, one dark night, the idea arose spontaneously amongst the girls while the men were out and was seized on with mischievous glee. On the men's return from town they were met by an excited Jenny.

"Where's the others?" Rob asked, staring through into the empty living room.

"We've got a surprise for you. Go in and wait!" Jenny turned to Malcolm. "And you too; leave the sandwiches alone and close the door." She turned the lights low and pulled the living room door closed adding, as she left, "And no peeping or you'll spoil it."

They heard music beginning to play in the kitchen. "What they doing?" Eric asked, looking round.

"Don't know," Rob replied. "I'll get us a drink. Beer Malc?"

"They said to wait."

Rob hesitated and Rita peeped round the door. "Are you ready boys?" She turned and gestured. "Ready girls?" and pushed the door open.

Naked to the waist, bearing sandwiches and drinks Rita, Helen and Jenny swayed self-consciously into the softly lit room and placed the food on the coffee table with mock oriental deference. "Your supper, oh lord and master," Rita said and Rob reached a hand towards her. "Ah, ah," she laughed, "mustn't touch."

Helen picked up a sandwich and offered it into Eric's mouth, her eyes looking boldly into his as he bit into the food, cradling her breasts in his hands. Jenny was teasing Malcolm with a drink, her breasts quivering as she drew back and laughing at his attempts to reach her. Unable to swallow Eric pushed the remains of the sandwich away and pulled Helen onto his knee. They began kissing and caressing and Rob said huskily, "Put the light out."

Now the room was dark the soft glow from the fire silhouetted Rita removing her skirt then someone opened the door.

"What...?"

"It's alright," Rob said. "We're just going upstairs," and they left the others to unrequited passion until they heard Rita's voice approaching beyond the door and Rob entered looking sheepish in the firelight.

"Don't put the light on." Suddenly bashful Helen and Jenny scrambled past Rob leering unashamedly at them and scampered through the kitchen where Rita, flushed and replete with sex was starting to make a drink.

Marlene watched their friendship with envy. There was an air of suppressed excitement about the six of them that transcended the staid business entertaining that predominated her life with Jim. So when Jenny asked Marlene if they were doing anything on Saturday, Marlene readily accepted. There was nothing in the diary, it would be a welcome change and she looked forward to an exciting evening in gay company...

On this Saturday they are at Malcolm and Jenny's and Rita's children are sleeping in carry-cots upstairs. No-one is quite sure how Jim and Marlene will respond but it is only innocent flirtation, not wife swapping, no not that, just kissing that's all, a bit of petting; a return to the heady days of courtship and the thrill of different kisses and the lingering trace of unfamiliar perfume. Better not go too far tonight though, no striptease but it will be alright and everything will fall into place. Jim enjoys the tour of the pubs, carefully sipping his beer and admiring the girls but he lacks the raw innuendo of the other three. And on their return, Jim notes with satisfaction that Marlene is enjoying her evening too.

It all happens so casually and naturally over supper. Rob is in one armchair and when Malcolm takes the other Rita sits on the arm of Malcolm's chair leaning against him with her coffee. The others do simultaneous mental calculations and Helen goes to Jim. She likes Jim; he is attractive in his quiet, businesslike way. She found it hard to put into words but... she has an innate sense that Jim is more respectful and there will be less groping in the dark. Jenny is smiling on Rob's knee and Eric is sitting rather formally with Marlene. After a few minutes Rita puts the light off and returns to Malcolm in the firelight.

Initially Eric is hesitant as memories of his first encounter with Rose Maybud arise. Marlene, with her vivacity and prettiness had seemed quite unattainable then; now she is in his arms. He puts his lips to hers and she responds with her lips slightly parted, pressing close and he feels her hand steal around his shoulders, caressing the hair at the nape of his neck. He breaks away, Marlene smiles then kisses him again with unexpected passion. "It's not very comfortable is it?" she whispers and wriggles and crosses her legs over Eric's knees, nestling against Eric's arm. "That better?" They kiss again and Eric opens a guilty eye and looks across Marlene's shoulder. Helen is on Jim's knee, stroking his cheek but Jim's response to Helen's kiss is no more than a polite formality. Then Marlene whispers, "Can we put the cushions on the floor? Shall we? Do you mind? It'd be more comfortable." They place cushions behind the settee and recline beyond sight of the others and kiss again. Marlene kisses him with devouring passion, pulling him to her in an unyielding embrace. Now Eric moves his hand down across her body and gathers a fold of her skirt but Marlene lifts his hand away, shaking her head as her lips move against his. He feels for her breast but again she denies him, only renewing her kisses, seeking his lips again and again, kissing him with an overwhelming need. It isn't sex Marlene needs but love, to be held and cherished and between each kiss she pulls him close again in her innocent, mute embrace...

Deep in the armchair, in the darkness of the shadow cast by the soft glow of the fire behind them Rita is curled on Malcolm's knee. She holds her breath, her heart pounding. Her blouse is open to her waist, the straps of her brassiere are off her shoulders and she is holding Malcolm's head against the softness of her breasts. The look in Rita's eyes is the look of a woman aroused, a wanton look of desire. Her lips are slightly parted and she lowers her head and whispers, "I want you." The words are indistinct but Rita moves her mouth to his ear, probing and sighing, "Oh Malcolm, I want you, I want you," and she pushes her hand into the waistband of his trousers. Malcolm gasps, Oh Christ! he is going to climax! Oh Christ! He pulls her lips to his and she holds his hand against her breast and they break away, breathless and gasping in the dark.

"I've got to see you." He is panting, and trying to keep his breath controlled and quiet Malcolm whispers again, "I mean it. Oh God Rita, I want to see you. Can we meet somewhere?"

"Shhhh," Her voice is no more than a breath. There are rustlings from other parts of the room. "I'd better fasten myself up," and she kisses him again, a parting, secret trysting kiss.

Husbands and wives reunite and Jim is suddenly preoccupied with the time. Helen says, "I hope you didn't mind Jim. It was just a bit of fun that's all," careful to keep a respectful distance, not even a touch of hands and Jim smiles back with restraint and looks at the clock again. The children are brought down whimpering in the light and Rob says, "We'd better be off then." Marlene slips her arm boldly round Eric's waist in an act of possession, hugs him and turns her face expectantly for another kiss. But Eric is conscious of Jim watching; there is something amiss, and Jim's polite, "Goodnight," removes any lingering uncertainty. Eric avoids Marlene's kiss and his eyes carry rejection instead of au revoir. It is cruel and Marlene turns from him and kisses Rob and Malcolm instead. And in the brief goodnight between Malcolm and Rita there is nothing at all.

Marlene and Jim didn't join them again and Saturday night continued as before, regulated by the unwritten rule that prevailed between Helen and Jenny; a hushed "No!" and firm resistance to the earnest entreaties in the dark and pushing aside the insistent hand trying to ease between her legs. That was taboo; she would not go that far and hearing similar hushed resistance from across the room Helen was reassured. But all the same…

It was the half time break in rehearsal. Jenny was over by the tea urn waiting for Malcolm to pass her cup and Eric said quietly, "There's nothing going on between Rita and Malcolm is there?"

"Rita and Malcolm?"

Eric looked around quickly and muttered, "Keep your voice down."

"Whatever makes you say that?" Helen exclaimed softly.

"I saw Rita today, that's all."

"You saw Rita?"

Eric shook his head at Helen's tone. "I didn't see her! Not to talk to! I was on my way to Faireys. You know, up near the university. Lunchtime, well, about quarter to two."

"What was she doing up there?"

"I don't know! She was skipping along like a kid out of school."

"With the kids?"

"By herself. And isn't Malcolm's showroom up there?"

Helen turned and began watching Rita and Malcolm. Malcolm and Jenny were moving easily amongst the other members and Rita was talking to Jim. Not a word was exchanged between them only... Helen turned away as Malcolm approached, his eyes fixed on Eric.

"Now then; you putting in for a part this time?"

"Don't think so." Modesty forbade. Singing in the chorus alongside somebody like Jim was alright, but singing solo!

"There's a nice little speaking part," Malcolm insisted. "You should go in for it."

Eric shrugged, his mind still on his earlier thoughts, and he was saved by Alice. "Are you putting in for a part this year Eric? You ought to you know."

Eric glowed with bashfulness. "I might," he said. Still, twice in one night!

Helen was in deep conversation with Jenny. "We have seen one and we're thinking about it."

"You ought to," Jenny replied. "Malcolm's dad's always saying 'put your money into bricks and mortar'."

"Well this job's better than the one he had before," Helen continued, "but it's over £800. Still they're offering a mortgage so who knows, we might have a place of our own soon."

The secretary began calling for everyone's attention and they resumed their places as Jim cleared his throat and began, "There are one or two notices and can members of the committee stay behind for a few minutes afterwards..."

The following Saturday Helen finally decided.

"You know you like it," Rita said.

"Well perhaps I do," Helen countered, "but it doesn't mean..." She faltered and lost the thread of her argument. She'd gone along with it because she didn't want to be thought a prude, and to be honest she rather enjoyed the thrill of appearing semi-naked in the soft light late at night but she was troubled by the recollection of Jim's barely masked disapproval on the night they had all been together. Jim's estimation of her mattered and she wouldn't want him to think she was...

"Oh come on Helen," Rita said, "You need another drink."

"No I don't think I do!" Helen put her fingers to her temple. "I've got a bit of a headache."

Rita looked at Jenny. "The boys'll be home soon," she said but Helen seemed to have dampened Jenny's spirits too.

"I don't feel very well really," Helen replied. "I think we'll go when Eric gets back."

"Get her a couple of aspirins Jen," Rita said. "She might feel better then. You'll be better by the time they're back Hel." She looked earnestly at Helen and Helen took the tablets with a reluctant smile.

Rob noticed the change in atmosphere on their return. "What's up?" he exclaimed, looking from Helen to Rita.

"I'm sorry." Helen turned to Eric, seeking comfort. "I don't feel very well. I've got this headache. I think it might be going to be migraine. Do you mind if we go home?"

"She's not had a drink all night," Jenny said.

Malcolm put his arm round Helen's shoulder. "I'm sorry Helen. Are you alright?"

She gave him a smile of apology. "I'll be alright later. I just feel a bit off colour that's all."

Eric grimaced at the others and fetched Helen's coat. They walked into the street with a half-hearted wave and heard them call, "Hope you feel better Hel," then the door closed and Helen linked her arm in Eric's.

"You don't mind do you?"

"As long as you're alright." To her surprise there was relief in Eric's voice.

"I just didn't feel like it. Not tonight."

"Have you really got headache?" Eric asked.

"Not really." Helen chose her words carefully. "I don't want it to go too far."

"I know."

They walked for a while in silence, their thoughts harmonising about them.

"You weren't jealous were you?" Eric asked at last.

"A bit," Helen confessed. "I never knew what you might be up to in the dark."

Eric was unexpectedly vehement. "I was jealous. I never really liked the thought of Malcolm running his hands all over you!"

"He didn't run them all over… And anyway…" Eric heard Helen's protest and let it pass. Be content and believe. Don't press for her confession and Helen won't press for yours and he heard her concluding, "…tried but I wouldn't let him go that far!" What had Malcolm tried, that Helen had needed to resist? To touch her and know her where no-one but he had the right? God! But the chase was over, they knew it and thank God they had not pursued it to its ultimate conclusion. And in the cold light of day, outside the unique forum of Saturday's late night fireglow Eric looked at Rita and Jenny and he thought, 'Yes, I lusted after you. I've seen you naked and held your breasts and kissed them and felt their heaviness resting in my palm and felt between your thighs and tried to coax you to let me… But if I asked you now?' And they saw the light of memory in his eyes and were able to laugh together as friends… It was strange. And meanwhile Eric took the plunge and they made an offer on the house and hailed it as part of their new beginning. It wasn't much different to Rita's except Helen's boasted a bay window with a tiny garden at the front and an attic under the roof. The main difference was their location. Rita's house was in the east-end, close to the beating heart of the city's industry whilst Helen's was across the city, away from the factories and close to her mother's.

Chapter 22 – 'The Emperor'

It was their final week in the flat; next weekend would be their last and then a home of their own. But now the perversity of human nature came into play. Eric's initial euphoria in his new job had quickly faded; the 'initial training' had failed to live up to its promise and for the first month Eric had been no more than fodder for Ted's ego, introduced to Ted's customers as 'my junior', relegated to the side-lines in meetings and showered with condescension to the point of nausea. "I'm supposed to be working on my own area," Eric protested and it had taken the intervention of Jacob Harker to prise Eric free of Ted's overbearing smothering. It was a side of Ted that had remained hidden when Eric had first seen him in the showroom; Ted's initial charm had masked the limitations of his intellect and Eric couldn't respect him like he'd respected Fred Robertson. But here he was, still having to submit daily activity reports to Ted and now another working day loomed. Eric faced it in a mood of disillusion.

It was raining steadily and looked like it was set-in for the rest of the day. Eric picked up his briefcase, ran for the bus and called on a couple of plumbers but it was no fun on foot in the rain and by eleven o'clock he had given up for the day. It was easy to justify it to himself; he couldn't do business looking like a drowned rat and they should give him a car so that he could do the job properly like the men in Wakefield and Leeds and Huddersfield. His discontent was fuelled by the uneasy suspicion that Ted followed him, checking up. If only Ted would leave him alone to get on with the job then he could really make something of it.

Eric returned to the flat and sat alone thinking in the silence of the house. He was going nowhere, stifled by Ted in a non-job. All his customers were out and there was a dreary air about the day; it seeped into the house bringing gloom and a sense of chill desolation beyond emptiness into the rooms. Eric's spirits were as low as the clouds outside and he felt the sourness of hunger gnawing at his stomach. He put on a tape – Beethoven – and slumped in the chair and closed his eyes. The music was soothing in its complexity, the brilliance of the piano in perfect balance with the orchestra. This was true creation stemming from the spirit, the fulfilment of an idea, a sublime dream. He decided to play it again. He had lived so much of his life without music, real music, music to move the world and he thanked God for Helen who had shown it to him.

He re-wound the tape and turned the volume higher than they had ever played it before, as loud as it would sound in a concert hall and this time he would conduct it. He would mount the rostrum and create a masterpiece! Eric found a knitting needle in a drawer and took centre stage facing the window. No – too public, people might see. Eric turned to face the hearth. Too mundane! He needed space, a horizon to fill and he turned to face the corner across the room with the living room door behind him. Better! The walls converging into the opposite corner gave a sense of perspective. He paused with his hand on the tape-recorder's switch. Now the world held its breath until the maestro was ready. Eric looked briefly around at the orchestra, nodded in satisfaction, flicked the switch and raised his baton. Ladies and gentlemen, 'The Emperor'!

Eric swept his arms aloft and held the mighty opening chord, holding the orchestra at the quivering baton's tip, released them to the piano then once more he wielded the awesome power that was his will. Oh! - how the music flowed at his command. What ecstasy! He closed his eyes, seeking perfection, gauging time and tempo, coaxing volume then quelling it to exquisite, delicate shades of softness. He took breath; the judgement of this descent towards silence just as profound as the most thrilling sound the orchestra was capable of. The concentration was intense, the music sublime. Eric's brow furrowed with concentrated force. Oh what joy! What love! He closed his eyes again and the whole world was encapsulated in the music, enraptured, enriched, banishing sorrow, lifting care away. The universe within Eric's mind was charged with the energy of creation and he felt a presence, a divine presence growing within the room. He opened his eyes. Before him and all around the room was grey, grey from its patterned walls, grey from the cold dead light creeping in from the world outside and Eric's movements became less certain. Now the music was overwhelming him, betraying his solitary presence and masking other subtle, unidentified sounds and he had a sense of the growing vulnerability of his back. What had he done? Behind him a force was gathering between him and the door and there was no way out except that door. Unexpected silence, Eric stood immobile and then a sigh of expectation! The Second Movement, the slow footfall of notes, a progression of sounds ringing from the keys. Once more he tried to raise his baton but the movement betrayed him, the slow progression of music was no longer innocent and Eric felt the chill proximity of the presence at his back. Oh God! Something was in the room and he stood rigid and felt the cold intensity of its presence. How long until the music ended? Silence, and Eric braced himself for flight then a flurry of sound, joyful, brisk, the Third Movement! Eric screamed in terror and ran blindly through the door, along the hall and out to the back garden.

He stood feet apart, leaning forward and rested his hands on his thighs gasping, taking huge draughts of the cold air. He felt ridiculous and hoped no-one from the houses beyond the fence opposite were watching. Oh God! He looked back through the kitchen, beyond the kitchen door into the gloomy hall. It was empty but something had been there, it had, he'd felt it! He was clear about that; there had been something in the room with him. Had he conjured it through the music or was it a phantom, a shadow from the oppressive gloom of the day? He could hear the concerto drawing to its conclusion and he raised his face to the thin rain now carried in the wind; cool and fresh on his face but his clothes were becoming damp. He took a breath, went inside to the kitchen, put the kettle on for tea and made some toast.

Silence hung about the house and he looked down along the hall. He didn't want to go into the sitting room. Not because he was afraid, he just needed to let 'things' in the atmosphere dissipate and get back to normal. Eric leaned against the sink units with his mug of tea and toast. He took a sip of tea and almost wished he was back out on his round of plumbers. No, he pulled himself up, he didn't wish that but where was he going? Helen, her mum and dad wouldn't be back for hours and the afternoon offered nothing at all. He took a step along the hall toward the sitting room then turned away with a sigh of resignation.

The doorbell rang.

Eric froze. A shadow was silhouetted against the frosted glass of the front door and a shiver of apprehension ran through him. Oh God! It looked like the bulky figure of Ted and here he was at home, framed in the light from the kitchen doorway. Oh God! Eric edged back into the kitchen and the doorbell rang again. Eric peered round the door but the figure was gone! Supposing he came round the side garden to the back door! There was nowhere to hide in the kitchen! Oh God! He had to get out! Eric edged along the hall to the living room with his heart pounding and stepped unseen behind the half open door. Then he leaned inside and risked a glance toward the window. The figure must have been peering inside the room; it was just withdrawing from sight and the doorbell rang again, insistent with the knowledge that Eric was inside. Behind the door Eric froze. Oh please God, why doesn't he go away! After ten minutes of silence Eric slipped swiftly upstairs and spent the rest of the afternoon behind the lace curtains in Alice Crawford's lounge window at the front, silently watching the road below.

He greeted Helen with inordinate affection when she returned from work. "Oh that's nice," Helen said, then, after a critical look, "Are you alright?"

"Yes why?"

"You look a bit... has something happened."

"No I'm alright," Eric protested. He gave her a smile. "I'm pleased to see you, that's all."

"Good. Sounds like you've had a good day. Tea won't be long."

Later, with the remains of the meal still before him Eric rose casually from the table and said, "I took the afternoon off."

"I knew there was something. You're not ill are you?"

"No. Oh I don't know, I just felt a bit down I suppose. It was raining and..."

"Nothing's happened has it? At work?"

"No. I was just feeling a bit – well, second rate. Trudging round Hillsborough, getting wet. Just not getting anywhere!"

"You're not second rate Eric," Helen protested vehemently.

"It's just that I wanted some time to think. But you can't do anything," he said with a pitying air, "not even take a couple of hours off. There's always something waiting for you."

"What do you mean?" Helen asked, "You sure you're alright?"

"Other people take time off. Why can't I?" It was that Greek thing hanging about him like a cloud. "You know," he said, "the gods watch what we're doing and just when we think everything's going alright they hurl a thunderbolt or something. Just to keep us on our toes."

"I don't know what you mean Eric."

"I only wanted a couple of hours out of the rain Hel…"

"Eric, what's the matter?"

He gazed wistfully round the room, so bright and comfortable with the faint sounds of activity from Alice and Frank above, so reassuringly different from the sombre atmosphere of that afternoon. But the memory was powerful and as Eric tried to explain the feeling that had built up in the room it sounded silly and inconsequential, like a silly fit of the jitters. "Anyway," he concluded, "that was it."

He looked so crestfallen and Helen smiled; what should have been a few pleasurable hours of stolen self-indulgence had been taken from him.

"Hubris," he said finally, "is inevitably followed by nemesis. I didn't deserve – no, that's the wrong word – it's as if I was taking something that I wasn't entitled to so I wasn't allowed to enjoy it."

"Don't you think that's just superstitious nonsense?" Helen asked gently.

"Perhaps," Eric replied earnestly. "But there really was something in this room. I could feel it."

Helen shuddered. "Stop it," she said, "you're making me go all funny."

"I know, I'm sorry. But then when the…" He was interrupted by the front doorbell.

They gave an involuntary start and their eyes met in apprehension. Helen recovered first. "It'll be somebody for my mum. Probably Mrs. Leavesley from next door."

Eric relaxed. "Yes. Sorry Hel. It was just…"

He hesitated and Helen rose from the table. "You stay there," she said. "I'll get it."

She returned with a look of concern and to his consternation Eric saw the figure of Ted following Helen into the room. "It's Ted. He just wanted a little word Eric."

Eric felt his heart sinking. Oh God! "Come in Ted," he said bravely with a quick glance at Helen. "We're just finishing tea. Well we've just finished actually."

"I'll just take these things out of the way," Helen said and Ted stood before the fire, looking round the room.

Eric gestured to a chair. "Sit down Ted."

"I'm not staying. I don't want to disturb you," he replied, his eyes on Helen.

"I'll just take these through to the kitchen then." Helen gathered their plates and cups and departed with an anxious look.

Ted's question came without preamble. "Where were you this afternoon?"

Eric tried to convey lingering illness. "I came home early. I wasn't very well."

"Why, what's the matter with you?"

"Er… I think I'm sickening for something."

"You weren't in when I called at two o'clock."

Desperately Eric fought to buy time, to see where Ted was leading. "Oh, did you call?"

"Where were you?"

"Well I'd… made a couple of calls. I was over at Hillsborough. Well you know that's where I was today." Ted watched him impassively. "And… it was raining…" God, how feeble that sounded, "and I was feeling a bit shivery. I started to feel like I was… coming down with something," Eric finished lamely.

"What time did you come home?"

Eric's mouth was dry. He could see where this was going. "Well," he faltered, "I'm not quite sure. As I say, I wasn't feeling all that good..."

"You only made two calls today," Ted said abruptly. "And you didn't spend long with them. Ambrose was out so you spoke to Eileen for two or three minutes then left. How long were you at Malin's?"

"About twenty, perhaps twenty-five minutes," Eric answered wretchedly.

"As long as that!"

Eric almost hung his head but he knew he mustn't; that would be the signal for Ted to strike. He concentrated his gaze over Ted's left shoulder with his brow furrowed as though searching for a recollection.

"Did you sell anything today?"

"No I... I wasn't feeling well."

"And yesterday? And the day before that?" Eric saw accusation harden in Ted's eyes. "So where were you today then? Eh? Where did you go?"

"I come home Ted. I told you, I wasn't feeling too good." Eric had no need to feign distress under Ted's examination.

"You weren't home were you!"

Eric was trapped. If not at home then where had he been? And if he admitted to being home why hadn't he answered the door? Eric tried to prevaricate. "What time did you say you called?"

"Look! You made two calls this morning. You didn't get to the first 'till nearly ten o'clock and the next one at about twenty past. Not a very good morning's work!" Eric raised his eyes to protest but Ted forestalled him. "It's not the first morning you've been late making your first call. Then you say you came home. Even if you had to wait for buses you'd still have been back here for twelve. And you weren't in when I called. Were you?"

Desperately Eric made the light of recollection appear. "Oh Ted. I'd gone to get something. From the chemist. It must have been then. I don't remember the exact time. I had to go out again in the rain." It was true, Eric told himself, he had gone out again in the rain, into

166

the back garden but that small kernel of truth helped him to assuage his conscience for the bigger lie. "I didn't want to go but I felt rotten and we'd not got anything in. I wanted a Beechams." A note of self-righteous reproach entered Eric's voice. "Sorry I didn't see you Ted. How long did you wait?"

Ted saw the lie behind the earnest expression. He also felt the tables turning against him and the difficulty of challenging Eric further. "I just wanted to see what was the matter," he said, adding silently, 'You cunning, lying pillock!' "Anyway," the solicitous enquiry merely a matter of form, "how are you feeling now?"

"I feel a lot better just now. I've had a nice tea and… It must have been a bug or something."

"Are you back at work tomorrow?"

"Yes Ted."

"Well you'd better come round to my place in the morning. Nine o'clock. Sharp! I'm having an office day. We'll go through your figures and see how you're doing."

"Yes Ted." Eric's heart sank at the prospect.

"And if you're unwell tell me. You can't just take days off when you feel like it!"

Eric was about to challenge the rebuke in Ted's words but he thought better of it. He had got away with it this time and it wouldn't do to challenge the gods further.

Chapter 23 - The black dog

It was the railway business all over again. "They were stolen off the float," Rob insisted defiantly, and Eric's look of disbelief triggered Rita into a vehement defence of him.

"It's not fair," she cried. "Just because he had a bit of bad luck once. Why won't you believe him?"

"Thought you had the money in a wallet fastened to you on a chain?"

It was a reasonable enough question; the same question the depot manager had put and Rob answered Eric with the same pained assurance. "The wallet split and the eyelet had come out; there was nothing to hook the chain on. I've reported it! I told 'em I needed a new wallet but they'd not done anything about it!" The depot manager had scrutinised Rob carefully, a grunt of exasperation masking his anger. It sounded almost true!

Eric shrugged and said, "It's their fault then?"

"You don't believe him do you?" Rita blazed with frustrated anger and Rob put his arm round her in an attitude of understanding and reconciliation.

"It's alright duck. They're all the same, looking for somebody to blame."

"Well I don't see why they don't believe you!" she said and tossed her head defiantly. "The manager was satisfied anyway and now he's got a new wallet. Pity they didn't give him one when he asked for it!"

Friday evening. The tension between Rita and Rob had begun to rise before tea was over and the children were packed off to bed early with Antony leading their protests, screaming and kicking. Rob closed the bedroom curtains, switched off the light and came downstairs to further confrontation with Rita.

"Well you tell me then Rob if you're so bloody clever 'cos I don't know what we're going to do."

"Oh come on duck. Things'll be alright…"

"They won't Rob, they won't! Not until you stop…" Rita gave a roar of exasperation and flung the tea-towel down on the sink and turned to face him. "You made a liar out of me Rob! To my friend, my best friend."

"I know love. I'm sorry." Rob put his arms about her but Rita pushed him away.

"No Rob, no. I don't want it…"

"You never bloody want it nowadays!"

"Can you blame me?" Rita cried. "Can you? I've nothing but worry and debts; you've no idea. I don't know where it goes!"

"But I've told you, it'll be alright. I promise."

"I've heard your promises before. And you've still not told me where that dairy money went."

"Didn't go anywhere. I told you." He spread his hands in the appealing gesture he'd used so often before. "It got stolen. Off the float."

Rita looked at him with scorn. "Oh come on Rob! I might have stuck up for you in front of Helen but I'm not daft you know."

"Well I've told you! Now shut up about it will you."

"No I won't shut up," Rita yelled. "You spent it didn't you? Almost ninety pounds! Gambled away, just like all the rest."

Renewed crying came from upstairs and Rob said, "Now look what you've done."

"Me!! You…!!"

"Rita!! You'll wake the kids."

"They're already awake!"

"Well what do you want for Christ's sake?"

"What do you think I want? I want them…" her eyes shifted uneasily to the back door, "out of our lives! It could have gone towards what you owe them!" She saw his look at the complicity of her words. "Well the dairy believed what you told 'em!" she cried defiantly. "I know it's wrong but… it could have helped us! It would have been a way…" She shook her head in desperation and turned to him, imploring, "Oh Rob. Don't you ever think about us? At least we wouldn't have that still hanging over our heads!"

"I've told you!!" Rob shouted, exasperated, "It's going to be alright. I'll take care of it."

"How?"

"How?"

"Yes Rob. How?"

"How? How? How bloody how?" he yelled. "That's all I ever get from you!" He retreated to the lounge and slammed the door, leaving Rita in the kitchen to deal with the kids...

The living room door opened. In a hollow voice Rita said, "He's here."

Rob sighed and heaved himself wearily from the chair.

"And don't wake the kids," she hissed as he passed by her. "I've just got Antony to sleep."

Rob opened the back door carefully; it was on the chain and he peered cautiously into the darkness. The voice was uncompromising.

"Come on. I haven't got all fucking night."

"Just a minute." Rob peered out into the narrow bar of light. "Where's the dog?"

"Don't you worry about him. He's alright." The man jerked the short leather strap and the dobermann emerged. Its lip curled and a low sound rose in the dog's throat. "Well come on then!"

"I need to talk to you," Rob said.

"Where's my fucking money?"

"Look, I can get it..." Rob glanced across his shoulder. Rita was in the living room on the settee, biting her lip. "I just need..."

"Don't fuck me about." The absence of threat in the voice made it all the more menacing. He knew how to talk to these people, hiding behind their doors, trying to pretend they were safe. He spoke in the manner of a reasonable man proposing a simple solution. "I'll kick the fucking door down."

"Look, look, wait..."

"Twenty five quid. I want it now. Stop pissing me about else I'm coming in for the fucking lot."

"No wait. I'm... I'll come out. I'm coming out. Just keep the dog away."

"He's alright. Don't you worry about him."

170

Rob stepped into the yard leaving the door ajar behind him. There was no light coming from any of the other houses in the yard and the dog's yellow eyes gleamed at him from the shadows. Rob struggled to keep his composure. "I need a... need another, a week. A few more days. I've got it - I can get it. It's just that..."

"Where is it then?"

"What?"

"You just said you've got it."

"I have... haven't! I mean," Rob stammered, correcting himself. "Not here. I... I can get it."

The man's free hand, fleshy with short strong fingers, reached down and gripped Rob's genitals, pulling at his scrotum and squeezing unmercifully. Rob doubled up helplessly against the wall and raised his left knee, trying desperately not to cry out. "Now you listen here. I'm sick of you fucking me about every time. I'm not leaving without my money." The voice became a snarl. "Or would you rather have the dog!" He squeezed harder, gave a final twist and released him. Rob gasped for breath and the man brought the dog forward and held it snarling a few inches in front of him.

"I'll get it I promise," Rob pleaded. He glanced along the yard. They were usually so bloody nosey! Why doesn't somebody come out! The knuckles of the man's hand were white from the pressure of the lead holding back the dog. Now he began to release it. "No wait!" Rob began to weep. "Take something else instead."

"What you talking about?"

Rob could hardly speak. He looked into the man's eyes, pleading. "Take my missus for... for this week's! Just... for... this week's, just until I can..." The sound was rising in the dog's throat again and its bared teeth were just a few inches away from... "Only don't... Please... Don't..." Rob whimpered.

The voice was contemptuous. "You think she's worth twenty five quid?"

"She's... She's a... she's a good... You wouldn't be disappointed."

The man gathered Rob's shirt in his hand and drew him to within inches of his face. "You offering me your wife?" Rob nodded with a sob. "She wouldn't fucking do it."

"She would," Rob cried in tears. "She'd do anything... for me. Anything."

"What's she like?"

"You've seen her," Rob whispered in his shame. "She's got a lovely... figure."

The man knew Rob was right. He'd seen her and fancied her. "I'll tell you what," he said. His manner became magnanimous. "You get her to let me shag her and I'll let you off the interest. Just for this week. But that'll still be seventeen quid this week you still owe." Rob swallowed and nodded. "And next week it's business as usual! Thirty quid plus this week's seventeen!"

"Thirty...?" Rob's mind was whirling; he tried to work it out but the man interrupted him.

"Interest my son. It still attracts interest! You don't get nothing for nothing. Or else the lot falls due now! And I'm not fucking kidding!" He allowed the dog to move forward. Rob felt it brush against his trousers and his face creased in anguish. "Well we'd better go and tell her to get herself ready then."

"Wait here..."

"What? I'm coming inside. Think I'm fucking daft or something."

"No. No, no, just for a second. We've got kids in the house," Rob pleaded desperately. "Just give me a minute to tell her. I shan't be a minute."

"I'm warning you..." The man grabbed Rob's bruised genitals again and yanked hard. "Don't think you can fuck me about. You come out with the money or I'm coming in with the dog. Kids or no kids!"

Rita looked up hopefully as Rob pushed the kitchen door closed but he was trembling and pale.

"Are you alright Rob?" He started to answer, his lips moved but she heard nothing. "What did he say? Will he wait?"

172

Rob snuffled and tried to regain his composure. He had to be quick, to tell her quickly and he took a breath and said, "I want you to do something for me duck."

"What? What is it Rob? What's the matter?"

Rob began to plead. "He won't wait. You know what he's like." Rob faltered. "He's got the dog with him again. He… he turned a bit nasty…"

"Are you alright?"

She reached out to smooth his hair but he pushed her hand aside. He hadn't time for her concern. "'Course I'm alright…"

"You sure?"

"Look, he's got to be paid. He won't take no…"

"But we've nothing to give him! How can we pay…" Suddenly Rita knew. Something in Rob's eyes; weakness, fear, shame, told her and Rita's head began to shake. He wouldn't, he wouldn't, no no no it isn't true… "No!!" Rita cried and recoiled from him.

"Shush Reet," he pleaded. "If there was anything, anything else; any other way. I'll give you anything you ask me…"

"No Rob. No!" Rita's voice rose in disbelief. "Rob I don't want to hear what I think you're going to tell me."

"It's the only way. Let him please. It's not as if you're a… Let him make love to…"

"Love!!" Rita cried, "Love!!"

"I've told him you will. Please Rita. For me. Do it for me!" Rob glanced toward the kitchen door; he'd be looking at his watch, losing patience. A spasm of fear ran through him. Bloody fool, he hadn't chained it! It was only will that was keeping the man and the dog outside. "Oh Christ Rita I love you, I do. Pretend it's me Rita, please, you've got to…!"

"I won't," she screamed. Rob clapped his hand over her mouth but she struggled free. "I bloody won't." She ran from the room and fumbled the chain onto the door as the door began to open; Rob caught her but she pushed him away. "I won't," she screamed again and Rob gasped, "Rita please! Rita!!!" but she started for the stairs. Rob caught the hem of her skirt and she kicked him off. He took hold of her skirt again but Rita broke loose, kicking and flailing with

173

her legs. Behind him Rob heard the deep baying of the dog and the man shouting, "Get this fucking chain off!" His fingers were inside, twisting for the chain and the dog's snarling and barking filled the house. Rob turned and put his weight against the door, praying for the chain to hold. Weight for weight Rob was no match for the man but his years on the railway had made him fit and hard muscled. Upstairs Rita gathered her screaming children, slammed the bedroom door, desperately searching for something to barricade it. Lights began to come on in the yard and Rob heard the neighbours calling from behind their half-open, carefully guarded doors.

"What the bloody hell's going on then…!"

"Who the bleeding hell are you…?"

"Fetch 'police, fetch 'police…!"

Better than the telly, watching repeats of 'The Saint', here was anger, real unpredictable violence. They gathered in a small knot at the far end of the yard, seeking safety in numbers and man turned on them and made a feint, the dog snarled and lunged and they retreated to the safety of their doors and grew silent and the word ran round, 'It's him. Him and his dog; Earnshaw's had trouble with him. Don't tangle with him.'

The man turned and gave Rob's kitchen door a parting kick. "I'm coming back! Don't you forget, I'll be back." And the neighbours became silent with relief and watched him depart into the night.

Chapter 24 - A fresh start

Tuesday afternoon. Malcolm parked the car, a new dark blue Zephyr bought on the advice of his accountant, stood back to admire it then he sauntered through the stone arch into the city's botanical gardens. The lawns had lost the smooth manicured look of summer and were pitted with the litter of autumn, wormcasts and dead leaves. Two gardeners were clearing a flowerbed and another was sweeping leaves into a pile. Malcolm walked past and turned into the seclusion of the water garden, crossed the shallow flagstone bridge over the pools and sat on a stone bench in the sunshine. The plants trailed dead stems and leaves over the water and there was an air of neglect about the pool's edge. He checked his watch; she was later than usual. Never mind, she'd be impressed by the new car. Rita liked nice things, going out, nice cars. She would never have anything like that with Rob; she was wasted on him but she'd like the Zephyr! It was the new model, long and low with a bonnet like the deck of the Ark Royal. He would take her into Derbyshire, find a bit of seclusion on the moors above Hathersage and lay her on that back seat... Malcolm's saturnine face creased with pleasure in anticipation of the afternoon's delights.

It wasn't that Jenny wasn't willing but somehow it lacked excitement. With the fiasco of their honeymoon behind them their sex life followed a typical pattern, if the magazines Jenny read were to be believed. Oh, Jenny was pretty, Malcolm would not deny her that, and he conceded she was highly fanciable but she didn't thrill him like Rita. Rita was much shapelier; she must have looked stunning when she was nineteen and even after two children Rita was - Malcolm savoured the nuance in the word - desirable. And she was voracious for it; she'd stopped doing it with Rob, at least that's what she told him. Well, more fool Rob.

Malcolm wandered back to the main path and saw Rita emerging through the arch carrying a suitcase. Malcolm's mind began to fill with surreal images. She's brought the washing? Bloody fool!

Shoplifting? Don't be daft! She smiled and trotted the last few steps towards him.

"I didn't think you were here," she said with relief. "I didn't see the car." She lifted her face, he kissed her and she hugged him and pressed close.

"Got the new one yesterday," Malcolm grinned. "Thought we'd try it out."

"Oh Malcolm." She spoke his name breathlessly, as though she had come to the end of a race and her eyes grew wide. "What, that big one at the gate? The blue one?"

Malcolm preened with satisfaction, "You like big ones don't you," and Rita giggled. "We'll take it a run into Derbyshire shall we?" They turned to leave the garden and Malcolm said, "Brought your washing?"

"I've left Rob," she murmured.

"Left him? What for?"

"He's been terrible Malcolm. I want us to get away from here. Go off somewhere together. Start a new life. Just me and you." She kissed him again eagerly. "Oh Malcolm, think of it, no more stolen afternoons, no more furtive meetings."

Malcolm tried to respond to her kiss but his mind was suddenly elsewhere. He took the suitcase and steered her back into the water garden with a quick backward glance, trying to hold down a rising feeling of panic. "Bloody Hell Rita. What're you doing?"

"I've told you, I'm leaving Rob. We can go away together. Like we said."

"What about the kids?"

"My mother's got them."

"I don't mean that." He looked about him, searching for escape. "I mean… Rita, darling… I can't go away with you!"

"You said you loved me."

"I… I do," he said wildly, desperately. "You know I do…"

"You said you'd do anything for me. Anything at all you said!"

"I know I did…" Christ, he never thought she'd take him literally! In the heat of the moment – and there had certainly been some heat, especially the last time! – well, God, you say all sorts of things. "…and I meant it," he concluded lamely.

"Well why not then? Oh Malcolm, Malcolm. You said…"

He knew what he had said. Lying in sexual abandonment with Rita beside him, his mind filled with visions of endless hours of consummating lust with this voluptuous woman he had said, 'Why don't we go away for a few days.' It could have been wonderful. Now he said, "I can't Rita. I can't go away with you."

"I don't understand! You said anything was possible. You know how it is with me and Rob. You said it was better with me than it could ever be with Jenny. You said…"

He couldn't think! Rita's voice filled his mind with all the rewards he had promised her, all she had needed to satisfy her, sex and promises. So easy to say words to get her knickers down, the lubricant of an afternoon's desire and the prelude to the removal of all his inhibitions. God, she had believed him just as he'd kidded himself that he believed them too but in his heart he'd always known the words were just part of the seduction. A flush of anger ran through him! So Bloody Stupid! Why does she have to go and spoil everything? What good will it do except bring everything tumbling about their ears! He didn't want to leave Jenny, of course he didn't and Rita knew it! It was such a bloody shame. They could have gone on forever! Why spoil it like this!

"You know I can't leave Jenny!"

"But you said…!"

"I never said I was leaving Jenny, Rita."

"You said we'd go away," Rita persisted desperately.

"I didn't mean… Not like this. I mean, not forever. Just for a few days. To be together… You know that's what I meant. A few days on our own…" But now? Panic crystallised into firm resolve. Not on your bloody life! "And there's the kids. What about your kids? Eh? Who'll look after them?" He saw the realisation in Rita's eyes. "I can't. I mean… how can I?"

Rita felt the bleak rejection in Malcolm's words. Where was her escape now? She couldn't go back to another night like last Friday. She couldn't carry on living with Rob's lies and betrayals, all the things she had turned a blind eye to; his... she was going to say affaire's but they weren't like her affaire with Malcolm; theirs was a real love affaire and she could have loved Malcolm as she had once loved Rob. She had been deceived into thinking that Malcolm really loved her but... in the end it was just like Rob. Only with Malcolm she had been the one who was there, every Tuesday, willing to let him use her, while with Rob it was a different woman every time. She felt such a bloody fool! The rosy scales of romance fell from her eyes and she felt pity for herself, for having been used as a plaything. She had given herself with such abandonment! Nothing had been withheld; everything she and Rob had done and more, for Malcolm had been uninitiated in the pleasures of sex. She had given him pleasures he would not otherwise have known and a vile taste rose in her mouth at the memory. God, what had she done!

"Rita. I'm sorry."

Malcolm's words brought her mind back to the present and the suitcase at her feet.

"What?"

"I'm so sorry."

Rita's eyes blazed with venom. "How could you! You deceived me into thinking you loved me."

"Rita, Rita you know I love you."

"Oh don't Malcolm!"

"If there was..."

Rita turned and bit her lip to suppress the rising sense of shame and anger and her mind went into reverse. She'd have to go back to her mother's and she needed friends like she had never needed them before. She couldn't afford to fall out, and with relief Malcolm saw the anger ebbing from her.

"I'm sorry Malcolm, I thought we had a dream together. Seems I was wrong! You'll just have to go back to your little Jenny won't you."

"I'm sorry..."

"Oh don't keep saying you're bloody sorry. It's so pathetic!"

"Sor..." He checked himself. "What are you going to do?"

"I'm going to tell the world!" With satisfaction she saw Malcolm go pale at her words and fear entered his eyes. "I've told you. I'm going to leave him." Then she relented. "Oh don't worry, I don't expect I'll say anything to anybody."

"Look, Rita, I'm sorry it's come to this." She was a good kid after all and he tried to assume an expression of contrite responsibility. "Was it... because of you and me?"

"Oh Malcolm." How he flattered himself! He looked so pathetic and she spoke with condescending pity, unable to resist another barb. "Do you really think I would leave him for you! You're only half the man he is in bed." She felt a small glow of satisfaction as her words deflated him. "It was over long before you. It's just that neither of us knew it." She sought refuge in attack. "You just helped me to make up my mind that's all. You can give me a lift to my mother's if you want."

Malcolm nodded in relief. "Of course. You'll get your ride in it after all." He picked up the suitcase and grinned at her hopefully. "Unless you'd..."

"Oh Malcolm," she said scornfully. "Do you really think I'd want to?"

Rita's mother glanced along the road as Rita walked through the door but Malcolm had dropped her off discretely at the corner. "You're back early," she said. "Raymond's in bed; he's not been asleep long."

She led the way along the hall to the kitchen. It was all so neat, clean and ordered. Antony was out in the garden and there was silence in the house. It must always have been like this Rita reflected, but when she was a girl it hadn't seemed so sterile. She hadn't even noticed it when she and Rob had lived here but then they had always kept to their own room. Now the sound of Antony's voice from outside only served to accentuate the emptiness of the house. Her mother pointed to the suitcase. "What have you got there?"

Rita placed the suitcase below the stairs and replied, "Just some old clothes for the charity shop." There! It was done. She couldn't come back. She had thought that 'home' – her mother's home – would provide her with a temporary bolthole but within a moment of entering she realised that it wouldn't.

"I've got some you can take as well. Remind me later will you."

"The kids been alright?" Rita asked, watching Antony at the kitchen window.

"So far. Are you alright Rita?"

"Yes, why?"

"It's not like you to be back so soon that's all."

"No."

"You and him's not had a row have you?"

"He's got a name mother," Rita replied irritably.

"There's no need to talk to me like that. You know how I feel about him."

"Oh mother, don't start that again."

"I'm not starting anything," her mother riposted primly. "I'll make us a drink when this kettle's boiled." She went into the hall and stood for a moment at the foot of the stairs, then she returned and regarded Rita shrewdly. "What is it?" she said. "Come on Rita; what's wrong?"

"I've told you…"

"I'm not stupid you know." Her mother made no reference to the suitcase but Rita saw it in the look that passed between them. "What's he been doing?"

"Nothing mother! It's just…" Rita hesitated; her mother would die if she knew what was really going on but… "We… we have a bit of a problem," she began.

"I knew it. I knew there was something. As soon as you walked in." Rita waited in silence while her mother brewed coffee in the pot. "Well, you might as well tell me what it is."

"We've run up a bit of debt." Rita said simply.

"What sort of debt?"

"Well… money of course!" Rita answered testily and received a withering look of reproof.

"I meant how much?" her mother said stonily.

"A lot more than we can afford," Rita countered.

180

"Oh I don't know. Here, have your coffee." She proffered the cup. "How can we possibly think of helping you if you won't talk to us."

Her mother's words lifted Rita's spirits. "Help?" she said.

"Well that's what you've come for isn't it?"

"Oh mother! I come every Tuesday! You know that." Rita stood at the window, watching Antony. At last she said, "It's about four hundred pounds." There was silence and Rita took a sip of coffee.

"I don't know Rita," her mother finally said and she shook her head. "I might have known. But you wouldn't be told would you! Well, you've made your bed and you must lie on it." She sighed again. "We'll have to see what daddy says." Rita turned to face her and to her surprise she saw Rita's lips quivering ever so slightly and there was the tiniest glint of moisture in her daughter's eyes.

It was Friday lunchtime. They were in 'The Shack' at the corner table by the door. Rita began with an apology. "It's been ages since we last had lunch together Hel."

"I know."

"How long have you got?"

"Oh I'm alright," Helen replied easily. "I told 'em I was meeting a friend. It won't matter if I'm a bit late back." The remark, made casually, came to Rita as clear as a gunshot, 'A friend' not 'My friend'.

"How's your mum?" Rita asked. "I don't seem to have seen her for ages."

"Oh she's alright," Helen said with an air of dismissal. "You know what she's like. Always got some bee in her bonnet about something. This time it's the floods in Bangladesh."

"I know. It's terrible but what can you do?"

"She keeps wringing her hands about millions starving in the world and saying we ought to do something. Next week it'll be something else I expect. How's yours?"

"Same as usual." No, that wasn't fair. "She's fine," Rita said with a burst of generosity. "Really. And she loves the kids and they think the world of her. Who'd have thought it, eh Hel?"

181

"Not much change between her and Rob then?"

Rita glanced at the menu. "What are we having? Same as usual?"

"Eric's been for another job," Helen said as the waitress brought their drinks.

"I thought he was settled."

"Well you know how restless he gets."

Rita tried to sound enthusiastic, but it wasn't easy. "What's it this time?"

"A rep. With a car this time. If he gets it."

"Oh, that's nice."

There was a pause while Helen masked her disappointment at Rita's disinterest then Helen said, "I'll just pop to the loo while we're waiting."

Rita watched Helen cross the café. She sensed the strain - or was it just her guilt - between them but she couldn't help it. She sipped her coffee meditatively and when Helen returned she leaned forward and said, "I'm thinking of leaving Rob."

"When?" The directness of Helen's question caught Rita off balance.

"Well, not yet. Soon."

"Where will you go? Back to your mother's?"

"Don't think so. I'm not sure. I've not got that far yet."

"What does Rob say?" And with sudden insight Helen provided the reply herself. "I don't suppose he knows yet does he?"

Rita shook her head, their meal arrived then she said. "I've been having an affaire."

Helen felt like the woman who knew too much. "I thought you were," she replied simply.

"You knew?" Rita had believed her liaison was a secret.

"Sorry Reet."

"But, how could you…?

Helen smiled ruefully. "You were seen."

"When?" Rita cried and glanced round. "When?" she repeated in a softer tone.

"Ages ago. You were on your way to meet him. It's Malcolm isn't it?"

Rita pondered silently then asked, "Who else knows?"

"Just me and Eric. As far as I know."

"What about Jenny?"

Helen shook her head. "Shouldn't think so or something would have happened by now."

A light of relief passed across Rita's face and she said philosophically, "Yes I suppose it would."

"It'll cause ructions you know."

Rita gazed out at the scene beyond the window then she turned back to face her friend. "It's not Malcolm Hel. I'm not leaving him for Malcolm."

"What? Who then."

Rita shook her head sadly. "Nobody. Anyway it's over with Malcolm. I… I had thought…" Rita's eyes grew distant. "But that wasn't going to work either." She sighed. "We… finished it. Tuesday. Three little days ago."

"I'm sorry Reet…"

"It's not that," Rita said earnestly. She leaned close. "You don't know Helen; you've no idea."

"We've known you and Rob were having difficulties. What with his gambling…" she paused as Rita suddenly pushed the uneaten meal from her. "Rita! What is it?"

"Can we leave? Do you mind?" She rose abruptly; Helen paid quickly and followed her into the narrow lane adjacent to the café. Rita was standing close to the wall dabbing tears from her eyes.

"Reet, what is it?"

Rita shook her head to compose herself. "I'll be alright." Her breathing calmed and she repeated, "Sorry Hel. I'll be alright in a minute."

They linked arms and began walking. It was easier to speak in the anonymity of the street and as they walked Rita began to talk. "We've got into terrible debt. You know he'd come home and boast of his winnings but he never said a word about what he was losing. But I knew; of course I knew; we'd never got any money!"

"We thought it was strange. I mean he always got good pay."

"You know that time he lost his wages. Well he did lose them but not in the way he meant. He lost 'em at cards."

"We suspected as much. Is that what happened to his 'bike? And the dairy money?" Rita nodded and Helen smiled sadly. "So now we know," she said, "and you're leaving him."

Rita's footsteps faltered. "No," she said at last. "You don't know." They paused before an antique shop window and the silence within Rita's mind gave way to the echoes of tumult as she stared at an ebony escritoire decorated with a delicate filigree of rosewood marquetry. "Nice," she said.

"Do you think so? You'd need a big house though."

"He offered me in payment of his debts."

Helen saw Rita's face reflected in the window; their eyes met in the glass and Rita made a small movement of affirmation. She could say it to no other person in the world but even so it made her feel dirty.

Speaking softly Helen said, "Do you mean Rob... offered you... to...?"

"Yes." Standing before the window filled with antique symbols of refined living Helen saw Rita's eyes mist with the memory of that night.

"Oh Rita..."

"You've met him. He comes with his dog."

"Him!" Helen exclaimed. She sought for words. "I'm so sorry Rita. We didn't know. I mean, we knew why he'd called... I thought he was just collecting the HP or something." Rita turned her face away. "He... You didn't...?" To her relief she saw Rita shake her head and Helen reached for Rita's hand and squeezed it. "I'm so sorry Reet." She felt the pressure of Rita's fingers tighten then Rita freed herself from Helen's grasp and moved from the window.

"Anyway we'd better get on or you'll never get back to work."

"Rita. We'd no idea. Honestly." They began to walk and Helen said, "But what happened?" Her brow furrowed. "Does he still call round on Fridays?"

"He's coming again tonight." She saw Helen's look of horror. "It's alright Hel. It's ok." Rita sighed. "I've had to go and ask my mother and father. See if they'd help."

"They don't know do they!"

"No. Well, not about... that! About him anyway! My dad would kill Rob if he knew." She gave Helen a look of reassurance. "They've lent me the money to pay him off. I've said it's a loan but I expect they've given it to me really. I only hope Rob told me the right amount! I can't go back and ask them for more."

"So...?"

"So he'll get what Rob owes him tonight."

"You're going back there then?"

"Oh Helen. What else can I do?"

Rob greeted Rita's solution with relief. He was quite incredulous. He had no illusions about Rita's parents and he grinned with delight. Antony, pale and watchful in the armchair with some paper and a plastic toy looked up and responded to his daddy's good humour with a grin.

"They've lent it to me," Rita corrected him. "It's for me. Me and the children!"

It didn't matter to Rob. The main thing was the solution had been provided and – wait a minute - he didn't even have to worry about where it came from! She'd just said, it was her responsibility not his. Overflowing with good intentions and gratitude he threw his arms round her. "You won't be sorry duck. That's all we wanted, somebody to believe in us and give us a second chance."

Rita stood unresponsive. "I've told you Rob. They've done it for the sake of the children."

He was suddenly suspicious. "They don't know, do they?"

"What do you think I am?" Rita tore herself from him. "Do you think I'd demean myself by telling them you tried to prostitute me to pay your debts! You're rotten Rob, a rotten little pimp, rotten through and through! It would kill them; it would kill my mother if she knew!"

185

Rob glanced towards the children. "I know duck; I know I shouldn't have done it." He switched to the boyish charm. "But what could I do? You saw what he was like. I'd have been maimed; finished up in hospital or something... It's not as though you're a vir..."

"You lousy, lousy rotten bastard..." Rita screeched, clawing at his face, "What about me!" Antony screamed and Raymond began crying. "What about the kids? You wanted to let him in the house! What would have happened to us? You didn't think about that did you!!"

Rob fended Rita off and held her at arm's length, laughing in the face of her rage. "Now look what you've done! You've frightened the kids!"

"What I've done...?" she yelled and renewed her efforts against him.

"Take no notice of mummy," Rob called, averting his face from Rita's slap. "She'll be alright when she's calmed down." But Antony's pinched little face screwed up in a renewed spasm as Rob pushed Rita from him. She landed untidily on the settee and Rob gathered the children up. "There, there," he said. "Naughty mummy to frighten you like that..."

Rita subsided, inwardly seething, fearful of upsetting the children again. Turning the tables on her like that! Naughty mummy!! If only they were old enough to understand.

"I'll get the kids' tea," she mumbled, "while you keep an eye on them."

"Oh don't you worry, I'll look after them."

"Same as you've looked after them so far!"

"Oh don't start again Rita!" Rob glanced at the clock. "Anyway you'd better look sharp; he'll be here soon."

Rita tensed herself to launch a further riposte then thought better of it and took her handbag from the sideboard. "Here!" She took a wad of notes, bound together in elastic bands. "There's nearly five hundred pounds. Don't give him a penny more than you have to."

Rob ignored her, crooning to the children, "There, you see. Mummy's better already."

Rita placed the money on the table. It broke her heart to do it. "And I want the rest of it back. Whatever's left! Do you hear me Rob!"

But Rob didn't reply; his problem was solved and he was happy.

And meanwhile a consequence of the end of Malcolm's affaire was that Jenny became pregnant. It was a biological atonement by Malcolm for his deception. And in her innocence Jenny was delighted.

Chapter 25 - A cup of faith

Eric's final disillusionment with Ted came in the summer when he was called for a meeting at Ted's home in the middle of a long row of sooty terraces overlooking the gasworks. "Biggest gasometers in Sheffield when they're full," Ted had said, pointing down at them with unaccountable pride from the patch of garden outside his back door.

The house was stiflingly odorous. Ted's wife, a greasy matron in a shapeless dress with an air of stale breast milk about her was kneading dough between ineffectually swatting at the flies infesting the kitchen. "Make us a cup of tea Margaret love," Ted ordered gracefully and he gestured at the roll of sticky flypaper dangling above them festooned with bodies. "It's this weather; can't do anything about 'em."

An earthenware pancheon of dough was resting beneath a damp cloth beside the hearth in the living room and Tony, the baby of Ted's brood, ten years younger than his brothers and sisters, was crawling about the floor. Ted placed his papers on the sideboard by the telephone and began making calls and Margaret brought tea in and swept the baby off the floor. Eric felt a surge of panic at the thought of her undoing her dress and putting out her sagging breast to the child but instead she spread him on her knee and began to change his reeking nappy. His tea was white with milk and sickeningly sweet. Eric sipped it reluctantly and looked with dismay at the squalor and mediocrity surrounding him. It was the spur he needed to secure that new job, the type of job he had always set his sights on…

The initial two weeks training was in London and the company's Sales Managers, men of stature, were brought in to motivate the stable of new recruits. The newcomers met in the hotel, sharing uncertainty and anticipation and Eric spent any free time in the evening in the pub along the road with his new-found friend Toby, playing bar billiards and laughing at their good fortune in having met each other and having new careers. On the final afternoon they parted fired with ambition.

"Do you know what your territory is?" Eric asked.

"East Somerset I think," Toby replied. "I'll know for certain on Monday. You?"

"South Yorkshire. I'm working out of Sheffield office but my manager's based in Leeds."

Toby affected a friendly sneer. "Of course. You're not selling Office Systems are you."

Eric replied with superiority. "No. I'm in Furniture division. We're a bit more specialised of course. Need more highly tuned selling skills. Not common or garden Systems."

Toby lunged, tried an arm lock and they fell against the wall, laughing. Then the security officer rose from his desk and announced, "Right gentlemen, your taxis are here."

"It's been great Toby. Let us know how you get on."

"I will. And you the same." They shook hands and were driven away and never spoke to each other again.

Helen left the hospital laboratory early to meet Eric at the station. They had never been apart this long before and last weekend Eric had passed on a joke he had shared with Toby. They knew it was a good company, he said, because they had been given 'inter-course leave.' But the weekend hadn't been the fun they pretended; he'd had to return on Sunday and the looming deadline spoiled it. But this weekend would be better, tonight would be better and in anticipation Helen was wearing her tailored grey suit with the pencil slim skirt and a flattering ecru blouse and her sexiest underwear with the delicate lace edging.

She saw him at the carriage window as the train drew into the station and with the harsh roar of the diesel echoing around her she felt a rush of excitement as Eric jumped down from his carriage looking for her. The joy of their reunion obliterated all the other activity around them as they kissed. "I missed you. Oh I missed you," Helen breathed. "I cried last week when you went away."

"It's good to be back. Gosh I've missed you."

"I bet you didn't. I'll bet you didn't have time," she teased. "I'll bet you never thought of me at all." And they emerged from the station into an evening that was light and balmy and a feeling that the world was theirs.

They celebrated that evening at the Berni Inn. Eric told her about Toby and going to Leeds on Monday to collect the car and report to Mr. Chatfield and it was a different world. He sat back with an expansive air of anticipation, watching their steaks on the grill. The wine arrived and Eric tasted and approved it without self-consciousness and they ate prawn cocktails and a phrase from a film jumped into his mind, one of those black and white New York detective things set amongst skyscrapers at night; 'He belonged in this city and the city belonged to him.' Eric smiled an enigmatic smile; Sheffield was his city and he would make his mark in it.

Their steaks arrived and Helen said, "Oh, I must tell you about my mother." Amongst the laughter surrounding them her voice carried a faintly disapproving air. "She's started collecting rice."

"Rice?" Eric had more interest in the steak before him.

Helen nodded. "She's going from door to door with a cup, asking for rice."

"Whatever for?"

"Oh you know what she's like. She's got this bee in her bonnet." Helen was embarrassed for her mother. "She says she's got this voice telling her to take from the rich and give to the poor. I think she's getting religion."

"But why rice?"

"Because of the floods in Bangladesh."

"But there's appeals and collectors on every street corner. Red Cross, that sort of thing."

"She says its food they need, not money."

Eric cut into the steak, spread French mustard on it and chewed with appreciation. Alice could be embarrassingly zealous. And for what, a cup of rice! He swallowed and raised his glass. "Well, here's to us love."

"Welcome home."

Eric returned from Leeds on Monday in a white Austin 1100 and Helen ran outside to admire it.

"Can we go for a ride?"

"Yes, come on. We'll go and show your mum and dad."

She sat admiring the way Eric's hands gripped the steering wheel and the decisive way he handled the car. Already in some subtle way Helen could see that he had grown in stature. It was nothing to do with the car but an innate sense of pride and self-worth seemed to radiate from him. "It's lovely," she said, placing her hand over his, and received Eric's approving smile in return and at her mother's they stood outside and admired it again.

"Ooh, look at you," Alice laughed, "Lady Muck driving around in a new car. Last time your father had a new car was before the war. Then we got married and he never had a new car after that."

They went inside leaving Eric to follow with her father still admiring their new possession. "What's in here?" Helen asked, pointing to a large corrugated box in the corner of the hall.

"Rice," Alice replied.

Helen stared with dismay. Every available inch of space was taken with packets of rice; brown, long grain, pudding, Patna, Basmati...

"Mother!"

"Why what's up?"

"Well... look."

"Yes I know," Alice looked at the hoard with pride. "You've no idea how generous people can be."

"But what are you going to do with it?"

"Send it to Bangladesh," Alice replied simply.

"But, what does my dad say?" Helen stammered.

"Well your dad doesn't say anything."

They drove across the city with the pleasure of expectation. Now Eric had something to show he was making his way in the world. Different to his father! He'd been apprenticed at fifteen and stayed with the same company for over thirty years with nothing to show for it. Eric parked behind his father's second hand blue Ford Popular and they went in. George Allenby looked up from his armchair with an expression of surprise and spoke without preamble. "What brings you here?"

"We've come to see you," Eric said foolishly, already feeling on the defensive.

"Helen too. Haven't seen you in ages."

"Hello dad."

"Sit down. I'll make us a cup of tea in a minute."

"It's alright dad, we've just…"

"Thanks dad," Helen said, "That'd be nice." They sat together on the settee under his father's gaze. "Eric's got a new job," Helen said before the silence had time to develop.

"Another new job. What is it this time?"

Helen forced her smile to stay bright and said proudly, "He's a sales rep."

"Another selling job. Like the last one?"

"Better than the last one," Eric said.

"He's got a car. A new one. It's outside."

George Allenby inclined his head to the window. "I can't see it."

"I've parked behind you. Come and have a look."

"In a minute. We'll have that tea first. Put 'kettle on will you Helen."

Eric struggled to keep disappointment from rising into anger. It was always the same; being pleased for him was too much trouble; enthusiasm was too much trouble; putting the fucking kettle on was too much trouble! "Sit down Hel," he said, "I'll do it." He left the room and heard his father say, "He hasn't parked it too close has he…?"

Why did he feel such need for approval in the face of such indifference? Whatever he did failed to please. Never any recognition of his achievements! He didn't deserve it and he knew he should raise his voice and demand respect but Eric couldn't confront his father. Somewhere in his mind were the words 'Honour thy mother and thy father,' and so he suppressed his anger and accepted the eternal rebukes in silence. Besides, he knew respect had to be earned and conferred, it could not be demanded.

"It's on," Eric said, returning after a moment or two. "Should be boiling in a minute."

"Your dad's just been saying one of their departments is shutting down."

"It won't affect you, will it dad?"

"No. They need people like me. Thirty four years I've been there!" And you can't hold down a job for more than ten minutes at a time! The unspoken words were in his father's eyes.

"This will be a good job," Eric said.

"Same as all the others?"

Why? Why? Why? Why? Eric tried to make his father understand. "No dad it's not the same as all the others! Anyway people don't make a career with one company any more dad."

"Never did me any harm and I had to provide for you. I couldn't go chopping and changing whenever I felt like it." He turned to Helen. "I wonder you don't take him in hand a bit more. You're his wife."

"Helen understands dad."

They heard the kettle whistling and his father rose from his chair. "Tea Helen? Or is it still coffee?"

"I'll have tea if that's what you two are having."

"I don't mind. You can have coffee if you want. It's only instant." At the doorway he turned and said, "All I can say Eric is it's a good job she understands you 'cos I don't."

Eric closed his eyes as if in pain and Helen placed a hand on his knee and murmured, "Never mind."

George Allenby returned with their drinks and said, "I'm going down to 'The Teagarden' for a pint later. I don't suppose you're coming for one?"

"I'd better not dad." He saw his father's look. "I've only just got the car today." Eric turned to Helen. "What do you think?"

"No," she said, "It wouldn't be wise, would it."

"Please yourself," his father said. "I can't remember the last time I saw you. It's nearly four months, I know that!"

They took their leave and his father came out to the car. "Very nice," he said, "You want to look after it," adding, "You would if it was your own. Still I don't suppose it matters."

"We could give you a lift down the road if you like dad. Have a little spin in it."

"No," he replied, "I'll walk. Does me good."

They drove off, Helen turned to wave but he was already disappearing into the house. "Never mind Eric," she said gently. "It's too late now."

"I don't know what I've done," Eric replied sadly. "Nothing I do ever seems to please him. And then he wonders why we don't go to see him." He drove away, his duty done for a few more weeks.

Don Chatfield congratulated himself on his new recruit and Eric formed a working partnership with the 'Systems' salesman in the Sheffield office. Arnold Brown viewed Eric with reservation at first but gradually Eric won Arnold's trust and Arnold began to put a few tit-bits Eric's way. "One of my customers is looking for a couple of chairs. He's thinking of going to Matthews, he always gets his furniture from them. But if you ring him he might see you."

"Thanks Arnold."

"But don't you go upsetting him. He's an important customer."

"I wouldn't dream of it."

"And ring him straight away. It's taken me ages to get his business and it makes me look bad if colleagues don't act properly."

Eric accepted Arnold's strictures in the spirit in which they were offered and Arnold began to respect Eric's integrity. Other introductions followed and over coffee and toast in the café the salesmen frequented behind the City Hall Eric said, "You know Arnold I'm really sorry I can't give you any leads in return."

"It's alright," Arnold replied absently, his nose in the Daily Telegraph. "Look at this." He folded the paper and showed it to Eric. "Rolls Royce are down to threepence."

They commiserated on the misfortunes of the great company, brought to its knees over an aero engine that nobody wanted and then Eric said, "I'm always on the receiving end. I'd like to give you something."

"It's different with systems," Arnold conceded. He put the newspaper aside. "We have repeat business, we get to hear of things." He paused. "There might be another job coming up. I don't want to say any more yet. It could be a big one."

"Who is it? Come on Arnold."

"I'll tell you when the time's right."

"But if it's as delicate as that... I might go in blindly and..." Eric let the implication hang and Arnold pondered Eric's logic. He was right. It would look incompetent if one of his colleagues were to blunder in.

"You're not to go anywhere near 'em. It's a firm of solicitors. They're in the middle of negotiations for new premises." Arnold paused, clearly nervous. "If news of it gets out before they've concluded the deal..." he hesitated again. "It's highly privileged." Arnold glanced around and whispered, "It's Morpheus and Jones." He fished in his pocket for his car keys. "Anyway I've got to go, I've got an appointment."

The following morning Eric was in the showroom collating brochures and Arnold was behind the screen at the back making telephone calls when the door opened and Johnny Horrocks entered from his office upstairs with his attache case and raincoat over his arm. A dapper, neat little man, he had emerged in an unremarkable career as manager of the Sheffield office. He conducted his morning briefings in stilted formality and Arnold invariably spoke of Horrocks with disdain. Arnold gestured with the phone and Horrocks looked at the clock on the wall and turned to Eric. "Still here Mr. Allenby?"

"I'm just putting a set of brochures together for British Steel at Treeton."

"It's nearly ten o'clock," Horrocks grunted. "I'll be in Hull office this afternoon if I'm needed."

Eric watched Horrocks disappear along the pavement. "You know," he said, "I'm glad I'm working for Don Chatfield instead of him. Pompous little..." Eric left the rest of his opinion unsaid.

"He wastes everybody's time," Arnold conceded carefully. "But you have to keep him off your back." He dialled a number and said unexpectedly, "Did you know he carries out hysterectomies on his chickens?"

Eric was dumfounded. "Who told you that?"

"It's well known."

"Whatever for?"

Arnold shrugged. "He says it stops them laying. Perhaps he enjoys it."

Eric put the brochures in his briefcase. "Why does he always go to Hull on Thursday?"

Arnold paused, grunted and replaced the handset. "It's fish day. Thursday is the wet fish sale on Hull docks. He goes with orders for the village and his wife sells the fish on Friday." Arnold shrugged, redialling a number. "He has to oversee Hull. Might as well be Thursday as any other day."

"But supposing something comes up in Hull say, on a Tuesday or a Friday?"

"Horrocks goes to Hull on Thursdays..." Arnold's next call came through and he raised his voice a tone. "Hello, is Mr. Blackledge there...?" He gestured urgently to Eric with his hand over the mouthpiece. "What are you doing next Wednesday? I've got to see Peter Blackledge at Morpheus and Jones. You can come with me if you like."

It was a mystery to Alice why Helen looked upon her project with so much disapproval. After all, she was only doing it to help the less fortunate in the world. And there was something in the simplicity of her idea that Our Lord would have approved of, going from door to door and asking for a small, symbolic gift of life. It was something that had to be done and no-one could refuse to give a cup of rice. The cup itself was symbolic; most people went indoors and fetched out a packet and those who had none asked her to come back and went out and bought one. And Alice's crusade for rice to feed the starving victims of Bangladesh began to receive wider attention.

A visit from members of the Asian community had mixed words for her. Who was this European white woman and what did she think she was doing? But they thanked her when they saw how much she had collected. The coat stand in the hall had gone up to the landing and in its place hundreds of packets of rice were piled from floor to ceiling. And they went away and spread the word that here was a gesture that could help their brethren in the Bay of Bengal. What if all the rice was not of the right kind! At least it was something they could all co-operate in together to help. But amongst Alice's family there was consternation. Even long standing friends wrung their hands and wondered what Frank was thinking of, letting Alice have her head in this way and they looked at the bursting packets and grains spilling over the hall carpet and predicted catastrophe.

On Saturday Helen and Eric went to lunch and Helen's spirits fell as she walked through the door. She gave a sigh of exasperation and called, "Where are we supposed to put our coats mother?"

"Here, give them to me," Alice said brightly, "I'll take them upstairs."

"Oh don't worry mother, I'll take them."

"People are funny," Alice mused to herself, and then to Eric, "Anyway come on through. Father won't be long."

Helen returned and buttonholed her mother. "But what good will it do? They're starving in their thousands. What difference is a few packets of rice going to make?"

Alice was unrepentant. "I've told you. It's going to Bangladesh. If everybody thought like you nobody would do anything."

"But you're just a lone housewife…" Helen pleaded.

"No I'm not!" Alice cried, "That's just where you're wrong. I'm not alone. Each one of those packets represents somebody else who cares. And if everybody did the same as me… The Victoria Hall's offered me a room and I'm going to have a coffee morning for people to come and bring rice, and 'The Star' is going to publicise it."

"But how are you going to get it there?" Helen pleaded.

"It'll get there. And I'm getting more publicity too."

Helen gave up. It was going to end in the most appalling embarrassment with her mother and father living off rice for years to come. She heard her father's car draw up outside and she went into the hall, kissed him in greeting and said, "Why do you let her do these things dad?"

"It's your mother's way of doing something," he said gravely. "You can't blame her for that. It's a pity more people don't."

"But how… I mean where's it all going to go to?"

"Well it's going to Bangladesh. You knew that didn't you? Didn't your mother say?" He went into the kitchen carrying the bag of pastries he always brought as a Saturday treat leaving Helen to work out whether he was being sarcastic or merely whimsical…

Morpheus and Jones, in the person of Peter Blackledge, the senior clerk entrusted with the job of managing the firm's relocation, were not interested in steel furniture. He was cautious and pedantic, fearful of making the wrong decisions. "We're replacing the partners desks that's all," Blackledge insisted. "They will want mahogany or rosewood, not steel. Any new chairs will come from the people who supply the desks."

Sensing Arnold's unease beside him Eric said, "The brochures don't do us justice. Why don't you come to the showroom?"

Blackledge demurred. "I don't think the partners will want to. They are going to visit two executive showrooms on Thursday to choose their desks." Unable to press the point Eric had to settle for a half promise to, "…try and come if time permits."

Outside the office Arnold was contrite. "Sorry. I told you it wouldn't be easy. You know what solicitors are like. Well, they want rosewood."

"You'll still get something out of it won't you Arnold?"

"You see my position Eric; I can't help you much. I can't prejudice our business."

"Don't worry Arnold. I'm just grateful for the chance. And you never know…"

But on Thursday Peter Blackledge was a very worried man. He had arranged to visit each showroom by appointment but they had been received with little more than a handshake and a cursory invitation to, 'Have a look round and then tell us what you'd like…' It was not what the partners of Morpheus and Jones expected and the comments within the group were critical and uncomplimentary.

"There's just one more," Blackledge said desperately. "It's on the way back, we may as well call."

Eric stepped forward in welcome as they arrived. It was immediately apparent that the visits were not going well and he gestured to a table prepared with sets of literature. "Please, come and sit down."

"We're not staying," the senior partner said before Peter could respond. "It's only because we were passing. Peter said he'd been talking to you."

"Thank you for coming anyway," Eric said. "Peter gave me an outline of what was in your mind and I've prepared some ideas for you to look at. Can we get you some refreshments? Tea? Or there's coffee if you prefer." The delegation consented to be led to the table and Sally, the showroom receptionist, brought out the china cups from the management suite upstairs.

"We're not really interested in steel desks," the senior partner said.

"That's why we're so pleased you were able to visit us. We don't just do steel." Eric saw two partners leafing through the brochures and beginning to confer. "Our system of office furniture has moved beyond the mere idea of a desk and chair," he began. "Oh, thank you Sally. Please help yourselves to biscuits gentlemen." He unrolled a plan on the table showing various configurations of furniture and they leaned forward as Eric engaged them in a discussion about their own ideas for the offices. "The modular design allows workstations to be designed to suit the needs of the individual and to improve the efficiency of the office…" Questions began to arise and Eric's responses were peppered with discrete references to Peter Blackledge. "Yes, Peter said that would be an important consideration…" and "Peter did explain that but we thought you might like an alternative to consider…" He needed Peter's goodwill; he might not have any contact with the partners again.

At the end of an hour they rose to leave and Eric shook hands with an appointment to discuss details of supply and delivery.

"Well," Arnold said, "that went unexpectedly well." He inspected the teapot for a final cup.

"We won't get the partners desks," Eric conceded, bursting with the pleasure of his achievement. "But they've agreed that their secretaries and some general office furniture needs replacing. And they're looking for a new boardroom table."

"Cup of tea?" Arnold said. "I'm going to make a fresh pot."

"Yes thanks," Eric called, disappearing behind the screen at the rear of the showroom. "I'm just going to phone Don Chatfield."

Chapter 26 - The miracle worker

Helen and Rita were walking in the park with Rita's children wrapped in coats and scarves against the cool blustering wind. Rita was mulling over past events and they paused by the stream under the bare budding trees. "He never really stopped gambling." Rita's voice was heavy with resignation.

"You'd think he would have tried," Helen said, "Especially after you'd bailed him out?"

"Well..." Rita sighed. "He promised faithfully but..." They sauntered on until they reached the children's playground and sat in the corner by the railings.

"How serious is it this time?"

"I'm not sure."

"But... you haven't got..." Helen spoke carefully, "collectors?"

"No," Rita said then added, "Not yet."

"It's a pity you couldn't have left when..." Helen stifled the rest and left it unsaid.

"Yes well."

They sat and watched Rita's children running across the playground. Antony was like a butterfly, fleetingly settling on a roundabout then moving to the see-saw, pushing it briefly up and down then dashing on. Helen couldn't help thinking how frail he was compared to his younger brother; he had an air that demanded watchful attention while Raymond was growing into a sturdy toddler.

"Were you really going to leave him Reet?"

"I thought I was." Rita paused, considering the question. "I was... You get desperate, you see something and it looks like the answer. But it wouldn't have worked." She laughed to herself, a little laugh of consolation. "You should have seen Malcolm's face. I knew then I'd made a big mistake."

"And Rob never knew?"

"Still doesn't know. If he does he's never shown any sign of knowing." The children's shouts drew Rita's attention. The roundabout was spinning too fast and she shouted, "No! Stop that Antony, he'll fall off." Antony released his grip on the safety bar and the roundabout lost momentum and Antony took his brother's hand and they ran off again, screaming and chasing one another. "Kids!" Rita said, "Who'd have 'em."

"So... What will you do Reet?

"I don't know. You have to do what you can if only for the sake of the children." Rita pursed her lips and added, "I can't go to my mother again. I know that."

"I wish I knew what to say..."

"There's nothing you can say really."

The children dashed back demanding to be pushed on the swings and they talked about holidays together at Trearddur Bay. It held happy memories for Helen and it needn't be too expensive but Rita said, "I wouldn't bank on a holiday together too much. It's no good looking at me like that Helen. If I know Rob we won't be able to afford it."

So it was going to be that all over again.

That evening at Helen's mother's they stood in awe before the mountain of rice in the hall. "There's some in the dining room as well," Frank said. Helen turned a face of incomprehension on her mother but she seemed totally unperturbed. In fact, she seemed to be more...? Helen searched for words to describe her. Eccentric, out-of-this-world, perverse, joyful, euphoric even? She turned to her father but he was as tranquil as ever although his expression carried a shadow of pain; it seemed to say, 'Don't rock the boat, it's alright, we'll deal with it.'

Helen spread her hands in despair. "But where's it all going to end mother? How much more?"

"Oh, I haven't finished yet," Alice announced. "I've had a letter from the Bangladeshi High Commission."

"Really!" Helen replied, unimpressed.

"They are very pleased with the initiative I've shown and they're looking forward to seeing it arrive in Bangladesh."

"You really think it's going to Bangladesh?"

202

"Of course," Alice cried, "why do you think I'm collecting it?"

Eric added his protest to Helen's and gestured at the piles of damaged rice packets around them. "But look at it! It's not in any state to be shipped."

Unperturbed Alice said, "Come on through, I'll show you the letter."

To their relief there was no rice in the lounge and they passed the letter between them. "But even so," Eric persisted, "they won't be able to ship it like that, all in little packets."

"You may scoff but I've been told this is something I've got to do." Helen closed her eyes to hide her embarrassment. "God told me. It's His way of showing the world what we can do. If we all did it think what a difference it could make. I am surprised that you don't do it Helen and get some of your friends to do it too."

"My friends would think I was going funny. I wonder you've still got any friends left…"

"That's no way to talk to your mother." Frank's gentle rebuke was spoken with regret.

"Oh dad." Helen turned to face him. "Can't you do something? It's not going to go anywhere. You know that. And then you'll have the job of trying to get rid of it. How much is there now?"

"Over two tons; must be nearly two and a half."

Alice replaced the letter in its place of honour on the fireplace. "Anyway I'll make us a nice cup of tea." She paused in the doorway and smiled at Helen. "I know you think your mother's daft, but I can put up with that. You'll see."

"Are you alright dad?" Helen asked on Alice's departure. "You look as if this is all getting you down."

Frank shifted to a more comfortable position in his chair. "I won't hear anything said against your mother. I know she's a bit melodramatic sometimes but she's absolutely sincere about this." He gestured vaguely toward the piles of rice beyond the door and looked at them steadily. "You've only to look around you to see." He was not a religious man, in fact he hardly gave religion a thought. He had listened to bible stories as a boy and tried to believe but like a true sceptic if he couldn't explain it, he didn't believe it.

He and Eric had had some inconclusive debates about 'faith' and 'taking things on trust', philosophies Frank couldn't subscribe to. But Alice had firmly held beliefs even though she didn't attend church, and her beliefs showed in small idiosyncratic ways. Now, and to his slight surprise, Frank found himself saying, "Not everybody thinks like you do Helen. If they did your mother would never have collected as much as she has. And nobody's laughing at her. Not one single person as far as I know has refused her. Did you know that? So this is just the first step. The next step is to get it to Bangladesh."

"But how?" Helen persisted.

Frank put his faith in Alice. "It'll get there."

They changed the subject and Eric talked about Morpheus and Jones, the satisfaction of pulling off the job and seeing it through to completion. But was there condescension in Eric's manner of speaking to them? Frank watched and listened carefully. Their relationship with their son-in-law was good. It would be a shame if success were to tarnish it.

On Saturday Eric rose at leisure and Helen put boiled eggs before them and they sat to breakfast. "I want to go into town myself today," she said. "Shall I come and meet you? How long will you be?"

"Hour. Hour and a half at the most," Eric replied and looked at his watch. "Gosh, quarter to ten! I ought to be going." He grinned across the table at Helen. "I don't want to get there and find they've left."

"Perhaps we could meet and have a sandwich or something in town."

"Good idea," Eric replied. "Come to the site at say, half past twelve. I'll show you the new office layout."

He drove into the city in a glow of anticipation and found the boardroom table, minus legs and still in its protective packaging leaning against the lift shaft at the foot of the stairs in the ground floor lobby. He took the lift to Morpheus and Jones' new offices on the second floor. One of the furniture erectors looked up as Eric stepped from the lift, said nothing and inclined his head toward the main office. Peter Blackledge and Joe, the foreman erector were in a heated argument. Standing a little distance apart the managing partner of the firm was glaring at them and impatiently consulting his watch. Joe looked at Eric with relief and Eric approached them in dismay. He knew Joe could be intransigent over trifles but surely even Joe wouldn't have upset a customer at this stage in the proceedings.

"It's that boardroom table," Joe said flatly. "We can't get it upstairs."

"Didn't you think of that when you had it made?" Peter cried petulantly. The charge was unfair, the table had been made to clients' specification but the reason for Peter's attack was clear. The senior partner was watching and listening to his handling of the crisis and Peter was close to tears of desperation, fighting to preserve his career. With a typist's desk, nobody would have taken the slightest notice, but the boardroom table…

Eric turned to Joe. "You've tried the lift?"

"It's too big. It won't go inside."

"Well carry it up the stairs then Joe."

"Tried that," Joe said. "It's too big…"

"I'll help. With six of us we should manage it…"

"It's too big to go round the curve in the stairs. It won't go round the first corner…"

The senior partner called Peter to him; it was clear hard words were being said then Peter returned and tried to adopt the same uncompromising tones in which he had been spoken to. "If it can't be delivered into the boardroom it won't be paid for. And we shall seek the cost of its replacement from you. And a considerable reduction in the final contract price as compensation for your failure to complete on time."

Eric's mouth began to go dry. This was crazy! What would Don Chatfield have to say? He turned to Joe. "Are you sure it won't come up the stairs?" he said desperately.

Joe nodded. "We've tried."

Under the critical eye of the partner Eric went to the landing and stood looking down at the staircase curving up around the tiny liftshaft. He felt their eyes upon his back, challenging him to find a solution or say he had failed. Eric composed himself and returned to join them.

"Is there any point in this?" the partner said acidly, consulting his watch. "I can't stay here all morning. I came expecting to see the installation completed as per the contract. You've got people in the office today haven't you Peter?"

Peter nodded. "They're packing all the files ready to begin transfer this afternoon."

The senior partner sighed. "This is very worrying. I shall have to speak to colleagues."

Desperately Eric sought a solution. "I suppose… We could always cut it."

His words met with a glare of hostility. "It's out of the question," Peter said.

"If we brought it up in two halves. And with a good French polisher…" But as Eric spoke he knew it wasn't viable and the partner advanced on him.

"If there is the slightest mark on that table we shall sue you. Do you understand?"

Eric fought to preserve his dignity and remain controlled. "It's alright, I'm just thinking aloud, considering possibilities."

The partner retreated and called Peter to him and then called Eric to join them. "What do you propose then?" he said.

"I just want to make sure we've tried to think of everything, every way first," Eric replied, playing for time. The table was a solid slab of timber two and a half inches thick with a polished surface. It towered above the tallest of them by some two feet and its curved sides were almost five feet wide at their extremity. He couldn't think with this pressure on him.

"Well?"

"I think the best thing you can do is to leave it with me," Eric said.

"Well I can't hang around here." The senior partner turned to Peter. "I'll see you on Monday morning!" And he strode from the office.

"Peter," Eric said, as calmly as he could, "I want you to go home."

"I want to see this table safely in place," Peter cried. "I want to see it comes to no harm! You've no idea how you've let me down!" His face was contorted with desperation. "It's got to be in the boardroom by Monday morning!"

"You can't do anything here Peter…"

"What are you going to do?" He was close to tears and the crew stood aside in embarrassment.

"I'm going to get it there for you Peter." As Eric spoke he felt a profound sense of release. He had no solution but he had to give this man reassurance; give him peace. God knows what had passed between him and the senior partner but the poor fellow was falling apart. "It will be in when you arrive on Monday morning. I promise. But you've got to go home. There's nothing you can do here."

"I want to know what you're going to do," Peter cried in anguish.

"I don't know myself yet. But it will be there. On Monday morning. I promise."

Reluctantly Peter prepared to leave. "Without a mark!" he said. "You are not to cut it!"

"I promise. Go home Peter. This is my problem now. We'll get it in for you." Peter turned, desperate to believe and Eric said, "I promise. Monday morning."

Eric watched Peter descend from sight and suddenly he felt like Superman. He had made a deep and sincere personal commitment to get this man out of trouble. Now he had to find the way.

"Well," Joe said, "You've dug a bit of a hole for yourself."

"Bit of a hole," one of the crew added. "Bloody big hole if you ask me."

"Anyway," Joe looked at his watch, "we've just got a couple of desks to finish then we're off."

"Just…" Eric began but Joe interrupted him.

"There's no 'just' anything. These lads have got to get back to Leeds." He began to walk away. "Let's get these desks finished, we've wasted enough time. Job's not contracted to go beyond twelve on Saturday." They left Eric with half an hour to find a solution.

"Is there a back way in Joe?" Eric called.

"Tried that one," Joe called over his shoulder. "No!" He followed the others, the 'old soldier' in him taking quiet delight from Eric's predicament. Joe was not a malicious man but he had seen these young whippersnappers before, making their wild promises then leaving him to make their promises good. All the same Joe couldn't see how Eric was going to solve this one.

Eric sighed and went down to the ground floor lobby. The table stood like a monolithic deity, challenging his ingenuity. He stared at it for a moment, then went outside. Maybe one of the adjoining buildings offered access. Maybe...? It was a wild thought, not really an idea, more like a strain of curiosity demanding to be satisfied and Eric clung to the thought lest it should escape before he had explored it to its conclusion. Then Eric strode back inside. "Joe," he called, and with a knowing look at the others Joe got up and sauntered across. "Joe, I've got a bit of an idea."

"Oh yes," Joe answered doubtfully.

"Just come and have a look. See what you think." Eric retraced his route, explaining as he went.

"Might work," Joe said adding with finality, "But anyway you can't do it on your own!"

"Come on Joe. It's not twelve; you don't have to go yet."

"It's up to them. But you won't get it in before its time for them to leave. And I can't tell 'em to stay."

"Ask 'em Joe."

"I can't authorise overtime either."

"Joe!" Eric pleaded. "Come on, it's worth a try. It might work, you just said so. Let's go and ask 'em. We're wasting time here just talking about it."

Joe relented. "But it's not up to me to try to persuade 'em," he said...

Helen arrived and found Eric standing at the corner looking up at the building. He turned, suddenly sensing her presence. "Oh, Helen. Sorry love, I didn't see you coming."

"Are you alright Eric?"

"Yes. Why?" Eric scratched his head. "Look, I'll be about another half an hour. Er…"

"Half an hour?"

"Yes. I'm just waiting for Joe. There's this last piece to get in. It's a bit heavy." He didn't want to go into detail; she would only kick up a fuss if she knew. "Half an hour should see it done."

"Half an hour?" Helen repeated.

"Yes."

She looked at her watch. "It's nearly half past twelve. I've got to go into Walsh's. I'll see you outside Cole's at half past one. That's an hour. Do you think that'll be enough time?"

Eric kissed her with gratitude. "It'll be more than enough."

On Monday morning Eric knew just how Scrooge felt. Oh, he had to be there first. At eight thirty he arrived and carried out a fast inspection of all the offices. Some staff were already in, still unpacking boxes of files but Peter had not arrived and Eric smiled with anticipation. He returned to the ground floor and at nine thirty-five Peter arrived with the partners. The senior partner regarded Eric without humour and proceeded to the lift and went upstairs without a word. Sensing Peter's anxiety Eric raced up the staircase ahead of the group and as they approached the boardroom Eric opened the door for them to enter. There were murmurs of approval. Eric had already switched on the subdued wall lighting, leaving the main overhead light off. In the centre of the room, surrounded by its chairs, the boardroom table gleamed softly. Eric remained by the door, allowing the delegation to absorb the atmosphere of the room, their seat of power, the inner sanctum. Peter discretely sidled towards him.

"You didn't…?"

Eric feigned innocence. "Didn't what?"

"You know…" Peter nodded earnestly. "To get it upstairs."

The senior partner was inspecting the surface of the table closely and Eric inclined his head towards it. "See for yourself," Eric murmured.

Peter went through a wide ranging inspection and bent to examine the surface, just as the senior partner had done. Then he crouched and peered underneath and ran his hand across the underside.

'I know what you're looking for,' Eric said to himself with satisfaction. He crossed to Peter and said, just loud enough for the senior partner to overhear, "You won't find it Peter. I've not cut it. I said I wouldn't."

Peter smiled at last and he began to relax. Now, with the project brought to a successful conclusion and his future secure, Peter spoke to Eric in a tone of confederacy. "So, how did you get it up here then?"

Eric smiled enigmatically. "I said I would didn't I Peter. Well…" Eric gestured expansively and received smiles of approval from the assembled partners.

When Alice announced that she was shipping the rice to Bangladesh her news was greeted with incredulity leavened with derision and Alice savoured her moment. She allowed the questions to accumulate then said, "It's going on a ship of course. There's a ship going to Bangladesh. All I've got to do is to get the rice to London."

"Ship? What ship?" Helen said.

"To London?" Eric added.

Frank shared in Alice's torment of the doubters. "We've had another letter," he said and Alice smiled benevolently on him. "The Bangladeshi High Commission have written to us again. That Mr. Kahn. He's ever so nice, he says there's a ship in London docks. If we can get the rice to London by next Thursday the captain has agreed to take it as cargo." Alice's eyes began to fill with the enormity of what she had done. "Free, for nothing," Frank concluded. "The ship's owners have said they'll take it there for nothing." Suddenly Alice began to cry, Frank put a comforting arm about her shoulder and through her tears she smiled in gratitude while he regarded Helen and Eric carefully and said in his quiet way, "It's a bit of a miracle really isn't it."

Chapter 27 - 1984 - A séance continued...

Trawling through her memories brought Helen neither comfort nor a solution. The short grey winter daylight was shrouded in drizzle beneath drab clouds and from the armchair by the window to which she had returned Helen saw the bare outline of Beauchief fading into the night. The yellow street lamps were on and the wintryness of the day matched the wintry desolation in Helen's mind as she roused herself from her reverie. Her only comfort now was physical; the protection of the house and warmth about her. In the two days since Rita's visit Helen had tried to make sense of the senseless but the memories only accentuated her despairing sense of loss for she and Eric had always been so happy, striving together and forging ahead with success the reward for every obstacle they overcame.

A miracle her father had said. Yes, she mused, perhaps it was. Eric had always insisted it was; he used to say it was biblical; against doubt and scorn her mother had raised something fleeting and noble in people's minds. A local haulier had arranged the free transport of almost three tons of rice to the docks and the rice had arrived safely. That one solitary effort of her mother had fed over two thousand families and Alice had been invited to a reception hosted by the High Commissioner to receive the thanks of the people of Bangladesh. Helen sighed and shook the thoughts away. Think what you're going to have for tea instead.

Jill would be in later, just for half an hour or so to see that she was alright, not too lonely. What did Jill know? Jill reminded Helen of the way she and Eric had been in that miraculous time, confident, fearless, assured. Now Helen knew she could never be sure of anything ever again. When they were young The Bomb, though it had been an indiscriminate threat, was viewed as personal to them, aimed at them alone! Why? Helen cried. We were innocent! Why?

She paused to look at a photograph on the small, carved oak table by the door; a single second in time framed in silver and she smiled for sorrow at the happy couple they used to be and guilt took the memories and twisted them into more questions. 'What did I do wrong?' And she sighed with determination and tried to turn her thoughts towards preparations for a meal. But now the stream of memories are in train there is nothing Helen can do to prevent them returning and they jostle in her head, teasing her with recollection. It isn't what people are whispering, she protested. I knew, I shared it all, we shared it together... It was the others whom you would have expected to have... to have... Rita for example! But other innocents were involved there too...

Helen sought release from her memories in sleep, in the vast expanse of the empty bed with the glow of lamplight outside and a sliver of amber light finding a gap in the curtains and shining a dagger onto the wall in the bay win... in the bay... The beautiful bay... Sunshine sparkling on the sea; the picnic on the beach with her mother and father, the carefree, endless day, her father discovering his cigarettes in the pocket of his shorts, insisting, "They'll be alright, they're still wrapped in cellophane." And on discovering they were soaked, his smiling tolerance and the weak, witty joke. "Well never mind. They're sea-weeds now!" as he laid them on the sea-wall to dry...

Fog rolling in at night, drifting over the headlands from Holyhead by Porth Dafarch to Trearddur and the mournful sound of South Stack punching its twin-toned warning through the fog. Helen heard the horn again, but this time it was sharp, without the resonance she remembered on Anglesey, and she woke. All was dark. The streetlamp was off; the dagger of light on the bedroom wall was gone. She stepped from the bed and pulled her dressing gown around her and drew the edge of the curtain aside but the road and the solitary car which had woken her was invisible. No garden, no road, only fog, grey and blank, masking infinity. Helen switched on the bedside lamp, went to the bathroom then returned to the window again and saw the unexpected reflection of her own face staring back like a ghost seeking entrance, giving her a fright. She switched off the lamp and sought the comfort of the bed; it was cold and she lay in the darkness seeking warmth in the covers and peace in her mind. But peace could not be found - 'Pace non trovo.' Only the solace of memories remained...

213

Ah, Trearddur, they had loved it so. Every year they had returned, and all the visits were as one, an endless happy memory. Her father had loved it and so had Eric. At Trearddur Eric and her father had become pals, scrambling over the rocks with a line and bucket between them, casting it into the pools and waiting for the voracious crabs to scuttle out of the seaweed for the limpet on the line, laughing like children as they dropped each crab into the bucket.

Poor dad, he hadn't told them about the fall at work. Why would he? Accidents happen, you shrug them off. It was a greasy steel floor; he had been carrying a steel bar on his shoulder and slipped, falling awkwardly, and gritted his teeth at the sharp pain where the steel had hurt him and shook himself down and within an hour or two it was forgotten. When was that...? It must have been towards the end of the rice business. And being the man he was he never spoke of it and for a year or so the injury lay dormant until something malignant had finally stirred into life...

Drowsing and waiting for the return of sleep, Helen sought refuge in happier memories and let them carry her where they would...

A time of rejoicing!

Eric recounting how he had surmounted the obstacle of the boardroom table, its appealing simplicity giving unexpected satisfaction to Frank, the secret anarchist when he was told. A skylight on the roof was the only access and Eric had persuaded the erectors to wrap the table in blankets. All thoughts of overtime forgotten and caught up in the challenge they hauled it up on the end of a rope, up four stories by the external iron fire escape onto the roof, clinging to the iron stair and nursing the dangling table up step-by-step and hanging like monkeys to fend it clear of the rail. No wonder Eric hadn't wanted to tell her when she went to meet him on that Saturday morning...

Eric's star had been in the ascendancy then and the real prize had come later when Sheffield Hand Tool Corporation announced they had decided to build a new office block and put the furnishing contract out to tender. How Eric had worked for that one... but even in that there was a price to be paid. Everything demands a quid pro quo. Was that the pattern she was seeking? The unconscious questions surged and receded like a tide in Helen's mind, sometimes emerging as dreams. But always lurking in the recesses of her mind was the memory of ....

PART 3 – 1970

MATURITY

Chapter 28 – Burolandschaft

….that Monday in September when the operatic society gathered to begin rehearsals for next spring's show. There was a rising buzz of chatter as members assembled and the talk was of summer and the holidays. Helen and Eric were greeted with nods and smiles for Eric had found his voice at last and after a series of 'character parts' had carried off his first major role in the last production. Jim was particularly effusive. "There'll be no stopping you now," he said cheerfully.

"Oh I don't know about that," Eric replied modestly. But looking back on his wasted years of diffidence he knew Jim was right.

Marlene smiled her coquettish smile and said, "Why should anyone want to stop him?"

"Nobody I hope. Ah, our new producer's arrived. We'd better go and say hello. Coming Marlene?"

"Oh duty calls." There was unexpected mockery in Marlene's voice. "One must respond when duty calls."

In the pub after rehearsal Malcolm unexpectedly said, "Why don't we all go to Majorca?"

Helen looked at him with surprise. "Majorca?"

Jenny nodded encouragement. "In February. Us four. Well, five," she added, "with Ralph. You wouldn't mind coming on holiday for a few days with Ralph would you?"

"Well, no," Eric replied after a careful glance at Helen. "I mean, we hadn't…"

"Only for a week," Malcolm said casually. "There's some real bargains that time of the year."

Eric was flattered by Malcolm's unexpected proposal. A midwinter break would give them something to look forward to; the furniture for Sheffield Hand Tool Corporation would be delivered in December and the commission would more than pay for it. It would be a marvellous way to set the seal on his year's work. "What d'you say Hel? Do you think you could get time off?"

"Wouldn't it mean missing rehearsals?" Helen asked cautiously.

"Only one," Jenny interposed, adding, "and if Rita and Rob came their kids would be playmates for Ralph."

Helen looked up sharply; so Jenny really didn't know. Malcolm turned to Jenny and said. "Do you really think they'd want to?"

"Rita would love it," Jenny insisted. "Where is Rita by the way? Why's she not here...?"

Rita had it all arranged. She would go to rehearsal while Rob looked after the children and she could go and have a drink with them afterwards if she wanted, then he could have his night out. Life wasn't much fun any more; and although they appeared to have got over that other business she hadn't really forgiven him. Still, the kids loved him. Antony, six-and-a-half, said Daddy was 'a carefree vagabond,' a phrase Rita had used back in the days when she used to laugh and tease him, in the days when he was seducing her and she was luscious, forbidden fruit. God knows where Antony had got it from but if that was how they saw him...

If only things ran as smoothly as planned. That Monday afternoon, when Rob returned from work Rita had looked at him carefully. Rob attempted nonchalance and she said, "What's up? There's something up. I can tell."

"What are you, bloody clairvoyant now?"

"All right then," Rita conceded, "there's nothing up. Where's your coat?"

"Here's my bloody coat!" Rob gripped his lapel. "Bloody wearing it. What's up with you?"

"You know what I mean!" Rita snapped. "Your blue coat. Your dairy coat."

"Oh that..." He removed his jacket and hung it behind the door.

"Yes that!" The bastard was playing for time, she could tell. He had that old shifty-eyed look about him again and Rita's heart sank.

"Forgot it."

"How d'you mean, 'forgot it'?"

"It's at the dairy!" He went into the sitting room. Antony was building a tower of bricks and unsuccessfully trying to protect them from his brother's attempts to scatter them.

"Tell him daddy." Antony gave Raymond a push. "He keeps knocking them down."

Rob bent to play with them. "Give him some of his own," he suggested.

"He wants mine."

"Oh well then…" Rob picked Raymond off the floor and began tickling him. "What have you been doing you rascal? Stealing Antony's bricks?"

Rita stood watching from the doorway. "You might as well tell me," she insisted quietly. "I'm not daft you know."

Rob continued laughing with the child on his knee. "Nothing to tell. Nothing that concerns you anyway."

"Oh come on Rob…"

He turned sharply. "I've told you. It's nothing!"

"What's nothing?"

"Oh for God's sake woman let it drop will you!"

Rita retreated to the kitchen and prepared a second assault while she made his mug of tea and brought it in to him. "Your tea!"

Preoccupied with the children Rob muttered, "Put it up there."

Rita placed the mug on the mantelpiece and said quietly, "Your collection book's not there either."

The play stopped and Rob's smile faded.

"Rob!"

"What?"

"It's written all over your face…"

Rob lowered Raymond onto the floor beside Antony. "Well! What do you want to know?"

"You tell me."

Rob sighed and his head began moving from side to side like an animal at the zoo, seeking escape from the peering faces. He saw Antony watching him with a look of innocent love and averted his eyes from the child. "Pass us my tea will you," he said quietly.

Rita passed it down and resumed her position at the fireplace. Rob sipped delicately, it was hot and he held the mug carefully, speaking softly. "I've been suspended." He sipped his tea again.

219

Eventually Rita spoke, calmly and with quiet authority. "Suspended? What for?"

"Nothing. I've not done nothing Reet," he protested. "No matter what they say, I haven't."

"Is it money?"

"That's what they're trying to say."

He turned from her and placed a brick on Antony's tower and Rita's sigh was the sound of defeated hope. "Oh Rob." She watched the children playing and silence hung like a cloud between them.

"So now you know," Rob said.

"Know what?" Rita cried, suddenly angry. It wasn't over; the explanation wasn't clear, even the accusation wasn't clear. "I don't know anything! They don't suspend you for nothing! What's been going on? What have you done?"

"I've told you. Nothing."

"Oh Rob, come on, I know you better than that!"

"Oh so you'd rather take their word against mine. Is that it?"

"You've been taking the milk money haven't you? You've had the takings."

"They can't prove…" he began but Rita forestalled him.

"Oh Rob. What d'you take me for? D'you think we're all fools?"

"It's a nice thing isn't it when a wife doesn't believe her husband." He pointed the mug towards her in accusation. "It's a nice thing when a wife would rather believe strangers!"

"How much?" Rita cried.

"There you go…"

"How much?" Rita persisted. "Come on Rob, how much."

"Seventy quid! But I didn't take it. That's what they're saying but I didn't…"

"Seventy quid!" Rita looked at him with incomprehension. The children abandoned their play and apprehension filled Antony's eyes. "Seventy quid!" Rita raised her hand to her brow; there was something else; he had said… "Suspended?" Rob's head jerked away; he turned and left the room. "What does suspended mean?" Rita shouted desperately.

"It means I'm bloody suspended!"

220

Rita followed him to the kitchen and whimpers of distress came from the children. "Well are you sacked or what…?

"'Course I'm not bloody sacked! I've just fu… bloody well told you!"

"And stop shouting will you, you're upsetting the kids."

"I'm not bloody shouting!" Rob raised an accusing finger at her.

"Yes you are…!"

"Well what d'you expect…!" He threw the mug into the sink and tea splashed over the windowsill.

"Well what's the point of being suspended if you've not been sacked!"

"I don't know do I!" he shouted. "What you asking me for?"

"Seventy quid Rob!"

"Aw shut up!"

"And when do you go back? Eh? I don't suppose you'll be getting any wages while you're suspended will you?" His reply was lost in a mumbled oath. "Well!"

"I don't know!! Not until they've proved it wasn't me I suppose."

"Who?"

"The dairy. Who the bloody hell d'you think?"

"Well how they going to prove that? Did anybody see the money being pinched? Did you see anybody?" Even as she asked Rita knew it was futile. Of course he'd taken it only this time the charm wouldn't work. These people weren't fools. He'd got away with it once; they wouldn't let him make a fool of them a second time. Rita's words were barbed with sarcasm. "Of course nobody saw it being pinched. It was you. Of course it was you!"

"That's what you seem to think. You're all the same, give a dog a bad name…"

"Oh Rob. We've been here before. So many times…" Rita hesitated and she went pale. "It's not…?" The memory of the black dog seized her with an overpowering feeling of terror, hands grappling at her, the children screaming. "You bastard!" Rita flung herself at him, clawing and punching. Rob felt her nail scrape across his cheek and Antony and Raymond screamed as blood welled from

221

his face. He pushed her away and Rita fell heavily onto the floor with a cry. The children screamed again and Rita winced in pain, unable to move.

Rob stood above her panting and consumed with self righteous anger. "No, we are not going to have... him... or his dog or anybody else coming!" he yelled, glaring down at her. "Why the fuck d'you think I did it!"

"Don't speak like that," she said quietly, "Not in front of the children." Antony ran and threw his arms around her and Raymond stood watching until Rita put her hand out to him and they buried their heads against her. "It's alright," she whispered, "Mummy's alright. It's alright. We're just a bit cross with each other that's all. It's alright, don't cry, don't cry..." She winced and tried to raise herself and Rob turned away. He hadn't intended it to be like this. He had planned on telling her in his own time, bluffing his way through. Even with the police on the job they couldn't prove anything and he certainly wasn't going to say anything about the police. Rita was struggling to raise herself and he bent to help. "Get away!" Rita hissed. "Get away from me. Don't you ever touch me again!"

Eric was working at the dining table on furniture layouts for Sheffield Hand Tool Corporation when Helen said, "By the way, Jenny telephoned. They've found a holiday at Camp de Mar in February."

"Where's that?"

"Majorca of course. She's bringing the brochure to the rehearsal next week. They'll want a deposit."

"Good," Eric replied. "I get the commission for this in January and then we can pay the balance. They won't want it all before then will they?"

"I don't expect so." Helen gazed at the floor plan Eric was working on, impressed by the curves and arrows covering the sheet.

"What are you doing now?"

Eric sat back in his chair and turned to her. "Workflow patterns."

"Looks impressive," Helen conceded. "Shouldn't it be easier not having separate offices?"

"Lot more difficult actually. Takes a lot more work and preparation."

"Oh. I thought these new American ideas were supposed to make life simpler."

"It's not American," Eric said. "It's German. Everybody thinks it's American but the proper name is burolandschaft – Office Landscape." Eric turned to the plans before him. "I'd better get on with this," he said. "Chatfield wants to take it in tomorrow. It's going to be a big day."

For the umpteenth time the following morning Rita looked at the clock. Rob had gone to the dairy at half-past eight and now it was after eleven! Knowing Rob he'd charm them like he charmed everybody and things would return to 'normal' for a while. It was a relief not to have been asked to go to Majorca; they couldn't have gone anyway with things as they were and it saved her having to invent an excuse. Rita laughed bitterly to herself and sighed. She was sighing her life away. She couldn't plan, she could barely think more than a couple of days ahead and if he wasn't going to be bringing any money in… Her head ached with the worry of it. At least he wasn't gambling – he had nothing to gamble with. Rita sighed again with determination. Well something would have to change that's all! She looked at the clock and tried to guess when he'd be back.

It was another hour before Rob returned. He looked drawn, like some of the life had been drained from him and he smelled of beer. He prowled uncertainly around the room; his eyes rested briefly on Raymond in the high chair with the debris of his lunch around his face and turned to Rita with a smile that made him look infinitely sad and vulnerable. Rita looked at the weakness in the man standing before her. "What did they say?" she asked.

"I've been sacked." He tried to raise his voice in bravado. "They've no right, not really. I'm going to a tribunal…"

"Rob."

"What?"

"Did you get any money?"

"Bit of holiday pay that was owing. I went for a drink. Only a half," he protested and reached into his pocket. "It's here."

Rita took the paltry sum and counted it.

"Rob I just don't know how we're going to manage."

"I'll get another job." His words sounded pathetic in their simplicity.

Rita's shoulders sagged and she took a deep breath. "Have you had anything to eat?" Rob shook his head. "Beans on toast?" A tremble quivered on Rob's chin, he took a hesitant step towards her but she turned from him. "I'll get you something to eat..."

She sat across the table and watched him mopping up beans with toast and sought the carefree, confident man she had known. There was a beaten air about him that had never been there before. "You'd better get down to the employment people and sign on."

"I'll nip out later and get a paper," he mumbled, chewing and swallowing. "Thursday's best but there might be something in tonight." He spoke as though he didn't really believe it.

"Have you had enough?"

Rob nodded and began to rise from his chair. "I'll go and put the kettle on."

"It's already boiled," Rita said, reaching for his plate but she was interrupted by a determined knock on the door. Rob made no effort to move and she put the plate down and said in a voice heavy with sarcasm, "No don't bother, I'll go!"

There were two men. Rita stepped back to close the door but they held up laminated cards with photographs, symbols and words she didn't have time to read. The man in front of her said, "South Yorkshire Constabulary. I'm detective sergeant..." but the rest was lost as she turned and saw Rob standing in the kitchen behind her with an unaccountable look of relief on his face.

Don Chatfield made lunch an occasion and took Eric to The Golden Dragon. "How long do they usually take here?" he asked.

"Shouldn't be too long," Eric replied. "They're geared up for the special lunch."

"Well, choose what you like."

They gave the order and received the waiter's reassurance that they could be out within the hour. Don said, "What time are Sheffield Hand Tools expecting us?"

"We're seeing them about two o'clock. Tranter's anxious to see you before you leave."

Don grimaced. "I thought he was ready to agree the new layout. You told me that was settled."

"It is," Eric said. "He seemed quite pleased when I spoke to him this morning."

"OK." The waiter presented them with soft bread rolls and Don leaned forward confidentially. "There's going to be some changes. I suppose you must have guessed. Leeds is full of rumour of course, most of it wrong."

"I wondered about that chap coming up from head office," Eric said carefully.

"We're re-organising the salesforce," Don said. "Paul Henderson's leaving."

"Paul!" Eric exclaimed. "But he's been with the company for years. When's he leaving?"

"Friday," Don said shortly.

"I'm sorry." Eric looked down at the tablecloth.

Don watched and understood. "Don't worry," he said. "It had to happen; he hadn't been doing very well at all. He was a nice enough bloke. The reorganisation presented the opportunity that's all. It would have happened sooner or later."

Eric turned his attention to the soup, a white, onion flavoured concoction thickened with a lacing of cornflower. "You'll have to find a replacement then."

Don shook his head. "No." They sipped in silence then Don said, "I hope the main course is better than this." He reached for the menu and tut-tutted. "And the price they charge for it!"

Eric tried to bring the agenda back into focus. "You'll have to alter the sales territories if you're not replacing Paul."

225

"The company structure is altering completely. Specialisation's going. Each branch is going to be selling all products." Don's voice became flat and there was a distant look about him, a look of regret. "You won't be working for me any more."

"Don?"

"You'll be reporting directly into Sheffield office."

"John Horrocks?"

"It makes good sense if you think about it. Every time we want to meet either you've got to come to Leeds or I've to come to you. Like today."

Eric sensed Don was trying to be loyal to the plan and he tried to generate enthusiasm for Don's words but it wouldn't come. "John Horrocks!" Eric pushed the unappetising bowl from him. "What about the contract? Sheffield Hand Tools? He doesn't know the first thing about it!"

Don signalled the waiter to take the dishes away. "The new structure doesn't come into effect until January the first. Well, January third by the day. So its good timing really; the contract should be complete by then." He looked sharply across at Eric. "It's got to be completed by then."

"It will be Don. Everything's on schedule."

"And it mustn't slip."

"No."

"I know what people say about him, but he knows the business through and through." Eric remained silent. "It's up to you Eric. You've got to make it work." Don looked for the waiters but they appeared to have vanished. "I've enjoyed working with you." He smiled. "And we've still got some work to do." He looked round and smiled again. "Bloody mistake coming here wasn't it."

Their meeting was successful and Don left early to drive back to Leeds. But Eric went home with mixed feelings. He couldn't bring himself to go back to the office, not if Horrocks was there.

A police car was parked in the street outside the house and as Eric locked the car an officer approached.

"Mr. Allenby?"

"Yes...?"

"South Yorkshire Constabulary. I'm here on behalf of a... ah, Mr. Rob Johnson."

"Rob...?"

"He's given your name as surety for bail. Would you be willing to stand surety for twenty-five pounds?"

"What does it mean?" Eric asked carefully.

"Mr. Johnson's under arrest. He's been granted bail until his appearance in court in the sum of twenty-five pounds."

Bail? Court? Rob? "What if he doesn't turn up for the trial?"

The officer suppressed a smile at the word 'trial.' It was merely a preliminary appearance. "Then the bail would be forfeit," he replied. "He'll remain in custody unless someone stands surety for him."

All Rob's past misdemeanours ran through Eric's mind, his betrayals and false promises. "I don't think I can," Eric stammered, "I can't. I'm sorry."

"That's alright sir. I'm sorry to have troubled you."

The officer returned to the car and Eric tried to reassure himself he had done the right thing. A stay behind bars might bring it home to him; Rob was always light fingered and careless in his attitude to money. Well it wasn't going to be their money. But all the same, in his heart Eric was troubled.

Chapter 29 - The landscape changes

The formal announcement of the reorganisation was made to the Northern Region in Manchester in the week before Christmas with the General Manager (North) presiding. It was no consolation to Eric that most of the salesforce assembled in the splendour of the hotel's gilded conference room shared his misgivings. The General Manager rose to dutiful applause led by the branch managers flanking him on the rostrum and outlined the far reaching benefits that would accrue from the new bonus and pay structure. He finished by congratulating them on being the ones chosen to remain and share in the company's destiny. Then the branch managers dispersed to different rooms to conduct interviews with individual members of their teams.

Eric sat with a disconsolate group waiting for Arnold to emerge from his meeting. Bob Roper, the surviving salesman from Hull was particularly scathing about his prospects. He had made vast amounts of commission from British Steel's expansion at Scunthorpe but now that programme was complete and there were no more easy pickings. They watched the faces of each salesman as they emerged with interest.

"Some's doing alright anyway," Eric said hopefully.

Bob Roper grunted. "You'll be alright. You've just got that big contract. It's the rest of us'll have to look out. What's Horrocks like to work for?"

"Arnold's your best man for that. He seems to get along with him alright."

Arnold re-appeared wearing his usual inscrutable expression and nodded at Eric. "Your turn." Eric rose and Arnold added carefully, "Don Chatfield's leaving."

Eric looked at him with incredulity and Bob Roper said, "Since when?"

"I've just heard," Arnold said, adding to Eric, "He's really pissed off. You'd better go in, they're running behind."

It was a simple room. The bed had been replaced by three chairs, two for Chatfield and Horrocks, the third in the centre of the room facing them.

Horrocks took charge. He spoke with nervous pomposity, in stark contrast to the confidence of Don Chatfield. "Sit down Mr. Allenby." The little grey moustache decorating his lip seemed to bristle as he spoke and his tone defied interruption. Horrocks cleared his throat and Don Chatfield returned Eric's look of regret. "Well, now you know commission is being replaced," Horrocks began. "The new bonus system is designed to reward consistent effort rather than opportunistic success and salaries are being revised accordingly." Eric listened with growing disappointment. Horrocks spoke as though he were the author of the scheme. For years he had laboured to command the same respect that Don Chatfield enjoyed; now at last fate had put him on top and even spiced the occasion by his rival's fall from grace. He could not know and would not have guessed that Don Chatfield had read the runes and decided of his own volition to take the step he had often dreamed of. For Don had bought a sub-post office and watching Horrocks's performance he felt relieved to be getting out of it. Horrocks droned on; Eric's new salary was presented as a fait accompli, the bonus hemmed in by 'performance parameters' linked to other members of the team. "...so it will be down to you," Horrocks concluded, "you and the rest of your colleagues." He tried to finish on a rallying note. "There is no limit to what the team can achieve for itself. But it is up to each member to pull his fair weight." A stick; "Not to let the others down by poor performance." Then a carrot; "And in the spring when the first quarter figures are announced we look forward to seeing some really good results from everybody." Horrocks leaned back relieved it was all going so well. Having Chatfield beside him had strengthened his resolve and he preened and stroked his moustache with his curled forefinger. "Are there any questions?"

Eric sensed a cut in earnings. "You said it comes in on January the third," he said.

"Yes." Horrocks sniffed, as though he'd just taken snuff.

"What about Sheffield Hand Tool Corporation?"

229

Horrocks' brow furrowed and his head dropped. "I don't understand," he said uncertainly. "What about it?"

"Well," Eric said, "the commission on all that furniture."

Horrocks moistened his lips with a brief flick of his tongue. "When was it invoiced?"

"It's only just been delivered. We're still installing it."

"Has it been invoiced yet?"

Don Chatfield shook his head and Eric's fears were confirmed.

"If it hasn't been invoiced you've missed the boat. All outstanding commissions will be paid to the end of December. After that it's too late I'm afraid."

"But I've been working on it for a year!" Eric protested. He sought a willingness to consider a special case, to make an exception. "Both of us. Me and Mr. Chatfield. The orders were placed in November; we're on schedule. We should be invoicing before the end of the year."

"Which means payment the end of January." The expression of smug satisfaction was barely concealed as Horrocks added, "If we're lucky! Like I said. You've missed the boat." He turned to Don. "Isn't that right?"

Unable to intervene on Eric's behalf Don Chatfield made a gesture of resignation.

"But there's nearly two hundred pounds!" Eric cried.

"I'm afraid those are the rules Mr. Allenby. Is there anything else you don't understand?"

There was a brief, interminable moment when Horrocks stared at Eric, challenging him and Eric regarded him with undisguised contempt. Then Eric caught Don's eye and saw the subtle shake of the head, a gesture that said 'Leave it before you go too far.' And then Eric understood. Despite the fine words spoken earlier to the survivors of the purge there were still no prisoners being taken. He turned to leave and heard the supercilious voice say, "You can appeal of course if you wish. Through the proper channels." Eric closed the door behind him and went to summon the next man...

Late February and the first flush of blossom was on the almond trees in Majorca. It was like springtime in England and along the promontories flanking the deserted beaches there was an elusive scent of pine. Eric and Helen hadn't been abroad since Italy and they savoured the unmistakable fragrances of the Mediterranean. Jenny appeared below their balcony, then Malcolm, kicking a ball for young Ralph to chase and Jenny waved up at them and gesticulated to the steps beyond the pool leading to the beach. "We're going to take Ralph on the sands."

They lingered on the balcony and watched the figures running to the sea. There were pinewoods sheltering the bay and a deserted jetty. Helen looked at Eric, searching for the pleasure they ought to be feeling. "I'll go and start unpacking a few things," she said.

"Imagine what it's like back in England," Eric replied.

In the evening they descended to the basement disco where the few guests assembled and swapped jokes, dancing before the deserted tables. Drinking 'Cuba Libre' lent a flavour of the exotic to their refugee existence and next morning, while Jenny paced their room in frustration Malcolm lay nursing a hangover with the covers pulled over his head. It was a ritual to be repeated most mornings.

After breakfast Malcolm and Jenny appeared, nonchalantly calling, "You alright, you two?"

"We're fine." Eric gestured towards the sea gently lapping against the shore. "Ralph's down there. We saw him about ten minutes ago digging in the sand."

Jenny hurried towards the steps and Malcolm rubbed his hands and said, "Right then. Who's ready for a drink?"

Day four, mid-afternoon. They were trying to make love. But it wasn't like Italy. The pool had chilled them and the quiet desolation of the bay denied them the abandon they sought. It wasn't warm enough to lie above the covers and Jenny might knock the door at any moment! It was no good, they couldn't relax; it wasn't going to happen.

"Later," Eric promised, kissing her gently.

"I'm sorry," Helen whispered.

231

"It's alright."

They lay listening to the sound of hot water, waiting for the bath to fill.

"Malcolm's hiring a car tomorrow," Helen said. "They seem to have endless money."

"It's alright," Eric reassured her. "He says we needn't worry about it. He says he always hires one."

"We wouldn't be feeling like this if we'd got that money the company owes us."

"Oh don't Helen."

"We can't keep up with them Eric."

Despondency began to cast its deadly cloud. There was nowhere to go except the hotel lounge and the tedium of keeping an eye on Ralph, looking across the deserted terrace to the beach, watching the descending sun, waiting for dinnertime and the onset of evening. "I wish we'd never come," Helen confessed as she departed into the bathroom.

The following morning Malcolm was up and dressed waiting for the car to be delivered, a small blue Seat.

"You going to drive for a bit?" Malcolm offered as Helen and Jenny arranged themselves in the back seat with Ralph between them.

"I thought it was only insured for you," Eric replied.

They drove along the coast and found a beach with slabs of flat, water-pitted black rocks extending like dark fingers out into the sea.

"Oh, this is nice," Jenny cried.

They laid a picnic of chicken, bread and fruit on the rocks and after they'd eaten Eric and Malcolm searched for pools, peering down into the crevasses at the clear sea surging beneath them. Occasionally the rock surface was levelled out with concrete inset with rusted mooring rings and they found a porpoise stranded on a small inlet of sand. It was obscene in death, bloated as tight as a drum and they stoned it to see what would happen. But the stones ricocheted off the glistening body and they moved on, laughing until Jenny called, "Ralph? Where's Ralph?"

"I thought he was with you."

They looked back across the dark rocky flats and suddenly felt a profound sense of desolation. The sea gurgled beneath the slabs and Jenny began calling desperately, "Ralph... Ralphy..." and Malcolm caught the panic too, his calls chiming with the cries of Helen and Eric.

"Listen! Listen!" Malcolm ordered but there was just the sound of water gurgling through the channels below their feet. They looked back to where the porpoise lay, its body scuffed with the faint marks of their stoning and superstitious images from the Classical age arose in their minds, though none would confess it; antique vases decorated with porpoises in turbulent waves and Poseidon, the implacable God. They had desecrated his creature in death and Poseidon would exact retribution. Jenny ran to the water's edge where a sludge of seaweed and decay lapped with quiet menace and their desperate cries continued as they spread across the shoreline.

Helen heard a sound, faint, over the surge of water. The sound came again, not just the sea below her feet but another. Close by, a rusted metal plate was set in a square in the rock and Helen bent to the rusty iron cover. The sound coming from beneath was distinct, a child whimpering. 'Oh God, the sea!' She raised the corner, just enough to see rough concrete steps leading below with the sea surging and falling then surging up over the steps again as though reaching for the child crouching there. "He's here!" Helen called, "Eric, Jenny, Malcolm he's here. Help me!" They raised the plate and Malcolm reached down and pulled Ralph out. Overwhelmed by their anxieties, Ralph burst into tears.

"How did he get down there?" Helen said.

Eric pushed at a corner of the plate. It wasn't located properly over the square and one corner pivoted down and then up again like an oubliette. "Looks like he stepped on it and fell through," Eric said.

They retraced their steps with Ralph securely between them. "Mind the porpoise," Helen said, "We don't want that bursting all over us," and they were glad for the opportunity to laugh and their laughter was heightened with relief...

Their return from Majorca wasn't completed without farce. It was raining as they waited for take-off and Eric took the safety instruction card from the seat pocket and scanned it with Helen. A droplet of water fell onto the back of Eric's hand and he brushed it away. The whine of the aircraft engines increased and another drop of water fell onto his hand. He turned to Helen. "There's water dropping on me."

They paused and watched an aircraft landing in a mist of spray.

"What are you going to do?" Helen said quietly.

"Don't know."

Memories of the Comet disasters arose. Metal fatigue, hairline cracks, aircraft disintegrating in mid air. The whine of the engines rose, the aircraft began moving again and Eric pressed the call button. A hostess reached for the bulkhead telephone then she unfastened her seatbelt and came along the aisle as the noise of the engines subsided.

"What is it?" The hostess glamour had gone, replaced by impatience.

"There's water coming in from outside."

"It's condensation!" She leaned across and closed the air vent over Eric's head and returned to the telephone, glaring as she spoke to the captain and snapped her seat belt closed.

"They'd have thanked me if it had been true," Eric whispered. Helen squeezed his hand and they braced themselves as the plane lifted into the sky.

Helen was filled with the anticipation of seeing Rita. She had another day before returning to work and she took presents for the children. It was a sharp return to reality. There was poverty in the thin weeds growing in the broken asphalt and grimy bricks in the back yard but Rita's initial caution at the door became a cry of pleasure.

"Helen! When did you get back?"

"Yesterday."

"Didn't expect you yet. How was it?"

"Majorca's lovely," Helen said. "We didn't half miss you Reet. The kids would have loved it."

They went into the sitting room and Helen proffered the bag she had brought. "A couple of little presents for the kids. And some castanets. And a scarf. It's nothing much. Hope you like it." She hesitated, "We didn't get anything for Rob I'm afraid. He's difficult to buy for," she finished lamely.

Rita put the children's parcels on one side then put the scarf around her shoulders and twirled, clicking the castanets. "It's lovely Helen. Really. Thank you. I'll be able to become a Flamenco dancer." She kissed Helen's cheek. "Wait until the kids see me."

"Wish you could have been with us Reet."

"Ah well… Next time eh." She laid the headscarf and castanets on the sideboard. "We've just got time for a cup of coffee before I go and fetch Raymond."

Helen followed her into the kitchen. "Did you get our card yet? How's rehearsals?"

Rita lit the gas and placed the kettle on the ring. "I don't think I'm going to be in this year's show." She paused. "It was Rob's case on Thursday." Her words fell between them like a stone.

"Oh I'm sorry Reet," Helen said. "How could I have forgotten? What…? I mean, did they…?"

"He got sent down. Six months."

"Oh Rita. I'm so sorry. I don't know what to say."

"He asked for another offence to be taken into consideration." She tossed her head, a rehearsed gesture of dismissal to the world. "He'll be out in four I expect."

"But that needn't stop you…"

"I can't." Rita's tone was adamant.

"There's no shame," Helen implored her. "Not for you. And you'll need your friends."

Rita smiled wryly. "I'm pregnant." She sighed and busied herself with cups and saucers. "It's his of course. Don't look at me like that Hel. I don't know why. He always had that effect on me. Right from the very beginning. Even when I told him I wanted nothing more to do with him." She laid a hand across her belly. "Rob's parting gift…"

They carried their cups through and Rita became introspective. "It's not that. But he's been making a fool of me with his women, his unfaithfulness. I didn't need to know who they were; I didn't even ask. But then one day you wake up and you think, he's a fool and everybody knew it and I had their sympathy. But then comes the realisation they'd seen me as a fool too." She raised her eyes to Helen. "Just a pair of bloody fools, to be laughed at and pitied."

"It wasn't like that Rita. It's not like that at all," Helen protested.

Rita let Helen's words pass. "You go blindly along and suddenly your eyes open and there's reality staring you in the face." She looked at the clock. "I'll have to go in a minute. I don't want to be late for Raymond. You can come too if you like."

"What will he do Reet? When he comes out? You know, for a job and that?"

Rita looked steadfastly at Helen. "I'm leaving him Hel. This time I am leaving him." And to Helen's surprise Rita's eyes moistened with tears. "I still love him Hel. I can't help it. But I really don't think I can take any more."

Chapter 30 - Singing the blues

Eric strode onto the stage and the light seemed to rise in intensity with the applause. He bowed and stepped back into the line and when the curtain finally closed the cast turned to each other in a frenzy of mutual congratulation. Max sought him out and laid a paternal hand on his arm. "Great opening night Eric. Well done."

Eric smiled at the little man. Max looked tired and relieved his job was over. He had worked hard to get the show ready but the final rehearsals had taken their toll and it was expected that 'The Gypsy Baron' would be Max's last show. Amid the general air of euphoria Jenny added her congratulations and planted a kiss on Eric's cheek. "There'll be no holding you back now," she said.

"Thanks Jenny. Have you seen Helen around anywhere?"

"She'll be in the dressing room. You're coming for a drink aren't you? Everybody's going to the Bear…"

It had had hardly changed since the day Eric sat eking out his half of bitter with Alfred all those years ago. Now he was no longer standing with his face pressed to the window, railing at the world, he was at the centre of things and he smiled with satisfaction as Jim caught his eye and called, "Can you take Helen's and Marlene's," as he leaned across, handing over glasses of Martini Rosso. Eric passed them across and Jim came over to join them.

"Is Rita coming to see the show?" Marlene asked.

"Saturday. Her mother's babysitting. She'll probably go straight back after the show," Helen said regretfully. "You know what it's like."

"Still, it'll be nice to see her. Be nice to have Rita back again." Marlene turned as a girl of seventeen came to join them, blond and elegant with the poise and confidence of a woman. "And nice to see we're getting some new talent in the society as well. How did you think tonight went Hayley?"

The girl smiled and said, "I thought it was very good. Especially after last night."

"Ah, we've had some funny dress rehearsals though, haven't we," Malcolm said. "Remember 'White Horse Inn? Went on until after midnight and we still hadn't got through the show…" and they fell to reminiscing.

Jim said to Eric, "You four going anywhere special for your holidays again this year?"

"No," Eric replied. "They're doing their own thing. Malcolm's been talking about the QE 2." He gave a shrug. "Don't think we'll be cruising somehow. What about you and Marlene?"

"Oh," Jim replied, "I expect we'll go to her parents' caravan in North Wales. We usually do."

Eric didn't want to be late for the Friday afternoon meeting with Horrocks. He'd had a good week, he was looking forward to the second night's performance and spring was finally on the way. He gathered his papers into his briefcase and smiled wryly at the thought of words of approval from Horrocks. He was on his way, he reassured himself, and he felt good so what was wrong with that? He wished no man ill; after all, if Johnny Horrocks could make it, anyone could.

Arnold looked up as Eric entered the showroom and called, "How was last night?"

"Great. Got a big round of applause at the end. I wish you'd come and see it."

"Not my cup of tea," Arnold replied and Eric went round to Sandy on the switchboard to see if there were any messages. She was on an incoming call and Eric stood admiring her legs until she finished. But before she could reply to him Arnold said, "You've missed Horrocks. He's only just gone. He wanted to see you."

"What about?"

"What do you think? He needed your figures to complete the week's returns."

"Aw bloody hell I've got 'em here. I wanted to see him too. That's what I've come back for." Eric consulted his watch. "God it's only… It's not even quarter-to yet. Where's he gone?"

"Home I expect," Arnold replied laconically. "He was muttering dark things about you being late reporting back."

"Late? Good God Arnold, I'm not late, he's left early!"

"No good going off at me."

"For Christ's sake, if I come in early he wants to know why I'm not out selling, and if I come in now he's already buggered off home and it's me that's in trouble!"

Sandy pulled a plug from the switchboard. "I do wish you wouldn't swear in the showroom," she protested. "They can hear you know."

"Well they shouldn't be bloody listening then should they!"

"There'll be complaints," Sandy muttered.

"Oh sod it. Any messages?"

"No," the girl replied shortly.

Eric looked on the bright side; at least he wouldn't be up there trying not to betray his impatience. For in his perverse way, if Horrocks suspected you were in a hurry he dragged it on as long as he could. "Give me the office key Sandy," Eric said. "I'll leave the figures on his desk. I don't want to be late tonight either."

Eric went up to Horrocks' office, a sparse room with a calendar and map of England hanging on the cream painted wall. The green linoleum desktop was bare except for a pen carefully laid on the blotting pad and a solitary tray labelled 'work in hand.' Eric laid his report on the centre of the blotter and placed Horrocks' pen across it. He hesitated. Behind the desk by the window was the filing cabinet. It would be interesting to see what files Horrocks was holding on him and conscious that he was in forbidden territory Eric listened at the door then tried the drawers. They were locked. He tried the keys on the office keyring but none fitted. Then he tried the desk drawers and they wouldn't open either. Feeling slightly ridiculous he wiped the drawer handles with his handkerchief, locked the office door and hurried downstairs.

"About time," Sandy pouted as she took the key. "What you been doing up there? I was beginning to think you'd gone home with it."

"I'm off," Arnold called. "Hope it goes well tonight. Better not be late Monday..."

Helen had tea waiting when Eric arrived home. "We haven't got a lot of time," she said. "I've had mine. I thought you were getting away early."

"Oh you know what he's like, he wanted to see me and then when I got there he'd gone home. Bloody good job too or I'd still be there."

"Come on then," Helen said, "I want to have time to get changed and do my makeup."

Eric ate thoughtfully. "He wants to see me on Monday now. He left a message with Arnold."

Helen regarded him carefully. "What for?"

"Because I was late with my report!"

"Well if you didn't get there until after he'd gone..."

"I got there early!" Eric cried. "Oh don't you start."

"Eric!" Helen chided him.

"Well I was early!" Eric protested. "Only he'd left earlier than me!"

"Well I don't know," Helen said. "Silly games you play with one another."

The light fades, the applause dies into a distant echo and mundane reality reasserts itself. Or was that the reality and this is just another long interlude until the excitement, the friendships and tensions, colour and laughter return again? The cast disperses from the afterglow of the Saturday night party and the theatre reverts to echoing emptiness. Depression sets in, Sunday comes with nothing to redeem it and Monday looms. Yesterday I was on the stage, bathed in limelight, receiving the applause of hundreds. Today I am at the whim of a fool.

Eric watched Horrocks enter the figures and write comments on his own report until finally he sat back in his chair. Did he suspect Eric had been trying to see the files? He would know that Eric had

240

been in the office. Horrocks cleared his throat and picked up Eric's report. "It won't do Mr. Allenby."

"I don't understand. What won't do?"

"This." Horrocks brandished the report.

Helen was right; the man was playing some sort of game. Eric took the report from him with a smile of innocence and said, "Is there some sort of problem with it?"

Horrocks the martinet thought he saw insubordination and said stiffly, "Yes, there is a problem Mr. Allenby. Your level of business is below that which we had been led to expect of you."

"But I had an excellent week. It's here, in my report."

"And your report was late." Now the play-acting was over.

"I brought my report in on Friday," Eric retorted sharply and heard the bell of caution ring in his brain. "It was here by quarter to five," he said in careful, measured tones. "I couldn't get in any earlier, I'd been with a customer but I knew you needed it so I got in as soon as I could. I'm sorry."

"I had some business to attend to. I couldn't wait for you any longer Mr. Allenby, you'd made me late as it was."

Eric lifted his hands in exasperation. "I don't know what else I could have done!" He continued in a tone of conciliation. "I mean, look at the figures. It was probably my best week. This will be my best month. And if the rest of the team do as well..."

"This doesn't concern the rest of the team. It concerns you."

"I... I still don't understand."

"We'll leave Friday out of it for a moment. You seem to think that all that's required of you is just going round picking up orders here and there." He retrieved Eric's report and jabbed it with his forefinger and looked for a response. Eric sat in stillness and Horrocks continued, "You were taken onto this team in preference to other good men because you had the potential to secure major furniture contracts. So far you have produced nothing beyond a smattering of chairs!"

Eric looked past Horrocks over the roofs of the world outside. Beyond the wavy ridges of old blue slate rose the clean square lines of the new Sheffield. "But there are no contracts," Eric replied, appalled by his own sudden helplessness. "Not of that magnitude anyway. They're not ten-a-penny."

"Nonsense." Horrocks had followed Eric's eye. "Look around you. Here in this city there are new office blocks going up."

"Most of them are already let and furnished," Eric protested. "Except for the ones that are still standing empty and I'm keeping close to all the major agencies. Of course when they come up for…"

"I'm not going to debate it Mr. Allenby. The evidence is there for you to see. It's all around you." Horrocks leaned back and steepled his fingers. "I stood up for you Mr. Allenby. They wanted others in your place but I resisted pressure from higher authority to have you on my team." Horrocks fished his handkerchief from his pocket and blew his nose then wiped it with deft flicks and stroked his moustache. "But I'm sorry to say you haven't lived up to my expectations." He returned the handkerchief to his pocket. "I want to see a different level of activity from you. The strategy of this division depends upon securing major furniture contracts. I can't have one member of my team letting the side down. And apart from that, your colleagues might have something to say, don't you think?" Horrocks reached for Eric's report again and brandished it before him. "This kind of thing won't do Mr. Allenby. We expected better from you." He looked at his watch with the air of a man with a pressing engagement. "I've nothing more to say. But if you are to stay on my team then you must show what you are capable of." He fiddled nervously with the sheet of paper; Eric waited and Horrocks looked up sharply. "Well I suggest you'd better start now."

Eric returned to the showroom and Arnold looked with some surprise at the expression on Eric's face. "What's up? What did he want?"

"What's the best paper for jobs?" Eric said flatly.

Arnold regarded him with consternation. "He's not…?"

"No." Conscious of Sandy listening at the switchboard Eric went to the stationery cupboard in the back room to collect some brochures and Arnold followed him.

"Not here," Eric muttered. "Are you going up to the cafe?"

"When I've finished here."

"I'd better not hang about. I'll see you up there."

As he turned to leave Horrocks appeared silently at the showroom door. "Still here Mr. Allenby?"

Eric held up the brochures and stuffed them back into his briefcase. "Just on my way out," he said and brushing past him went straight to Mary's Café to wait for Arnold. The euphoria of show week had vanished completely.

He felt dispirited and depressed. Leaving Arnold to his newspaper in Mary's Eric browsed round the stores in the high street as the morning dragged on. It was just like the day he'd played truant from school with Dave. After two hours they'd become bored, and beset with hunger they'd shared a chocolate bar and sneaked back just in time to re-join the class en route to French with Miss Jones and basked in the admiration of their peers. This time there was nothing to sneak back to. Eric bought a paper and took it to the Central Library. He scanned the appointments pages and found a couple of jobs he might apply for but the heat and silence of the reading room were oppressive and he wished he was with Helen; to share an hour together would make him feel better about things. Of course! Bloody fool! The mood of lassitude dissipated in the instant and he strode out to the car...

The hospital laboratory annexe was in the grounds of a converted mansion with a winding drive and undulating lawns lined with rhododendron and laurel. The laboratory itself was a small red brick building at the rear. Eric drove to the car park and went round to the laboratory door but it was locked. He knocked and a lab assistant in a white coat came down the staircase. Eric signalled to her and she opened the door cautiously. "I think I'm in the right place," Eric said hesitantly. "I'm looking for Helen Allenby."

She indicated the staircase. "Up there. Second on the right."

"Thank you."

"Are you Eric?"

"Yes," he replied and she smiled as she led the way.

An atmosphere of quiet concentration permeated the building and Eric approached the lab cautiously. Peering in through the small window in the door he saw Helen at a bench in a white lab coat with

243

her eye to a microscope. A woman maybe ten years older with a look of uncompromising authority saw him and touched Helen's shoulder. Helen looked up with a grin and ran to the door.

"Eric. What brings you here?"

"I just wanted to see you. I thought perhaps we could have lunch together. I mean, if you can."

"Come on in," Helen said with a laugh of pleasure. "It's alright, come and meet the gang."

The atmosphere in the lab was overlaid with the aroma of formaldehyde. Two young women in white coats were engaged in activity with slides at microscopes; others appeared pre-occupied with small objects in fluid in small dishes and beakers. As Helen introduced him Eric sensed his appearance was a welcome diversion from the routine of the day.

"This is Eric," Helen said, gesturing an introduction. "Marcia – she runs the lab."

"So this is him is it?" the older woman said with warmth and unexpected playfulness. "No wonder you kept him from us."

A woman at Helen's bench said, "Take no notice of Marcia. She's only jealous." And catching Eric's eye she dropped her head and delicately began lifting something from the pungent preserving fluid in her dish and onto a glass slide.

Helen glanced at the clock and began to unfasten her coat. "You don't mind do you Marcia?"

"Well if you don't go I will," Marcia replied.

"Won't be long. Come on Eric."

"Don't rush," Marcia called.

"Right," Helen said, "This is a lovely surprise. Where are we going?"

"I don't know really," Eric replied. "How long have you got?"

"I ought to be back in an hour."

"Do you fancy a burger? Uncle Sam's?"

"Yes," Helen enthused, "Uncle Sam's. That'd be lovely. Oh Eric, what a nice surprise."

244

Chapter 31 - The triumphal return

Rob came through the prison gates on a Thursday morning in May filled with new resolutions but little remorse for the past. Arriving at Sheffield he stepped off the train from Wakefield and looked along the platform but there was no-one to meet him and he lingered beneath the clock at the corner of the station, clutching his parcel, looking across at the city. Now he understood what Percy had been talking about; the air was different and he breathed deeply, filling his lungs. It was the air of freedom, he was home and free.

He had twenty minutes to kill. Great, he could have a drink, just a quick one, a drink of his own choice before the bus came and he strode past the bus platforms to the old Queen's Head in the small cobbled cul-de-sac and joined the late lunchtime crowd in the ancient bar and savoured the taste of malt in the beer and it had never seemed so satisfying. He drained the glass greedily and called for another and promised himself he would have another tonight. But now it was time to go home; anyway he needed to save the little money he had for tonight's celebration drink.

Rita had only visited him twice. The first time she had dressed prettily in a fine woollen sheath dress and Rob had to endure the other inmates' looks as they fantasised about her and he pretended to laugh with them, listening at night to the grunting and coarse breathing in the bunk above him and missing her more than he thought possible. On the second visit Rita told him she wouldn't come again. "I don't want them looking at me when I'm pregnant," Rita whispered, lowering her eyes and when Rob protested it had all fallen apart because he didn't want the visit to end with them at odds with each other.

Four months! The terraces were silent like the grainy black and white photographs of anonymous industrial streets seen in studio exhibitions, with kids in darned pullovers playing in shiny puddles in the gutter. Someone passed him without a glance and Rob was conscious of feelings he couldn't explain. He was from somewhere alien. Before Wakefield they had lived with his peccadillos, his

245

laughter and devil-may-care gaiety, at one with the people around them. But now Rob knew in his heart, even if he couldn't express it, that it would be different. All the same he wished – no, he hoped it could be as it used to be before…

He was nearly there and an image arose of the way she would look, a memory rooted in the past. The kids would be out, Antony at school, Raymond at nursery until…? It was only half past two and she wasn't so far pregnant… Were people watching? Did it matter? Did he care? It was all such an anti-climax. Rob closed the kitchen door behind him in expectation.

"Rita…?" The house was silent and an expression of disbelief crossed Rob's face. "Bloody hell!" He tossed the parcel he was carrying onto the table and stood with his hands on his hips. The house didn't look deserted. There were clean pots on the draining board and a tea-towel hanging carelessly from the cupboard door. The sugar bowl was on the table with the funny shaped sugar spoon Rita always insisted on using. So where…?

The back door opened and Rita stood with a smile combined with sadness in her expression. Her head moved in imperceptible nods like she was weighing something up, evaluating him. "Hello Rob." From across the yard Rob heard the faint sound of water flowing into the toilet cistern.

"Reet." He spoke without moving, imprinting the image of her on his mind.

"You look well anyway," she said, and pushed the door shut.

"And you," he replied gently.

"I wasn't sure when…"

"I had to wait for a bus…"

He wanted to run and throw his arms round her and lose himself in the softness of her kisses but there was something unapproachable about her and Rob saw the joyful homecoming evaporating before him.

"When did you last eat?"

"This morning," he replied with hope rising in his breast.

Rita crossed in front of him and reaching for the kettle she paused. "You've been for a drink though."

"I had to wait for a… Aw come on Reet. Two halves of bitter. What was I supposed to do? Walk about? Form a queue? Just sit on a bench?"

"First thing you think of isn't it Rob, eh? The nearest pub! As soon as you're out." There was neither rancour nor accusation in Rita's tone, just resignation. It was Rita's confirmation, removing the last remnants of doubt that had begun to surface at the prospect of his return. She indicated the brown paper package on the table. "What's in there?"

"Just some things. They return your things when you leave."

Just some things. All that Rob possessed in a brown paper parcel. She saw the eager need for approval in his eyes and started to feel sorry for him. Where was the carefree vagabond? It was supplanted by something in his face; a shadow, a sense of wariness that hadn't been there before.

"Egg and bacon?"

He smiled an eager smile. "That would be wonderful Reet." He moved to put his arms around her but she pushed him from her and turned to the cooker. He tried to become busy and willing at her side. "Here, let me help you," he said but Rita forestalled him.

"You go in there and sit down. I'll bring your tea through in a minute."

He went through to the sitting room and stood examining the small changes since he left. A new toy, correspondence stacked on the corner of the fireplace behind her mother's figurine.

"A bit cold in here," he called, "can I put the fire on?"

"If you must."

He bent to the gas switch and hesitated. "It's alright. Must be the beer..." and he grimaced at his words and wished he'd never said them.

Rita brought him a mug of tea and found him standing in sunlight at the window. "You can put it on if you want," she said.

Rob shook his head. "It's alright. I wasn't thinking. It's just that you get used to the central heating…" He reached for the tea and curled his hands gratefully round the mug. "Thanks Reet. My first real cup of tea."

"I'm going to have to go for Raymond shortly."

Rob's eyes lit with pleasure. "I'll come with you."

"No… no. I'd rather you didn't."

"Rita…!"

"Not today. He's not expecting you. Well we didn't know what time you were… Anyway there'll be others there waiting for their kids too." She turned to go to the kitchen. "Your bacon'll burn if I don't go and look at it." She returned with a plate of bacon and egg and fried tomatoes with slices of plain white bread in a basket. "I'll get your knife and fork. Do you want sauce?"

Rob smiled his appreciation. "It smells great." He pulled a dining chair out and turned it at an angle to the table, his arms open in invitation. "Come here a minute. I don't want sauce. Come and say hello to me properly."

"It'll get cold if you don't hurry up and eat it," Rita responded. "I'll just get you the salt."

Rob sighed. How much of this treatment was he going to get? Perhaps she'd relax a bit more when the kids returned. He tore a corner of bread and dipped it into the egg yolk. "It's wonderful," he called.

Rita watched him as he ate. She knew how desperately he was trying to please her and she found herself faltering as she watched him. He was so vulnerable and weak she wanted to mother him. Sensing her eyes on him Rob raised his face with a grin of appreciation.

"Great," he gulped, and took a swig from the mug. "Bacon and egg and a cup of tea. Perfect." Rita gave a wan smile. "We'll have bacon and egg every day. Just like this." He was nearly finished, mopping the remnants from the plate with bread. "If I'd known I was coming home to this…"

"Rob."

He looked up, pleased at the sound of his name on her lips.

"Rob."

There was a faint sad smile on Rita's mouth and hesitation; Rob smiled encouragement and pushed the plate from him. "Thanks duck. That was…"

"Rob." She turned away, searching for an opening. "I... I don't want you to come home." The smile on his face decayed leaving an expression of misunderstanding in its place. "I don't want you back... to come back..." she faltered, "I want... I want a separation. A divorce."

Rob raised his hand to his face and began to rub his mouth and chin. He stared quizzically at the empty plate on the table and raised his eyes to Rita's with a look of disbelief and her eyes held his with pleading, compelling him to understand.

"What are you saying?" he asked, stupidly.

"I want you to leave Rob. I don't want to live with you any more."

"Just like that!"

"No," Rita protested, "Not 'just like that'. I can't..." Rita caught her breath. "I've had time to think about things," she pleaded, "while you've been away."

Rob raised his head. "Yes well I've been thinking about things too."

"It's... it's over Rob. Finished."

"How d'you mean it's over? What's over?"

"Us! I can't go back Rob. Not to the way it was before."

"Nor me. That's over! You're right. That's well and truly over. Come on Reet, we haven't had a chance to talk yet. I've not been home five minutes! I've got plans, ideas..."

"I don't want to hear them Rob."

"Rita!"

"I want you to go. Now! Before the kids come home."

Rob shook his head, a violent, dismissive movement as if trying to shake Rita's words from his mind. What was going on? Before this she hadn't said a word, neither during the visits nor in any of her letters. Now she had cooked him a meal and told him to leave. "What's going on?" he cried at last, his voice rising in accusation. "You've got a bloke! That's it isn't it? You've got yourself a bloody feller while I've been away and now I'm in the way and you want me to leave!"

"No Rob! It's not like that!"

"What is it then?"

"I've told you. It's all the debts and gambling…"

"I've told you that's over!"

Rita shook her head. "I don't believe you Rob."

"No!" He rose from the table and began pacing the room. "And I don't believe you either. I know you…"

"What does that mean?"

"You think I didn't know about you and Malcolm? Eh? Eh?"

He jabbed his finger at her and Rita pushed him away. "How dare you! When you've had women all over the place…"

"What are you talking about?"

"For years," Rita cried. "I've had to turn a blind eye for years while you went off shovelling coal to London in your best suit. D'you think I'm a complete fool!"

"You were a bloody fool if you thought you could carry on with him and me not know about it. Oh yes," he sneered, "you thought you were fucking clever didn't you! And now you've got somebody else you think you can pack me off just like that." He snapped his fingers in Rita's face. "Well, I'm not going 'just like that.' I've got my children to think of."

"Your children!" Rita yelled. "Whenever have you given a thought to your children?"

"Always assuming they are mine!"

"Get out!" she blazed at him. "How dare you! Get out of here. I've finished with you. And take your bag of 'things' with you. I hate you Rob; I hate you!"

"This is my ho…"

"Get out! Out! Out! Out!" Rita pushed him from her, out into the kitchen and slammed the door shouting, "And take your prison things with you!" and collapsed onto the chair, weeping and sobbing. She felt ashamed and it was his fault for making her feel like this. Why didn't he just go? She'd been nice to him. They could have parted friends. He wasn't a bad man, just weak and silly. But he had done such hurtful things, said such dreadful, hurtful things. And the tears came again and she sobbed in great gulps and didn't hear the door opening behind her until she became aware of Rob's presence; she turned quickly but he was just standing there with the parcel.

"Rita…" There were tears in Rob's voice. Rita snuffled and tried to wipe her eyes with the back of her hand. "Rita…" there was pleading in his voice. "I'm sorry. I…" Rita remained silent, snuffling back her tears. "… I want… I'm sorry for what I said. What about the kids?" Slowly Rita shook her head. It wasn't denial, only… "I still want to see the kids. Rita?" Her head nodded in resignation and she sat with her eyes lowered. "There's my other things too."

The defeat in Rob's voice fuelled Rita's distress; she began to softly weep again and berated herself. Whatever had happened in the prison to rob him of his spirit? Oh God, how could she be so cruel to him now, how could she, but what else was she to do?

"Upstairs," he continued pathetically. "My suit. A couple of shirts. And things…"

Rob's defeat was unexpected and total. He stood pathetically before her and Rita knew she had won. But there was no triumph, just a conflict of feelings and regret for what she was doing. "Where will you go?" she asked with an overpowering sense of guilt.

"Back to my mother's I expect," Rob mumbled.

"Oh." Back to the home Rita had despised and refused to live in when they married. "Will you be alright?"

Rob fumbled for his handkerchief. "I expect so."

"I'll have to go in a minute," Rita said with her eye on the clock.

"But what about the kids Reet? I want to see 'em. You can't stop me."

"I don't want to stop you Rob. But not today. Perhaps… in a couple of days. The day after tomorrow. Come back at the weekend and you can collect your things then."

"It's not fair Reet."

"Don't Rob. Don't start again please."

"Why are you being like this?"

"Rob. Rob, listen Rob. I've got to go. For Raymond. I don't want to leave him hanging about at the gate…"

"Can I come with you? Let me come with you Reet. I won't interfere. Promise. I just want to see him."

A rising sense of pity tore at her and her resolve was hanging by a thread. Rob was right, she ought not to deny him, he was like a child himself and she wanted to comfort him But a deep instinct guided her and Rita knew she had to break now. If she didn't it would never happen and they would be condemned to their relationship.

"Saturday Rob. Come back Saturday. There'll be more time."

"You're a bloody hard woman Rita! I never seen you like this! You can't keep me from the kids. They're my kids too, don't you think you can."

"I'm not trying to but I've got to go Rob. Please, I don't want him to see us like this." She stood at the mirror and looked at herself with shock. God, what a sight! Her face was smeared with mascara, her eyes were red and there were red blotches on her face from crying.

"I should think you bloody don't!" Rob said sneeringly. "What an image! Look at you. Who'd want to come home to that anyway?"

"I've got to get ready," Rita implored him miserably. "Please Rob. I'm sorry."

"Don't be sorry for me," he replied bitterly. "You'd better be in on Saturday that's all." He turned with a flourish and Rita leaned against the mantelpiece and rested her head on her arms. Through tears she heard the back door swing against the latch and suddenly the house was silent.

Chapter 32 - Love is lovelier...

Eric's job applications lacked sparkle and two failed interviews fuelled his de-motivation. Trapped in indecision Eric followed Arnold's advice and did enough to keep Horrocks' eyes off him but whenever possible he collected Helen for lunch.

Marcia commented, 'You've got him under your thumb then,' but Helen only smiled for Eric's discontent brought other consolations. It had begun in June on an unexpectedly hot, perfect summer day. They drove to the outskirts of the city where rising farmland gave way to heather moor and Eric parked against a drystone wall bordering a copse of silver birch. "So we're going in the woods are we?" Helen smiled coquettishly and they walked into the dappled shade. Out of sight of the road Eric drew Helen to him and kissed her then they left the path and pushed deeper into the trees, listening, alert for the sounds of intrusion, stepping carefully through bracken and fallen branches; hearts pounding and the heat of desire rising between them until they reached a small fern-covered clearing. Silence all about them broken only by small, furtive sounds and the rustling of birds in the branches above. Now breathing is heavy and heat rises in the silence as Eric kisses her and begins to caress her. "Wait," Helen's urgent entreaty as she reaches beneath her skirt, wriggling. "I don't want to get them messy," and stepping then kicking her knickers aside. "Oh, Now, oh, oh yes," 'and everything around them recedes in breathless, timeless oblivion as they give themselves to each other in an ecstasy of unbridled lust and love...

Passion spent.

Smiling in exhaustion, Eric gazes at Helen lying in a shaft of sunlight beneath the canopy of branches. She is smiling up at him, a slow endless smile until they suddenly become aware of the return of time and Eric turns away and Helen, suddenly modest tosses aside the tissue, smooths her skirt over her legs and turns to look at him. "Do you think anyone saw us?"

"It's alright. Don't worry. I didn't hear anybody..." Eric's breathing began to slow. "You alright? Did you...?"

Helen kisses him gently. "Course I did. You know I did. Couldn't you tell?"

"Yes. It's just... As long as you're alright."

She kisses him again. "Of course I'm alright. How do I look? My skirt's all creased. Does it show?"

"You look lovely." He helps her up to the path, brushing the creases from her skirt. "What does it matter anyway?"

Back at the car Helen sits repairing her make-up. "Do you think Marcia'll know?"

Eric smiles, replete with satisfaction. "She'll know what she's missed..."

As summer progressed they became bolder. They took a blanket and lay in deep bracken on a moorland hilltop, safe from intrusion with the midday sun on their skin, their clothing cast about them in disarray and below them the distant vista of the city softened in the heat haze. Freed of inhibition, the scent of earth and the fragrance of broken fern rising around them, Eric lay raised on one elbow and marvelled at the beauty of Helen's body. She was lying on her side, regarding him, her eyes languid with content as he drew her open blouse aside and began moving his hand slowly down along to her waist, his fingertips scarcely touching her. The heat of the sun was upon her skin as his hand travelled slowly through her waist to the rising curve of her hip, another beautiful curve, unexpectedly erogenous. "You like that don't you?" Helen said, mildly surprised, for he had caressed her slowly, tenderly as a prelude to their lovemaking, touching her with the intense, delicate perfection of lovemaking they had learned and shared together. And now he was tracing another contour with his fingertips and smiling that enigmatic smile. The thought of her constantly excited and aroused him; the way she yielded; teasing, coaxing and demanding until finally they emerged gasping in climax together. He kissed her again, gently, then smiled and glanced down at his watch. "Better go," he sighed and reluctantly they rose to their knees and began to dress.

Once a low flying helicopter startled them, briefly hovering and banishing passion but no matter, for there was always the anticipation of the night to come and meanwhile through the endless hot days of that summer Eric continued to seek the consolation of reckless passion in Helen's arms...

Rita lived a different life. For a few weeks in June and July Rob was regular in his visits. They fought and fussed over Antony and Raymond, and speculation about Rita's plight was a prime topic at operatic rehearsals. Rob determined that Rita would not keep the children from him and Rita pleaded with him to stop his harassment. "I've never denied you the children," she said tearfully and then the visits abruptly stopped. Rumours abounded at society social gatherings. Rob had been seen working 'in a betting shop' and everyone hoped for the best. Then a new story began to circulate.

"Guess who I bumped into at the weekend?" Malcolm announced. "Rob."

"How's he doing?"

"Couldn't say," he replied laconically. "I was on my way to meet Jenny. I gave him a wave but as soon as he saw me he turned off and went straight down St. Paul's Parade."

"Perhaps he didn't recognise you," they said generously.

"Oh he knew me. Looked straight at me and as soon as he saw who I was he made off like he didn't want to be seen. Funny bloke." Malcolm shook his head unctuously. "You know I feel sorry for Rita. Still married to him and living on her own..."

Rita's baby, a girl, was born at the end of August. Her mother shared Rita's delight and gave up a week to stay with Rita to look after her and the boys. The baby's name – Susan – was greeted with approval and the society sent a bouquet congratulating Rita on Susan's birth. But of Rob there was no sign.

The operatic society picnic in September was the last social event of summer. "Oh do come," Helen pleaded, seeing Rita locked in a life of celibacy, "You never know, you might meet somebody," and she immediately bit her lip, cursing her clumsiness.

"Don't you know I've finished with men," Rita replied bravely, clinging to her battered self-esteem. "Anyway who would I meet on a picnic with three kids?" Rita cuddled the children to her. "Anyway we're happy as we are, the four of us," she protested defiantly. But she went all the same.

They converged on Clumber, a park with an ornamental lake, once the estate of the Dukes of Newcastle and parked in a semi-circle under the trees with open meadow before them. "Hey! Picnic first," Rita admonished vainly as Antony ran off screaming. "And look after Raymond. Don't let him stray."

After everyone had eaten a game of rounders got under way.

"Come on Rita," Marlene called, "men versus women."

Rita shrugged. "I'll sit this out. I've got to look after the kids."

"They'll be alright," Jenny said, "Raymond and Antony can play too."

Rita laid the baby Susan sleeping on the back seat of Eric's car and enjoyed an hour of glorious fun. Malcolm was caught out by Jenny who screamed with pleasure and stuck her tongue out at him and Jim hit a long ball that sent Rita chasing across the meadow. "Last base! Last base!" the girls yelled; Rita threw it to young Hayley on fourth base and she caught it with a scream just as Jim arrived and they fell to the ground in a flurry of arms and legs.

"I wasn't out was I?" Jim said, helping Hayley to her feet and Hayley shook her head with a brief shy smile. She wouldn't humiliate him, not even in fun.

Then the girls went in to bat; the men cheated unmercifully but Rita and Marlene challenged every decision and they scored a runaway victory.

At half past six the picnic began to break up. "We're going up to t'Millstone," Malcolm said. "You coming?"

Eric shook his head. "We're going straight back. We're taking Rita and the kids home."

"See you at rehearsal then."

God, yes! Rehearsals start in a couple of weeks.

One by one they began to disperse and the semi-circle of cars broke up. Sitting in the back seat of Eric's car with her children Rita was unexpectedly contented; it had been more fun than she had imagined it could be and she sighed wistfully. "Sorry you've got to take me back Hel," she said. "You could have gone to the Millstone with the others."

"It's alright Reet. No problem."

Rita settled back for the short journey home. The evening was still warm and the house would be oppressively hot. Suddenly she was tired and the euphoria of the afternoon faded. Antony would still want to play when they got back and Susan needed her feed and...

"How long's that been going on then?" Rita asked suddenly.

"What's that?" Helen turned to look over her shoulder at Rita.

Either Helen was being extraordinarily discrete or impossibly naïve and Rita answered in a tone of bitter disillusion. "Don't tell me you didn't see Jim with Hayley. She was all over him."

"There's nothing going on there Reet." Helen turned to Eric. "Is there?"

Eric shook his head. "Just horseplay Reet. You alright there?"

"A bit tired that's all." Rita fell silent in a confusion of rising unhappiness. Her brave words about being finished with men had risen like a spectre during the afternoon, triggering her assertive gamesmanship alongside Marlene. She'd seen the look Hayley and Jim exchanged as they tumbled together on the grass and she knew she wasn't wrong. It wasn't fair. Jim and Marlene had everything, money, security; he couldn't want for any more but he was taking it all the same! And with pretty, nubile Hayley; far too bloody young for him while here she was, almost thirty with three children, her life whizzing by and going nowhere. Finished with men? Fat chance of getting one! Raymond was drowsing beside her and Rita put her arm about him and held him close as they drove through the outskirts of the city. If she'd known Jim was... but she recalled his manner on that one Saturday night he and Marlene had tried to join in the fun and decided, no, she wouldn't have. Not with Jim anyway.

Rita rejoined the society and auditioned for the second female lead. She was pipped to it by Hayley but got a small part, a consolation prize to say welcome back. It was another sign that she wasn't getting any younger and Rita took no consolation in seeing Marlene get the lead.

"I thought you'd put in for a part this year Hel," Rita said.

Helen glanced over to the piano where Hayley and Marlene were working out a harmony and smiled wryly. "I think I'm too old to play swooning virgins."

"Well if you're too old, where does that leave Marlene then?"

"Miaow," Helen laughed. "She still looks good though doesn't she? But she'll have to look to her laurels with Hayley around."

"Yes, you're right." Rita regarded Helen shrewdly and glanced round. "She'll have to look out in more ways than one."

"How d'you mean?" But there was no time for Rita to answer.

And then a whisper arose and began to intensify, fuelled by the revelation that after a rehearsal Jim had stayed behind to help Stewart with some props and Hayley had been there too. "They locked up together." The speaker had given a sniff and added, "Stewart said it was getting on for midnight when they finished."

Jim? No, can't be, not Jim. Somebody's got it wrong. Jim's a pillar of the society with a solid career, destined for the board, some said. And then Marlene unwittingly added to the speculation. Proclaiming Jim's dedication to the success of the show, she laughingly revealed that Jim had returned home, "... well after midnight; it was getting on for one o'clock," with a lame excuse about 'difficulties'. "And," Marlene confessed, she had been, "pretty cross with him at the time." Her revelation gave rise to a new frenzy of whispers.

"Jim? Not Jim!" they protested. "Why, Hayley's young enough to be his daughter!" But now the pack was in full cry and Hayley became the focus of their disapproval, "Flaunting herself in tight jeans and see-through blouses." It wasn't Jim's fault of course and there were commiserating nods. If she'd led him on who could blame him. Now discretion became the watchword of the watchers, for Marlene didn't seem to have noticed. Rita listened to the gossip with mixed emotions and when Jenny mentioned that Marlene, attractive and vivacious Marlene had begun slimming, Rita stood before the mirror and began to examine herself critically…

And so rehearsals continued through autumn and the whispers died away for lack of fuel to feed them. Besides, another rumour was being discretely whispered in certain quarters, ever so quietly for no-one wanted to cause unnecessary embarrassment. But all the same there was no denial either.

The rehearsal came to an end and all eyes were drawn to the door. Through the small square glass panes they could see a figure waiting in the corridor. The first women to leave passed him with shy curiosity and their smiled 'Goodnight' were returned with quiet restraint. He was clean cut with lightly waved brown hair, medium build and smartly dressed in a light brown sports jacket. Not much above thirty with a nice speaking voice, might be a baritone. Gwen plucked up courage and asked, "Are you waiting for anyone?"

He glanced at his watch. "Rita," and glanced at the watch again. "She said about half past…"

Gwen gave him a girlish smile. "She won't keep you. She'll be out in a minute," and she rushed to catch up with the others. "It looks like Rita's got herself a feller," she reported breathlessly.

Helen looked again at Rita and gave a slow smile; yes, Rita was carefully made-up; of course, she should have realised.

Jenny said, "You're a dark one. What's his name?"

"Gerald, Gerry," Rita corrected herself. "He doesn't like Gerald. Come and meet him." She waved and hurried to the door. "Gerry. You should have come in. We were only chewing the fat." She put a protective arm round Gerry's waist. "Anyway we've got to go."

"You coming for a drink?" Jenny asked hopefully.

Rita exchanged a bashful grin with Gerry. "Next time," she said as they hurried out.

"Where did she meet him?" Jenny asked as they followed down the stairs.

"Bonfire night," Helen replied. "We took the kids to that bonfire party remember? Only she asked us not to say anything in case –

well you know. In case he didn't want to see her again. I think they're getting serious."

"She knows how to pick 'em." Marlene said with interest. "Is he coming to join us?"

"I don't think so," Helen said. "I don't think this is Gerry's scene. Not according to Rita."

They arrived at the schoolyard in time to see the rear lights of a small two-seater disappearing through the gates. "She certainly seems to have done alright for herself," Marlene said.

"Well they seem alright together," Malcolm observed drily.

"What's the matter with you Malcolm?" Jenny chided him. "It's the happiest she's been for ages. Nothing wrong with that is there?"

Chapter 33 - Deck the halls...

Christmas was almost upon them and Marlene was laying out crisps and nibbles on small tables, waiting for Rita, Helen and Jenny to arrive. There were drinks on the tray and she reduced the lighting so that it reflected softly on the Christmas tree twinkling against the French window. She hadn't planned to host a party for the whole society this time; she had done it for the past few years and it was coming to be expected but a little get together with the girls was something to look forward to. Jim had gone on a 'men's night out' with Malcolm and Eric. With the tables all set she placed a stack of records on the hi-fi including Cliff (of course), Beatles, a selection of show albums and set the music softly playing in the background.

Rita arrived first. Marlene hugged her and gave her a look of critical approval as Rita went through to the lounge. "A real tree again Marlene? You always manage to get trees that smell of pine. It's so Christmassy." She sat on the settee, admiring the tasteful trimmings and holly over the pictures frames.

The doorbell rang. It was Jenny and Helen arriving in high spirits together. "Oh Marlene, it looks lovely," Jenny said. "Good idea this, turning the 'men's night out' to good account."

"Things don't change do they." For Rita it was a moment to savour and they raised their glasses to one another.

"Well come on," Helen said. "Tell us then."

Rita hesitated, teasing them but the twinkling smile betrayed her. "We're great," she said. "We couldn't be better."

Helen turned on her with mock exasperation. "I wish you'd come out with it."

"Out with what?" Jenny asked in bafflement.

Rita paused on the point of revelation and refilled her glass instead. "What? What?" she said, teasing them mischievously and Marlene took the bottle from Rita and passed it around.

Jenny gave a sigh of exasperation, looking first at Rita and then to Helen and Marlene said, "What is up with you two?"

"Come on Reet," Helen prompted.

Rita sipped her drink then, trying to appear casual she said, "I'm moving in with Gerry. We're going to live together."

There was a chorus of glee and Jenny cried, "When?"

"In time for Christmas."

"Really...!"

"Next week."

"Oh Rita, that's wonderful!" Marlene rose and picking up the Cinzano bottle she dashed into the kitchen. "I'm putting this away," she called. "We've got champagne somewhere."

"We're so pleased for you Reet," Helen murmured.

"So what's his house like?" Jenny asked.

"It's nice. It's only a maisonette," Rita replied modestly. "One of those new Vic Hallam type houses." Enthusiasm took over. "They're ever so well designed. It's got a lovely big lounge and a modern kitchen. And a garden. Not as big as here of course but it's got a nice lawn. And it's safe, you know with a fence all around it. It'll be lovely for the kids to play in the summer."

Marlene entered, struggling nervously with the champagne cork. "I'm not very good at this," and they watched with apprehension as the cork shot from the foaming bottle and hit the ceiling. "What'll we drink to?"

"It's Christmas time! Rita's happiness of course."

"Rita and Gerry."

"Rita and Gerry."

They wrinkled their noses at the bubbles and Marlene re-filled their glasses. "What's he like, really?" she asked earnestly. "We're going to have to meet him properly soon you know."

"Helen's met him," Rita replied. "You tell 'em Hel."

They turned to Helen in expectation. "Well," Helen said, "he seems very nice. Quiet – you know – well mannered." She gave Rita a smile of apology. "Sorry Reet, I'm making him sound terribly old fashioned."

"I suppose he..." Rita hesitated. She so wanted them to approve. "He's not really. But he is well mannered. And he's got a lovely home. And he's really intelligent."

"So that's why you're going to live with him is it?" Jenny said, "His brilliant conversation!"

Rita laughed with them and the twinkle returned to her eyes. "Oh that as well. After." And they laughed again, happy for her at last and continued to question her like girls giggling under a blanket in a dorm. No, Gerry didn't have any children. And yes, Rita's own children did know and they were looking forward to it. Gerry had his own fine furniture of course, the residue from his own unhappy marriage, "...and it's better than mine anyway," Rita concluded. "I'll be glad to see the back of it."

"Won't you take anything?"

"Oh just a few personal mementos..."

Then Jenny said, "What about Rob?" Her question dropped into their midst like an icicle.

"Rob?" Helen said glancing from Jenny to Rita.

"What... about him?" Rita replied.

"Well you know, the kids, going to live with another man?"

To their relief Rita said, "It's nothing to do with him."

Jenny tried to recover her composure. "Oh I didn't mean... It's just that... don't you have to let him know? If it affects his children?"

"He's not interested. He never has been."

"Anyway," Marlene brandished the bottle again, "Come on, we've this champagne to finish."

"We'd like to move," Helen said, turning the conversation. "We'd like a nice semi with a garden."

"How's Eric doing?" Marlene asked and Helen pulled a face.

"He doesn't get on with his boss. Not like the one before. He's looking for another job. I sometimes wish he'd been an accountant or something. Like Jim." A phrase flashed into Helen's memory – 'Jim, destined for the board' - and she added, "A steady job. With prospects."

"You chose the right word, steady," Marlene said unexpectedly. "Steady." She repeated the word almost to herself, raised her glass and took a deep draught of champagne and gave them a wry smile.

"I didn't mean..." Helen began but Marlene forestalled her.

"It's alright. You settle for what you've got Helen. You're better off than you think you are."

"It was just…" Helen protested and Jenny gestured at the comfort around them.

"Well you can't say you're not well off Marlene."

The remark was disingenuous and direct; it caught Marlene off guard and she said, "Houses don't make happiness Jenny."

"Are you alright Marlene?" Rita said.

Marlene responded to them with a bright smile and she raised her glass and swept her arm round. "Of course I'm alright. Look around you. Who wouldn't be?" They heard unexpected contempt in the tone of Marlene's voice as she raised her glass and doffed it at Rita. "To happiness then!" and drained the remains of her champagne. "Anyway, that's enough of that. Come on, there's more yet, it'll have to be finished."

"I'm alright just for a minute." Rita showed her glass and smiled.

Marlene spoke again but now her voice was low and sincere with none of its previous hardness. "Be happy Rita. Just… Be happy."

"I am." Rita turned to Helen and Jenny to break the mood which had suddenly descended. "I will be; I am." She did a little twirl before them. "Come on girls, I'm as happy as can be! And yes, I will have some more champagne…"

The Christmas holiday was two days away and it was time to fulfil a duty. Eric drew into the space behind his father's car and sighed as he switched off the engine. He felt Helen's hand on his arm. "You sure you're alright?" she asked gently and Eric sat in the darkness of the car's interior and sighed but made no effort to move. Helen waited. He sighed again. Two more days and then no more work for almost two weeks. But Eric remained still and silent, consumed by the blackness of his mood. Everything conspired to thwart him, so what was the point and he resigned himself to despair. Christmas? Some Christmas! It had started when he came home from work and Helen had had to coax the reason from him.

"Bloody Horrocks!"

"They've not…?" Her unspoken fear hung between them.

"No. Not yet." Eric raised his head and looked at her. "Oh don't worry. He's not sacked me."

"Eric! What's going on?"

Eric sat and ruminated. "Regional Manager's been down. We all thought it was 'well done' time and a bottle of sherry apiece. We went in; one by one and I thought... I mean, I've had a good year and I thought..." Eric paused, overwhelmed by recollections. "It's not bloody fair!" he said at last.

"Shall I get you a drink? Come and talk to me while I get tea ready."

Eric followed her and leaned against the kitchen wall. "Horrocks sat behind the desk with him, the pompous little chuff. He introduced me, 'And this is Mr. Allenby'," Eric mimicked, "as though I were the prize exhibit or something. Then he said, 'Mr. Allenby's not living up to expectation I'm afraid.' I couldn't believe I was hearing it!"

"But I thought you were doing well," Helen protested.

"Yes! So did I!"

"Well how could he say that then?"

"Oh Helen," Eric groaned.

"Well I don't know do I?"

"He sat and watched me like a cat with cream. He knew what was coming; he'd set me up for it! Bloody coward; he's had it in for me all year but he can't do his dirty work himself! Had to call on somebody to do it for him." Helen placed Eric's drink on the table and waited. "I said to him, 'I don't know what you mean!' I told him I'd won a prize in that competition for selling chairs over summer."

"Didn't the Regional Manager have anything to say?"

"He agreed with Horrocks. He said that didn't matter. They were very disappointed." Eric breathed a great sigh of exasperation. "Sorry Helen, I'm on the way out. I'm sorry."

"It's so unfair," she cried. "Come here; come here Eric." She threw her arms round him and he stood unresponsive with his arms at his side.

"I'm sorry," he muttered in desolate self pity, "I'm sorry."

"It's not your fault Eric..."

Her words hadn't helped, even though she was right. It wasn't his fault and that didn't make it any better. He'd been looking forward to the holidays; now he felt rotten. And he would go on feeling rotten. And angry, and impotent! He'd done nothing wrong except dislike the little twat! And now, on top of everything, they had chosen this evening to come and bring his father's Christmas present. From the darkness beside him Eric heard Helen say, "Would you rather go home?"

But there was a duty to be done and guilt for past neglect added to his mood. "Oh come on," he answered sulkily; with luck it'd be no more than half an hour at the most. He reached for the door handle and felt Helen's restraining hand on his arm.

"Eric?" Helen pleaded.

"Aw let's get it over with."

"I'm not going in with you if you're going to be like this."

"Like what?"

"It's Christmas. You can't go and see him like this."

He sighed and drew himself up in his seat. "That better then?" he asked facetiously

"Oh Eric…"

"Oh come on!"

Helen retrieved the parcel from the back seat then Eric locked the car and led the way into the blackness of the backyard. He rang the doorbell and heard his father calling, "Who is it?"

"Eric. It's me. And Helen."

The sound of the key turning and a bolt being drawn then his father peering through the narrow gap of the door. "That you Eric?"

"Yes. Me and Helen."

The chain rattled out of the slot and his father said, "You'd better come in. It's cold out. Just the two of you?"

Well for Christ's sake who else would be with us! "Yes dad. Me and Helen."

"Hello dad," Helen said and they stepped inside.

The kitchen was icy and his father ushered them into the sitting room while he relocked the door. "You can't be too careful," he said. "It doesn't do to be careless. Especially round here." He pushed the woollen snake against the bottom of the door. "Draughty hole this," he said reaching to the gasfire. "Better turn this up a bit. Get some warmth back into the place."

Eric shifted an assortment of magazines and newspapers laying on the cushions to one side and sat next to Helen on the settee. Helen offered their parcel in its wrapping of holly paper. "We've brought you a little present dad."

George Allenby said, "Ta," and placed it on the floor beside his chair. He gestured at the television; a panel game was showing. "Turn that thing off," he commanded. "It's rubbish anyway." Eric switched it off and the sudden silence was profound. "I haven't got your present yet. I've not had time," his father said.

"It's alright dad," Helen protested.

"I'm giving you a cheque instead. You can choose for yourselves. I think that's best don't you? No good buying you what you don't want is it?"

"Thank you very much," Helen said.

Eric sat stony faced with suppressed anger, listening to Helen and his father. 'I might as well not be here for all the bloody notice he's taking of me,' he fumed. Finally he said, "How are you doing dad?"

"I'm alright. Ready for a holiday. Too much bed and work. Twelve hour shifts. Does you no good. When do you break up?"

"Day after tomorrow. Then two weeks off. Helen's got the same."

"Two weeks! Bloody hell." George Allenby spoke with undisguised resentment. Thirty years at the bloody firm and all he got at Christmas was half of Christmas Eve, Christmas Day and Boxing Day. Then New Year's Eve afternoon and New Year's Day itself. His eyes rested coldly on Eric. In and out of soft jobs and ten days off over Christmas! He rose from his chair and spoke to Helen. "Would you like a cup of tea?" She nodded graciously and he corrected himself, "Oh you're coffee aren't you," ignoring Helen's protest, "I'll put kettle on." He strode into the kitchen, the open door bringing a chill into the room and returned and warmed his hands at the fire. "Won't be long," he said. "Well, what've you been up to?"

What to say? His part in this year's show? His father had stopped going to see them years ago despite his professed interest in music. Work? What could he say? 'I'm in the firing line,' and suffer his father's satisfied, 'I told you so, why don't you get a proper job?' "Nothing much," Eric replied sullenly.

"Are you keeping alright dad?" Helen asked.

"I have to," he answered shortly and a thin, shrill sound began to rise in the kitchen. "Kettles boiling," he said and left the room.

Eric looked at Helen with unconcealed irritation. "Waste of bloody time."

Helen, the peacemaker, mouthed, "Just a bit longer."

His father called, "Do you take sugar, I can't remember?"

Eric's response was another sigh of exasperation.

"I don't. Eric does." Helen rose from the settee. "I'll go and help him."

Eric rubbed his temple and wondered, as he always did, what else he could have done…

They sat with their drinks and Helen asked recklessly, "What are you doing over the holiday dad?"

The reply was pointed; it made them squirm as was intended. "I'm going up to our George and Myra's. Good job. Otherwise I'd be going nowhere."

"We've got to go to Helen's mothers," Eric replied. He didn't add that Christmas dinner would be late, that Alice would be exasperated despite having been up at six o'clock to start preparing the meal, that daylight would be fading when they finally sat down to it and Alice would be full of apology and grumbling at Frank, who would respond with passive good humour; that despite Alice's protests the dinner would be excellent and it was where Eric preferred to be, in the happy, chaotic, welcoming atmosphere of Helen's family. "… only, she asked us ages ago," Eric excused himself lamely.

His father's head inclined towards him. "Would you like a drink? I've got plenty. Whisky, vodka, brandy? Or you can have a rum…"

"I'm driving dad."

"How about you Helen. Tia Maria. Drambuie? Sherry, have a drop of sherry. I've got a nice one." He turned back to Eric. "Or there's beer if you want."

Eric relented. "A small sherry then." It was churlish to refuse. What a pathetic, lonely man his father was, with a house full of drink and no-one to share it. It made him feel so guilty? 'But why?' Eric cried in silent desolation, 'it's not my fault, look at you, look at this place! It used to be my home!' They raised their glasses and tried to make the salutation 'Merry Christmas' sound as merry as the words, but the spirit wouldn't dispel the chill of their relationship. Eric looked at the clock; he could stand it no longer. "We'll have to be going," he said and drained his glass with a gesture.

"I've got that cheque for you." His father went to the sideboard and produced a cheque made out for eight pounds. "That's four pounds each," he said.

Helen thanked him and wished him 'Merry Christmas' with a kiss on the cheek and a hug of George Allenby's rigid shoulders. She would have liked to offer a warmer demonstration of affection but it was as close as he would allow. Eric shook hands and looked for reconciliation in his father's face but there was none.

"Why do you leave it so long," his father demanded at the door.

"I'll try to get round a bit more often," Eric lied and from the darkness at the corner of the yard they turned to raise a hand and Eric called a final 'goodnight' but the door was already closing, cutting off the thin shaft of light from the house. They heard the rattle of the chain and George Allenby returned to his armchair with their gift lying unacknowledged on the floor beside him.

On the evening of Helen and Eric's visit to his father Rita and Gerry moved the last of Rita's things into Gerry's house. Gerry had prepared for Rita's arrival with meticulous care. The pale, heavily embossed coffee coloured wallpaper blended unobtrusively with the new off-white paintwork and the brass light switches and sockets were a further concession to gracious living. The furniture was a blend of style and colour; a red three-piece suite upholstered in tapestry, a sapele sideboard, a matching open plan room divider with half empty shelves of unread books and beyond the divider a rectangular table set against full length fawn curtains on a carpet of orange starbursts. The sound of banging and children's voices came from upstairs.

"They're excited," Rita said. "They'll settle down. I'll give them their supper and put them to bed in a bit."

"They'll be alright," Gerry said. He gestured to a large brown corrugated box overflowing with bric-a-brac on the table. "Where d'you think this ought to go?"

"It's Susan's things. Oh, and I think there's ornaments as well. Perhaps they'd go…" Gerry's Capo di Monte figurine on the sideboard caught Rita's eye and she changed her mind; it was too soon to impose herself on his room yet. "Can you take it upstairs in the kids' room. I'll find a place for it."

Gerry grunted and raised the box. "It's heavy, I know that. Good job you weren't bringing furniture too." He edged past her to the lobby at the foot of the stairs. "Watch it you lot," he called, "I'm coming up." There were renewed screams and scampering as they tried to hide and he heard Antony's stage whisper, "Shush you two. Uncle Gerry's coming…"

Rita made the children's supper in a haze of happy exhaustion. The kitchen was so much more modern and better equipped than the one she had left and she grinned with pleasure sliding cupboard doors open until she found dishes. Everything was so well organised she felt like a new bride; it was so long since she had found such contentment. She carried the children's suppers through to the lounge and found them quiet at last. Antony was reading to Raymond and as she sank with pleasurable weariness onto the settee Gerry passed Susan across to her.

"Tired?"

Rita smiled and shook her head. "It's been a big day." She cuddled Susan close. "You going to bed now? In your nice new room daddy's made for you?" Antony looked up at her. "Come on then you two," Rita said, "hurry up, it's bed time. I want you all to go to bed together tonight."

"Aw mum!" Antony protested. Being the oldest he was used to older brother privileges like going to the shops on his own and going to bed after his brother and sister.

"Bed time," Gerry said evenly. "Do as your mummy says." He turned to Rita. "Will you want a hand with them?"

"No." Rita smiled at the boys. "You'll be fine won't you?" They nodded dutifully and resumed their supper. "I'll just go and get this little one to bed." She held Susan to Gerry for his kiss then it was the boys' turn. "Say 'night-night'." They each received a moist kiss then Susan was carried up to bed.

"Right then," Rita said when she returned. "Have you finished you two? Come on then, come and say 'night night'."

Raymond approached Gerry's chair. "Night-night," he said.

Gerry tousled his hair, replied, "Night," and Raymond wriggled away smoothing his rumpled hair.

Antony approached cautiously, hoping he wasn't in for the same treatment. He wasn't sure about kissing either and murmured hesitatingly, "Goodnight... Uncle Gerry."

"Night," Gerry repeated.

"Come on then," Rita said brightly. "Upstairs, both of you." She smiled at Gerry, another hurdle safely crossed. "Shan't be long," she said.

Rita returned to find the lights turned low and Gerry mixing drinks in the kitchen. Exhaustion overwhelmed her and she threw herself into a chair. The room looked pretty and Christmassy with the lights subdued. The tree in the window twinkled against the darkness outside and the baubles hanging from the room divider reflected the light from the fire. It was Christmas; against all the odds suddenly it felt like Christmas. Gerry came in and gestured with glasses, "Gin and tonic," and sat on the settee, patting the cushion beside him. "Come on, come and sit over here," he said.

Rita crossed to Gerry's side. "Thanks Gerry," she murmured and snuggled against him.

"You don't have to thank me." He kissed her gently. "Happy?"

"Oh yes, Gerry. You know I am. You?"

He nodded and rose. "I'll go and close those curtains." Rita watched him. She was tired, but perhaps not too tired. "Will the kids be asleep yet?" Gerry said, drawing her close to him again.

"A minute or two. Just give 'em a few minutes."

They reclined together, waiting in the soft light.

"You know," Gerry began hesitantly, as though giving voice to slow forming thoughts, "Susan'll be alright."

"Hmm? Yes. Why shouldn't she be?"

"She will that's all. I just wish…"

"What?"

Gerry gave a slight shrug. "Do you think you can get the boys to call me something else? They ought to call me something other than 'Uncle Gerry'."

Chapter 34 - Mr. Blue Sky

Throughout the winter Eric hung on. He increased his rate of activity, made more calls and put in his reports diligently. And all the while the eyes of Horrocks were on him like a cat, waiting and watching, and like the mouse he had become Eric knew that each day was leading to an inevitable end. Now he was writing for jobs in earnest but the responses were slow and how he wished he'd kept up the flow of letters. And meanwhile he endeavoured to tease out a furnishing contract. No matter how far in the future, it would be a lifeboat. But the paradox was that despite his success under Don Chatfield's regime Eric was unable to succeed under Horrocks' rigid control. "I know I can do it," Eric constantly reassured himself, "I've done it before." But the cold demotivating hand of Horrocks fell like a weight upon him and stifled his endeavours.

Eric confided his frustrations to Arnold over tea and toast at Mary's. "Loyalty is a two-way affair," he said. "That's something Horrocks will never understand, something he's never given me." Arnold sipped his tea silently. "There's a better way than this to manage people," Eric insisted. "He's never supported me from the start. Not the way Don Chatfield did. I could show him."

"Yes well," Arnold observed, "I doubt you'll have the chance. How's the jobhunting?"

"Rubbish." Eric's voice carried the bitterness of failure. "Only one interview so far."

Arnold's eyebrows rose in surprise. "Didn't think you'd had any."

"Well I'm not going to advertise it am I? He finds out I'm going for interviews and that's the end isn't it! It was some agency in the Grosvenor House. I was in and out in an hour."

"Any joy?"

"Nothing." Eric sighed and checked his watch. "Anyway, I've got to go. See you later?"

Arnold nodded and turned to the business pages of his newspaper.

In the third week of February the snow came, driving down from the moors. The Snake was the first road to be blocked and then Fox House was cut off by drifts as high as the door. By mid afternoon traffic in the city was struggling, the tracks in the snow filled white again almost before the following vehicle found them and the roads climbing from the city centre were becoming impassable as the snowploughs fought their losing battle against the blizzard. By three o'clock shops began sending staff home and the office closed soon after. It brought two days unexpected respite for Eric but by the middle of the following week the snow was slush. Dampness hung in vapour round the miserable amber street-lights at night and the passionate mid-day interludes of summer were just a memory. But still they sought the comforting warmth of each other's company and when Eric drove to the laboratory to collect Helen for lunch there was an aura of excited curiosity about her. As they approached the car she said, "You've had a telegram Eric," and fished it from her handbag.

"Who's it from?"

"I don't know, I haven't opened it. It came just after you left this morning. I was just leaving for work when he came."

Eric opened it and re-reading it his expression changed from curiosity to surprised delight. "I've got an interview." He sounded almost incredulous and he read it out to Helen but the words revealed nothing; "Ref your recent application please telephone the undersigned to arrange interview at your earliest convenience. Andrew Brock; International Converting Emulsions." He looked at Helen. "I'd better go and call them."

"Who are they?" she asked and Eric shook his head, trying to remember the companies he had written to. They drove until they found a call box and Helen watched from the car while Eric made the call. Finally he hung up and returned with a faraway look. "You alright Eric? You look..." Eric started the engine but made no attempt to move and Helen saw the dreaminess again. "You sure you're alright? You did get the interview didn't you?"

"Oh yes." Eric was savouring every second that could be squeezed from the moment. He turned to regard Helen as though committing every aspect of her face to his memory before he spoke, and when he did it was with a gentleness that was utterly compelling. "They've asked me to fly to London to meet them."

"Fly?"

"To London. On Tuesday. To their office in Uxbridge."

"Fly??"

"Yes." He grinned, all thoughts of cold and greyness forgotten. "I told 'em we didn't have an airport in Sheffield." The smile broadened. To fly for an interview! "Anyway I'm going on the train instead and they've moved the interview back. I'm seeing 'em on Tuesday at two o'clock."

But with the perversity of human nature Eric's euphoria began to wear off and by the middle of the afternoon he became prey to anxieties. Had he heard them correctly? Had he got the date and time right? And if he didn't get it he'd be back with no prospects. Superstition kicked in, they told no-one and held their breath.

On Tuesday morning Helen went with him to the station and Eric ran through the timings again. "My interview's at two o'clock. Say that lasts an hour; then I've got to get back to London. Then it depends what train I can get. Could be… eight? Nine o'clock even before I get back."

"Don't let it worry you," Helen said. "It doesn't matter if you don't get home until midnight. Just concentrate on the interview and give them what you've got Eric." She hugged him as if to protect him with her love. "You've got a lot to give Eric, remember that." She saw modesty resisting her flattery. "You have," Helen persisted. "They'll be glad of what you've got to offer them. Just remember that." Her voice was drowned by station announcements and the growl of diesels as his train drew alongside the platform. "You look nice anyway. I could fall for you myself." Helen raised her hands with her fingers crossed. "Good luck. I'll be thinking of you." She kissed him hurriedly and pushed him away. "Go on, get on, you don't want to miss it after all that." He boarded and slammed the door but barely had time to lower the window to say another farewell when a whistle sounded, the locomotive gave an answering blast of its horn and as the train began to move Helen took two steps

275

after it. "Good luck," she called but her voice was lost in other sounds.

Eric returned late. He produced a folder and Helen's reaction was an immediate, joyful, "You got it then!"

Eric shook his head. "Not yet." He handed the slim document to her. It contained information about the company and its products and the cover was strikingly simple. It read, 'There's an 'I' in your future.'

"What's the job?" Helen asked.

"Selling industrial resins. Nothing very glamorous."

"But you don't know anything about… industrial resins."

"No but," Eric repeated their words of that afternoon. "It's not product knowledge they're after. They said that can be taught."

"Were there many others?" she asked.

Eric settled before the fire. "Four of us." He took the folder back from her. "And when we came out, we were all milling around in the foyer and one of the managers gave me this." Eric looked at it thoughtfully. "I was the only one to get one." It was a powerful signal and Eric gazed at the folder as if it was a talisman of good fortune. "So, we'll just have to wait."

The following morning Eric pleaded sickness and diarrhoea to explain his absence to Horrocks.

"Why didn't you phone in?" Horrocks demanded petulantly.

"We're not on the phone," Eric said shortly.

Horrocks' eyebrow lifted. "Your wife could have phoned."

"She works at the hospital. It isn't easy for her."

Horrocks gave a grunt. "You are required to let this office know if you're sick."

"I'm sorry Mr. Horrocks," Eric said disarmingly.

"Did you go to the doctor?"

"No…" Eric saw Horrocks' face pucker with suspicion. "I… I needed… I stayed inside. I didn't want to be far from the… You know." Eric feigned delicate embarrassment.

Horrocks lifted his chin. He had an acute sense that Eric was laughing at him but there was nothing he could do except go along with... with... this charade! "And are you better now?" he asked.

Eric's face brightened. "Yes thank you."

It was unchallengeable and Horrocks dismissed him and watched for any sign of cockiness in the departing figure. 'I've had enough of this,' Horrocks muttered and with sudden determination he reached for the telephone. Illness wasn't a sackable offence but in his eyes mute insubordination was.

The letter arrived on Thursday. "It's next Tuesday... " He was reading carefully. "I've got to see the marketing manager. It says arrive midday and the interview will take place over lunch." He paused. "Anyway," checking his watch suddenly, "I'd better be off or I'll be late."

"Take care," Helen called. So much excitement, so much enthusiasm; all of a sudden so much at stake. Do take care...

Eric escaped from Horrocks as soon as he could and joined Arnold in the cafe. "Don't know why he always keeps me waiting until last every morning," Eric said.

"It's his way of showing his authority."

"Funny way." Eric sugared his tea and took a sip. "He's always bleating on about how I've got to be out there finding business, then he keeps me hanging about."

"Have you heard anything?" Arnold asked.

Eric put the other thoughts aside and grinned. "Second interview!"

"Well done. When is it?"

"Tuesday."

Arnold sucked his teeth. "They don't hang about do they..."

Eric sat with the marketing manager of International Converting Emulsions in the corner of a discrete restaurant by the Thames, struggling with the particularly bony fish he had ordered for his lunch. The towers of Windsor Castle were just visible through the mock regency window, there were few other diners and Eric was acutely aware he was under scrutiny.

Bill Ronson had the appearance of an intellectual. His thinning hair was smoothed back from his high forehead and his conversation and choice of phrasing betrayed a man with serious interests in art and life. But he was not without a sense of humour and it amused him to see how people behaved in such situations. Eric seemed to be coping with the pressure but Ronson could see that Eric regretted the choice he had made and smiled inwardly to himself. Eric's plate had become a pile of inedible debris and he wished he'd followed Ronson's lead and ordered steak. Eric would have preferred steak but had opted for the fish to demonstrate his independence. What he could not know was that as far as Bill Ronson was concerned, Andrew Brock and Ritchie Black had made their choice and that choice was sitting before him, trying to create a good impression while picking unhappily at the food on his plate. Finally, to the relief of them both Eric placed his knife and fork on the plate and pushed it away.

"I think I've exhausted all the possibilities that has to offer," he said.

Bill Ronson chuckled his agreement. "Dessert?" Eric declined; he wasn't here for the lunch. "What time's your train?" Ronson asked.

"I've got a choice actually." Eric reeled off alternative times from mid afternoon onwards. "I wasn't quite sure how long lunch would take."

"We'll get back to the office then." Bill Ronson called for the bill. He was satisfied; he wasn't going to veto either Andrew or Ritchie's decision and as they drove back to the office Ronson talked about the company. "Is there anything you need to know that we haven't covered?" he asked finally as they drew into the car park.

"I don't think so," Eric replied, racking his brains for some meaningful questions. It was all so disconcertingly low key and Eric was wary of making a mistake. There was no doubt, these people weren't fools but now he felt it was time to make a bold assumption. "Except for practical details. They didn't say anything about the type of car. Oh and salary, expenses. That sort of thing."

Bill Ronson took a dismissive tone. "Car's a Hillman Minx I think. You'll get whatever's already allocated to the territory. Salesmen get a choice when it comes up for renewal. As long as it's four door. You're expected to do a fair amount of entertaining and we don't want customers struggling in and out of two-door cars. Your licence is clean?"

"Yes." He almost added 'of course' and checked himself.

"We'd better go up to my office. I thought they might have covered salary with you..."

Eric rose to their defence. "We were mostly talking about the range of responsibilities." Eric smiled deprecatingly. "I assumed salary wouldn't be a problem."

Bill Ronson was suddenly serious. "We'll get that sorted out. I'll introduce you to Szelnick in Personnel and we can get you on your way..." And there it was. A sudden feeling of euphoria swept through him and he wanted to shout 'I've got it!' all the way to Yorkshire for Helen to hear. Light-hearted and happy he was barely able to concentrate on what Bill Ronson was saying, "... and we'll confirm all this in writing to you of course. How much notice do you have to give?"

"Erm... a month. I might be able to join you sooner..."

"A month." Ronson consulted his diary. "Middle of April." He made a note. "Monday the fifteenth?"

Eric took out his diary. "Yes," he said. "That's perfectly fine."

Ronson gave a smile of satisfaction. "We've got another new man starting then. Tony Reeder. You'll do induction training together." He became brusque and rose from his desk; it was clear he was pleased with Eric's successful recruitment to the company; now he was anxious to move to other, more pressing things. But it was an exquisite moment, and Eric treasured it enormously.

The following morning Horrocks was waiting. A second unexplained absence had given him the confidence he needed and he was keyed up and ready to deliver the coup-de-grace he had been planning since last week. He had cleared it with Regional Office and he half smiled in anticipation. "Ah, Mr. Allenby," he crooned. "Come in. Sit down will you."

Eric crossed the floor and took an uncompromising stance before the desk and reached into his pocket. "I'm handing in my notice," he said, and passed the letter of resignation to Horrocks.

Horrocks sought to regain the initiative and laid the envelope on the desk before him. "Where were you yesterday?" he demanded.

"I'm leaving." Eric gestured towards the envelope. "There's my resignation. From today, four weeks notice."

Horrocks did a rapid calculation. Four weeks, effective from today? That means he's got a starting date. He made a final sally. "You can't resign midweek," he said with a smirk. "It will be effective from next Monday." Adding stupidly, "Assuming I accept it."

Eric ignored the remark and said equably, "Next Monday then. If you want whole weeks."

Horrocks opened Eric's letter and scanned it briefly. "It would help if you waited until we recruited your replacement."

Eric looked at him stonily. "Four weeks from Monday." He glanced at the calendar on the wall by Horrocks's shoulder. "I'm leaving on the twelfth."

"There's still work to be done," Horrocks cried petulantly. "And I shall want to go through your records with you."

"Everything's up to date."

Horrocks sighed with the practised air of a harassed businessman. "So who are you going to work for? Anybody we know?" He rattled off the names of competitors in the city, small beer that he could taunt Eric with.

"I'm joining an industrial chemicals company." Eric savoured the opportunity to get back at Horrocks. "I flew to London to meet them for the final interview yesterday." He noted the effect of his words, 'flew to London' with satisfaction. Horrocks was a man who imagined those beneath him had even narrower horizons than his own. It gratified Eric to see their positions reversed at last.

"Yes well," Horrocks said in a final rearguard to preserve his own self esteem, "I only hope you've made the right decision Mr. Allenby."

"I'm sure I have," Eric replied calmly.

"It's a hell of a programme," Eric said, examining the schedule which was enclosed in the bulky brown envelope. A six-week course at Uxbridge supported by customer visits with different salesman to see the company's products in use in a range of industries. "I'm at Uxbridge for the morning on the fifteenth then driving to Tewkesbury in the afternoon to meet Ritchie Black then on Tuesday we're driving to Wigan for a seminar with a customer." He looked down the addresses on the list and back to the programme again. "It's going to be all over the country."

"Six weeks." Helen pulled a face. "What will I do while you're away for six weeks?"

"I'll be home at weekends," Eric said.

"Oh yes," Helen said smiling, "and don't forget to bring me your dirty washing will you."

But it was the start of a great adventure and on the first day Eric left home early. "I'll write," he promised, reaching for his suitcase.

"I'll look for the postman every day," Helen replied. She kissed him and he turned to wave at the corner. At the station he was overtaken by exhilaration; the train was taking him to a new future and he was doing it for them both and it felt like the fulfilment of a dream. He thought of Arnold, getting ready to go through the sterile formality of the meeting with Horrocks and he gazed through the window with an endless smile of pleasure. At St. Pancras Eric mingled in the bustle as he had on the days of his interviews, hurrying across to Paddington but this time he belonged. He wasn't just a stranger, a North Country boy passing through; he was one of the chosen, a man with a purpose, on his way to fulfil his destiny.

The confirmation letter had said, 'Telephone Anna at the office when you reach the station,' and after a short wait at Uxbridge a car driven by Bill Ronson's secretary arrived to collect him. The welcome formalities were brief; a tour of the lab and introductions to heads of departments and then with keys to his new car Eric was free to get on his way. The car delighted him, a brown Hillman Hunter, the top model in its range and he had the rest of the afternoon in which to enjoy it. He nosed it carefully from the car park, savouring the space around him after the confines of the little 1100, and followed the afternoon sun along the motorway to the west…

There was a song that became forever associated with that time. They heard it on their newly acquired stereo and it became an anthem of happiness in their lives:

> 'The sun is shining in the sky,
>
> There ain't a cloud on high…'

Helen turned up the volume and it made her feel more than happy, it was a feeling of bliss. Their dreams were coming true and they were really moving up in the world. Eric was fulfilled at last in a job he liked, working with people who respected him and within the year they would move into a new, modern house. The change in fortune had come for Rita too; she had her new man and a new home. 'Mr. Blue Sky' was reaching its conclusion in a chorale of exultation and Helen closed her eyes and cleared her mind and immersed herself in the music.

Chapter 35 - Suffer little children...

It was Sunday afternoon and they were on their way to the park. Eric and Gerry were swinging Susan between them; Antony and Raymond were running ahead and Helen and Rita were strolling behind deep in conversation when Helen stopped and reacted to Rita's words with disbelief. "Marlene told her that?" she asked incredulously.

Rita nodded. "She says she can't remember the last time."

"You'd want to keep that to yourself wouldn't you? I mean, Marlene's an attractive woman."

"Well, that's what Jenny told me."

At the park gates Susan let go Gerry's hand and ran ahead to join the boys and Eric said, "You are coming back for tea aren't you? It's ages since you've been over."

"Well I..."

"Helen's mum and dad are coming too," Eric continued. "Be a nice little get together. They think a lot of Rita."

Gerry prevaricated. "I don't think she'll want to. It's school tomorrow. Things to do... kids' bathtime..."

Eric despaired of ever understanding him. There was something in Gerry's manner; not just churlishness, it was the isolation that Gerry displayed, an unwillingness to freely accept their friendship. Well, Eric decided, he wasn't going to plead; Gerry could get off home if he wanted.

Meanwhile still loitering behind Helen and Rita continued their conversation. "So what made her tell Jenny?"

Rita shrugged. "You know how thick they've been getting. Well apparently Jenny said something about Malcolm having an eye for the ladies and were all men like it and Marlene said, 'I wish they were,' and then it came out. Just like that."

Helen recalled Marlene's mood at her Christmas party. "You know," she mused, "I used to envy Marlene." Rita gave her a knowing look and Helen added thoughtfully, "Even so he did spend a lot of time with Hayley. And he was late back from dress rehearsal that time."

"Yes but according to Marlene nothing happened."

"She can't know that," Helen persisted. "What makes her so sure?"

Rita hesitated; had it been told to her in confidence? But having come so far she could hardly hold back. "Because she told Jenny they had sex when Jim came home. He woke her up for it." Rita looked at Helen with a pitying sort of sadness. "She says it was the first time in more than a year. Quite unexpected and completely unsatisfactory."

Helen compared Marlene's existence with her own fulfilled life. Finally she said, "It takes some believing Reet. Do you remember 'Camelot'?"

"I wasn't in it."

"Jim was playing Lancelot opposite young Grayson. It must be one of the best he's ever done. We all said there'd been just the right touch of..." Helen searched for words, "...understated passion between them. It must have been terrible for Marlene, watching Jim as the lover of the young queen."

"She says he actually likes women; he enjoys their company, it flatters him. It's the sex he's no good at."

"Platonic passion on the stage." Helen shook her head and changed the subject. "Anyway how's you and Gerry? Still love's young dream?"

Rita smiled. "He can be quite demanding sometimes. Mind you, I'm not complaining."

They paused at a park bench. Helen watched Rita's boys chasing each other in circles across the meadow and heard Gerry call sharply, "Look after Susan. Raymond! Antony! Look after your sister!" They were so happy; a real family together. She returned to their earlier conversation. "I can't imagine Marlene putting up with a life of celibacy, can you?"

"Oh I don't know," Rita replied distantly; after Rob her life had been celibate until Gerry. She called to the children, "Half an hour on the swings so make the most of it. Then we're going to Aunty Helen's."

"Yes but more than a year Reet. Imagine…" but Gerry joined them before Rita could reply.

"What've you two been gossiping about then?" he asked.

"Talking about you," Helen teased and they laughed together but Helen's laughter wasn't reflected in Gerry's eyes.

After an early tea Rita and Gerry left Helen and Eric sitting in the garden with Helen's parents, their chairs up against the wall, soaking up the heat radiating from the bricks.

"Oh I think you've got your garden lovely," Alice said. "Has Eric's father seen it yet?"

"He's coming next week," Eric replied shortly.

"Would you like another cup of tea?" Alice asked. "I could do with one."

She rose and followed Helen inside, leaving Eric and her father dozing like Mexican peasants. Too warm for conversation they made observations to each other at leisurely intervals with each reply made slowly as though the words had to be chewed over and regurgitated before the meaning could be divined. "Be nice if it stays like this for Trearddur," Frank murmured and received a lazy "Hmmm," from Eric in response.

Alice appeared followed by Helen bearing cake and placed a tea-tray before them. "You don't want to sit in that sun too long," she said. "And where's your hat?"

Frank turned to Eric with a laconic grin. "I thought it was too good to last."

"He won't hurt, will you dad?" Helen said. "Bit of sunshine'll do him good."

"Vitamin D in sunshine," Eric said helpfully.

Helen passed her father a cup of tea. "Anyway we don't often see you sitting and relaxing, do we?"

"No," Alice replied, "He spends all his spare time down in that cellar. Heaven knows what he does down there. We never see anything come out of it!" Having delivered the expected rebuke, to which no one paid any regard Alice turned to Helen. "I don't like him sitting in the sun. Not with that thing on his shoulder."

"What thing?" Helen asked. Eric looked at them carefully and took a bite of cake.

"That thing," Alice repeated. "Didn't you know...? I thought I'd..."

"It's nothing," Frank protested. "Anyway it's covered up."

"Show our Helen," Alice commanded.

Helen looked at him with concern. "Do you want me to fetch your hat?" she offered but Alice overrode her.

"Come on Frank, leave your tea for a minute; come and show Helen." Frank rose wearily and followed her inside; he had lived long enough with Alice to know that resistance was useless. Alice unfastened his shirt and drew it down from his left shoulder then she stood back for Helen to see. The flesh below the collarbone was swollen into a grotesque protuberance like an oversized marble, veined and discoloured with a delicate skein of pale red and blue arteries under Frank's white skin. "And he says it's nothing," Alice said in a voice of accusation.

"Does it hurt at all dad?" Helen extended a careful finger and Frank made to shrug his shirt back on.

"Wait a minute!" Alice demanded. "Let her have a proper look."

"I won't touch it dad," Helen said, and she pressed the skin delicately around the discolouration.

"No," Frank said, "It doesn't hurt." He gave Alice an accusing glance. "It's only when people start messing about with it."

"I've told him. He should go and see the doctor about it," Alice said, ignoring him.

"You should go dad," Helen said gently.

"I don't want doctors messing with it and poking about." It wasn't bravado but Frank's matter of fact approach to the thing. It only became a hindrance when Alice remembered and began taxing him.

"It's ever since he had that fall," Alice cried. "He wouldn't go and have it seen to."

"Nothing to do with it," Frank protested.

"You said it hurt you," Alice persisted.

"Well it did when I fell. Then it went off and it's been alright since. It's just that... over this past week or so..." Frank dipped his head and stroked his chin against his shoulder.

"Anyway I wish he'd go," Alice said.

"I think you should dad," Helen repeated and Frank answered with a sigh. "Anyway," Helen said, "come on or your tea'll be cold."

Alice's sigh was equal to Frank's and she raised a warning finger at him. "And just you make sure you keep it covered. Especially out in that sun."

Meanwhile back at Gerry's it was the children's bedtime. Susan was already in her nightgown, clutching her soft doll and sitting before the hearth with Antony and Raymond. "Come on you two," Gerry ordered. "Pyjamas. Both of you."

"Aw it's not bedtime yet," Antony protested.

"School tomorrow. Your sister's got hers on look."

Antony's dignity was affronted. "She's younger than me. I go to bed after her."

"I didn't say you were going to bed," Gerry said. "But you can get your pyjamas on."

"Aw do I have to?"

Rita entered with Susan's drink. "Do as daddy says," she admonished him.

"What about Raymond," Antony snuffled. "He hasn't got to get his on!"

"Yes he has," Gerry insisted. "And get a handkerchief and blow your nose."

Antony sniffed again defiantly. "I haven't got a cold."

"Well stop sniffling then. It gets on people's nerves. Always sniffling like that."

Rita drew Antony to his feet. "Come on love. Get them on like daddy says. And you too Raymond."

Raymond went to fetch their pyjamas and Antony turned to Rita. "Can't I wait a bit mum? Just until she's gone to bed."

"'She' is your sister," Gerry said unctuously.

Rita gave Antony a hug and ruffled his hair. "Come on; be a good boy for daddy."

Antony turned sullenly to his brother. "Come on Raymond! You as well!"

"Give him chance," Gerry said.

Rita picked Susan up and carried her across to Gerry. "Say night-night."

Susan put her arms about Gerry's neck and kissed him. "Night-night daddy."

"Night-night sweetheart." Gerry kissed her with affection. "Sleep tight."

"Now Antony and Raymond."

She kissed her brothers and disappeared in Rita's arms. Gerry called, "Straight to sleep," then turned his attention to the boys. "Half an hour. Then it's you two."

"We haven't had our supper yet," Raymond said.

"You had it at your Aunty Helen's," Gerry replied.

"That wasn't supper," Raymond protested, "It was tea." He turned to his brother but Antony was sitting with his head bowed, intent upon a comic. "We usually have Weetabix," Raymond insisted but Gerry was adamant.

"You had all that trifle. And some cake." He turned his attention to the television; Raymond reached out for Antony's comic and Antony tugged it back with a protest. "Hey you two!" The voice of authority came from the chair. "You'll go to bed now!"

"I'm still hungry," Raymond muttered defiantly to himself.

Rita returned. "She'll be alright. She's tired out bless her. She'll be asleep in a minute." She turned to the boys. "Now then, what are you two having for your supper?"

"We're not allowed to have any," Raymond mumbled.

"Oh. Who says?"

Antony glanced in Gerry's direction. "He does."

"And who is 'he'?" Rita demanded. "Do you mean daddy?" Antony nodded and Raymond echoed his brother with a vehement nod. "Well that's not very nice, saying 'he' is it?" Rita said. "Now why don't you go and say 'sorry' to daddy."

The boys stood before Gerry's chair and mumbled, "Sorry." Rita waited for 'daddy' but it didn't come. She turned to Gerry with a weak smile. "Give them time," she said and went into the kitchen to prepare the boys' supper then returned and perched on the arm of Gerry's chair. "It's only natural after all," she whispered softly. "They still remember their real daddy."

"I expect you're right." Gerry placed his hand on Rita's leg and began stroking her, savouring the sheer smoothness of her stockings. "Anyway we'll have an early night shall we?" Antony glanced up furtively and saw his mummy's skirt was pushed in folds above her knee and he saw the secret look of pleasure on Gerry's face then their eyes met; he had been caught looking. Antony flushed and dropped his head and began spooning furiously at his dish.

Chapter 36 - Orphans of the storm

Helen and Eric returned from holiday refreshed and tanned. Once again Trearddur had lived up to its promise and they had enjoyed a week of relaxation on the beaches, enlivened with sightseeing and revisiting favourite places. Frank had bowed to Alice's instructions to keep his shirt on at all times but Eric and Helen had sunbathed recklessly. They left Anglesey and drove through the mountains in a mood of bittersweet content but it always surprised Helen how quickly Eric could switch from holiday to work mode as soon as they got home. She began sorting the washing from the suitcases and returned to find Eric with his briefcase open going through the accumulated post.

"We've got a marketing meeting in Uxbridge week after next."

"Does that mean you'll be away?"

"Just for one night I think," Eric replied. He took his diary from his briefcase and entered the dates. "Monday. I'll probably be late back Tuesday."

Helen shrugged. The company made demands but the rewards were worth it. Eric was happy and their lives were more fulfilled than ever before. He was valued and the company showed it in unexpected ways; the Christmas hamper, personal notes in the margin of memos, not just from Ritchie Black but from Bill Ronson too. The opportunities for dining at the company's expense when they entertained; the choice of car when it came up for renewal, (which wouldn't be long now, the number of miles Eric was doing). And a commission structure that rewarded success. All these things went into the balance of Helen's mind and she was content. "You'll miss the first rehearsal," she said.

"Can't be helped," Eric replied.

On the Monday evening Helen had left herself short of time to get ready for rehearsal and she was expecting Eric to telephone when the doorbell rang. She sighed in exasperation, tweaked a wayward curl into place, threw the comb onto the dressing table and dashed downstairs. To her surprise Gerry was standing on the doorstep with Antony and Raymond. "Gerry?" Helen exclaimed. She hesitated then stood to one side. "Come in." She glanced at her watch; it was after seven o'clock and time was ticking away but she sensed something was wrong; the boys were too quiet. "Where's Rita?" she said. Gerry hesitated and Helen shoo'd the boys through to the lounge. "Go on Antony; you too Raymond, I think there's something on the television you'll like." She closed the lounge door on them and turned to Gerry.

"I'm sorry Helen," Gerry blurted out suddenly. "Rita's missing."

"Missing?"

Gerry nodded.

"Missing?" Helen repeated.

"She's not at home," Gerry said simply. "I thought she might be here."

"Here? Why would she be here?"

"I don't know. All I know is she's gone." He began to get agitated. "I've got to find her."

"What makes you think she's missing?"

"I got home from work at four o'clock and she wasn't there." Gerry's eyes flickered briefly towards the lounge door. "It's a good job I was or there'd have been nobody at home for those two."

Helen's voice rose in disbelief. "And she's not been back?"

"No."

"But where's she gone to?"

"I don't know," Gerry cried in anguish. "If I knew that…"

Helen's mind was whirling. How could Rita have gone? And without the children? The children! "Where's Susan?" Helen cried.

"She must have taken Susan with her," Gerry answered. He began fiddling with his watch. "I've got to find her. She's been missing hours."

"What about the police? Have you been to the police?"

"Not yet," Gerry said desperately. "I thought she might be here."

"You must go to the police Gerry. Do you want to phone them? You can use the phone."

"I've got to go and look for her," Gerry said. "I'm sorry Helen, can I leave the boys with you for a bit?"

Helen's mind was filled with conflict. Why would Rita have left? They were happy together; Rita had said so, almost too happy. She would have said something, she would have confided. She wouldn't have just left the boys. And what about Susan? All thoughts of rehearsal driven from Helen's mind she said, "Yes. Yes of course, leave them with me…"

The telephone rang and Gerry looked up in alarm. "Hang on a minute Gerry," Helen said quickly as the boy's heads appeared at the lounge door and she picked up the receiver. "Hello."

"Hi Hel, it's me."

"Eric! Er, yes."

"You alright Hel?"

Helen's mind was in turmoil and Gerry was gesturing at the door. "Hang on a minute Eric." She beckoned Gerry to stop. "Gerry…! Eric, just hang on a minute… Gerry! Gerry, just…" But Gerry was already disappearing; she heard his car door slam and turned back to the boys and Eric's voice on the telephone.

"Helen, what is it? What's going on?"

"Oh Eric. It's Rita. She's left Gerry."

"Left him? What for?"

"I don't know," Helen replied. "Gerry's just been round. He's gone to look for her." She turned and saw Antony and Raymond were still at the lounge door listening, their faces pinched and afraid. "Can you call me back in a bit Eric? I've got the boys here."

"The boys?" he exclaimed.

"Yes."

"What about rehearsal?"

"Well I'm not going am I…"

"You sure you're alright Hel?"

"No I'm not! I'm not sure of anything," Helen replied desperately. "I'll… Call me in a bit Eric, will you." As she put the phone down the children ran and clung to her to her. "It's alright," Helen said, stroking their heads. "Mummy will be back soon. You'll see."

"But where's she gone Aunty Helen?"

Helen looked down at the imploring faces. "Oh, she's probably gone on an unexpected visit to see a friend."

"Which friend?"

"Well, if we knew that…" Helen replied enigmatically.

"She doesn't want us," Antony said with uncompromising insight.

"No," Helen protested. "Don't say that Antony. Your mummy's got lots of friends. She'll have been held up that's all. You'll see. Now, who'd like a drink? Let's see what we can find." But for all her brave reassurances Helen felt the same hand of fear as the children clutching her heart.

Eric telephoned an hour later.

"You wait in there," Helen said, cradling the handset against her breast, "It's only Uncle Eric phoning from work." She closed the lounge door.

"Is there any news?"

"Nothing."

"Not even from Gerry?"

"No."

"Have you tried phoning his house?"

"Well of course I have." Worry added an edge to Helen's voice. "There was no answer."

"What about the police?"

"Gerry's supposed to have contacted them." She heard Eric's sigh of exasperation. "I'm sorry love," Helen said. "What with all this I forgot to ask you. How was the meeting?"

"Oh, fine. It's you I'm worried about."

"I'm alright." Helen spoke with as much reassurance as she could muster. "I'm wondering what to do about the boys. I don't know whether they're going home or what. I've got work tomorrow. I can't just send 'em off to school wondering if I've got to leave early…" Helen's voice tailed off.

"Oh God! I wish I was there with you!"

"So do I." Then, "Don't worry Eric. Please. We'll be alright. If I can't look after a couple of little boys…"

293

The conversation ended on an unsatisfactory note. They couldn't devise a real plan of action and Eric promised to telephone first thing in the morning. Helen promised in return to telephone the hotel the minute there was any news. She returned to the lounge, the boys sat with her in the chair and Helen put her arms around them and smiled reassuringly.

"Uncle Eric sends his love. Would you like another drink?" Raymond nodded and she went out to make it overwhelmed by a feeling of total inadequacy. "Here you are boys," she said brightly, handing the tumblers to them. "I shan't be a minute then I'll be straight back."

"Where are you going?" Antony cried, leaping to his feet.

"It's alright," Helen said soothingly. "I'm not leaving you. I'm just going to make a telephone call that's all. I'm only going to be in the hall."

"Leave the door open," Antony pleaded.

"Alright then." She pointed to the telephone table at the foot of the stairs. "I'm only just there, look." Antony squatted on the floor close to the door, keeping her in view. Helen went to the telephone, lifted the handset and dialled. Gerry didn't like Rita's mother and the feeling was mutual. Perhaps…?

"Oh hello Helen. How nice to hear from you." There was warmth in the greeting. "How are you both keeping?"

"Fine thanks. Is Rita there?"

"Rita? No. Why? If she's not at rehearsal she'll be at home."

Helen said, "She's… not at home."

The way she uttered the words put Rita's mother on guard. "Not at home?"

Helen stole a glance towards the lounge. Antony's eyes were on her; she smiled and spoke quietly and clearly into the mouthpiece. "Rita is missing. I've got Antony and Raymond here with me."

The shock at the other end was palpable. "Missing? Rita? How do you mean, missing? Helen…?"

"I'm sorry." Helen felt Antony's eyes still on her and forced another smile. "I can't say too much. Not over the phone. It's not easy… The boys are here. Eric's away as well."

"Where's Gerry?" the voice demanded.

"He brought the boys round. Now he's gone to look for her."

"Has he called the police?"

"Yes. I think so. Yes... Yes he has."

"How are the boys? Are they alright?"

"Yes, they're fine. They're going to have their supper in a minute."

"What about Susan?"

"I... we think she's with Rita."

"Just hold on a minute will you Helen."

Helen waited and gave Antony another reassuring smile. She could hear Rita's mother and father talking and sensed the phone changing hands, then Rita's father said, "Are you still there Helen? Don't do anything; we're coming straight over…"

Eric telephoned later. "I just wondered whether you'd…?"

"Rita's mum and dad came. They've taken the boys back home with them."

"What about Rita?"

"I've not heard anything. From either of them."

"Are you alright Hel?"

"Yes…. I'll be alright. I'm just worried about Rita." Helen suppressed a snuffle with her handkerchief. "I wish you were here Eric. I need you."

"I'm sorry Hel. I wish there was something I could do."

"Just come home Eric. As soon as you can. Please. Come home."

Chapter 37 - Schism

The following evening Eric was home by eight o'clock. Helen kissed him with relief and said, "I've not heard anything. From either of them."

"What about Rita's mother?"

"She hadn't heard anything when I spoke to her."

"And she's still got the kids?"

Domestic priorities began to assert themselves. "Let's talk about it later," Helen said. "I've got a lasagne in the oven; I wasn't sure what time you'd get here."

Eric looked at Helen closely. "Smells great. You sure you're alright?"

Helen nodded. "You must be tired. Go and have a wash. It'll be ready when you come down."

Eric nodded gratefully and went upstairs to change.

"So," Helen said when he returned. "How was it?" She spoke brightly but the brightness was forced.

"Excellent," he said. "Bill Ronson's setting up a series of Task Forces to focus on different markets." Helen placed the dish of lasagne hurriedly on the mat and began to serve. "I'm heading up one of the Task Forces."

"Promotion?" Helen exclaimed.

"Well," Eric said modestly, "not exactly. I'm heading up a team to target a particular market and build up knowledge and expertise, to become the experts in our field." He was paraphrasing Bill Ronson. "Each team has a dedicated chemist doing technical back up and I've been chosen to lead one of the teams. Of course I'll still be reporting to Ritchie," Eric added. "I've still got my sales area to run."

"Do you get a pay rise?"

Eric laughed. "No. But it's a hell of a career opportunity. Gives me a chance to show what I can do. It's what I've always wanted Hel. To work for a company that recognises potential and gives you the opportunity to show what you can do." He looked at her earnestly. "You don't know where this can lead Hel."

"Is there more travelling?"

"Some. We'll have quarterly meetings. My sales area's still the main priority." He reached for her as though physical contact between them was needed to convince her and Helen squeezed his hand.

"Oh I'm so pleased for you Eric."

"The money'll come Helen. Don't worry about that."

"I'm not." Her eyes sparkled on him. "I'm very proud of you."

The brief celebration passed and Rita's crisis gathered like a cloud over them.

"I'm sorry you missed your rehearsal Hel."

"It's not your fault is it." A frown creased Helen's brow. "I just wish somebody would phone. I'm so worried about that little girl!"

Eric checked his watch. "Perhaps we should try Rita's mother again. Just to see how the boys are. It's only just nine o'clock."

"Give me a hand with these things first then," Helen said and drew the curtains.

By the time they'd finished clearing away it was nearing half past nine. "Do you want to speak to her or shall I?" Eric asked.

Helen hesitated. "You don't think it's too late do you? If they'd heard anything I'm sure they'd have…"

Eric dialled the number. "Come on Hel," he called, handing her the phone, "It's ringing."

Helen braced herself and Eric saw her expression undergo a series of rapid changes as she listened. Caring concern gave way to shock, then to disbelief and Helen began shaking her head. She prompted the conversation with brief, pointed questions and disbelief became incredulity. Eric went to the kitchen and returned to see a look of the utmost sympathy on Helen's face. She replaced the handset and remained still, afraid to move. It was as though movement would make her lose the words she had heard and she stood waiting until the distillation of information in her mind was complete. Finally Helen turned to Eric and said, "She's at home!"

"At her mother's?"

"No." Helen's voice had an ethereal quality; like a visitor to a holy shrine then her eyes focussed on Eric with recognition and anger. "At Gerry's. How could she!!!"

"Hel?" Eric took a step towards her. "Helen? What is it?"

"They've thrown the boys out!"

"What! Who...?"

"Rita and Gerry! They've thrown them out!" She wandered into the sitting room, shaking her head in disbelief. "Antony and Raymond. They've thrown those little boys out."

"What about Susan?"

"Susan's with them! Oh, they've kept Susan." Helen began pacing the room. "Her mother's been trying to reach them all day, but every time she phoned Gerry there was no answer. She took the kids to school as normal and she went to fetch them this afternoon hoping she'd meet Rita at the school. But of course there was no Rita so she brought them home again. Rita's dad was all for going up to Gerry's when he came home from work but, as her mother said, 'What's the point? There's nobody there.' Then after tea Rita rang her mother." Helen paused, marshalling further recollections.

"But why didn't she phone you Hel?"

"You haven't heard the rest of it yet," Helen said grimly. "She didn't want to speak to the boys. She said it would only upset them. She told her mother they're keeping Susan but Antony and Raymond have got to go." It was as though Helen was describing some obscene, blasphemous ritual. "It's true but... I just can't believe it!" Helen's pacing came to a stop.

"So what's happening to the boys?"

"Rita's parents have got them. Oh, and there's more! All day, while her mother was ringing up and getting no answer they were there all the time, not answering the phone! And we've all been sick with worry!"

"So what's happening now?"

"Gerry won't have them. They won't accept him as their father and Rita says it's causing a rift so they've got to go!" Helen concluded suddenly. "It's not Rita, it can't be Rita."

"But why Susan...?"

298

"Oh Susan's alright. She calls him her daddy. Poor mite doesn't know any better."

"The bastard!"

Helen subsided into a chair. "I don't believe it. He must have got some kind of hold over her."

It was a week before Helen saw Rita face to face. She braced herself to telephone and Rita suggested 'The Shack.' The little café was neutral ground and Rita knew Helen wouldn't make a scene there but Helen declined icily.

"Well where then?"

"I don't know." Now Helen was actually speaking to Rita her mind wouldn't work.

"Well if you don't…"

The sarcasm in Rita's voice brought Helen's mind into focus. "Barkers Pool. Outside the City Hall."

"If you like," Rita said. "What time?"

"One o'clock," Helen replied shortly.

"See you there then." Rita rang off leaving Helen infuriated at her lack of contrition.

Helen arrived at the City Hall to see Rita waiting beside one of the pillars under the portico watching her approach. Rita's scrutiny put Helen at a disadvantage but Rita descended the steps and they greeted one another without affection.

"Are we going for lunch?" Rita began.

"How could you?" Helen responded.

"You don't understand," Rita said.

"Oh! I don't understand? Really!" Helen responded with passion. "I understand you've thrown those two lovely children out with nothing but the clothes they were standing up in."

"Well that's not true anyway."

"Oh yes it is."

"I don't know who you've been speaking to…"

"Your mother actually! She took those two boys back to Gerry's and you made them wait outside while you fetched their belongings.

You sent them away with all they possessed in a carrier bag. How could you Rita!" Helen cried in anguish.

"My mother's going to look after them. They'll be better off with her than with me and Gerry."

"They need their mother Rita!"

"They weren't happy…"

"It takes a little time! And effort!"

"Do you think we didn't try between us, all of us? Anyway what do you know about bringing up children…?" She saw the hurt in Helen's eyes and wished she'd never said the words.

"I don't know you Rita," Helen said quietly. "I thought I did. All the years we've been friends and now I look at you and I don't know you."

"Is that all you've came to say? 'Cos if it is…"

"What sort of hold has he got over you?" Helen pleaded. "This isn't like you… It's not like you at all. What do you see in him?"

Rita's reply was low and simple. "I love him."

"You can't," Helen cried desperately, "Not if he makes you give away your children. You always thought the world of them, even through all that business with Rob."

"It's nothing to do with Rob. There's no need to bring that up!"

"Oh Rita," Helen pleaded. "Don't do it. Don't, please."

Once more Rita's voice became cold and unemotional. "It's nothing to do with you either," she replied. "Anybody would think I was selling them or something. They're going to live with my mother. They'll be well looked after. They'll be looked after there much better than I could. You're so wrapped up in your own little world with Eric you don't really know what goes on."

There was a twisted logic in Rita's justification that Helen couldn't answer. She attempted a smile of superiority but her chin was quivering and the smile became lopsided. Embarrassed under Rita's gaze, Helen bit her lip to control it. "I'd rather have my little world than yours any day. Goodbye Rita." Helen turned and walked away. She had achieved nothing, but she wouldn't let Rita see the tears filling her eyes.

Helen took the afternoon off and went to see Rita's mother. They shared tea in the chintzy lounge overlooking the park where the trains ran through the trees and Helen was dismayed at the change in the woman sitting opposite her. Bitterness was etched in the deep lines running to her mouth, sagging into permanent disapproval, and her eyes were lined from weeping. Worry had made an old woman of her.

"What really hurt," Helen said, "was Gerry standing there, bold as brass, telling me Rita had left him. And all the time he was lying. Lying to my face."

"I know Rob had his faults," Rita's mother said, her head bowed in defeat, "but he never put her up to anything like this."

Helen extended her hand but her gesture elicited no response. How times change, Helen reflected; she had never thought to hear Rita's mother admit to any redeeming quality in Rob. She withdrew her hand, gave a wan smile and nodded. "You're right. Whatever else he did, he never neglected the boys." They sipped their tea. "How are they getting on?" Helen asked presently.

"It's not easy for them. Antony's very quiet. He spends all his time with his head in a book. But Raymond's a little terror."

"I thought he was the quiet one," Helen observed.

Rita's mother shook her head and her expression took on a new look of anxiety. "He's been the most upset by it. I've never known tantrums like it. He keeps saying nobody loves him."

"Oh, surely," Helen began and stopped. There was something different about the room, a change so subtle that Helen hadn't noticed it until now. The immaculate tidiness with everything carefully placed and not to be touched, all the ornaments and tasteful little nick-knacks that used to adorn the mantelpiece and small tables were gone apart from a few remnants, protected behind glass in the china cabinet. She remembered all the high expectations; now all that pretension had been swept away and Rita's mother began speaking as though in a confessional.

"Raymond once told me, just before it happened..." she took a handkerchief and dabbed briskly at the corner of her eye, the subterfuge a relic of earlier times. "Grit," she said. "I was in the garden this morning. There I think it's gone."

"You were saying...?"

"Oh yes. Well, one day when the children were here I saw Antony looking strangely at Susan. Of course when I asked him what was the matter he wouldn't say. But Raymond told me. They'd wanted something – I don't know what, some little treat – and Gerry refused them. Then they saw Susan with it. And when Antony asked why she could have it and they couldn't Gerry said, 'Because Susan's more important; she's my favourite.' I mean, fancy saying that to a child. There were other things too. I should have known. I should have seen it coming." She glanced at her watch. "I'll have to go and collect the boys from school."

Helen said, "I'll have to be getting back too."

"What about you and Rita?"

"I... I don't think so... I'm too upset. When I think about those boys, the way they were that night. I still don't know how she could do it."

"I'm sorry Helen." Her face grew wistful. "When I think back to you and Rita, the way you used to be... It's a pity to lose friendship like that."

Chapter 38 - A Wild West hero

And so friendship was cast aside as Helen wrestled with her conscience and tried not to think too much about her erstwhile friend. Determined to have nothing more to do with Rita, Helen's resolve was strengthened by the struggle Rita's parents had with the boys; their insecurities, resentment and violent rejection of her love for them. How could she? Helen repeated endlessly. No matter how she twisted the facts round in her mind, Helen found no justification for Rita's cruelty and her anger was compounded by the way Rita had deceived her. As for Gerry…!

Meanwhile Eric's career prospered and they began enjoying the fruits of his success. He arranged to take the car abroad and use it for their holiday; clearly virtue was bringing its own reward.

"You mean you're not going to Trearddur this year?" Alice said, crestfallen.

"We want to do something different this year mum. I mean we still want to go to Trearddur of course. Perhaps we could all have a weekend together later in the year."

"Me and your father might give it a miss this year."

"Oh mum… We don't want you to miss your holiday," Helen protested.

"Well, we've been thinking about it. And if you're not going... Besides, there's things wants doing to the house. Your father'd be better off doing them this year instead."

"Perhaps next year then eh?" Helen said but in her heart Alice knew they had already had the last of their holidays together.

Summer. The long German autobahn was behind them and they stopped for the night at an inn on the Romantikstrasse and ate a simple, wholesome dinner. Replete with contentment and wine they strolled outside and meandered into the garden behind the restaurant, and in the darkness beyond the faint glow of light from the curtained windows made love daringly between the flowerbeds, screened by trellis beneath the stars.

"Do you think they heard us?" Helen whispered.

"Doesn't matter if they did. We shan't see them again anyway."

The following morning, having braved the knowing enquiries of the hausfrau they continued south, speeding along with renewed vigour. A smudge on the horizon like a low haze of smoke appeared and slowly began to coalesce. Helen felt like the heroine of one of her mothers' old operettas as the Bavarian Alps rose before them. Now the undulating meadows were a lush carpet of green with peaks towering beyond the trees. Eric slowed and lowered his window and they were assailed by birdsong and the scent of meadow grasses. He stopped the car; ahead of them, perfectly framed in a bend in the road rose a solitary massive peak.

"Do you want the camera?" Helen asked reaching into the glove compartment.

Eric shook his head. "No. I can't see to drive," and Helen saw tears in his eyes.

"Are you alright?"

Eric nodded. "It's so beautiful." But the afternoon was passing and after a few minutes he started the car and they continued their journey.

They checked into the gasthaus at Alterschrofen and Helen asked, "Are we near the castle?"

The owner smiled back. "Yes. Both castles."

"Both," Eric exclaimed.

"Yes. You didn't know? This is the land of castles."

"Neuschwanstein?" Eric asked.

"Oh yes, of course. But also Schwangau. Und if you have no…" she sought for a simple phrase, "misgivings to drive there is Linderhof. Also Chiemsee. Oh ja, we have plenty of castles for you." She examined the register and handed Eric the key with a smile. "So. You are room eleven. You can bring in your luggage round through the back. Or here," she shrugged. "Where is your car? Do you want a hand with bags?"

Their room smelled of freshly polished wood and the window opposite the bed was curtained. "Might be the balcony," Helen said, recalling the description from the brochure. "Some rooms have balconies."

Eric drew back the curtain. "Come here Hel. Look at this." Just beyond the village, high on a shoulder of the mountain was the fairytale castle of King Ludwig...

They saw the castle of Neuschwanstein by moonlight and made love in the hour before dawn with the castle gleaming white under a brilliant moon beyond the window, then stood outside on the balcony in the chill morning air, waiting for the arrival of daylight until, under the lightening sky, the castle began to fade. They showered and dressed and returned to the balcony. Now the sun was rising above the mountain and the castle was illuminated in dazzling shafts of light streaming between the peaks...

Mid-morning, it was already hot and Helen and Eric were sitting in a hotel garden by Lake Aachensee with coffee and cognac, watching diamonds of sunlight flickering on the surface of the lake. "If we're going back into Salzburg I'd like to try and get some of that perfume," Helen said. It was a perfume she had worn when they first met. Musky and sophisticated, she had only worn 'Tosca' on special occasions.

Eric gave a sigh of contentment. "You know what I'd really like?" he said.

"I know," Helen said lazily, "apfel strudl? I'll bet it's not as good as we had in Kitzbuhel."

Eric smiled in recollection. In Kitzbuhel it had begun to rain and the café in the old part of town town opposite the church was like a set from an old film; waitresses in dirndl skirts and pinafores, posies of fresh flowers on the tables and discrete Alpine music. They despaired of getting seated but a smiling waitress found them a table, found time to give them a menu in English - though God knows, Helen thought to herself, how could she tell? - and reappeared promptly and took their order, delicious, mouth watering warm apfel strudl and 'vanilla sauce'. "It's custard," Eric had cried in delight, surprised that he should find it so surprising... Happy with the memory he beckoned the waiter and ordered two portions of apfel strudl.

"You'll make me fat," Helen murmured.

Eric merely smiled. His thoughts were busy with his ambitions, reflecting on the different managers he had worked under. The exceptions stood out. Men like Don and Ritchie could motivate; they led, not by bullying and coercion but by example and their ability to release the potential in others. Free of obsession about their own status, they commanded the respect of their subordinates and stood tall amongst their peers. Looking at these men Eric recognised his own ambition. To be a leader of men, a guide and mentor; wise enough to know when to intervene and when to stand back and win admiration for bringing them success. Like a Wild West hero, tall and strong; modest and forgiving in triumph, ruthless in opposing wrong. The sun burned down and Eric gazed across the lake into the middle distance, his mind busy with images of 'Shane' and the hero-worshipping cries of a boy with blond hair as Shane departed from the ranch, the job done, the town cleaned up, the people safe and secure once more. Suddenly he became restless and sat up. "Come on Hel," he said, "let's go."

Helen blinked reluctantly and said, "In a minute."

But the languor had gone from him and a few minutes later he stood up and stretched and shook himself like a swimmer emerging from water. "I think I'll just go and have a wander round the garden," he said. "See you in a minute or two."

"Alright. I'll be ready to go when you come back." Helen adjusted her sunglasses and sipped her coffee, immersed in the pleasure of the view across the sparkling blue lake...

They drove to Salzburg and Helen got her Tosca from a small shop near the Glokenspiel Café and they worshipped the birth of genius at Mozart's Geburtshaus. They decided to have a celebration dinner and drove out to the Salzkammergut and St. Wolfgang, from where the steamers plied their way to St. Gilgen, the birthplace of Mozart's mother. Eric had intended they should dine at the White Horse Inn. "Remember, that was the first show I ever saw you in," he enthused but, "...we should have booked," he said ruefully.

Across the lake the light on the mountains was turning to mellow gold as evening approached. Helen threaded her arms through Eric's. "Never mind love. It's nice just being here and watching the lights across the other side." For now tiny points of light were twinkling and in a cafe beside the lake tables were set under a grove of trees. "We could eat here. Look, there's a table by the waters' edge. I know it's not as grand as the White Horse Inn but we can see it from here and watch the steamers as well." She kissed him; a fleeting touch of her lips on his cheek and Eric loved her then for her spontaneity and lack of pretension as he led her to the lakeside table. And so the holiday came to an end and they retraced their journey home with the mountains receding behind them.

"I'm going to speak to Ritchie when we get back," Eric said. "About getting into management. I want to show them what I can do."

"But we're doing alright aren't we Eric?" It was only a mild protest but to Helen the status quo at the moment was perfect. "We've got a lovely home. And this lovely holiday."

"I know. And it's been great hasn't it. But I'm only doing a part of what I'm really capable of Hel."

"You're not unhappy are you?"

Eric turned and grinned at her. "Of course I'm not unhappy. Why?"

"Well," she said, "this sudden talk about change."

"But we could have even better things Hel. Anyway, it's not sudden. I've been thinking about it for a while. The task force project is going well and I could go on to bigger and better things. What's wrong with ambition Hel? If I hadn't been ambitious I'd still be at the co-op selling kitchen tables."

"I know Eric. It's just that we're happy and I don't want anything to change. But I don't want to stop you doing things. Not if you really want to. You've got a lot of talents Eric, in all sorts of ways. I mean that."

"Well, there you go then." He settled back with satisfaction and concentrated on the road. There was still a day's driving ahead of them...

They took gifts of Mozart chocolates and an alpenstock for Helen's mother and father. "How's my dad?" Helen asked.

"He's alright," Alice said, touched by Helen's concern. "He's down in the cellar as usual. I don't think he knows you're here yet."

"I don't suppose there's any news of Rita?"

"Not a word," Alice replied. "Which reminds me, I must give her mother a ring and see how she's coping with those two little boys."

Frank emerged from his workshop beaming owlishly through his glasses and wiping his hands on a piece of rag. "Have you had a good time then?"

"Oh, it was lovely dad. You'd love the mountains. All the little trains running through the valleys. We've brought you both a little present."

Frank took the alpenstock and laughed and Alice said, "I'll make us some tea, we'll have it in the garden. It's a lovely day. You can tell us all about it. Oh, by the way, we're getting a new producer, did you know?"

Back to work. Eric didn't mind, he was looking forward to it and he waved Helen off and went inside to begin planning his week but the telephone rang and he gave a grimace of exasperation. It was Tony, his correspondent at Uxbridge. Of course, Tony was always early, always ahead of the game. They exchanged pleasantries then Tony said, "You heard about Reeder?"

"I didn't get back until Saturday. What's happened to him?"

"There's been a big reorganisation. They've created a third sales region covering the east. Reeder's been made Sales Manager."

"Reeder?"

"Yes," Tony replied. "It's on the notice boards today. I expect your memo's in your post."

Eric felt a sense of loss and disappointment. "I'll go and check; I've got a pile of stuff here. Call you back in a bit Tony."

Eric rang off and went through his mail but the announcement wasn't there. Reeder, a salesman with little apparent sales success to his credit and disliked among his peers. The appointment of Reeder appalled him. He called Ritchie Black.

"Welcome back Eric." Ritchie's lugubrious voice was secure and comforting." How was the holiday?"

"Great thanks Ritchie. We've had a fabulous time. Have you ever been to Austria?"

"Never," Ritchie said. "Emmy likes her sun."

"We got our suntans too."

Anxious to cut through the chat Eric said, "I hear there's been some changes."

Ritchie detected the edge in Eric's voice. "Ah," he said, "you've been on to the office. I was rather hoping to speak to you first."

Well you could have called me, Eric thought. Instead he replied, "Tony called me. Just now."

"So what did Tony tell you?"

Eric tried to sound off-hand. "About the new Eastern Region. Is it right, Reeder's been appointed sales manager?"

"Yes." Ritchie had no intention of indulging Eric's petulant disappointment and his tone was unequivocal. "What else did he say?"

"Nothing. Just that. I've only just put the phone down."

"Good." The smile in Ritchie's voice returned. "You've not been left out either. That's why I wanted to talk to you before you spoke to anyone else."

Lunchtime was approaching. Helen glanced through the window and saw Eric waving. "I'm going out for lunch by the looks of it," she announced with delight. Their midday trysts of summer had long ceased; it must be something special to bring him to her during his working day.

"Must be love," Marcia replied but Helen was already on her way.

They swept down the drive and Helen said, "So what's brought this on then? I thought you had lots and lots of work to do."

Eric settled back comfortably and swung the car down past the park. "I'll tell you when we get there. Uncle Sam's alright?"

"Mmmm. That'll make a nice change. Like old times."

They took a table in the window. "I've been on to Ritchie," Eric began. "There's been a reorganisation. Reeder's been appointed manager of a new sales region. You remember Hel. He joined the company same day as me. We did our initial training together."

Helen remembered how dismissive Eric had been of Reeder at the time. Her mind turned to their conversation by the lake and she laid her hand on his. "I'm sorry Eric. It should have been you."

"Yes, well. I'm more sorry for the fellows that'll be working for him."

The waitress brought two glasses of water. Eric acknowledged her with a nod and his smile returned. So that wasn't all. Helen could always tell when Eric had something to say, he became keyed up, waiting for her to tease it from him. "Well?" she said, "What else is there?"

"What makes you think there's anything?"

"Oh come on Eric." Helen twiddled with the cutlery in the paper napkin hoping it was something she could be glad about too.

Eric spoke carefully. "I've got a new assignment. If I want it Hel. They want me to take responsibility for Ireland."

"Ireland!"

"Four days a month. If I want it," Eric said earnestly. "For two years; certainly no more than three."

"Ireland?" Helen couldn't keep the dismay from her voice. "What have you said?"

"They want me to think about it. You know, talk it over with you and then let them know."

Helen fell silent. Last night's news had seen a march in Londonderry end in violence. Before their holiday there had been images of flames roaring out of a bombed out shop in Belfast. The news was of nail bombs and car bombs, kneecappings and murders. And then there'd been Bloody Sunday and the carnage of the Birmingham pubs. "Have you got to go?"

"It'll only be in the South Hel, in Eire. It doesn't include the North," Eric pleaded.

"It's still Ireland though."

Their meal arrived and they drew apart. "Relish tray?" the girl asked. Eric nodded and Helen began to eat silently with her head lowered.

"It could be a good career move Hel. Hel...?"

She hesitated, gazing at the food on her plate. A career move! Had she heard him aright? "Can we talk about it later," Helen said, glancing quickly around. "Not here."

Part 4 – 1979

DECLINE

Chapter 39 - Figures in a landscape

The initial reaction to Eric's arrival in Ireland had been scepticism. "Another new face. When will your company learn, you'll never do any business until you have somebody permanently over here." But Eric had persevered, revelling in the easy informality, what Uxbridge called the 'manana' culture of Irish business. He sensed there were bridges to re-build and business relationships to be restored and with sensitivity and patience the formality of the English mainland was replaced by, "Come and see me towards the end of the morning and we'll go home and have a bite together. You won't mind ham and eggs? You can meet Sheilagh and the kids."

"I'm supposed to buy you lunch Dermot."

"Ah, I can't be bothered with all that. Buying me dinner won't make me alter me decision." No, but genuine friendship might; and Eric began to score small victories and as his commitment became clear the victories became bigger.

It was a revelation to him the way the people of Eire regarded Ulster as a different country. "Me flight home from holidays was cancelled," the buyer from AMP in County Cork told him over coffee in his office, "and they wanted to send me to Belfast and take a connecting flight to Dublin. I soon put 'em right." They laughed together. It was alright for Eric to laugh for his Irish friends laughed at themselves. But no politics! If ever politics was taboo in business, it was anathema for an Englishman.

In the second summer of his assignment Eric organised their holiday around a week's programme of entertaining that included an opportunity for Helen to meet his customers and their wives. Then they drove west for a week in County Cork before heading north to Connemara. They crossed the Shannon in blazing sunshine while travellers on the ferry entertained them with jigs and reels to the accompaniment of spoons, and lived in a field in a cottage which they filled with smoke from a slow peat fire and drank milk drawn fresh from the cow, still warm in the pail. They visited the impossible site where Alcock and Brown had landed their Vimy bomber amongst the boulders in a bog of peat and were stunned by the vibrancy of Dublin when they returned from the empty landscape of the west.

"It's such a shame," Helen said, "when people can't live in peace together."

But the politics were too convoluted and the history of conflict was too long and deeply ingrained for there to be any end in sight to the Troubles in the North. And now it was his third year.

August and the sun was still high as Eric flew over Anglesey. He had completed his week's business unexpectedly early and caught the Friday mid-afternoon shuttle to Manchester. In an hours time Dublin airport was going to be bustling with tired, frustrated businessmen anxious to get home and he smiled a self congratulatory smile. A good job done this week and a perfect way to end it. His good humour ran ahead of him and Helen greeted him with, "You look like a cat that's had the cream."

Eric followed her into the kitchen. "You remember that proposal I made for marketing that new resin? I had a message from Bill Ronson, they're getting the advertising agency to build a sales campaign around it. Ritchie wants me to make a presentation to the salesforce."

"Oh Eric! That's great."

"So forget about cooking; we're going out to celebrate." Eric checked his watch. "I'm just going to run a bath and have a soak…"

The Chequers was an old country pub situated half way down the road dropping from the moors to the Derwent in the valley below. It was only just seven thirty but already the bar was almost full. "Are you dining tonight sir?" the barman asked. Eric nodded and they took their drinks through the tiny coffee lounge into the dining room. The music playing softly in the background was one of their favourite pieces, a Mozart adagio and Eric sat back and smiled. Helen began to fidget under his scrutiny.

"Something wrong?" she said in a low voice and pulled a slight adjustment to the neckline of her dress. "Am I showing too much?"

Eric breathed in her perfume and his gaze became intense. "I was just thinking how lovely you look."

Helen blushed with pleasure and leaned forward, returning kisses with her eyes. "I love you," she murmured then drew back as the waitress placed Parma ham and melon before them. "Do you think she heard?"

"I don't care if she did. I love you Hel. That's all that matters."

They finished their starter and leaned close, sipping wine in complete contentment one with the other and planned their weekend.

"By the way, you haven't forgotten it's my turn to do the animals tomorrow?" Helen said. "It won't take long and then, if it's nice again we could go up to…" She broke off as the waitress arrived with their steaks and dishes of vegetables.

Feeding the animals in the sheds behind the hospital was a weekend chore shared between the laboratory staff every eight weeks. Topping up the drinking water was the main priority but the feeding instruction on the cages varied according to the nature of the experiment in progress. Some animals were desperately listless, others grossly obese. In the nursery cages some animals lay pregnant whilst others were nursing tiny pink litters amongst the straw. Helen didn't mind the rabbits but the rats made her nervous. "I don't know what I'd do if one escaped," she said. "You wouldn't want to be bitten by one."

"This one's absolutely desperate," Eric said, watching a rabbit sucking furiously at the tube of a water bottle.

"Something to do with its condition," Helen replied.

They finished in an hour. The animals were clean and both sheds had been fed and watered until Monday when the laboratory staff returned. Eric watched as Helen locked the doors securely behind them. "We never go in that one." He indicated a third shed behind them.

Suddenly Helen became wary, speaking of things forbidden. "Nobody's allowed in there," she said, "It's… It's to do with our work, up at the lab."

Eric's interest was aroused. "Really? What is it?"

315

"The professor regards it as his own private domain." She studied the bunch of keys in her hand. "I don't even know if I can get in. This one's for shed number one, this is shed two, that's the lab where I work, this one's..." Helen counted them off until she reached an unidentified key. "I'm not sure about this one..." Helen inserted the key gingerly, the lock turned and she hesitated. "Would you really like to see? Only you must promise not to tell anybody." She glanced around but they were alone and they stepped inside quickly and Helen closed the door behind them.

The shed was filled with large blue plastic barrels and a smell in the atmosphere that made their nostrils twitch. Eric suppressed a sneeze as Helen loosened the toggle on the locking ring of the nearest barrel and lifted the lid off. The odour immediately became stronger and Eric peered inside. It was filled with plastic bags floating in formaldehyde and inside each bag, pale and deeply creased, a human brain, the spinal cord still attached trailing deep into the liquid.

"Babies," Helen said.

"Babies?" Eric looked with dreadful fascination, seeking recognition as she read the label.

"This drum is the Hydrocaphs." Helen replaced the lid and snapped the locking ring securely closed. Eric turned to look at the other drums around them and felt a tightening sensation round his heart. "Better go." Helen switched off the light before opening the door and they walked away, feeling guilty and grateful for fresh air. "They're used in... one of the projects." It was the Holy Grail of research. "You must never tell anybody Eric," she entreated him.

"What do their parents say?"

"I shouldn't think they know. They're delivered to the professor following autopsy. He's got to keep them somewhere Eric," Helen protested.

"So... what have the parents buried?"

"I don't know," Helen replied awkwardly. "Whatever's..." but his question was unanswerable.

They walked on in silence as Eric tried to unscramble the incoherent thoughts jostling in his head. Children taken and stored in spirit; the deception of grieving parents; there was something about it he couldn't reconcile himself to. And his Helen was somehow complicit in the deception. He wished she hadn't shown him. They paused as they reached the car and Helen took his arm and turned him to face her. "I'm sorry Eric. I didn't mean to upset you."

"I'm not upset Hel. It's just… I'd no idea."

Helen regarded him earnestly. "They're trying to find the causes of disease and disfigurement. Think about what it means; it would save thousands of baby's lives if they could. The children are already dead Eric, they're not hurt in any way," Helen pleaded. And she saw the look of accusation in Eric's eyes as he wrestled with another thought, 'Is this where our child was brought?' He unlocked the car and Helen looked across the car roof at him with a final attempt at justification. "You'd get used to it Eric; yes, even you. You'd have to, just as they have had to. They don't regard them as babies but they're not monsters. They see them as, well, just as tissue." She hesitated. "They don't even refer to them as babies; you've seen them, seen how they are preserved. They call them toffee apples. It's a sort of self-defence mechanism Eric. You have to be that disinterested."

"Toffee apples?! Oh Jesus Christ Hel, who thought that one up?"

Back to Ireland. Eric was driving north to one of his major customers in Dundalk on the Ulster border. He normally arrived in time to do his business and have lunch in the company dining room before driving back through Drogheda to Dublin. But his plane had been delayed and Eric was late for his appointment. He hurried through the lawns and over the landscaped stream. The girls on the desk looked up with a smile. "Hello Mr. Allenby. You're later than usual today. Peter waited for you but then he had to go to a meeting." She saw his disappointment. "But he says he can see you after lunch."

Eric smiled with relief. "Thank you. I'll see you in about an hour then." He drove slowly from the car park. There was a hotel out on the Dublin road but the entrance was shielded from car bombs by a necklace of oil barrels filled with concrete strung around the door.

317

Eric decided the town centre would be better and headed in towards Dundalk instead.

The bar on the street corner had once been bright red but that had long begun to fade and the interior with its worn counter and polished overhead shelf retained the memories of a hard drinking past. Beneath the opaque window, frosted and etched with brewers' insignia, a long horsehair bench running the length of the wall was occupied by three or four drinking men at a table. Eric nodded a brief acknowledgement to the watching eyes and turned to the bar. "A pint of Guinness please." The sound of his voice, an English stranger's voice caused a drop in the quiet conversation. Eric watched the slow ritual of the Guinness with anticipation as the stout began to settle and the publican went off to serve the man who had followed him in standing some distance away along the bar. Then the publican returned, topped up Eric's glass, skimmed off the excess froth with a spatula and handed it to Eric.

"Do you have ham sandwiches?" Eric asked.

"No sir."

Eric pondered briefly. "Cheese?"

"I have no sandwiches sir."

The low conversation behind him fell to silence and Eric, poised to take his first drink indicated the board on the wall. "Well, anything..."

Eric saw the publican's eyes flick past his shoulder and, "I cannot serve you sir," the man said softly. His impassive eyes met Eric's and Eric's mouth became dry; he looked at the drink in the glass in his hand and saw assent in the publican's eyes then the publican moved away and began washing glasses, paying Eric no further attention.

Eric squared his back and began to sip, carefully and steadily, not rushing, listening to the murmurs behind him, waiting for the sudden pause, the scrape of a table leg, a chair being moved. After five fearful minutes the blessed glass was empty. He placed it on the counter and walked stiffly out of the bar, his back prickling with intense awareness. He reached the car without looking round, felt for his keys with shaking hands and drove to Dublin. He telephoned

318

Peter in Dundalk from his hotel, pleaded a prior appointment then he sat in his room for the afternoon and promised himself a good meal in the hotel restaurant to make up for it.

It was an aberration, that's all it was. He shouldn't have gone there. Stick to the well-worn path and it would be alright; it had been alright for the past two years; more than two years now. And so, Eric decided, he must say nothing to Helen and carry on. She had become reconciled to it, bolstered by Eric's reassurances. And he still had a job to do and his reputation to build. Three more days in Dublin.

He flew back to Manchester and a welcome return to the normality of home, friends, singing and rehearsing with Helen. Back to the people and the customs he knew. Sitting in the comforting familiarity of his car a deep sense of weariness overcame him and he drove home, crossing the Snake in deepening twilight.

"How was it?" Helen asked, busying herself with Eric's supper.

"Very good," Eric replied from the armchair in the lounge. "I'm getting another major customer soon, the way things are looking."

"Oh, that's good. I've done you something light." Helen appeared at the door. "Is Welsh rarebit ok? I assumed you'd have something at Dublin as usual."

Eric smiled. "Yes. That's fine."

"Do you want it on your knee or are you coming to the table?"

"Here please Hel. I'm a bit tired."

She brought the tray through and studied him. "You alright Eric?" He seemed drained.

"Fine," he protested, "I'm fine Hel, fine. Just a bit tired."

Helen curled at Eric's feet and began talking of inconsequential things. "You know I said I thought there was something going on at the operatic? Well, you'll never guess. Desmond's resigned and Marlene's left Jim."

Eric tried to register interest in what she was saying and shrugged, "I suppose it was bound to happen."

Helen continued doggedly, "We all thought it was strange when neither of them turned up for rehearsal."

"Who?"

"Jim and Marlene."

"Oh. So what's happened?"

"As far as we know they've run off together."

"Who?"

Helen's eyes sparkled with a 'you'll never guess expression' and she repeated, "Desmond."

"So who's resigned then?"

Helen sighed in exasperation. "Eric! Desmond! Marlene's run off with Desmond."

"I didn't even know they were seeing each other."

"Nobody knew. They kept it very quiet. They reckon it started when Marlene began having private rehearsals with him." Helen laughed scornfully. "Private rehearsals! Well now they've run off together. Left his wife with both of the kids. Fancy being left like that."

"I wouldn't have believed it."

"You sure you're alright Eric?"

"Sorry Hel. Just a bit tired. It was a... strenuous trip. Been overdoing things a bit I think." He smiled wearily. "We'll have an early night eh?"

Helen took Eric's plate into the kitchen, beset by divided loyalties. It was three years since the split with Rita and now she was faced with another choice. She sought reassurance from Eric. "I mean, you can't be loyal to both sides can you."

"Do we have to take sides?" Eric asked.

"It wouldn't be fair to Jim. If we kept seeing Marlene and Desmond it would be like condoning it. I don't see how we can." Helen compressed her lips in regret. "I just wish... Why can't things stay like they used to be..?"

But the condemnation of Marlene and Desmond was widespread. "I mean," the gossipers said, "that Desmond wasn't all that to look at was he? Overweight and not particularly handsome."

"He was good company though," someone said by way of compensation but even that was turned against him.

"Yes, well, you can see why she was attracted then can't you." Sniff. "Just for the good time!"

"There'll soon be nobody left in the society," Eric said. "Old Max was the producer all those years and now we'll have had two in almost as many years. What with Rita, now Jim and Marlene…"

"Oh we think Jim's coming back. But you're right. When you think about it…"

Chapter 40 – Kismet

But there had been no premeditation. Desmond knew nothing of Marlene's unhappiness and it had been triggered quite innocently and unexpectedly. "You seem a bit tense Marlene," Desmond had said after Marlene's first tentative rehearsal in the part of the siren 'Lalume' but Marlene had shrugged off Desmond's suggestion of coaching her away from onlookers; she didn't mind rehearsing in public; she was an experienced actress. But Desmond had suggested the extra rehearsal, "… to get the characterisation of Lalume out of the way so that I can concentrate on the others." So, for the good of the society and because she was a trouper… just so long as he wasn't going to waste her time.

Marlene tried but she was trying too hard and after twenty-five minutes she glanced at her watch in frustration. "Look," Desmond said, "come here, try to relax a bit more. Like this." He reclined across the two chairs in a provocative pose, apologising for his ungainliness and then moved self-consciously across the floor in the way a seductive woman like Lalume might move. "Now you do it Marlene, just like that, then walk towards me." Marlene started towards him with no more intent than to get the characterisation right and then go home. "And then he'll take you in his arms and kiss you," Desmond said and in the sudden hiatus Desmond put his hands on Marlene's shoulders and kissed her. "There. Like that." He blushed and hastily added, "Sorry. Anyway I think that's it, you'll be great Marlene. I think we'll call it a draw for this evening." But neither of them moved and Marlene looked at him with an expression of sad understanding.

They told themselves it was the innocence of newly discovered friendship and arranged to meet for dinner at a village pub in the Hope Valley and within the week they became lovers in a highly charged consummation in the dark against a drystone wall a hundred yards from the car park in the lee of a disused barn and emerged panting and revelling in their mutual rediscovery of lust. Desmond's eyes were shining and the blood was coursing through his body while Marlene's satisfaction was enhanced by the elation of paying Jim back in his own kind. But the affaire could not continue in secret forever and when the secret began to leak they left to begin a new life together. And speculate as they might, no-one really knew the truth of it.

Alice had other concerns. After years lying dormant the swelling on Frank's shoulder suddenly began to grow with startling rapidity until it could be ignored no longer and Alice made him go to the doctor. She fretted alone until he returned, for he refused to let her accompany him, and her fears were confirmed. "It's your father," she said to Helen with the anger of desperation. "I told him to go but he wouldn't. You know what he's like! Now..." Alice bit her lip. "Well I only hope he's not left it too late." She snuffled and rearranged ornaments on the mantelpiece. "I wish he'd gone years ago," she muttered.

"It might not be anything mum," Helen said bravely, denying what intuition had already told her. The stupid part of it was, Frank still appeared strong and robust but they took him into hospital anyway and did what they could to trace the extent of it and suddenly Helen was reporting, "I don't like the look of my dad at all. He looks so...." She hesitated with the memory of Frank's grey pallor and the hollowness of pain in his cheeks.

"He's in the best place though isn't he." Alice sought reassurance in meaningless statements of hope.

"Course he is. Come on mum, Eric'll be back soon, he's only in Leeds today; I'll get him to run you home after tea. You are stopping aren't you?" adding before Alice could reply, "'Course you are. Here, come and sit down for a bit. I'll put us some music on."

The music soothed fear and brought respite and Alice began to relax in the recollection of her memories. "Oh 'Yeomen'. I did this in 1950 with Tom Blackwell. You won't remember, you were only a little girl then. He made a lovely Jack Point." Alice's eyes became faraway as she mouthed the words and the finger on her lap began to beat the time. "Ah, the spinning wheel. I used to love this song." Alice took refuge in the music, humming to herself while Helen went out to make tea and when she returned there was moisture in her mother's eye.

"Shall I take it off mum? Put something else on?"

"No," Alice said, "leave it on. This is one of your father's songs. Your father's always singing this." She closed her eyes, beating time, listening, but to which voice Helen didn't know, the voice on the tape or the voice of memory within her head, 'Attend to me, and shed a tear or two. I have a song to sing – O.' A chorus rose in soft reply, 'Sing me your song - O,' and as the gentle harmony died away the voice sang to her alone:

> 'It is sung to the moon
> By a lovelorn loon,
> Who loved with a love lifelong - O
> The song of a Merryman and his maid...'

The song ended and Alice became still. Finally she sighed and said, "Lovely show, but not easy. Oh no. Not easy." And neither was Frank's passing. He lingered into spring, smiling at his visitors from his ashen face, quietly indomitable. "I'm going to bring him home," Alice said. "I can get a nurse to come and help me to look after him."

"Do you think you should mum?"

"Why not? He'll not be left to himself, just lying in bed for hours on end."

"It'd be a lot for you to take on," they cautioned and Alice bridled.

"I took it on years ago, the day I married him. 'For better, for worse; for richer or poorer; in sickness and in health,'" and Helen braced herself. It was going to take more than zeal and her mother's determination to care for her father as he should be cared for, as she would wish him to be cared for. They went with Alice to tell Frank of her plan and sitting round him it seemed, as they listened to his voice, that Frank was holding his own. "It would be a shame to move him now," Alice declared as they turned and waved from the door. "Just when he seems to be looking better."

Four days later Frank died.

"It was very peaceful Mrs. Crawford. The night nurse was with him. He just went to sleep."

"He wasn't in any pain was he?"

The nurse gave a sad, brave, comforting smile. "No. He was just as you left him earlier. He seemed quite content."

"Yes," Alice replied, "that was Frank. He was a very contented man. I've been a very lucky woman."

The service for Frank was simple. "A cremation," Alice instructed. "He wasn't a religious man but he liked nice music. I want something nice for him; can I choose? I'd like that piece from Peer Gynt. Ase's Death. He liked that."

After the service Helen stood with her mother as the mourners filed out with their murmurs of sympathy and suddenly she found herself facing Rita.

"I'm sorry Hel," Rita began nervously. "Hope you don't mind. I saw it in the paper."

Helen's lip started to tremble. "Rita…" She began to cry and felt the touch of Rita's hand on her shoulder and said, "Are you coming back Reet?"

"Well I…"

"I think I'd like you to. If you've got the time."

The people behind began to press and Rita said, "Thanks Hel. I'm so sorry. I… I can't." She hesitated and began to walk away. "Tell your mum for me. I always liked your dad."

Helen's deep sense of loss was heightened by the unexpected encounter with Rita and she grieved over memories of their happy times together. "Are you sure you're alright Hel?" Eric asked.

"I didn't think I'd miss him so much. He's just… gone. There's no memorial, not even a plaque. Not like your Granddad; you can go and visit his grave and there's something tangible about it." Helen's logic ignored the fact that the unkempt mound of earth where Eric's granddad lay hadn't been visited for years. But at least it was there…

One evening Alice unexpectedly confided, "I say 'goodnight' to your father every night."

Helen gave her mother a smile of understanding.

"I keep his ashes down in his workshop," Alice continued, "and I go to the top of the cellar steps and say goodnight to him."

The smile on Helen's mouth died. "I didn't know you'd got his ashes."

"They're in a little urn. I keep it by his lathe."

"In the cellar?" Helen protested. "Why not…" she hesitated, "in the spare bedroom. Or even your bedroom? You could keep it on the dressing table."

"I wouldn't want him in the room, not at night, not when I'm asleep." Alice's fear of the dark was like a child's. "Anyway that's where he spent most of his time."

There was something brooding and Gothic about the nightly ritual her mother was going through and to her own surprise Helen said, "Can I…? Can I see it mum… see them?"

"Whatever for?"

"Oh, I don't know. I miss him. Just… I want to say my own goodbye I suppose."

"I'll take you down next time you come to visit."

The dark in the cellar was total blackness. Eric lowered his head and felt along the ceiling joist for the light switch. It was as he remembered; metal racks and shelves carrying tools and small machine parts were ranged against the uneven whitewashed walls and a bulb on an extension cable drooped above the lathe. Frank's bench was littered with tools; two files, a scribing block; spring callipers; a centre punch and ball-pein engineer's hammer, all lying in a layer of iron filings. Below the bench were piles of ancient newspapers with Frank's pin-ups hidden amongst them. Alice pointed to a burgundy coloured plastic jar standing on the lathe bed. "I thought he would be happy here." She sighed with an air of resignation.

Helen's eyes travelled round the cellar, wondering at all the time her father had spent amongst this… clutter. Beneath the coal chute he had hoarded lengths of wood, hardboard panels, sheets of aluminium; brass and copper bars of varying length and diameter; a lifetime of careful husbandry, the accumulation of raw material for...? Helen sighed, Eric placed his hand on her arm and Helen sighed again. "What are you going to do with it all mum?"

"Nothing yet. It was your father's. I expect some day it will have to go. Anyway, I'll leave you for a minute. Come up when you're ready." She turned to leave. "You won't touch anything will you."

Helen shook her head sadly. "Don't worry mum. I just want to... have a few minutes alone. That's all."

Alice departed, thankful for the light, grateful to leave someone remaining behind her. Helen reached for the jar and Eric watched as she gazed at the coarse grey powder.

"Hel...?"

"I'm alright. Honest. I'll be alright."

"Do you really want to be alone?"

"Just for a couple of minutes. Do you mind?"

"You won't be long?"

"No," Helen answered quietly.

Eric paused at the foot of the steps. "Leave the light on when you come up Hel. I'll come and turn it off."

He left her to her meditations.

"Is she alright down there?" Alice asked.

Eric nodded. "She won't be long..."

He returned to the cellar and found Helen with her hands beneath her coat and a guilty expression. "Eric, don't think I'm being silly will you." She drew out a small plastic bag of grey ash from beneath her coat. "There's not a lot," she said. "My mum will never notice."

"Helen!"

"I want to scatter it somewhere. Somewhere where he'll be happy."

"Helen." Eric took it from her. "We can't make a shrine. I know how you feel love. But... Come here." He took Helen in his arms and held her close. "I wish I could feel about my dad the way you feel about yours."

"It's as though he's just been dismissed from our lives and forgotten," she said softly.

"Your mum's not forgotten him."

327

"No but I can't keep asking if I can come down the cellar can I?"

Later, at home, Eric glanced across at Helen but her thoughts were faraway. "You know," he said gently, "if you really want him to be happy, somewhere you could say goodbye to him properly, why don't we take them to Trearddur and scatter his ashes over the bay? He loved it there."

Sunday. A day for pottering in the garden, indulging themselves, relaxing and filling their minds with inconsequential things. Surveying the lawn and borders with a mug of tea in the comfortable morning air; brunch beneath the parasol; the arduous effort of going in for cold drinks.

Six fifteen and the long afternoon drawing to a close. They roused themselves and Helen said, "Salad, or do you want something cooked? I've got some lamb chops."

Eric replied lazily, "Just salad. On its own. I'll come and help you." He followed Helen inside to open a bottle of wine...

The heat of the day lingered into evening and they left the door and windows open and went back outside and reclined in carefree weariness in the garden with a last glass of wine as the daylight faded into dusk.

"I could drink the tap dry," Helen said, rising.

"I'll see what's on television," Eric said. They cleared the lawn and put the neglected tools away and went reluctantly indoors. "Why don't you make us a nice pot of coffee and I'll get you an Amaretto."

"That would be lovely," Helen replied. "With ice."

The sound of the percolator and the scent of roasted coffee drifted from the kitchen and Helen placed a tray with coffee cups and brown sugar and cream on the coffee table. "I thought we'd have the best china cups," she said, "and round the evening off properly. Something good on?"

Eric was standing with the liqueur bottle in his hand and he gestured her for quiet, his face creased in consternation. On the television a man was being interviewed, masked and in silhouette, speaking with a high pitched brogue and the twisted vowels of

Ulster. "I know him Hel." Eric turned to her. "Oh Hel. I know that voice."

The announcer was speaking with pride, bringing the interview to a close, "...prominent member of the INLA who, for legal reasons, must remain anonymous..."

Helen clutched at her breast. "You know him? Who is he?"

"I can't say," Eric replied, the words burning in his brain, INLA; a group with a reputation for ruthlessness and more unforgiving than the IRA. Eric's disquiet was betrayed in the softness of his voice. "I... I'm sure it's him." He looked with sudden distaste at the bottle in his hand; it was heavy, as heavy as the stout in the Dundalk bar and he put it down and as the programme ended he switched off the television and began to pace the room in silence, pondering and sifting the nuances of the voice. "Yes," he said, "I'm almost sure."

"But how? How do you know him?"

Eric turned, drained of all the vitality garnered from that carefree, happy day. "He's one of my customers. I... I see him from time to time."

"You've got to stop going there Eric."

"I know."

"Please. You're not to go across there any more."

"I know." Eric went into the hall and locked the front door. Helen closed the windows and drew the curtains then stood quietly listening while he spoke on the telephone to Ritchie.

Chapter 41 – Heartsease

The tension was evident in Eric's voice and he glanced at Helen before he spoke.

"Sorry to disturb you Ritchie."

"You must be keen, telephoning this time on a Sunday evening."

"Have you seen that programme that's just finished?"

"We're watching a film," Ritchie said.

"They were interviewing someone." Ritchie caught something in the inflection in Eric's voice and waited until Eric continued. "It... he was a member of the INLA."

"Really?"

"I can't be sure. But I think I know him."

"Who is it?"

"I can't tell you." There was a momentary pause. "It's a customer. Somebody I... have dealings with."

"You're not to make any more trips over there."

Eric's eyes closed in a brief prayer of relief and Helen choked back a sob of thanks. "I can't be absolutely certain Ritchie. It's just that you hear different things. I mean... I've been handing out my business card and it's got my home details on it and..." He stopped, conscious of Helen listening behind him.

"I've told you, I don't want you going over there again."

Eric offered on-going commitment. "I'll need to look after the business of course until you find my replacement. Then do the handover when you've appointed him."

"Is it just tonight or have you had any other occasion to be worried?"

"Well..." Eric checked himself. What could he say about Dundalk, that he'd been spooked before and was losing his nerve? Anyway that was months ago. "No. No, nothing."

Ritchie spoke with quiet perception. "I wish you'd said something to me before this Eric."

"I'm telling you now."

"No more trips," Ritchie insisted, "You've already done longer than the usual secondment."

Eric began to feel wretched. "I don't want to let anybody down Ritchie."

"You're not. You've done great. We should have replaced you before now; we would have done if you hadn't been making such a success of it."

"Thanks Ritchie."

"There is one thing."

"Yes."

"I need to know his name."

"Ritchie... I... I can't."

"I want his name. The company he's with."

"I can't Ritchie."

"Come on Eric."

"No. I can't. Suppose I'm wrong?"

"Eric, do you think we're going to go up to him and ask if he's a terrorist? Do you think we're going to go to his boss?" Ritchie's voice was cajoling. "So come on, which customer?"

"It's not that."

"What is it then?"

"If you knew you'd never be able to do business. He'd know you knew."

"Don't you think you owe it to the man taking over from you?"

"Ritchie I... I'm still not absolutely sure. Supposing I'm wrong? I can't tell you. I'm sorry, I'm not going to say."

There was a sigh of acquiescence. "You'd better bring your files and customer records to me. Come to the house? Not tomorrow." There was a pause then, "Wednesday. Eleven o'clock?"

"Thanks Ritchie."

"And no more contact. Not even on the phone. You understand?"

"I'll have to let them know Ritchie. It's only courtesy..."

"No more calls Eric." Ritchie was unyielding. "Leave it all to me from here."

"Alright Ritchie. Oh, and thanks. Sorry to disturb you." Eric replaced the handset quietly and turned to Helen. "That's it. I'm out. I feel as though I've let everybody down."

The affair hung over Eric like a cloud. He said to Helen, "I feel as if I've had to be rescued because I became frightened. Because I've failed in some way."

"Eric, you mustn't think that."

"But where do I go from here?" Ireland had been a career stepping-stone but instead of striding on to increased responsibility and status he'd lost his footing and slipped off and Eric castigated himself for his haste. Why hadn't he waited until Monday to allow the jitters to subside then said to Ritchie, 'Look Ritchie I've done my three years, what's next?' instead of having to be bailed out? Was this it? Was it all over in his mid-thirties? Slipping off the stone was bad enough but now he had fallen into a career backwater.

Summer returned with a final flurry in October; St. Luke's Little Summer but there was precious little opportunity to enjoy it. A persistent, disquieting rumour was running through the salesforce and Eric phoned the office. Tony answered cheerfully, "You've heard then."

"Is it true?"

"Yes. Reeder's moving on. Eastern Region are throwing their hats in the air."

"Where's he going? Not leaving is he?"

"No." Tony paused for effect. "He's coming south."

"What?"

"Southern Region Sales manager. Harry Dartford's resigned."

Eric was incredulous. Southern Region was a career springboard; Bill Ronson had once had charge of it and he'd gone on to become head of marketing. Eric's mind went into overdrive; now there was a vacancy in the East. "I'd better draft out my application," he said.

"What? For the East? Shouldn't bother. John James has got it."

"James?! But he's only just out of college."

"You should worry. We've got Reeder for our sins." Tony's voice changed. "He's just walked in," he whispered, "up the far end of the office." His voice rose artificially in greeting. "So, Mr. Allenby, what can I do for you this fine morning…?"

Eric made two more calls and then went to the lab to see if Helen was free.

"You hadn't got anything planned for lunchtime had you?"

"Why, no," Helen replied, "I thought you were in Leeds."

"Change of plan. I'd rather spend it with you."

They drove to an old stone pub on the outskirts of the city where farmland surrendered to the moors and sat in the cold solitude of the bar.

"But surely they wouldn't promote him if he wasn't any good," Helen said. "They wouldn't promote just anybody."

"Wouldn't they!" Eric replied. "You don't know him Helen. James is all mouth, full of himself. It's always them that gets on. If I had to apply for my own job I wouldn't get it now." His mood was made worse because the opportunity had been denied him. "They never even advertised it," he complained bitterly.

"You're too modest Eric, that's your trouble."

Eric didn't answer. The truth of Helen's observation hurt more than he could say. He had clung to the naive belief that merit would bring its own reward and promotion would come in due course. Now he realised opportunities did not come to those who wait and soon it would be too late. Eric gazed outside in silence. The day was bright but the ancient pub was cheerless, devoid of comfort in its isolation. The beer was cold and thin and he needed to visit the toilet again. "Better get back I suppose." He stood and said, "Are you bothered about coffee?"

Helen shook her head, musing as he disappeared, 'I wish you could get the recognition you deserve.'

They left the inn and Eric drove with no sense of purpose until their wandering brought them to the Surprise View at the edge of the plateau. "Come on," he said irritably, "I want some air," as he swung into the car park.

"I'm not dressed for walking," Helen protested, glancing at her watch. "I really ought to be…"

"Not far," Eric said. "Just over there. Just to look at the view."

333

They crossed the road and he led the way along a narrow sheep path through heather and fern growing tall amongst boulders and slabs of rock. "It's not good for you," Helen said, "being like this. If that's the way you feel you ought to tell them."

"You just don't understand." Eric's voice was bitter with disappointment. "It doesn't work like that."

"Why not? If you're a good salesman..."

They reached the edge, the outcrop dropped away and they stood overlooking the valley. "That's the trouble." He spoke through gritted teeth. "If you're a good salesman that's where they want to keep you! Out in the field, selling." Below them the River Derwent meandered through rich farmlands and Eric stretched his arms wide, embracing the air blowing from the Pennines rising on the distant horizon. It was clean and scented with nature, the scent of grass and earth. A line from 'Ruddigore' came to him; 'You must strut it and stump it and blow your own trumpet, or believe me you haven't a chance.' It all sounded so naively simple... It just needed resolve. Did he still have enough credibility? Eric faltered. He didn't want to set himself up for another fall. And then another old saw from some poem or other entered his thoughts: 'Faint Heart never won Fair Lady,' and the confusions in his mind started to clear. Unexpectedly he put his arm round Helen and hugged her. "You are right love," he said and his depression began to lift. "I'm going to talk to Bill Ronson this afternoon."

Helen turned her face to his, happy at his change of mood and they kissed and stood for long moments together like lovers silhouetted against the landscape.

A cold December wind was whipping across the deserted city-centre square swirling scraps of dry litter around the base of the old king's statue. Sallow lamplight did little to relieve the early darkness, only adding to the air of desolation and Eric wrapped his overcoat round him and pulled his gloves from his pocket. It was Eric's regular evening pilgrimage; when he missed the local collection he drove into the city and posted his day's reports at the sorting office. He strode briskly to the ancient steps in the corner of the square and

334

descended into the dark street below. A figure detached itself from the shadow round the statue's plinth and followed him into the darkness.

At the far end of the street, beyond the Post Office building the deserted bus station glowed like a film set. A handful of travellers stamping their feet against the cold added to the sense of isolation, accentuating the darkness where Eric was standing. He checked the address one last time and as he posted the letter he heard his name spoken. Eric turned warily; across the road a figure was standing in the shadows. "Rob!" Eric shook his head with a grin of incredulous relief.

He surveyed Rob carefully. His features had a pinched, weaselly look. His dark, slicked back hair was thin, in the first stages of baldness and there were creases in his face, deep folds in his cheeks and beside his mouth that hadn't been there before. He looked old and worn. His jacket collar was turned up against the cold and his hands were thrust deep in his jacket pockets and hunching up his shoulders Rob gave Eric the old, devil-may-care smile. "It's been a few years hasn't it?"

"A few, yes," Eric replied cautiously.

"Anyway how are you doing?" Rob stepped forward, appraising Eric. "You look alright."

Eric shrugged. "Still a salesman. Well actually I'm..." He was about to launch into his recent meetings with Bill Ronson and Ritchie but he couldn't, not to the man standing before him. "Well," he said, "with a different firm though."

Rob nodded, a jerky movement to disguise his shivering and convey understanding but Eric saw the insecurity in Rob's eyes as Rob began to edge towards a face saving departure. "I thought it was you. Anyway..."

"What about you Rob?"

"Oh," a flash of the old bravado. "Been working abroad. Just got back from Germany. In time for Christmas." He nodded at Eric. "Good job then?" his nod inviting approval.

"Look... fancy a pint Rob? Queen's Head's just round the corner. I were going to pop in for one." Eric tried not to sound too magnanimous. "Come on. For old time's sake...?"

"Well... Yeah. Why not? Too cold to stand out here chatting..."

It was almost eleven o'clock when Eric returned home. Helen greeted him with surprise and mild disapproval. "Thought you'd got lost."

Eric threw his overcoat over the banister rail in the hall. "You'll never guess who I met." His voice was weary with pity. "Rob," he said quietly.

"Rob? How is he?"

Eric pursed his lips. "He's er... Having a bit of a struggle. I took him for a drink." He stood before the fire warming and rubbing his hands.

"Where did you go?"

"Queen's Head. In town."

"So what's he doing now?"

"Says he's been working in Germany. How marvellous it is over there, miracle economy and all that. Back home for Christmas with the family." Eric sighed. "He asked me for a loan. Said his wages were coming but they hadn't arrived yet and gave me some cock and bull story about exchange controls... You know what he's like Hel. I bought him a couple of drinks and lent him a fiver."

"You won't see it again."

"I know. He's just out of prison. You can tell. Just by looking at him."

"Where's he living now?" Helen's glance flickered towards the door.

"Don't know. Said he was going home to this girl he lives with. I reckon he's at his mother's." Eric gazed into the fire. "He was asking about the kids."

"Whatever did you tell him?"

"What could I say?" Eric made a small deprecating movement, "I just said Rita had moved in with somebody and they'd been together for a year or two and left it at that." There was a moment's reflection. "He never mentioned Rita at all." Eric shook his head

336

slowly. "It's such a shame about the kids though. He thought the world of them."

Eric's four words struck deep into Helen's conscience. 'He never mentioned Rita.' She never mentioned Rita either and Helen recalled her shock seeing Rita at her father's funeral and Rita's refusal of her invitation. At least Eric had taken Rob for a drink but between her and Rita it was all strangely unfinished. She had said her piece to Rita on the steps of the City Hall and felt justified in doing so and yet, her first reaction on seeing Rita again was... she couldn't deny it... pleasure followed by disappointment at not being able to see her. Helen felt so confused. 'Let those who are without sin cast the first stone.' She couldn't reconcile the words to her feelings but a profound sense of disappointment lay within her. And so, a few days later Helen made up her mind, took an afternoon off work and hoped Gerry would not be at home.

Walking along the avenue towards the house Helen felt a strange sense of isolation. She and Eric had once been familiar figures; now she felt like a stranger, as if eyes were watching. Just so long as Rita wasn't watching as well. She looked for changes but it was as she remembered; the neat garden, the small wrought-iron gate clanking loud in the silence of afternoon. Helen rang the bell with trepidation and felt a rising sense of relief when there was no immediate answer. A moment's indecision; to ring again or leave quickly? The door opened and Rita stood before her.

"Oh! - Helen."

"Hello Rita."

Rita gathered her composure. "Come in. Please, come on in." She raised her hand to the side of her head as though catching at stray hair and stood aside. "Is Eric...?"

"No. No he's at work. Gerry...?"

"No." Rita followed Helen into the sitting room. "Just me, you've caught me all alone."

The room was different; Rita had established her personality in the informal way the furniture was arranged and in the subtle colouring of the walls. It was less spartan, less precise. "You've got it done nicely," Helen said and Rita gestured her to an easy chair and sat on the settee with the polished walnut coffee table between them. "Is Susan…?" Helen began, glancing quickly around. Nothing in the room betrayed the presence of a child.

"She's at school."

"Of course. School? Time flies." Helen winced inwardly.

"She's just started."

The looming silence built on their awkwardness and Rita said, "I'll make us a cup of coffee. You are staying for a bit aren't you?"

"If… that's alright."

Rita went to the kitchen leaving Helen with her thoughts. She didn't know what she had expected. The house was comfortable and Rita looked settled. If anything she had lost weight but…

"Won't be long," Rita said resuming her seat. "Well, how are you and Eric?"

"Oh fine," Helen replied. "We think he's in line for a promotion. He's been working in Ireland. But that's finished," she added quickly, closing that line of conversation off.

"You must be relieved."

Helen gave a shrug. "We are a bit. How about you and Gerry?"

"Yes," Rita nodded and completed her affirmation with a bright, silent smile.

Helen let her eyes wander about the room. "I er, like how you've got it Reet."

"It needed a woman's touch. He'd been living on his own for too long."

"And Susan?"

"Yes, she's fine."

Helen took the plunge. "Do you ever see anything of…?"

"Oh there's the kettle," Rita said rising to her feet. "Shan't be a minute."

This was terrible. Why ever had she come? She remembered how it used to be between them and now she'd got to stay and drink coffee. "Do you want a hand Reet," she called.

"No I'm alright. Shan't be a minute."

Helen sat upright against the cushions, unable to relax, a stranger listening to the sounds coming from the kitchen until Rita arrived with a tray. "I've brought us some biscuits. You're not on a diet or anything are you?" Helen shook her head with a weak smile. "Help yourself to milk and sugar Hel."

Helen poured milk with the rigour of politeness and refused the sugar bowl. "Mmm. Nice," she said with the relief that the small activity brought her.

Rita reclined against the arm of the settee. "So, what brings you here after all this time Hel?"

"Oh Rita. I don't know. I've just been thinking about things lately and..." She sighed. "I wanted to say thanks for coming to the funeral. It would have been nice if you could have stayed on for a bit." Rita said nothing and sipped from her cup. "I just wondered..." Helen continued desperately, "you know... if you were OK. You and Gerry. No particular reason," she added hastily. "It's just been such a long time..."

"Yes."

There was no regret in Rita's voice and again Helen's heart sank. This wasn't the Rita she remembered, this was a woman who had turned her back on her past, a new, self sufficient woman whose life had taken another direction. It was no good Helen decided; she would just have to say how she felt, try to explain her feelings without any criticism or censure and then leave. Helen put her coffee on the table and said, "Eric bumped into Rob a little while ago." Rita's expression froze into immobility. "He didn't say much. In fact Eric said he never mentioned you."

"The feeling's mutual."

"Oh Rita. I've not come to stir anything up or interfere. That's the last thing I'd do. We were always good friends."

"It's not my fault..."

"How can you say that Reet...?"

"You said some pretty awful..."

"Rita." Helen's voice was a sharp appeal. "I only said what I felt for those boys. How do you think we felt when Gerry dumped them on us and told us you'd run off and..." Helen checked herself. She was going too far and she didn't want to get into all that again. What was done was done. "It's just that Rob was asking after them." Rita remained withdrawn and silent. "Eric told him you'd met somebody and you were all..." it took Helen an effort to say it, "happy together."

The defensive air surrounding Rita weakened. "Thanks for that anyway." A sudden look of alarm passed over her face. "He didn't tell him where I am...?"

Helen shook her head. "No. I doubt if we'll see him again. But we've not heard anything of the boys. We saw your mother a couple of times but... You lose touch."

Rita finished her coffee in silence then held her hand out for Helen's cup. "Would you like another? There's some left. I'm having one."

Helen nodded. "Yes. Thanks Rita. That would be nice."

Rita fetched the cafetière from the kitchen and placed it on the table between them. "I don't expect anybody to understand," she said at last.

"I've not come to sit in judgement Rita."

"You don't know what it was like. Gerry is a very intelligent, sensitive man. After Rob, I didn't think I was going to find anybody else, not with three children. But – we hit it off together. He's never had children of his own but that didn't seem to matter. He was looking forward to being a family man. He joked and said he wouldn't have to go through all that pacing about with all the other expectant fathers. It was a new life for me Helen, especially after all I'd been through with Rob. You know that, you must surely understand." Helen nodded and Rita continued, "And it was alright, everything was alright. Sex between us was – is – wonderful. I saw myself turning into a frustrated old maid and then Gerry came along and it's as if we'd both discovered it again. The fact that I'd already got children didn't seem to matter. That wasn't the issue. He... he'd been alone for a long time and for a while I wasn't sure that it would work, not with four of us barging into his life. But we discovered something wonderful. I could begin having intelligent conversations again. Suddenly life was stimulating." Helen tried to reconcile the Gerry that Rita was describing to the taciturn man she had met, the man Eric described as the boring moron yet here was Rita protesting

Gerry's intellectual virtues. "The kids liked him. We were all getting along famously." Rita paused then heaved a sigh and poured herself more coffee. "We were all going to be happy together."

"You don't have to tell me if you don't want to Rita."

There was unexpected bitterness in Rita's reply. "It's what you came for isn't it?"

"No I…" Helen protested. "I don't know what I came for. I just wanted to see you, that's all."

"Anyway," Rita sighed again and tried to draw herself together. "You might as well know. We were alright at first." Rita's brow furrowed and her breast was heaving. "He wanted them to regard him as their daddy that was all. Just to call him daddy. But they wouldn't."

"It must have been difficult for them," Helen murmured.

"How do you think it was for Gerry? In his own house, the home he'd decided to share with us? They didn't call him anything! At first, when they were first introduced they used to call him Uncle Gerry but once we'd moved in together he said it wasn't right. And it wasn't Helen, it wasn't right," Rita insisted earnestly. "He wanted to be their daddy." Helen reached for the cafetiere but it was cold and she withdrew her hand and waited. "It became an issue," Rita continued. "'They must call me daddy,' he said. 'I'm not having them talking to me as if I'm nobody, just here to provide meals and a bed for somebody else's kids. I've given them my home!' You can see, can't you Hel? It was starting to come between us." Rita paused, her hand smoothing the stray hair at her temple, recalling memories from the distance then she looked at Helen again. "It went on for ages, this… this attrition between Gerry and the kids. And I started to feel I was prostituting myself for them. Every time he wanted to make love I was thinking, what am I doing it for? Your mind begins to play tricks."

"But he understood surely? You've just said, he's an intelligent man. They're only children."

"We're not all the same Helen. Gerry's wonderful but after his wife left him he got used to having things his way. Those were his rules."

"So…"

"Susan was alright. She wasn't old enough to know the difference. She's always called him daddy." Helen pursed her lips in silence. Finally Rita said, "Anyway I knew my mother wouldn't see them taken into care."

"But what about Gerry's mother? Couldn't she have helped?"

"I thought you knew. She committed suicide. Years ago, when Gerry was a little boy."

"Suicide!"

"She gassed herself. Gerry found her."

"Oh Rita! I'm so sorry Rita. I don't know what to say."

"I'm sorry too Helen. I didn't want to…" Rita checked herself. "Perhaps you had a right to know. I don't suppose it makes it right in your eyes but," she closed her eyes, "well, there it is. Sometimes you have to…" Rita opened her eyes to Helen's censure but there was none. "Anyway," Rita began to stir from the settee, "coffee's gone cold. Would you like another?"

"I really think I ought… Well if you're having one then." Helen accompanied Rita into the kitchen and they rinsed the cups and drained the pot and replenished it together. "What about Antony and Raymond?" Helen asked. "Do you see them?"

"Of course I see them," Rita said but her indignation was muted. "My mother was…" Rita shook the memory from her head. "It was understandable I suppose. She's alright now though. I go to see the boys. They won't come here. I have to go alone. My mother won't have Gerry in the house."

"And you and… Gerry?"

Rita's smile was a little too forced. "We're fine. He has his moments sometimes but… No we're OK."

Helen sought justification for Rita and tried to blame Gerry for coercing her but Rita would not allow it and refused the olive branch Helen offered saying, "It wasn't just Gerry's idea."

Helen shook her head disconsolately. "I don't think I'll ever understand it Rita."

"No, I don't expect you will," Rita responded. "Your life has always been so calm and placid."

"Oh I wouldn't say that. We've had our moments too."

"Yes…" Rita said wryly, "Well. But Gerry's not as bad as you all make him out to be. Anyway." She glanced meaningfully at the clock on the wall.

They agreed to meet again but the thaw was still not complete. Helen had hoped to begin their friendship anew but now she wasn't sure. After the unexpected intimacy Rita's mood was defensive beneath a superficial air of bright 'new woman' independence. It was difficult to define; no-one was more loyal than Helen was to Eric but there was an intensity about Rita's relationship with Gerry that made Helen uncomfortable; it was as if she were being subjected to a new doctrine. And then Rita telephoned and put Helen off; she 'couldn't make it this week.' But two days later she telephoned again and suggested lunch at 'The Shack'. "It'll be just like old times," she said.

There was a strained look about Rita when she walked in. It was evident in Rita's pale complexion under the carefully applied makeup.

They engaged in small talk, re-establishing the ground between them until drinks and their salads arrived.

"You know," Helen said, "The last time we were here, I think that was the time you told me about that fellow who used to call on you. You remember, him with the dog?"

"Oh I remember," Rita said. "You know, it's amazing how things like that can happen and you survive them. You put them behind you and move on, get on with your life. But at the time it was awful."

"I know. I couldn't believe it. Who would have thought that Rob…"

Rita's eyes took on a faraway look. "They're all the same really," she said.

"Eric's not like that."

"You're lucky then." Rita pulled herself up sharply. "Sorry Helen, daydreaming."

Helen leaned across the table to her and kept her voice low and intimate. "You alright Reet?"

"You don't want to know." But then she raised her head and flashed a smile and protested, "Of course I'm alright."

"How's the boys? Still not coming to the house I suppose."

The sound of scraping chairs announced the departure of the couple at the next table and Rita pushed her fork round the residue of salad in the small dish. "Mum's having some trouble with them. They're talking about taking Raymond into care," Rita said softly. "He's been... He's..." She gave a helpless sigh. "He's stealing things. From the neighbours. They've had to have the police. And he gets so violent! He goes around the house, smashing things and swearing... and..." Rita exerted another effort at self-control. "Sorry Hel, I don't know why I'm telling you."

"It's alright. I'm sorry Reet. You have to tell somebody."

"He's still only a little boy really." There were tears in Rita's voice.

"How is your mother...?"

"I know it sounds awful but..."

"Is it Gerry? It's Gerry isn't it?"

Rita made no response.

"What about Antony?"

"Oh he seems to be coping," Rita replied through her misery. "He's very quiet. He doesn't say anything. I don't know how my mother would cope if they both went..."

"And doesn't Gerry see? Surely... Doesn't he want to help? They're your children after all. If he loves you I would have thought..."

"Oh you just don't understand," Rita cried suddenly and she looked round sharply in case her outburst had attracted attention. "You've no idea," she added softly.

"What is it Reet?"

Rita drew a deep breath. Oh what the hell, she'd already said more than she'd intended. "He has these fixed ideas. Nothing must... must come into his life that he doesn't approve of. He won't have the boys. And if I push him too far..." Rita pulled herself up sharply and Helen saw something else in Rita's eyes, something that must remain unspoken.

"He's not mistreating you is he?" Helen asked gently.

Rita's voice rose in a challenge. "How do you mean?"

"Well..."

"What are you saying?" Rita cried and she looked around again.

"Well, just, listening to you it..."

"You've no right to..." Rita's voice tailed off. "Anyway every man does," she continued helplessly. "I dare say Eric..."

Helen remained silent. It was all a façade; somewhere beneath it was the real Rita, her friend of all those years. But Rita drew another breath and composed herself and raised her wrist to check the time and, examining herself discreetly in the mirror from her handbag she applied another touch of lipstick, "Anyway I'd better be off. It's been nice Helen. Almost like old times. Only I've got to get something for Gerry's tea."

"Reet?"

There was something compelling in Helen's tone and Rita sat back heavily in her chair. "Look Hel," she said, "I've got too much to lose. I know what you're thinking but don't. I love him. He loves me and... and I've got Susan to think of." She turned away abruptly and glanced round the room. "Anyway. How much was it? Have we had the bill yet?"

"I'll get it." Helen cast an expectant look at Rita and smiled. "You can get it next week."

Rita hesitated and bit her lip, then she nodded and this time her smile had nothing hidden behind it except... gratitude. "Yes. Alright Hel. Next week. Oh – and thanks."

For Rita their restored friendship was an overwhelming and unexpected relief. There were no recriminations. Helen was pleased to have her friend back and they began to meet regularly, making up for the time they had lost. But the friendship was confined to the two women alone. For although bright and overconfident in public, Rita was in conflict with her other self who lived a private life of stultifying wretchedness under the dominance and neat precision of Gerry.

But now Helen felt she could confide to Rita that Eric was in line for a promotion. He'd been on an external appraisal and flattering things had been said about him but as the weeks went by nothing happened.

"Never mind Hel," Rita said. "You're comfortable. Happy. What more do you want?"

"He's ambitious Reet. He keeps saying, 'just this last step, one more step and I've made it.'"

Rita shook her head. "The grass is always greener isn't it? Still, he tried Hel. He can't say he didn't try."

And then Eric got a call from Ritchie. Another restructuring. The company was growing and they were pleased that Eric had made his ambitions clearly known; it had focussed the boards' mind with regard to the next phase of the company's growth. But it would mean relocation. Perhaps he would like a couple of days to think about it, but they'd like to have his response by the end of the week.

"Who else is in the frame Ritchie?" Eric asked.

"Nobody. There's no-one else in the frame at the moment Eric."

Eric grasped it with both hands, determined not to let it slip into someone else's. "Take this as a provisional 'yes' Ritchie. I'll have to talk to Helen of course but I'll confirm it tomorrow."

Chapter 42 - Scotland the brave

Eric didn't know there were reservations about his appointment but they had begun to surface during his meeting with Bill Ronson in the autumn. "Men have usually made their first step into management well before this," Ronson said.

"Churchill was in the wilderness for years before he became Prime Minister," Eric parried. "He didn't get to be the Prime Minister until he was in his sixties."

"He'd held high office long before."

"I thought that's what my assignments were. Heading up the task force. And Ireland. They were key responsibilities weren't they?"

"Not man-management though."

Nevertheless Eric made an impression and Bill Ronson consulted with Ritchie and Andrew Brock; then confided his doubts to Sczelnick in Personnel.

"Get Anderson Barleymore to look at him," Sczelnick suggested.

"Do you have any idea the amount their rates have gone up this year?" Ronson said.

Sczelnick shrugged. "If you want to know the answer Bill, you've got to ask the question."

And the answer had confounded Bill Ronson's firmly held opinion and thrown his judgement into doubt for the first time since…? He placed the report from the industrial psychologist on his desk and leaned back in his chair, considering the conclusions that leaped out at him. The candidate was intelligent and clear thinking. Communication skills were good. In strategic thinking he was in the upper quartile of senior industrial management. Bill Ronson couldn't remember the last time his judgement in these matters had been so seriously challenged. He called Ritchie in to see him. "I'm still not sure. He did well at Anderson Barleymore but," he pursed his lips, "there's something. He gives me the impression of being soft."

"Don't know what makes you think that Bill."

"I don't mean soft in the head!" Bill liked to play games when teasing out a problem. "Ireland for example. It seemed very muddled at the end."

Ritchie shrugged. "OK, I wouldn't have handled it the way he did but…" Ritchie spread his hands.

Bill Ronson shook his head and sat in silent contemplation. "I'll do it Ritchie but only if you are comfortable. It'll be on your shoulders."

Ritchie gave a sardonic grin. "Oh. Thanks Bill."

"You've got to go into it with your eyes open Ritchie."

"He's a good fellow Bill and he wants it. He's hungry for it."

"Pity we didn't see his hunger before then," Ronson replied drily and tapped the finely sharpened pencil on the pad before him. "There's plenty of up and coming young turks in the salesforce."

"Bill. I've said I'll do it. Everything else he's done has been good."

"Not necessarily outstanding."

"What do you want Bill?" Ritchie spread his hands with good humour

"Peace of mind," Bill Ronson laughed. "Alright Ritchie. You want to sound him out?"

"I'll phone him tonight."

Eric turned with the phone still in his hand, savouring the feeling that was coursing through his body. He could hear laughter on the television in the other room and his own smile silently spread across his face and he drew himself erect. "Helen," he called, "Helen, Helen." He stood before her, grinning. "I've got it! Got it! They want me to," he sought the right phrase to capture the moment. "I'm being promoted. Sales Manager."

Helen rushed to him. "Eric!"

"Getting my own team."

"When?"

"Straight away. Ritchie's going to start advertising for my replacement."

"Oh Eric…"

348

"You were right Hel. All it needed was for me to ask. Nine months," he said, "that's what it's taken. Nine months since I decided to go for it. You remember? That day up on the Surprise?"

"Will it mean moving?"

"'fraid so Hel. It's Scotland."

"Scotland!"

"They're creating a new sales region. Carving up Ritchie's team. He'll be responsible for everything up to Carlisle and I'm taking responsibility for the rest of the team in Scotland. Ritchie will have a watching brief."

"Is that fair?"

"Well, yes," Eric replied staunchly. Nothing must spoil the moment, no doubts, no second thoughts. "Ritchie knows the markets up there. He'll be a big help until I get my feet under the table. It's what I've always wanted Hel."

"And you'll be manager? With the proper title and everything?"

"Yes."

"Eric?"

"Sales Manager (Designate). Oh don't you see Hel, the title doesn't matter. It's what I can do that really counts." He needed Helen's enthusiasm and tried to make her see while she regarded him shrewdly, quizzically. "Do the job, show them what you can do, that's what counts."

Helen looked at Eric, clutching at the opportunity. She couldn't know how reluctantly it was given, she only saw the determination to make it work, to build their future. What was the phrase? – 'damned with faint praise.' Other questions began to rise in Helen's mind; what about salary? Relocation costs? Where would they live? What about timescale? When would Eric have to start going there? Was it forever? But all the questions of practicality faded before the most important question of all: would his team, the men who until today had been Eric's colleagues, accept him? Eric knew Helen was struggling to be enthusiastic but he had to take it; to refuse would be to close the door forever while younger men took over. He cast small nuggets before her. "There'll be an extra fifteen hundred a year Hel. And an annual performance bonus."

He heard Helen say, "I wish it was south. It's cold up in Scotland."

"It'll be alright Hel. We'll have nice holidays. And no more relying on commission to make up my salary."

"We have nice holidays now," Helen said.

"Oh I know we do Hel. But you know what I mean."

"It means leaving all our friends here."

"We'll make new ones. Come on Hel. I thought you'd be pleased."

Helen relented. "I am Eric, you know I am. I wish... I just wish..." She put her arms on Eric's shoulders and kissed him. "Congratulations love. You deserve it."

"Thanks Hel," he said.

"Thanks? What for?" she smiled.

"Oh, just for putting up with me. Coming to Scotland. Trusting me..." Eric shook his head. "Oh I don't really know what I mean myself. You could have said 'No'."

Helen said earnestly. "I just want you to be happy. I'm like Ruth: 'whither thou goest, I goeth'. That's all." There was something awesome in Helen's simple words. Eric made no reply and she took Eric's hand. "Are you sure you're alright Eric?"

He nodded. The promotion was what he'd always wanted. He had seen so many other managers and been subject to their failings, their self-interest and pettiness. Few had the golden ability to motivate and lead. Eric vowed he would apply the lessons he had learned. "You know I've always been a bit of a dreamer Hel. It's as though there's something in me, a small flame, always there, burning steadily and sometimes I feel as though I could conquer the world. No! Not even that, not conquest, nor pursuit of money. I know it sounds a bit daft but it's like a feeling of destiny."

They took the news to the operatic society. Helen told everyone with pride that Eric was going to lead a new team that had been created and they basked in the congratulations of their friends.

"When will it be?" Jenny asked.

"As soon as we reasonably can. Eric's taking over the office in Edinburgh and we've got to find a house."

350

The news brought admiration amongst the society's older members.

"I remember when you first met him Helen and brought him into the society. We all looked at Eric then and – I'm sure he won't mind us saying this, will you Eric – we wondered what he was going to do with himself. He seemed so shy and bashful. Now look at him. A captain of industry."

Eric gave a deprecating smile and said, "Well I…"

"Will you be able to be in the next show?"

"No," Helen said. "That's it. 'South Pacific' was our last."

It was different with Rita; she wanted to be pleased but she said, "Oh Helen, what am I going to do? I feel as if I've only just got you back and now you're going away and leaving me."

"You'll be able to come and visit us Reet. You've never been to Scotland have you? And Susan'll like it too. Anyway, it'll be ages before we move."

"Tell Eric I'm very pleased for him," Rita said.

Eric started for Scotland early. He left home at five am, took the Great North Road to Edinburgh and five hours later, after a brief stop at Berwick he was climbing through Portobello and passing the distinctive mound of Arthur's Seat. Here the epithet 'the Athens of the North' took on meaning with classical architecture overlooking the city and as he began the descent into Princes Street, driving like a sightseer and admiring the skyline above Waverly Gardens, Eric felt an immediate affinity; Edinburgh was his capital too. He was invigorated by the bustle. There was an innate sense of pride, style and confidence in the people swinging alongside him on the pavements and at the traffic lights by the statue of the Royal Scots Greys Eric took stock of his directions. The office was in the New Town amongst the wide streets sweeping down towards Leith and he left Princes Street and drove amongst Georgian squares and crescents until he arrived at the elegant building which housed the small suite of rooms the company maintained as its Scottish base.

He was here at last! He had come a long way since the day he sat with Alfred nursing his half of bitter in the Brown Bear all those years ago. Eric paused on the threshold and turned to look back along the road, seeing in his mind all the people who had influenced his destiny; Fred Robertson, Ted Wainright, Don Chatfield, even Johnny Horrocks. If only the doubters could see him now; he had beaten them all. He savoured the city's smells, the air sharpened by proximity with the Firth of Forth carrying the smell of barley and oatmeal and coal fires rising in the chimneys. It didn't matter that his newly created fiefdom was the smallest in the company; Eric's smile was illuminated by pride in his achievement. Scotland, you are mine! He turned and entered the building.

He had called a meeting of the sales team after lunch and Ritchie had provided Eric with a set of office keys but he didn't need them. The office door at the end of the corridor was open and Mark Lambie, one of the salesmen, rose from the desk adjacent to the window with a humourless greeting. Eric laid his briefcase on the table alongside the desk and glanced through the window into a dingy back courtyard two stories below enclosed by rough-hewn stone walls. "This it then?" he said laconically.

"That there's the storeroom. It doubles as a kitchen." Lambie gestured to a door opening into a small room in the corner. "This'll be yours through here." Lambie threw open a door opposite and Eric had an immediate sense of deja-vu; it was like Horrocks' office with a desk before the window, two visitor's chairs and a filing cabinet. A single red rose in a tumbler stood on the windowsill. "From your wife. It arrived first thing this morning. Interflora." Eric bent to smell the rose, opened the card and smiled with pleasure. Behind him Lambie was lounging against the filing cabinet. "You'll find customer files and order records in here. They're alphabetical. You'll no doubt want to introduce your own system." Eric opened the top drawer. "In the bottom drawer there's things to do with the office, lease and suchlike. Memos from Uxbridge, that kind of thing." Eric turned to the desk. It was clear apart from a plastic tray containing an old order acknowledgement and a sheet of lined A4 paper with some doodles and incomprehensible notes scribbled in pencil. Eric opened the desk drawers. "You'll maybe find one or two things of mine," Lambie said. "I've been acting head of things up

352

here during Ritchie's absences." Then he added, "Are you no going to try your chair?"

The chair was impressive and nothing would have given Eric greater pleasure than to assume the seat of his authority but not with Lambie watching; that moment was reserved to himself alone. He gave the chair a push and it swung smoothly. "Anything I need to know about?" Eric asked.

"No I don't think so. We know what we're doing; everything's running smoothly."

"Sounds like I'm going to have an easy life."

Lambie was uncompromising. "The whisky industry's in recession; it has been for a year." He shrugged. "It's tough!"

Eric allowed Lambie's resentment to pass and went back out to the general office. "So, where do we get a cup of tea then? It's been a long drive. Then we'll go through the key accounts..."

After an hour and a half at the table in the outer office they broke for lunch. Lambie went out for sandwiches and Eric stretched with relief and returned to his office and tried his chair for size. It felt good and he sat gazing at the rose on the windowsill. Then he went to the small storeroom and put the kettle on.

The rest of the team began to arrive as Eric and Lambie were clearing the debris of their lunch away. The first was Leslie Farquhar, a brash graduate of twenty-two, barely six months with the company and the youngest member of Eric's team. He was followed by Alan, a fresh faced man seven or eight years younger than Eric. He greeted Eric with a handshake and brief congratulations but it seemed to Eric there was something hidden behind the words and Alan went across to Lambie and began discussing a situation he was faced with. Eric pursed his lips. "Is this something I need to know about?"

"Sorry Eric, I..." but Alan's apology was overlapped by Lambie.

"It'd take too long. It's alright. We've got a strategy all worked out. Alan's just bringing me up to speed."

Eric's face hardened. He didn't relish an open confrontation so early in his tenure but it would have to be dealt with. He took a step toward them but he was forestalled by the door opening as Tom

Ridley walked in, the final member of his team; a no-nonsense Scot in his early forties, with a brusque manner befitting an ex-Chief Engineer in the merchant marine. Tom flung his briefcase down and offered Eric his hand. "Congratulations boss. I'm not late am I? You said two o'clock." He turned to the others. "Where's the coffee then? Have I got to do everything round here?" The moment for addressing Lambie's snub was subsumed in the bustle and activity surrounding Tom's arrival, but it gave rise to a sudden sense of isolation. Tom Ridley was the man Eric had been briefed by Bill Ronson to 'take urgent action' with. It was a nice euphemism for 'sack him.'

Alone in his office Eric reviewed the afternoon. It had not been the start he had dreamed of and he found himself revising his opinion of his former colleagues. There was activity but no sense of purpose and the group lacked motivation. Mark Lambie wasn't the successful, mature man he thought himself to be but he had assumed a role as the confidante and mentor of both Alan and young Leslie. Clearly Alan, potentially the strongest member of his team, was torn by divided loyalties but he had been under Lambie's domination too long and Ritchie, Scotland's erstwhile absentee manager had done nothing to discourage Lambie's pretensions. Eric couldn't afford to let Lambie's attitude to remain unchallenged and he sensed the way he dealt with him would be carefully watched. And then there was Tom Ridley. His credibility was already at stake.

On Friday Helen took the day off to join Eric in Edinburgh. "I know I've got to work my notice," she said to Marcia, "but we've got to start house hunting and neither of us knows the city at all. The company are paying for three weekends for us to find somewhere. It doesn't give us very long does it?"

"Three weekends in Edinburgh at the company's expense." Marcia smiled with envy. "My word, we are hard done by."

Eric met Helen at Waverley Station. As she stepped off the train a small group of people congregated round the door of a first class carriage and a piper in Highland regalia began to play as a smartly dressed couple stepped down. The drone of the pipes rose above the sound of the locomotive and the station announcements became lost in the skirl of welcome. The party moved towards the exit and Helen's eyes were misty with emotion as they followed the sound of the pipes. "It's wonderful," she murmured. "All along the coast, it's beautiful. Crossing that bridge at Berwick. And now this."

"I laid it on 'specially for you Hel. We'll freshen up at the hotel," Eric said, "then have a little run to look at a couple of places I've seen. Then we'll have dinner in the hotel. Or there's a nice little Italian restaurant I've found. Not far from the Usher Hall."

"Whatever you say Eric. I'm just pleased we can be together..."

They opted to dine in the hotel. Eric laid the menu aside and looked intently at Helen. "I've missed you," he said.

"And I missed you. Oh you don't know how much I missed you. How has it been?"

"It's been a tough week Helen. You know, when you are given authority over people, you see them with different eyes. But I don't want to talk shop, I've had enough of that all week." He told her of his pleasure at seeing her rose and they went on to map out a schedule for the next two days. "It doesn't have to be in Edinburgh," he said as he refilled their wine glasses. "Could be anywhere really, just so long as it gives me reasonable access to the office."

But it wasn't easy. Living in the city in the type of house they wanted was beyond what they could afford. "I don't want to live in a semi," Eric protested, with an innate awareness of his new status. "I know it might sound a bit snobbish but we can't live just anywhere." They returned to the hotel at the end of the afternoon drained of energy.

"Three weekends," Helen bemoaned, "and this one's half gone already." They lay on the bed with brochures scattered about them, trying to remember which house and development matched which location. "I liked Stirling," Helen said.

Eric shook his head. "It's really too far out Hel." He picked up a another brochure and studied it. "Falkirk?" He pulled a face. "Could be OK I suppose?"

Helen's expression matched his. "Nothing there though," she sighed. "Anyway I'm going to start getting ready for dinner." She went to the bathroom and began to run the bath.

"We'll go over to East Lothian tomorrow," Eric called.

"Where's that?"

"Other side of the city. Along the Forth. The way you came in. Then perhaps we could take in Livingstone and... What's the name of that other town?" Eric furrowed his brow. "Cumbernauld?"

Helen re-entered. "What about Bo'ness? It's right on the coast or river, or whatever you call it. I've always wanted to live at the seaside..."

The following day their frustrations continued. They retreated from the Pentland Hills and toured Dalkieth and still the spark of discovery eluded them. They grew impatient with one another and by mid-afternoon Eric had had enough. There was still outstanding business with his old customers to be concluded and contemplating the five hour drive south that lay ahead he pulled into a lay-by to consult the map. "It could be a real drag getting into the city from here," he said irritably.

"Tell you what," Helen said. "Let's just go and have a quick look at Bo'ness and if we don't see anything we like we'll call it a day." Eric sighed with frustration; it meant driving back across the city. "Come on Eric, just for me. I've got this feeling. It could be just there. Waiting for us. There were some new houses at Grangemouth too. We could go and see them. It's only just past Bo'ness. Just a quick look, while we're there."

"Right!" Eric's nod barely masked his irritation. "We'll go there first then! And then let's call it a draw Helen. We've still got a long journey ahead of us."

They left Edinburgh behind them, passed the airport and drove along the motorway in silence. Helen pointed through a gap in the embankment, "Look!" she exclaimed, "There's that castle we saw yesterday." Eric fleetingly saw a medieval building on a green island then the embankment rose again and the view was gone.

"Next exit," he said.

Grangemouth was a network of overhead powerlines, petroleum tanks and the vast skeletal pipe-works of chemical plants with clouds of vapour rising from them. Helen laughed in a mixture of relief and confession.

"I don't think so," Eric said.

"I'm sorry Eric."

He shook his head. "I should have known. It didn't register when you said it."

"Well, just Bo'ness then while we're here. And then we'll go home?" They drove down by ancient stone villas to a disused waterfront on the Forth; neglected warehousing; a neglected, narrow town. A notice on a boundary fence proclaimed an attempt to develop the abandoned railway into an area of industrial preservation. They cruised the outskirts, looking for redemption, trying to console themselves with virtue by not rejecting it out of hand but its solitude defeated them and they left. "Sorry Eric," Helen repeated wryly.

"Come on love. Let's go home."

The following Friday they returned to Scotland. "We'll take a break at Carlisle," Eric said. He was driving purposefully, with concentration and Helen selected a tape – ballet music – and settled back into her seat as the huge landscape of the Cumbrian Fells rose about them, coloured in glory by the afternoon sun. Shap was a joy; they swept past lorries grinding towards the summit and the broken landscape of the Lakes gave way to vistas of moorland with tantalising glimpses of a railway line briefly emerging from within its folds. And then the landscape mellowed and they began the descent to Carlisle. At the services Eric stood watching the traffic and he turned at the sound of Helen's footsteps. "Everything alright?"

"Yes," she said, "What are you looking at?"

He gestured at the endless streams of freight on the road. "There's something dramatic about standing here on the border, watching the commerce of Scotland on its way to all the different markets they serve. We might be in a recession but they're fighting back." He turned to her. "We're going to be part of this Hel. You and me, we're going to do our bit to keep this country prosperous. I'm glad I didn't get the south. We've got an identity here, a border that defines us. It's a different country with its own culture and customs. It's not all bagpipes and kilts." He shook his head. "I don't think half the people in England realise that. They think it's just another county on the top of England where people speak differently. But it's huge. How long have we been travelling? We've only just reached the border and Edinburgh's still a hundred miles away. And there's all the Highlands beyond that."

Helen smiled at Eric's enthusiasm. He was a romantic and she loved him for it, for his ability to speak to her about his feelings without embarrassment. "We're going to do a good job up here," she said, "And we'll make lots of new friends and have a good life together." She slipped her arm through his and drew him close. "So long as you give me plenty of summer holidays."

They renewed their house-hunting and by lunchtime the following morning they had found two areas they liked tolerably well and worth a second look. Once more they sat and consulted the map. "There's a place we haven't seen," Eric said, peering closely. "We must have passed it on the motorway."

Helen leaned across. "It must be near where we saw that castle. Lin... I can't see it properly."

"Linlithgow. It's not far from that Bo'ness place," Eric said.

Once more they crossed the city and headed West and as they came off the motorway they saw the town sign and beyond a small stone farm on the outskirts an area of land with bulldozers and dumper trucks standing amidst wooden ground markers. A collection of houses stood in varying degrees of completion and Helen pointed to a board proclaiming a development of 'tasteful dwellings in a variety of different styles'.

"We'll go and look at the town first, shall we?" Helen suggested.

They passed open parkland lined with an avenue of trees and a country hotel on rising ground, then a brief glimmer of water. They entered the town and as they drew up to park Helen shook her head and blinked. "I'm seeing things. I've just seen a ghost. Three ghosts.

358

Along there." She pointed up the street. "They had head dresses and long gowns. I wasn't imagining it Eric."

Ahead of them a pub declared itself 'The Four Mary's'. "Well you saw three of them," Eric laughed.

"I did. Really," Helen insisted and as she spoke the ghosts reappeared and hitched their skirts and skipped across the road towards the precinct and the parish church.

"Must be something going on," Eric said. "Never mind." He laughed again. "We'll go and have a cup of tea shall we."

The sales office had a plan of the site on the wall with plots and houses shown in outline. "You'll have to come back and see the sales negotiator," the site foreman said. "We're closing up for the day. I was just on my way."

"We're only here for the weekend," Helen pleaded, "then we've got to go back to Sheffield."

"There should be somebody here tomorrow from ten until four o'clock."

Eric pointed to the coloured houses on the plan. "Are they sold?"

"Aye. Phase One's nearly sold out."

"Is there a Phase Two?"

The man retrieved his jacket from behind the door and gestured through the window. "Across by yon tree." He relented as he ushered them out. "The best plot for my money's Plot 35."

"Why is that?" Helen asked.

"It's on a big area of ground." He pointed. "On the cul-de-sac. And it's an Athol."

"Is that good?"

"The Athol's the top house for my money. You'll no find better." He locked the hut and drove away, leaving them to wander about the site. They took their bearings from the tree and tried to remember the position of the house. Eric wandered to a concrete platform. "This must be it," he said.

The following morning they returned early. The Athol was as good as anything they had hoped for, protected from further development at the back by a wide strip of land dedicated as a

359

thicket. They went through the range of options the sales negotiator was offering. "And you've yet to put your house on the market," the negotiator said, making a final check of the notes he'd made.

"It's a company move." The words filled Eric with confidence. "The company will provide bridging finance."

"And you've got your mortgage?"

Boldness was the only answer. "I'll confirm it to you tomorrow. When will you need a deposit?"

"When you've got it all lined up." The negotiator closed his book and they shook hands and emerged from the hut glowing with exhilaration. It had only taken an hour; now the day was theirs and there was nothing more they could do. The mortgage would be more than they had planned for but... They walked over to the plot and tried to imagine the house standing there.

"Linlithgow." Helen savoured the name and pictured herself telling their friends, Rita, her mother. "Burghmuir," she murmured. "That's what this area's called. Sounds nice doesn't it?"

As they drove off Eric said, "By the way there is a loch here. I asked them at the hotel."

"Oh let's go and see it," Helen cried.

"And a palace."

"That castle place we saw last week?"

Eric nodded. "Not a castle; it's a palace. Where Mary, Queen of Scots was born."

"There," Helen declared with triumph." I told you this was where we were destined to come."

"You said Bo'ness," Eric laughed, but it didn't matter.

They parked in the high street and walked up to the church with its funny little aluminium spire of thorns, and came upon the ruins of the palace on a grassy promontory overlooking the Loch with the motorway from where they'd seen it visible in the distance. The sailing club was out and a small flotilla of yachts were criss-crossing the sparkling water. Helen said, "Let's just sit for a bit." The laughter of children came to them from the water's edge and all around the world was filled with sounds of content. Helen leaned against Eric's shoulder. "Oh Eric, I'm so happy. Thank you for bringing me here. I love you Eric." She kissed him. "And I don't care who's looking," she teased, and kissed him again. "I love you."

Chapter 43 - Casting the die

The Scottish sales team convened for their first formal sales meeting and Eric stood before them, surveying them like a performer judging his audience. His gaze rested briefly on each; Lambie, lounging in exaggerated indifference, displaying his perpetual air of boredom in Eric's presence; Tom Ridley with a quizzical expression, nursing his habitual mug of coffee, Alan and Leslie Farquhar in varying degrees of cynical expectation, waiting for the usual statistics and the latest Uxbridge theory, or the reaffirming comfort of last year's theory re-hashed.

Right! – let it begin. Eric peeled back the flipchart; it said simply, 'Welcome, Scottish Division,' and began to speak. His words were not Bill Ronson's nor Andrew Brock's or Ritchie's; they were his own, simple and sincere without exhortation. This is who I am, Eric declared in his love for them. This is between us in this room, the Scottish Team. He couldn't talk like this with Ritchie or Bill Ronson or any of the others; they would think he was messianic. Eric's words were reserved for his new team. And he saw their doubt and knew they didn't believe him. "We have a recession," he began, "with Scotland's most prominent industry in disarray, hundreds laid off and the Highland distilleries mothballed and all over the country people being thrown into unemployment. We have the toughest conditions any of us can remember. But we work for a good company and we have good products to sell."

"We've got good competitors too," Mark Lambie said with a sneer. "And they get good support from their companies."

"I don't believe they're better than us," Eric replied.

Tom Ridley rode in support of Mark Lambie. "They're undercutting us everywhere. We're losing business because we can't compete." Eric glanced at the two younger men and saw them nod in agreement.

"If you've got any tricks up your sleeve to deal with that…" Lambie said, and let his challenge hang between them.

Eric understood and he forgave them their weaknesses for he had scarcely begun. "I want to talk about us first," he continued. "We sell what the people in our factories make. And they don't make rubbish; we wouldn't have customers if that were the case. They don't go to work to do a bad job…"

"Neither do we," Lambie said. "They have no idea how tough it is trying to sell in a recession."

"Well I'll tell you how tough it is." Eric replied to Lambie with passion. "Those people are no different to you or me. They have wives and families to feed, mortgages to pay and debts to deal with. And if we fail what happens?" Tom Ridley lifted a hand but Eric's look forestalled him. "I'll tell you what happens to them if salesmen fail," Eric said with unexpected vehemence, "the first thing is his overtime gets stopped and his wife and family feel the pinch. He's faced with short time and being laid off. The holiday gets cancelled, the mortgage falls into arrears." Eric's voice rose in a cry of indignation. "But without them we would have nothing!" He paused, looking for a sign that they understood. But all he saw was their bland faces waiting. "So what about us?" he continued. "Us, the salesforce, on whom their jobs and their prosperity depends? We are given cars; they have to buy theirs. We get expense accounts and meals out at the company's expense. The worst thing you have to face is a bit more pressure from the boss while they are facing the prospect of life on the dole if we fail. Ok, you think you're working for yourself. Do you think you are just working for your family? Yes you are, and your family includes all those men and women in our factories and their families too!"

"You can't say that," Alan ventured.

"Well Alan, I do say that," Eric replied without compromise. "I believe that. It's not just about money. There are other motivations too."

"Well don't think all this is going to motivate us," Lambie said. "You can't motivate anybody."

Eric refused to rise to the bait, his agenda was more important. "Mark," Eric said evenly. "I know motivation is a personal thing. It's personal to you all in different ways and the door to motivation is locked on the inside. My job is to create a climate where you unlock that door yourself. But it's up to you."

"We're working for the money," Tom Ridley insisted.

"Do you really think so Tom? I know it's not; if it were you'd be off selling computers or something else instead and getting twice or three times what you do now. There are other reasons. And in my case the reason is what I've just said; all those people in our factories depend on us and I'm not going to fail them." Eric looked at each in turn and his voice became quiet and intense. "I haven't come here to fail."

His statement signalled a pause in the proceedings. Tom Ridley rose from his seat and looked at the others. "I need to take a break. Anybody want coffee?" He left the office and went into the small kitchen. Mark Lambie began to make a phone call. Alan and Leslie stood in quiet discussion by the window overlooking the dingy area below until Tom returned with coffee and they began to reconvene, with the exception of Lambie who was conducting a lengthy telephone conversation. Eric sat watching the others carefully. They grew restless and Alan turned to Eric but Eric waited to see what peer pressure would do. Finally Tom Ridley growled, "Come on Mark or we'll be here all afternoon and all night as well."

Mark Lambie brought the call to an end without apology and said, "Some of us have business to look after."

Eric ignored him and addressed the others. "Mark was asking if I'd got any tricks up my sleeve. Well, the answer to that is, yes! But first I want to talk a little bit about where we're going." He noted with satisfaction a glimmer of alertness lighting their eyes as he announced, "We are going to grow this business."

Now he had them. He saw three looks of expectation except for Lambie who lowered his head over his folder and muttered, "What, in the middle of a recession?"

But Tom Ridley's eyes held the light of battle; he became animated and began rubbing his hands. "A price war!"

"No!" Eric said vehemently. "Look, our competitors are still in business so we know there's business out there and we know where most of it is. So we're going to increase our share of the market, and if there's no natural growth we'll get it by taking business from the competition. And..." Eric paused and looked at them keenly, "we're not going to lose any! Not without a bloody good reason!"

"What I said," Tom enthused. "A price war. You've got to give us the weapons to do it. If we're going to beat our competitors we've got to beat their prices."

"No!" Eric repeated, "No price war. All that happens in a price war is prices get reduced and profits shrink and very little business actually changes hands. We finish up by reducing our prices just to retain what we've already got! And that's bad for everybody." Eric had reached the crux of his policy and it was essential that he took them with him. "There's a better way. You want a trick? Here's a trick for you. We're going to take away our competitors weapon - price! That's the weapon they use so we're going to render it useless."

The light began to die as doubt and confusion coloured their faces. "But you said..." Tom began.

"Be a nice trick if you can pull it off," Lambie said.

"Look fellers, we've got to begin outselling them. We needn't be ashamed of our prices. We have fine products. All we have to do is sell them properly, capture their true value in the market place; sell extra value."

"But if they're ten percent cheaper than us..." Tom persisted and silent looks were exchanged around the table.

"Then we have to find a way of demonstrating ten percent extra value in our products. Look! We can either go around doing what they do, become order takers using price as a blunt weapon to get business at any price. Or we can use all the skill we've got and begin to sell properly."

"Yeah - That's easier said than done." The sotto voce comment was reinforced by nods from the others.

"Well of course it's not easy! But it's a damn sight more effective. Can't you see," Eric declared scathingly, "if the customer buys our fine product in preference to the competitor's cheaper product, then clearly price is not the deciding factor." He saw scepticism in their eyes. Why were they resisting? "Value for money is what matters!" Eric insisted. "A price reduction isn't going to help our competitor to beat us if price is not the issue in the first place! If the product doesn't do the job the customer wants, then reducing the price doesn't make it do the job. We don't have to engage in a price war." It was so blindingly simple. Eric had hoped that an appeal to pride and esprit de corps would help him to win the argument but he saw disbelief and unwillingness instead.

"So we're always going to be at a price disadvantage then?" Alan asked with dismay.

"No! Look, if we need to, if we really need to, then we will compete neck and neck. But you will need a strong justification. I will not undercut our competitors. It's up to you."

They dispersed unconvinced, prepared to see Eric's policy proved wrong. As the meeting broke up Eric asked Tom Ridley to stay behind. "Close the door Tom."

Tom examined the jug for the last dregs. "Coffee?" he asked.

Eric shook his head and stood contemplating the man and his heart began to pound as he searched for the words he wanted to use. Tom poured himself a cup and observed, "Well all I can say is it's lucky for us we work for a good company that can carry us through until this recession's over." It was the opening Eric was looking for.

"That's the problem Tom," he said icily. "There's no room in this company for passengers."

"Well we know that Eric."

"I'm not sure you do." Eric felt his heart rate begin to increase; now he was committed he felt unsure of the outcome.

"Nobody's resting on their laurels," Tom said indignantly, "if that's what you're thinking."

"You've got no laurels to rest on Tom."

Tom's expression froze then turned to anger. "There's a bloody recession up here. You people from the South don't seem tae understand just how bad it is. And you come here wi' your fancy half brained ideas and expect us tae succeed."

"Your sales are down Tom. Your call rate is down. It's pissing with rain out there and you're holding an umbrella over our competitors."

Tom began pacing the room. "I'm working bloody hard! If you know of any business out there that I don't know about then you just let me know and I'll go and get it!" He dashed his half empty cup onto the table and began fumbling for a cigarette. "Och I'm out o' bloody fags!" He tossed the empty packet away and stood fuming before the window.

"I need to see an increase in your sales Tom. No excuses. We need to increase business up here."

"Aye and what about the others?" Tom barked, turning to face him.

"We're talking about you Tom. Your business."

"Or else what?"

"You know what. There is no room up here for passengers."

"I never expected this." Tom began to pace again, his anger rising. "I thought you'd come up here to do some good but you're all the bloody same once you get intae management! You just come up here tae gie us a bloody good kicking! You come up here tae tell us tae get more business then you put the bloody prices up. How the hell are we supposed to win wi' people like you running the show? We're on the end of a rope with a noose around our necks and you and all the others down at Uxbridge are yanking us about at the end of it."

"Yes," Eric said, "you're right." His passion matched Tom's own. "There is a noose round your neck. All salesmen have that same noose, with management holding the other end..."

"I'd better start looking for another job then."

"But there's a difference Tom! I've come up here to succeed. But I can't succeed without you if you've got the guts for it. And Mark and Alan and young Leslie Farquhar. You're right, there is a noose round your neck. But I'm hauling the other way, taking the strain from Uxbridge to give you a bit of slack. Room to perform. I know you can't win if you're being jerked about. I'll help you, I'll support you, but it's you that has to do it. And if you can, we can all be successful."

Tom looked at Eric with resentment. "We all want tae be bloody successful."

"Well… that's what it's all about Tom. I'm giving you a written copy of our discussion today…"

"Discussion ye call it!"

"It'll serve as a first written warning. And then I want to sit down and work out some objectives with you. Then in three months we'll review them."

The anger flared again. "Three bloody months!"

"It's the way it is Tom."

Silence hung between them. "Is that it?" Tom asked at last.

Eric nodded. Tom picked up his briefcase and strode from the room without a word.

Eric savoured the calm that remained. Through the door adjoining his office he saw his desk, the one he had so much wanted to occupy. He tried to see himself as the others saw him, but all he saw was the weight of their suspicion. His mind returned to the ultimatum he had just given Tom. It had been easier than he thought and a phrase jumped unexpectedly into his consciousness; 'Red in tooth and claw'. It was a realisation of the power he held. Eric frowned and turned to look at the empty places round the table. The day's agenda lay on the table and he pushed it to one side. He hadn't come to take his colleagues' jobs from them, he wanted to motivate and lead them to success. But the cause of Eric's frown was the realisation that he had enjoyed seeing Tom struggling with the ultimatum he had delivered, and suddenly he knew that if it came to sacking Tom he would enjoy it. It was a disturbing revelation, a paradox at odds with Eric's beliefs and experience. His gaze returned to his chair in the office and he tried to recognise the figure he saw in his imagination, and wondered if Helen would recognise him too.

The following Monday Eric received a telephone call, followed by a letter of resignation. It was from Alan…

Eric's first management meeting at Uxbridge was conducted in an atmosphere of convivial self-congratulation in the boardroom and at lunchtime the caterers arrived with the buffet. Ritchie poured two glasses of wine and passed a glass across to Eric. "Bit different to sandwiches and crisps eh? How's it going up there? You had a chance to talk to Tom yet?"

"I've given him a written warning."

Ritchie grinned. "You don't hang about do you!"

Bill Ronson sauntered over and caught Ritchie's remark. "Hang about at what?"

"Eric's getting to grips with the Scottish team. Just issued his first written warning."

"Who to?"

Ritchie inclined his head and Eric replied, "Tom Ridley."

"Oh yes." Ronson gave Eric a sardonic look. "Just remember to follow the correct procedure. Well done." He took a sip of wine and said, "Come and see me before you leave Eric." He nodded at Ritchie, placed his wine glass on the table and went in search of mineral water.

"Any problems?" Ritchie said.

"No. Apart from Tom, Alan's resigned. Nothing I can't handle."

"How about Mark?"

Eric shrugged. "He's a funny bloke."

"Sounds like you've got your hands full up there already."

Across the room a group had assembled round Bill Ronson and John James raised his glass in mock salute. "Getting stuck in early eh! Quite right Eric. Don't hang about. Two down, two to go." Beside him Reeder managed a cold smile then turned to Bill Ronson. Andrew Brock gave Eric a nod and Eric grinned back. But James' tone rankled. Even offering congratulation, he couldn't do it without the supercilious wing commander voice he affected.

By four o'clock the meeting was over and Eric made his way to Bill Ronson's office. Bill gestured to a chair and spoke without any preamble. "Are you still using that manky bureau for your letters?"

"They send a girl in a couple of mornings a week. She's alright I suppose."

"Alright won't do. Get yourself an office secretary. Full time. We don't want to be relying on couldn't-care-less strangers and it'll improve the turn round on your quotes. Try and get an ad in next week if you can. We need someone we can rely on to man the office.

Salesmen are supposed to be out selling, not lounging round the office."

"I've already made that clear to them Bill. And I'm beefing up the reporting procedure."

"You need to be out as well," Ronson continued unexpectedly. "There isn't enough work for a full time man-manager with only four men. Scotland is important to us but you've only got a small team. The other sales managers are running teams of seven or eight and they work damned hard. I want you to take responsibility for a market we're interested in. You've got skills Eric and we don't want to see them wasted. It's a big opportunity if we can get into it."

"You mean, manage the team and the Scottish office and take responsibility for a new market as well."

"Yes. You'll have personal responsibility. That's why you need to get the office organised. From now on you'll be reporting directly to me." Eric nodded, conscious of Bill watching his reaction as he outlined his ideas. "There's opportunities for us in the clothing industry. Resins for suit liners and stiffeners…"

Eric caught the early Edinburgh shuttle and sat in isolation from the passenger at his side, his mood soured by a strange sense of disillusion. He turned to the window, gazing out at the clouds in the golden glow of evening. Ritchie had acknowledged that he'd already got his hands full. Now he'd be re-joining the ranks of salesmen too and what sort of message was that going to send to Tom and Mark Lambie? On the other hand having a full-time secretary and reporting directly to Bill put him on a similar footing as Ritchie and his other management colleagues. All the same he felt his status had been compromised.

Half an hour into the flight the captain gave them his message of reassurance and advised that the Isle of Man was coming into view. Eric craned to look down through the window. Sheffield was somewhere beneath him and Helen was alone in the house below and he was filled with a sudden yearning as he passed unseen high above her, back to Scotland and the solitude of his hotel...

At the end of the week Helen finally finished working. The girls in the lab gave her a party and even the professor added his name to the card. They all expressed envy and promised to visit her in Scotland and there hadn't been time to feel anything but excited. But there had been small tears, helped by the sherry and swiftly dabbed away, bittersweet smiles and then a final lonely walk down the drive. No more standing here waiting for the bus. No more dashing through blustery rain between the trees. No more slides, research notes and secrets; the camaraderie of being involved in research that might someday assuage grief. Goodbye to friends. Thank God Eric was coming home tonight.

Helen sighed; they had never spent so much time apart. This was worse than Ireland but it was a price she was willing to pay while Eric consolidated his career. They were due one more weekend at the company's expense and then they could be together again. She checked the time, it was seven o'clock and Eric would be on the road for another two hours at least. Yesterday he had been to a meeting at Head Office and must have passed overhead twice, once in the morning and again on the way back to Scotland. Last night she had meant to go into the garden to look for his plane and wish him 'God Speed' but... She made a cup of coffee and settled down before the television to wait but she couldn't concentrate and hopped from channel to channel until at last she heard the sound she was waiting for, the unmistakeable sound of Eric's car pulling onto the drive, then the expectant silence as she went to the door to greet him and Eric was home.

Chapter 44 - Sweet sorrow

Eric kissed her and threw his briefcase and overnight bag into the hall and sank gratefully into a chair.

"How was it?"

Eric yawned and smiled. "Not bad." The single-minded focus that had kept his concentration sharp during the five-hour drive was receding against a tide of weariness. "Bloody long journey though."

"Are you ready to eat now?" Helen asked.

"In a bit love. I'll just sit for a minute." He yawned. "The house is really coming on. We should be ready to exchange contracts soon."

The phone rang.

"If it's Ritchie or any of the boys tell 'em I'm not home yet," Eric called wearily.

It was Rita. "Oh hi Hel." Anxiety betrayed in the inflexion of her voice. "Are you er..? You're not busy or anything?"

"You alright Reet?"

"Yes!" Briefly defiant then, "No. I'm not interrupting you am I...?"

"Er, I'm waiting for Eric. You know what Friday's like. As a matter of fact I thought you were him." Thoughtless, unnecessary falsehood.

"Gerry's left me."

Oh no, not again! Helen recoiled with a rush of deja-vu. "I don't beli... Left you?"

A trembling affirmation. "He's gone. Walked out."

"You mean... he's walked out of the house?"

The sound of Rita's voice on the edge of tears. "We've had a terrible, terrible row."

"Rita..."

"I'm sorry Hel"

"I don't know what... Eric's due back soon." Helen bit her lip, trapped in the cruel futility of her careless lie. "Can I..?"

"No, it's alright Hel really... I had to tell somebody... Susan's terribly upset."

"When did he go?"

"Teatime. It was all over nothing. He gets so terribly jealous."

"He's not hurt you...?"

"Oh, no. No! Well not... I mean - I know he flies off the handle sometimes. This was worse."

"But he's got nothing to be jealous about."

A snuffle; a choke in Rita's voice. "It was the boys. He gets jealous of the boys."

"The boys! But..."

"I go to see them. Well you know I do. At my mother's. I never bring them home. They wouldn't come here anyway. He gets... He thinks I put them before him. But I don't Helen, I don't and it breaks my heart to say it." Rita began to cry and guilty tears welled in Helen's eyes. "I'm alright," Rita gulped. "I just needed to talk... To tell..."

"He won't do anything foolish will he?"

"Foolish?" A brave, failed attempt to ridicule the suggestion, "No..." and silence.

Helen had to end the conversation somehow. "Damn phone. It's so inadequate. I just wish I could... Oh, I think Eric's here," she said awkwardly. It made her feel terrible.

"It's alright Hel."

"Are your doors locked?"

"I'm alright Hel, really. He won't be coming back." Another silence followed Rita's words, the hollow sound of hopelessness.

"If there's any trouble at all call me. Promise me Reet. Or the police. We'll come and..."

She replaced the handset and Eric heard the news with disinterest. He was tired, impatient of gossipy chatter. Besides, there was the memory of the trick Gerry had played on them before. "Of course he's not left her," he said wearily.

"You can't say that Eric. You should have heard her. She was terribly upset. Crying." Helen left him and went into the kitchen.

373

Presently Eric rose from the chair, drawn by the smell of frying bacon. "Anyway," he said, "he wouldn't walk out on her would he? Bloody fool if he has. It's his house."

Helen cut the sandwiches and passed the plate across. "I want to go and see her," she said. "Just to make sure she's alright."

"Not tonight I hope," Eric insisted glumly.

"Tomorrow then."

Eric sighed. "Can't you just phone her? We don't want to become embroiled in their affairs again. Besides, what can you do? We won't be here much longer."

"I must go," Helen insisted. "She's my friend."

Saturday. No deadlines, no appointments, only their own time at leisure. The morning sun was tantalisingly bright against the curtains. Helen stirred and sighed; Eric drew her towards him and she purred sleepily and snuggled against his knees and they lay in contented silence like spoons in a drawer.

"'time is it?"

"Don't know," Eric murmured.

She turned to face him and opened her eyes. "Do you want a cup of tea?"

"Tea? No."

They began to caress, and made love, and lay afterwards in exhausted fulfilment, so different to the debilitating weariness of last night. Helen reached for her dressing gown and looked down at him, replete with love. "Tea," she said, and disappeared through the door.

Eric lay with the smile faintly stirring the corners of his mouth listening to the sounds from below; water running into the kettle, the placing of cups on saucers, a silence, Helen's gentle footfall on the stairs, water flushing in the bathroom, a door closing and silence again. Another sound reached him, music, an adagio as gentle as sunlight on the placid waters of a lily pond. Ah, Saint-Saens. The brightness outside accentuated the shade within, warming the room and Eric lay at peace. In his mind he saw swans on the waters, a picture of perfection. Somewhere he had been told swans mated for life and he saw them now, gliding in unison, faithful to each other

374

just as he and Helen were. Helen appeared with a tray and settled against him in the bed. "Is it loud enough?" she asked. Eric nodded languidly but the sounds of the day outside would not be denied and Helen drew away and reached for the clock. "Heavens," she cried, "it's nearly half past ten. We've got to go up there remember."

Eric clung to the languor of the morning. "I don't want us to spend all day there Hel. We've got other things to do as well."

"Nor do I," said Helen. "But I'll have to go. I said I would..."

Parking outside Gerry's house was always a problem at the weekend. The houses had no driveways and the road was lined with cars but they eventually found a parking space. At a distance they saw Gerry's car in its accustomed place. Eric exchanged a glance with Helen but made no comment as they approached the house.

Rita opened the door with a shock of guilt, the look of a child caught stealing from the pantry. She hesitated in the doorway and said quietly, "I was going to ring you," then turning to the lounge she announced in a bright voice, "Helen and Eric's here."

Gerry was sitting at leisure on the settee in comfortable fawn slacks and open neck polo shirt. He smiled easily at them and said, "Hello."

"Um. Hi," Eric replied uncertainly.

Gerry's glance rested briefly on Rita. "What brings you here on a Saturday morning?"

"We... er..."

"Where's Susan?" Helen said.

"She's up in her room," Gerry replied affably.

"Can I get you a cup of coffee?" Rita asked but Gerry's eyes carried no invitation and Helen hesitated.

"Yes please," Eric said.

Once more Gerry's glance flickered across to Rita. "She didn't say you were coming."

"Just come to see you," Eric said lamely. "It's been ages."

Helen took the plunge. "Rita said you'd had a quarrel." Her voice carried all the assertion she could muster in the face of Gerry's disquieting blandness. "She called last night and said you'd left her."

375

"We had a bit of a row that's all."

"Well she was very upset," Helen persisted.

"I expect you two have arguments sometimes…"

"And she said you'd walked out."

"Now why would I want to walk out of my own home? I went out for a breath of air that's all. To let things calm down a bit." Gerry's eyes rested on Rita again. "She can get very violent you know when she's upset."

"Well you shouldn't upset her then."

"You weren't here," Gerry said, speaking with an unnerving smile, "so you wouldn't know."

Rita stepped forward. "It's alright Helen. Anyway Gerry's back now so…"

"When did you get back?" Eric asked and Gerry looked sharply across at him.

Rita intervened again, too quickly, "Not long after I phoned. Weren't long after were you love?" The endearment made Helen squirm. "I was going to phone you back Hel but… you know… making up… after a quarrel. You know what it's like." She tried to put conviction into her voice but failed and turned away. "Anyway I'll go and make that coffee. You having some love?"

"Yes please," Gerry replied.

Susan came down briefly with a storybook, drawn from her bedroom by the sound of Helen's voice. She stood by Helen and Rita returned with a tray of china cups and saucers. "Is Aunty Helen telling you a story?" Rita said.

"She's showing me her storybook. Aren't you Susan?"

Susan nodded silently.

"Come here," Gerry said, patting the arm of the settee; Susan obeyed and sat beside him, long enough for the tableau to be observed then she scrambled down again.

"I'm going back upstairs now," she announced, and collected her book from Helen's knee and ran from the room.

Rita brought coffee in and began to pour. "She plays lovely by herself with her dolls." She perched on the arm of the settee, unconsciously mimicking Susan's pose against Gerry's shoulder.

"Anyway we're alright now aren't we love?" speaking lightly, trying to recreate the informality they had been used to, her voice bright and conciliatory. "Sorry if I worried you Hel. I didn't mean to." She smiled encouragement but there was pleading in Rita's eyes and they watched, helpless, as the charade was played out before them. Finally they left and Rita called from the doorstep, "I'll see you next week then Hel."

Helen waved and called back, loud enough for Gerry to hear, "Looking forward to it Reet."

The following week Rita insisted that normality had returned. "It was just one of those things," she said. "We just got a bit carried away. That's all."

Helen gave her a knowing look but Rita wouldn't be drawn. Helen sighed and said, "If there's anything…"

"We're alright Hel. I've told you, it was just… just a spat." She gave Helen a sad smile. "Sorry."

The summer wound on with unremembered pleasures between Eric's absences in Scotland. Anxiety alternating with impatience plundered their emotions, consigning them to a kind of social limbo as the weeks passed. But in September the house in Linlithgow came to completion, a date was set for them to take possession and suddenly the time of imminent departure was upon them.

They went to see Eric's father. "So it's finally come has it? When do you actually go then?"

"Next Friday."

"And what about your house? You've still not sold it."

"I've told you dad. The company provide bridging finance." Eric tried not to betray his exasperation. "We've got a lovely house up there. Just wait 'till you see it. You'll be able to come and stay with us. Have a holiday. We'll be able to show you around; I'll take some time off."

A non-committal, "Hmm."

What's that supposed to mean? Helen added her plea to Eric's. "You will come and see us won't you dad?"

Eric watched his father weighing up reasons to avoid making the journey. Why? Eric asked himself, why did he constantly have to justify himself? All his life! He tried to look beyond the criticism implicit in his father's eyes, his mind screaming, 'Be pleased for me dad! Be proud of me!' but all he heard his father say was, "Don't suppose I'll see you at all now then." His words were sullen, his eyes unforgiving.

Another plea for reconciliation from Helen, "Dad…"

"Well I don't see much of you now so it'll be even less when you're up there."

Eric groaned and they drew the visit to an end. As they drove away Helen said, "Perhaps he's jealous."

"Jealous?"

"You know; envious of your success."

"He's got a funny way of showing it."

"You don't know Eric. For all you know he might brag you to heaven with his mates." It was a singular thought. Eric would have liked to believe but he found no comfort in Helen's words.

It was different with Helen's mother. "You are lucky," Alice said. "I've always wanted to go to Scotland."

"You'll be coming to see us mum. You'll be able to stay for a holiday."

"Oh I shall." Alice turned her laughter on Eric. "You'll be having your mother-in-law coming to stay with you. I just wish your father could have had the opportunity that's all." Alice allowed the passage of a memory to still her laughter, but only for an instant and her smile returned. "Anyway, you'll just have to put up with me on my own."

"You'll enjoy it mum," Helen replied, and Eric nodded approvingly at her side.

Thursday. The removal van came and by mid afternoon the contents of their home had been loaded. All that was left were the suitcases with the clothes they would need until they saw the van again on Saturday.

"We should have decorated," Helen said, looking with shame at the discoloured squares stencilled by the missing pictures on the wall. "I wouldn't want the new people to think I was dirty."

Eric went upstairs to make a final check. The rooms, bereft of everything that defined their life appeared cold. He picked up the extension in his study but the phone was silent. With all the time in the world to indulge himself he was in limbo until they could pick up the rhythm of their lives in Scotland. Helen joined him. "I hate the thought of leaving it empty like this," she said gloomily, wandering in desolation from room to room. "Are you sure the loft was empty?"

Eric nodded. "It's too late anyway. The step ladder's gone."

It was no good; the house had nothing more for them and they loaded their luggage into the car. Helen remained standing in the drive watching Eric lock up for the last time and he heard her say, "Goodbye little house, we've been very happy here." Then she climbed in and Eric climbed beside her and they drove to Helen's mother's.

That evening they went out for farewell drinks. Nothing formal, just a few special friends; Malcolm and Jenny, Rita was expected of course and they were pleased to see Jim there. He and Grayson arrived together and, they said, Jim looked better than he had for ages and that was the important thing. And, the voices added discreetly, Jim was better off without Marlene and everybody agreed Jim and Grayson made a nice couple. Only as friends of course; it was platonic, anybody could see that; Jim was far too much of a gentleman and Grayson was a career woman in her own right. Although why that was relevant none of them could say and turned to another subject.

Jim raised his glass to Eric in a gesture of salutation, "You'll do alright Eric," and Eric felt a glow of pleasure for Jim's simple words of approval meant a lot to him. Eric told Jim how he had stood in the wings all those years ago feeling he was unqualified to join them and Jim laughed and Eric laughed with him.

"How long do you think you'll be gone?" Jenny asked.

Helen shrugged. "If Eric does well it could be years. We may never come back. I mean, he might end up at head office. Who knows?"

Malcolm passed a pint across to Eric and called, "You got your kilt packed?"

"He's got tartan underpants too, I'll bet," Jenny added.

"He won't need them," Malcolm said with a wink. "They don't wear 'em."

Helen scanned the room. "I've not seen Rita yet," she said, looking around her. "Have you seen her Jim?"

"I wouldn't worry," Eric said. "You know what Gerry's like about the operatic crowd. Doesn't want to come himself and won't let her come." There was a nervous laugh from everyone and he added disarmingly, "He can be a bit funny at times."

And so the evening wound to its end and the landlord began calling for their glasses and long goodbyes began with advice about places to visit; things to see until eventually they began to disperse and the pub door closed behind them and Helen and Eric stood at the edge of the car park, waving as the last car drove away leaving them in the cool night air with a rapidly waning feeling of euphoria.

Friday degenerated into an unnecessary rush. Alice rose early and laid the table, having promised them "a nice break-fast. You've got a big journey in front of you," and they rose to the sound of the kitchen radio mingling with the sounds of Alice bustling about below. Helen savoured for the last time the familiarity of the house, its memories of her childhood. "But I must see Rita before we leave," she said, busy with hairspray and Eric suppressed a sigh. "Well I can't go without saying goodbye," she insisted as she capped the spray and turned to face him. "It won't take a minute," and Eric glanced pointedly at his watch. Their leisure to enjoy the long drive ahead was being taken from him.

"… so we've just got to see Rita before we go mum," Helen said as she joined her mother in the kitchen. "Then we'll come back and say goodbye to you properly."

Alice barely acknowledged Helen's kiss. "I've set the table in the dining room. Go and help yourselves. There's fresh grapefruit. And cereals. You can have both." She returned to her efforts, berating herself for failing to bring everything to completion at the same time. "Oh Helen," she called, "Come and take this plate of bread and butter through will you."

Helen glanced at Eric. She knew what he was thinking but it was no use trying to rush her mother; she would only become more flustered. Alice finally joined them, fluttering and apologising for the delay, hoping it wasn't cold, hoping it was alright, sorry that she was delaying them and fussing about the length of drive before them. Eric went to load their final belongings into the car. At least, he consoled himself, when the time came they'd be ready for a quick getaway! But even so, despite Alice's endeavours it was almost ten-thirty before they were ready go.

They felt strange visiting Rita in the middle of a working day. Helen rang the doorbell and they heard it echo in the quietness within.

"Perhaps she's out," Eric said hopefully.

Helen rang again and Eric paced back along the garden path and looked back up at the house. The sitting room curtains were barely open; the bedroom curtains were the same. Helen raised her finger to try the bell for a third time but she was forestalled by the door opening carefully on the chain, just enough for Helen to see Rita peering out at her from the gloom.

"Hel..." Rita's voice was toneless and she remained in the shadows.

"Reet?" Helen said, her mind working quickly. "Reet. We're... er... it's today we go. We've come to say..." and heard Rita mumble something in the darkness. "Sorry Reet. What did you say?" More mumbled words and Helen gestured to Eric standing behind her. "Oh Eric? He's just dropping me off."

To Helen's relief Eric read the signal; he raised a casual arm and called, "Got a couple of things to do Rita. Can I leave Helen here with you? See you in a bit eh?" He gave Helen a meaningful look, tapped his watch, walked back to the car and drove away.

"Can't I come in Reet?" Helen gave an artificial shiver. "It's a bit cold standing here." The door closed silently and Helen heard the chain drop. She entered hesitantly but the hallway was deserted and she went into the gloomy sitting room. Rita was standing with her back to her, leaning against the fireplace.

"Rita?"

Rita's reply was a whisper. "What did you have to come for?"

Helen stepped forward quietly and reached out, "Rita?" and felt Rita flinch at her touch and heard a sound, a stifled sob repeated in the subdued shaking of Rita's shoulders.

"Why did you have to come and see me like this?" It was a voice filled with shame, her words almost incoherent with tears. She reached onto the mantelpiece and picked up a pair of large sunglasses and hesitated, then turned to face Helen with the useless sunglasses dangling from her hand. Helen pressed her knuckles to her mouth and suppressed a gasp. Rita's cheekbone was purple, raised in a bruise and above the swelling her left eye was discoloured and almost closed. Her mouth was lopsided, distorted and still weeping blood from the split in her swollen lip. "Now you know," she mumbled.

"Oh Rita!" Helen reached out to her but again Rita flinched and as she raised her arm to put on the glasses Helen saw her wince with pain. "I'm so sorry Reet."

"You... needn't... be..."

"I'm sorry because... because... we knew." Helen hung her head with a sigh of regret.

"I wish you hadn't come. I didn't want you to see me like this." Rita snuffled and hesitated. "Do you want a drink?"

"Oh here Reet let me..." Helen protested but a blazing look from Rita's eye stopped her.

"You can stop as long as you like Hel. But I don't want Eric to see me."

Helen raised her hands in a gesture of helpless submission. "Can't we...?"

"No! OHHH!" Rita grimaced with pain and regretted her vehemence then continued softly, "Promise me you won't let him in."

Helen nodded. She went out into the hall and replaced the chain on the door, and stood alone in the darkness. When she returned Rita was holding a bottle and two glasses. "Or you can have coffee if you'd prefer," she said.

"Coffee. If that's all right." Helen didn't want to appear puritanical. "It's just that... we're going to have to go. I'm sorry."

Rita poured vodka into a glass, took a small sip and winced as the spirit passed over her lips then went into the kitchen carrying the bottle with her. "You mustn't think anything about this," Rita said, studying the drink in her hand.

"I wasn't Reet. It's just that we've got this long dri..."

"It's just a consolation." Rita closed her eyes to shut out the world and its memories. "Numbs the pain. Just the physical pain. Nothing can dull the other."

"Shall I put the kettle on?" Helen said gesturing helplessly. Rita left her to it and wandered back to the sitting room. Helen found her back at the fireplace and took the glass from Rita's unresisting hand.

"Come and sit down Reet."

"Can't. Can't settle."

Helen put her hand out and hesitated with it hovering over Rita's shoulder as she sensed her stiffen. "Will you let me look? Come on Reet," she said gently, "let me take a look."

Rita looked for prurient curiosity but it wasn't there. She looked for pitying condemnation and found none. She took a step toward Helen and unfastened the buttons of her dress and eased it from her shoulders and let it hang at her elbows. Rita's upper arms were discoloured with bruises and there were bruises on her back. Holding back the rising tears Helen said, "You've got to see a doctor Rita."

Rita's head slowly moved from side-to-side in a gesture of infinite sadness. "What's the point." Painfully, slowly she raised her arms and Helen drew the dress back around her.

"Look at you Reet," Helen pleaded.

"Be better in a couple of days."

"How long has…?

"A couple of… A few months. It was alright until… a few months ago…"

A car drew up outside. Rita looked up sharply; then they heard the door rattle against the chain. Helen looked through the gap in the curtains. "It's alright," she said. "It's Eric."

"Don't let him…"

"I won't."

Helen went out closing the lounge door behind her and Rita heard subdued conversation in the hallway. When Helen returned there were two cups on the table and Rita was pouring coffee.

"I've only got an hour Reet. I'm so sorry."

"I know," Rita said.

"You're going to have to leave him."

"I can't go running back to my mother again…"

It all seemed so futile and Helen racked her brain seeking reason. What perversity in her nature bound Rita to him? Everything Rita had aspired to, all her dreams lay smashed in Gerry's brutality, so cunningly hidden beneath his veneer of softness. And not just the violence, though God knows that was bad enough. It was the coercion, the deception! He'd deceived Rita, just as he'd deceived them all with his air of self-effacing solitude. Yet beyond all reason Rita still clung to him... She became aware of Rita speaking to her.

"You look for peace in your life," Rita was saying. "And what do you find? Certainly not that. We're all looking for it Hel but 'Pace non trovo'." Helen looked at Rita quizzically. "Peace not found. It somehow seems more civilised if you say things in Latin but it doesn't take the reality away does it? It's all gone wrong Hel; first Rob then the kids. Now Gerry." Her chin trembled. "But when it's alright it's lovely. You've no idea." Helen looked around at the neat and tasteful decoration, the lack of ostentation. Rita had tried to make her mark but its sterility proclaimed it was still Gerry's. Was it worth this? "I look at you," Rita continued. "You and Eric..." She turned away and stared at the window and snuffled. "As if this wasn't enough I think I've got a cold coming on too."

"I hate to say it Reet but... You can't stop with him if it's going to be like this."

Rita stayed silent and Helen knew her words, her appeal to logic and all her entreaties were falling on deaf ears. Once more they heard Eric's car draw up outside.

"I'm sorry love," Helen said. "I've got to go." She reached to embrace her but conscious of Rita's injuries and sudden look of alarm she could only hold Rita within the framework of her outstretched arms, her hands hovering, unable to touch her. "Oh Rita." Helen wept, "I hate to leave you like this."

"Go on Hel. Eric's waiting. Give him my love." Rita followed Helen to the sitting room door to watch her leave. "Oh, and good luck." She gave a brave, distorted smile from the shadows. "You will phone won't you...? Promise...?"

Chapter 45 - The swan's song

Before the year was out the business in Scotland had begun to grow but Eric's manner of achieving it exposed the dreamer within. "We will be successful," Eric declared. "You give me more than I expect and I'll give you more than you expect."

There was no other way for him and seeing the dreamer standing before him, Mark Lambie sneered, "You think you can walk on bloody water. Well I know you can't." But Eric let such remarks pass. If only these men would listen and follow him he would show them. It didn't require walking on water but he had to try and get them to dream for themselves.

His staunchest ally was Edna, the secretary he appointed. She was in her fifties, experienced and overweight, and likely to break his leg, she said, if she sat on his knee. She was also supremely confident and a rapport quickly developed between them as her understanding of him grew. One lunchtime, sharing what they called a picnic together Edna said, "You're different to the other managers. You're not as…" she searched for a word, "forceful."

"The results take longer," Eric replied, "but it's more satisfactory. Anybody can dish out orders. We need more than that if we are to succeed."

"Do you think Tom's going to make it?" she asked.

Eric nodded. "I hope so. He's talking to people he didn't know existed a year ago. He'll do it."

"I don't like Mark Lambie," she said candidly and Eric smiled ruefully as she added, "He's got a chip on his shoulder."

"Thinks my job should have been his."

"Och," she said scornfully, "he's no the mon for it. You are. But ye should mak' him respect you." She watched Eric shrewdly. "Aye, I've seen how he talks to ye. I wouldna' stand for it."

Eric nodded slowly. "It's like a poison Edna. I've got to let him work it out of his system."

"Maybe you're right," she conceded, "but it's a dangerous road you're walking. I've seen memos. Lambie wouldn't dare speak to your predecessors like he talks to you."

"I don't care Edna," Eric replied vehemently. "If I can turn Mark round like Tom we'll have a hell of a team." He paused. "Actually I do care. I find it hurts. And it's offensive…"

"Then why don't you make him respect you?"

Eric looked at Edna, grateful for her concern. "Respect has to be won Edna. I can't order him to. I've worked for bosses who tried to demand respect on account of their position and the title on the door. I'm not like that. I want him to work for me, not my position."

"You know what I think Eric? If you don't mind my saying so, what you're looking for is personal loyalty. But they're only salesmen Eric. They don't really care; you don't have to like them and they don't have to like you."

"Words don't hurt," he answered reflectively.

She took their plates away into the small kitchen and sighed wistfully to herself, 'Oh but they do Eric. You may not know it but they do. They hurt you and undermine your authority.' She reached for the tea-towel. 'Aye and they hurt me as well.'

The annual reviews were a prelude to Christmas. Eric saw each man on separate days and Edna maintained sphinx-like inscrutability as each man arrived. But at the sound of Lambie's voice raised in a tirade beyond Eric's office door she winced. When Lambie finally emerged she was icily formal until he left then she took coffee in to Eric.

"Well," Eric said, "how much did you hear?"

"All of it." She shook her head. "You shouldn't have to put up with it."

Eric tried to grin it off and raised the cup she had brought him. "Thanks Edna."

"You look tired."

"Yes," Eric conceded. "It's wearing."

"You won't have that trouble with me."

"I don't have to review you Edna."

"Och I know. It was just my wee joke."

At the end of the week Eric went to Uxbridge for his own review and returned glowing with satisfaction. Bill Ronson had been relaxed and chose to be forgiving about Eric's lack of progress in the 'rag trade' project as he scathingly referred to it, except to remind Eric that it was a responsibility against which he would continue to be measured.

"Did you ask about your title?" Helen asked. "After all you're no longer 'designate' surely?"

Eric was dismissive. "The review isn't about things like that Hel. It was about status and stature. Status is conferred but stature has to be earned. That's what gives you authority. It was a good review Hel. He liked my ideas on reorganisation." He showed her the note Bill's secretary had passed to him before he left and she read, '...to use your phrase, the best is yet to come. I look forward to enjoying it,' and she forgave him his diffidence.

"Anyway Hel, time for a little celebration. I've booked two extra day's holiday so we can leave early. Christmas in Sheffield with the family eh?"

They approached the border in driving rain, passing trees stunted and bent by the incessant winds that blew across the lowland moors and suddenly Eric felt the pangs of homesickness as images of a gentler land arose, an idealised landscape of soft greenwoods and deep in his heart Eric yearned for England. "I don't see us living there forever," he said.

Alice welcomed them with kisses and ushered them in. "Your bed's ready, I've aired it. How was the journey? You must be tired Eric, driving all that way. How was the traffic? And in all this rain too. I've got you some tea ready... Have you seen your father yet?"

"No not yet, we're going to go tomorrow. We came straight here..." Eric sank into a chair and tried to forgive Alice her fussiness.

"I've asked Rita and Gerry to come for tea on Christmas day." Alice placed cups on the coffee table before the fire. "I thought it would be a nice surprise for you."

Helen exchanged a look with Eric. "Thanks mum," she said. "I'm going to phone Rita anyway."

"Oh and there's a Christmas Eve party at Malcolm and Jenny's. You'll meet all your friends. I shan't go. Well it wouldn't look right to go to a party and then straight to Midnight Mass. Besides, I can get my preparations done for Christmas dinner. I want it to be nice for you," Alice protested gaily.

"I think I'll just go up for a wash," Eric said. "I'll take the luggage up while I'm going."

Helen found Eric sitting on the edge of the bed with his jacket draped across his knee. "Close the door," he said in a low voice. "Doesn't she know?"

"What? About...?"

"Gerry! The way he's been treating Rita?"

Helen shook her head. "She can't do. Well I've said nothing anyway."

Eric grimaced. "It's going to be a fun Christmas Day!"

The village had been absorbed into the western suburbs of the city but still managed to retain a village feeling. The small cluster of shops had a Christmas card look with lights, artificial snow and trees twinkling in the windows. Malcolm and Jenny's house was a stylish sandstone bungalow in a cul-de-sac with a low roof undulating over a casement window, a detached garage by the shrubbery and lamps shining in the stone gateposts. The drive was already full of cars and Eric parked on the avenue. They were greeted at the door by Jenny.

"Helen!" Kiss and hug.

"Just thought we'd come and pay you both the compliments of the season..."

"Eric!" Kiss; bottle offered and accepted. "Come on through. It's only a 'drinks and nibbles do'."

Basking in their admiring comments Jenny took their coats then steered them towards the sparkling buffet. They were greeted with cries of welcome. They told of the wonderful life they were living and how different Scotland was and how the winter was colder and the nights were longer but summers were... and the people too...

But it was short lived and the talk began to revert to next season's show, how Jim wasn't putting in for a major part this year but Grayson was going to be wonderful as Julie. Malcolm kept everyone supplied with drinks and cheer and Jenny, a perfect hostess was kept busy with more arrivals and some early departures...

"Got to get back. We've still got to wrap the kids' prezzies. We've left her parents looking after them. You know what it's like Jen, Christmas Eve..."

"Don't want to break up the gathering. Lovely party Malcolm. Have to go; only we promised to look in at Paul and..."

"I wish people would come straight in," Jenny said as the doorbell rang again. "Can you go Malcolm; I'm just getting Roger a drink..."

Though time had set a distance between them it was nice to see friends and be remembered and they refused to submit to wistful envy except for a brief, sharp pang as they finally left and stepped out under the stars to cries of 'Merry Christmas...' leaving behind echoes of merriment and laughter.

They returned to the smell of warm baking.

"Would you like some supper?" Alice asked. "I decided not to go to church after all. I got the vegetables finished instead. We're nearly ready. And I've done some more mince pies." Days of fret and worry concentrated in a final burst of Christmas Eve activity, a last minute act of self-sacrifice.

"I'm going to bed," Eric said with an abrupt yawn. "It's nearly one o'clock."

Helen rinsed the cups and kissed her mother. "Don't be long mum. It's a big day tomorrow."

"I won't," Alice said wearily. She followed Helen into the hall and called, "Goodnight Eric. Merry Christmas..."

One meal, one indulgence, with all the essential ingredients of guilt and inadequacy. "I managed to find some brandy butter after all," Alice said as they cleared the plates for pudding. "I had to go right back into town for it. Did you like that Eric? There's white sauce or custard; the brandy butter's for the mince pies."

"That was excellent."

Alice allowed herself the satisfaction of Eric's compliment and Eric wondered how the world got through the rest of the year without brandy butter.

"Me and Eric'll clear away and do the washing-up won't we Eric."

Alice joined them in the kitchen. "I'll just put the kettle on for a drink," she said. "Then we can all sit down..."

Exhausted with eating they watched television with heavy eyed disinterest as the daylight faded. Until the doorbell rang, forcing them to stir. They heard Alice's greeting in the hall and Helen went to welcome Rita. "We were just dozing," she said. "I think Eric's still asleep."

"We can't stay very late I'm afraid." Susan was standing behind Rita with a new doll. "We've got to get this little one to bed. She's had a big day haven't you sweetheart?" Susan nodded and moved further behind her. "Come on silly," Rita said, drawing her forward, "come and say hello to Aunty Helen."

Susan mumbled a shy, "Hello," and retreated again, biting her lip.

"She's getting to be a big girl now isn't she," Alice said. "How old is she? Seven? Come on, let's get this off." She helped Susan out of her coat. "That's it, make yourself at home. Come on in Gerry love. I've made a nice trifle."

Helen winced inwardly but Gerry responded with bland politeness. "That's very kind Mrs. Crawford. We mustn't be too late."

"It won't take long. Eric's about somewhere. Where's Eric," she called. "Helen? Have you seen Eric?"

Rita said, "She doesn't change does she Hel?" and Helen raised her eyes to heaven.

Rita entered the sitting room feeling somewhat awkward, unsure of who knew what but Gerry strode in and Eric lifted a dismissive hand in token greeting. Rita kissed him and said, "Merry Christmas Eric. Susan, come and wish Uncle Eric a Merry Christmas."

Susan whispered, "Merry Christmas," and began undressing her doll on the floor in front of the fire. Gerry extended his hand and

Eric half rose and took it, repelled by the touch. It was just as he remembered, flaccid and soft, and he tried to reconcile the weakness in Gerry's grip with the bruises inflicted on Rita. He said "Merry Christmas" and sat back with a glance at Helen as if to say, 'Well what else would you have me do?'

"I must go and help my mother," Helen said.

"I'll come too," Rita said eagerly. "I haven't seen her for ages. You don't mind do you Gerry?" She smiled at Susan. "You'll be alright playing with your dolly won't you?"

The child nodded silently.

Tea was a tortured affair. Alice bustled and chattered, cajoling them to eat; Eric struggled to raise smiles with weak jokes; Helen and Rita sought refuge in memories and Susan sat withdrawn, hardly eating, her eyes flickering between the adults. When tea was over Rita whispered, "I'm sorry Hel but would your mum think it was ever so impolite if we left?"

"It's alright Reet."

"Come on then." Rita rose from the table. "I'll help you with these dishes first."

"Oh you're not going are you?" Alice cried with dismay.

"They've got to go mum," Helen said.

"Oh," Alice said, nonplussed, "I am sorry." She proffered the teapot to Gerry. "There's plenty more if you'd...?"

"No thank you."

Helen gave Rita a look of understanding. "Leave the pots Reet; we'll do them later." She followed Rita into the hall and they began searching among the coats on the hallstand. "You alright Reet?" Helen whispered.

"Yes," Rita replied. "Tell your mother I'm sorry. Only if we..." as Gerry emerged from the living room with Susan. "Oh look, here it is!" Rita held Susan's coat out to her. "Here you are love," and they prepared to depart in a gush of farewells.

"Lovely to see you again Rita," Alice said. "Now you will come again won't you."

"Of course we will Mrs. Crawford. Sorry we've got to dash like this. Hope you understand..."

It was time to return Scotland. Eric began to accelerate out of the city along the motorway, crossing the long viaduct in fading light and Helen turned for a wistful look back at the city silhouetted under a dusky red sunset.

"We'll catch up with the rest next time Hel," Eric said.

Helen replied distantly and fell silent as they sped north. Poor Rita, she was a fool for love. It was uncharitable to think it, but she wished her mother hadn't asked Rita and Gerry to tea. It had been a terrible mistake and afterwards Helen had been forced to tell her mother the reason. And the following morning while Gerry was at the Boxing Day football match Rita had telephoned, profusely apologetic and Alice had been sorry and forgiving for both of them. It had all been terribly unsatisfactory. "I wish I'd known," Alice castigated herself. "They must think I'm terrible."

"Why are you terrible!" Eric said, irritated that Alice should take Gerry's guilt on herself.

"I don't know what the world's coming to," Alice said. "Me and your father were happily married all those years..." Her eyes clouded with memory as she ransacked her conscience. "Anyway, what's Rita going to do?"

"I know what I'd do," Eric said.

But it hadn't been all crises. The visit to Eric's father had been marginally better than previous times and they still had Hogmanay in Scotland to look forward to. Helen turned to Eric and saw her smile returned. "Not be long now." She settled back in her seat and behind them the sunset faded into darkness.

In February Eric changed the way the salesforce was organised and called Tom into the office. He arrived relaxed and confident and Edna said, "I suppose you'll be wanting your usual?"

"I need my coffee," Tom replied.

Edna rose and headed towards the lobby.

"I'll do it Edna," Tom offered but Edna forestalled him sternly.

"You'll do no such thing. You're here for a meeting with the boss." She gestured towards Eric's office. "You'd better get in there. He's been waiting for you. I'll bring your coffee."

Tom went in, nodding over his shoulder, "She's a real dragon that one."

"She's alright," Eric replied, amused at the exchange.

"Oh aye, she's good alright." There was respect in Tom's voice.

Eric sat back. "I want to run something by you Tom. Most salesmen naturally gravitate towards customers they feel comfortable with." Eric shrugged. "It's human nature to seek the comfortable option." Tom watched Eric carefully. He was being 'foxy' again and Tom wasn't sure which way this was going. "Take you for instance. There's customers you go to because you regard them as important. And then there are those you never get round to calling on at all."

"Och we can't be everywhere, we're not Superman. I know you'd like us tae be."

Eric waved Tom's protest aside. "It's alright Tom. It's not a criticism. I know you can't be everywhere. But I'm reorganising things and I'd like your views." Eric reached into his drawer and pulled out a plastic folder. "If we're to succeed we've got to play to our strengths." He turned the pages until he reached the one with Tom's name at the head and pushed the folder across the desk. It showed a map of Scotland patterned with dots and Eric swept his hand over them. "These aren't all your customers Tom, but they do represent the markets where you've had most success." Eric flicked to another page with Mark Lambie's name at the head and different coloured dots in a different pattern. But the pattern overlapped onto Tom's area. "I'm abandoning geographical sales territories," Eric said, "We're going to focus on markets instead."

"What does Lambie think about it?"

"Nobody else has seen it yet. You're the first – apart from Edna of course."

Tom nodded sagely. "What about Uxbridge?"

Eric shrugged. "It's up to us to make it work."

Tom considered carefully. It wouldn't do to reject it as daft but...
"It could mean all of us going to the same town. Me and Lambie
both going to Stirling for example?"

Eric nodded. "If you are visiting different customers in different
markets, yes."

Tom raised his eyes in an expression of enlightenment. "It could
work I suppose."

"That's what I think Tom." Eric saw doubt replaced by interest.
"It's what I mean about playing to our strengths. As you become the
expert in your chosen market you'll develop even more expertise.
And customers will have an acknowledged expert in their industry to
turn to."

The plan was greeted with unrestrained mockery by Mark
Lambie. He lost no opportunity to phone and tell his cronies in other
regions. "Its bloody chaos," he sneered. "He's got us running all
over the fucking place," and the comments percolated through the
salesforce. Abandoning sales areas? It was heresy. Bill Ronson sent
Eric a note of encouragement but Lambie continued to deride him
and marks of strain begin to appear in Eric's face as the continuing
attrition with Lambie took its toll. For although within six months
Scottish sales were up again, Lambie wouldn't concede any credit.
"They'd have been up anyway," Lambie grunted to his cronies.
"Some of us are putting in a lot of work to make him look good."

As the weeks went by Helen watched Eric carefully and decided
to broach the Lambie question. Eric was laying a sunken patio,
sweeping dry sand and cement into the spaces between the paving
slabs. "Come and sit down," she said. "You look worn out."

"In a minute," he replied, sweeping with an obsessed air. "Got to
finish this."

Watching him Helen said, "Why don't you get rid of him Eric?"

Eric paused. If only it were that easy. Lambie's figures were
acceptable and at the end of the day that's what Eric's management
was designed to achieve. The problem was intractable. "I can't sack
a man just because he doesn't like me," he protested, adding
unhappily, "Just because his face doesn't fit!"

"You're looking so tired."

"I am tired." He gestured with irritation at the paving and the rockery. "Course I'm tired! Doing this makes you tired!" He swept the rest of the mix between the stones and looked at it critically. "All I want is for him to do the job without a continual fight. It's so hurtful, so... ungrateful! I don't mean the man any harm. All I want is for us all to be successful together." He let his gaze wander over the garden. "Anyway," he tossed the sweeping brush aside. "What d'you think Hel?"

"I think it's brilliant. Now come and sit down."

Eric pulled chairs down onto the new paving. It would be a shame to spoil the weekend. "There," he said, flopping down, "Would madam like a Pimms?" Helen smiled with relief and nodded eagerly, entering into his sudden mood of play and Eric said, "Well we haven't got any." They sat together enjoying the long Scottish evening. "We're going to have a nice holiday again next year," he said. "I know this year's been tough. But it's what I came here to do Hel and I don't care what the others say, it's working. I know Lambie's a bit of a swine but look at Tom, he's a hero. Leslie's a bit of a plodder but he's catching up. And Denis is coming on. He's going to be a really outstanding salesman." He smiled. "Edna was a real find. I'm glad I took her on. You know Hel, no team is perfect but I reckon we've got the makings of a really first class team here."

At the end of August Rita wrote to ask if she could bring Susan for a short holiday. "Gerry won't come," Helen said and continued reading from the letter, '...and I'm sorry it's such short notice but I'm sure Susan would enjoy seeing Scotland. And it would be so good to see you again Hel.'

"It's next week. You don't mind do you Eric, just for the week? They'll share the same bedroom."

"Course I don't."

They welcomed Rita with a spontaneous burst of pleasure and Rita hugged her friend with gratitude. "It's awfully good of you Hel," she said, looking fondly on Susan. "You're ready for a holiday aren't you sweetheart?" Susan smiled quietly.

"We'll go into Edinburgh and look round the shops," Helen said, showing Susan and Rita up to the bedroom. "And if it stays like it has been we'll have our tea out in the garden. And Uncle Eric says he'll take us into the Highlands to Glencoe and we'll show you the palace and the castle..." She gave Rita an earnest look. "Make this your home Rita. Don't feel you've got to... well, creep about." She tousled Susan's head. "Anyway, it's lovely to have you. I'll leave you to it, come down when you're ready."

Downstairs Helen looked at Eric and shook her head. "I expect she'll tell us when she's ready," and for two days nothing was said. Helen indulged them in an afternoon by the loch and tea in the town and showed them the palace. "Do you learn about Mary Queen of Scots at school?" she asked and received a look of incomprehension from Susan. "Oh, well, we'll have to get Uncle Eric to tell you all about her. He's a much better storyteller than me." For the end of the week they planned a trip to Loch Lomond.

On Tuesday they caught the train into Edinburgh. The one o'clock gun being fired from the castle ramparts made them jump and set pigeons wheeling and they squeezed their way into a café for lunch. Then they window shopped along Princes Street beneath flags and banners proclaiming the Edinburgh Festival and descended into Waverly Gardens to see the squirrels. "Can we come and live here mummy?" Susan said as they made their way through the gardens toward the station.

"Nice to be out of the crowds for a bit," Rita said. "It's a beautiful city though."

"I'm so pleased you like it."

Susan pointed to a vendor at the end of the path. "Can I have an ice-cream mummy?"

"Here," Helen said, "I'll get you one. No, put your money away Rita. Let me get it."

They found a bench and watched Susan skip away. "Take care and come straight back. We'll wait here." Then Rita said, "She's really enjoying it Hel."

"She's starting to come out of her shell," Helen replied.

"She's such a quiet little thing. This last two or three days has really done her good." It was peaceful beneath the trees and Rita said, "I'm leaving him Hel."

Helen nodded quietly. "I'm sorry Reet."

"Don't be..."

"I felt awful at Christmas," Helen persisted. "So helpless to do anything. I couldn't help thinking about you all the way home."

At the van along the path Susan was collecting her ice-cream and reaching up to hand the money over. Rita turned to face Helen. "How do I look?"

"You look fine. Why?"

"He broke my nose."

Helen focussed into a closer examination of Rita's face. "It's..." The words choked in Helen's throat, "It doesn't... Oh Rita how could he...?" She looked up and saw Susan lingering by the van, licking the edges of the cornet. "He didn't hit...?"

"He wouldn't dare," Rita interjected quickly.

Helen looked at Rita and studied her in bewilderment. "Why Rita, why?"

A look of pain passed like a shadow across Rita's face but the question was without answer except for the single, enigmatic word, "Anyway..." Rita's lips compressed in a hard line. "I'm sorry Hel; I... We needed somewhere... just for a few days... I... hope you don't..." There was so much more she needed to say but Susan was coming back along the path and it was time to resume the make-believe of their afternoon together...

"Oh Rita," Helen said, "you can stay as long as you like."

In the end Rita stayed three days longer than intended. Helen would have made them stay longer but Rita was adamant. "We have to get back," she insisted over Helen's protests. "I need to see the boys again. I... It's time I started to try and make up for..." she faltered, "Well... you know."

"You're sure you'll be alright?" Helen asked repeatedly, standing at the door with Susan while Rita loaded their luggage into the car.

Rita's smile carried more confidence than Helen's. "I keep telling you Hel, we've got this little flat. My dad's been doing it up for us while we've been here." She took Helen in her arms and laid her cheek against Helen's. "Thanks for everything Hel," she whispered. "You've been brilliant. And Eric." An intense look of friendship passed between them. "Keep in touch won't you."

Helen nodded to Susan. "Come on then," she said. "It's your turn now."

Susan's face broke into a smile. "Thank you Aunty Helen," she said.

"You've got everything Reet?"

Rita nodded and slammed the car door and wound the window down. "Everything that matters." The car gave a brief lurch, they turned the corner and were gone...

Helen waited for news that Rita was happily ensconced in the flat, that there had been no trouble with Gerry, that... But a week went by without a word. And then a letter came; a blessed letter that all was well and more profuse thanks for the haven of shelter they had provided for her and Susan. "I'm so glad," Helen said. "She does worry me." But Helen need not have worried. In October Rita wrote again to say she had taken out an injunction against Gerry harassing her and citing his cruelty. Helen immediately telephoned and offered Rita a statement about the abuse she had witnessed if she needed it.

At the end of the month two major prospects Tom had been working on became customers. Relief and joy combined to lift the look of strain from Eric's face. "That'll show 'em," he cried. Bill Ronson was talking of introducing Eric's ideas more widely and he paced the office with excitement.

"But surely they're not still doubting you...?" Edna said.

Eric turned to her. "They wanted me to sack him! Let 'em doubt me now."

But Eric's official title still rankled with Helen. "Perhaps they'll make you Manager without reservation now," she observed icily. "You deserve it."

"I am Hel. You know that. Everybody knows it. Perhaps they've forgotten! What does it matter anyway?"

"It matters to me Eric. I've not forgotten and I'm proud of you. I'm proud of all the things you're achieving. I want to see you recognised. Can't you see? It's important, not just to me but to your team. You deserve it."

A memory flashed into Eric's mind from way back. Sightseeing in London they had seen the inscription on Christopher Wren's tomb: 'If you seek his monument, look around you.' But... was that enough? Suppose Helen was right after all? Suppose Edna was right and Lambie's insidious mockery was beginning to percolate and hit its mark? There were jealousies amongst Eric's colleagues in the other regions and at the last quarterly business meeting whilst laughing over dinner Knight had called petulantly, "Don't you ever get sick of the sound of your own voice!" and Eric had hesitated while the conversation shifted away, leaving him isolated. Suppose among his peers at the management table he wasn't considered their equal? He put a call through to Bill Ronson.

"It's about my job title Bill."

"Your job title?"

"Yes... 'Designate'. I've proved Scotland is viable as a Region in its own right. It should be corrected, deleted."

"You're doing a good job up there Eric."

"Yes. Well - I should be manager Bill, not manager designate. It's like being offered a meal and then being denied it. Well I'd like to taste that meal now. It devalues the status of my team. They're doing well and they deserve more."

Ronson pondered for a moment. "You've got your annual review after the sales conference. Can we talk about it then Eric?"

"Yes, alright. Thanks Bill."

He told Helen. "I'm going to get it after the conference Hel."

"Well I should think so. It's a pity they didn't correct it before."

But the Sales Conference came first. Eric assembled the Scottish Team in the lobby of the hotel and they walked proudly into the conference hall, making an immensely satisfying entrance compared to the piecemeal way the other sales groups assembled. When the afternoon business was concluded and it came to the evening awards for achievement, Tom was pronounced 'The Salesman of the Year'. It was a moment to savour. Bill Ronson made a speech of congratulation and awarded Tom the company's trophy, a pair of silver 'Fighting Cocks' to keep for the year and Eric applauded him as loudly as anyone else in the room. Then Bill Ronson stood again.

"I have another announcement to make. Since Eric Allenby took over Scotland it has flourished and I know Eric would be the first to acknowledge that this is a magnificent effort by everyone involved. However, his leadership has played an important part. His promotion as 'Manager' is confirmed and Eric's title will no longer be manager designate. It is long overdue and well deserved."

Once more there was applause and Tom extended his hand and offered Eric the fighting cocks saying, "These are yours."

"We'll share them Tom," Eric replied.

A short distance away Mark Lambie was applauding slowly, almost derisively but Reeder's applause had already ceased and he was in conversation with John James, apparently oblivious to the mood of congratulation around them.

Chapter 46 - Swirls and eddies

Eric concentrated on consolidating his progress. Successful and impregnable to the chill winds of change beginning to eddy and swirl in corners of the company he listened to Bill Ronson musing, "We must make room for younger men; create opportunities for them," and heard himself agreeing. Bill was talking of a new, independent division, a kind of 'super task force.' Its manager would hold a senior position and be someone who could exploit the uniquely different sales strategy that he had created and it was clear to Eric that he had managed to create an opportunity for himself that no-one could have foreseen. In the run up to Christmas he flew to Uxbridge for his second review.

Bill greeted Eric with smiles, Anna deposited the tray of coffee on his desk but as she closed the door behind her the smiles fell away. "Well Eric," he said, "you've had a year of mixed fortunes."

"Well, pretty good I thought."

Bill glanced at the papers on his desk. "You've certainly made good bonus."

"We've done good business Bill."

"You've done well with Tom." Bill's chin lifted assertively. "The others aren't quite so outstanding."

"Lambie's figures are pretty solid. I grant you, he could do better. I'm working on him." Eric gave a confident nod. "We'll get there."

The reply was uncompromising. "You should be there by now. You've had nearly two years." Bill selected a sheet from the papers on his desk. "Let's look at other areas shall we…?" He examined the printout briefly. "You've done nothing on your own assignment. Why?"

Valiantly Eric tried to escape as an unexpected blanket of criticism was drawn over him. "I judged my priority to get the group performing successfully. I concentrated on that. You've seen the Scottish figures Bill. I thought I might have been in line for some praise."

"A review's not about praise, it's about performance. You're expected to accept your responsibilities and perform to the standards set. In all areas. Achieving them is no more than your job. As a manager you should know that. You were given responsibility for opening up a new market for us. We thought you were the man to do it. Now we're two years behind."

"Sorry Bill." As Eric said the words he regretted them. Determination, not contrition, was the only way forward. "I wanted to get the team performing. Error of judgement I guess." Dammit, wrong again. "I should have listened to my own lectures on time management." Eric suppressed a self-deprecating smile and set his jaw. "It will be done Bill. It's not that I…" He stopped the flow of self-justification. "You're right. I'll give it the attention it deserves…" Bill Ronson waited for Eric to finish then picked up the sheaf of paper and began to review the performance of Eric's team in critical detail…

At the end of the interview Anna entered to clear their coffee away and Bill switched to the public face of harmony and invited Eric for lunch in a fish and chip bar along the High Street. Eric assumed his usual familiarity with Anna but his discomfiture showed.

"I'll be back in an hour," Bill said to her, then to Eric, "Will you be coming back here afterwards or…?"

"I'll get the earlier flight if we've finished," Eric replied. "Things I need to get on with."

Bill nodded. "I'll drop you off at Heathrow." He turned to Anna. "Give Sczelnick my apologies. Tell him I'll see him when I'm free."

There were still two hours of business left when he landed at Edinburgh but instead of going straight to the office Eric turned west out of the airport and drove home.

"What a lovely surprise." Helen's eyebrows rose quizzically. "Eric?" As he placed his briefcase in the hall she saw the lack of joy in his smile. "What's wrong?"

Eric told her of Bill's assessment. "Oh the others are doing ok - not as well as Tom but – no, it's bloody Lambie! And the rag trade."

Helen tried to console him. "But the others aren't as experienced as Tom."

"Lambie is. But he's a bloody fool," Eric retorted. "He treats me like his enemy. He just won't listen." He grimaced. "They don't know... I can't sack a man because his face doesn't fit!" He turned to the window, gazing at the gloom outside. Eight hours ago he had been on top of the world with opportunity beckoning and a clear view of his future. Now far from being ahead he was trailing behind. Did Ritchie suffer the same detached criticism? Or Knight? Did they come out feeling the dejection that Eric felt now?"

"It's not fair," Helen said softly, "I'm going to write to Bill Ronson. They don't appreciate the work you're doing up here."

"I wish you wouldn't."

"Why not?" There was a light of determination in Helen's eyes. "I don't understand it. And after they got rid of that silly title too. Didn't you tell him?"

"Oh Helen! Of course I did," he replied wearily...

Eric sought to bring Lambie's shortcomings home to him, to make him see that his attitude wasn't helping him, but in the way of the man Lambie made the issue personal and accused Eric of trying to engineer his resignation. "... and I'll take you and the bloody company to a tribunal if you try that one on," he said, rising to his feet and standing over Eric, jabbing his finger. "My figures are as good as anybody's!" He swept from the office leaving Eric tight lipped and breathing hard to regain his composure.

Edna called from the outer office. "Bill Ronson on the 'phone. Shall I tell him you're engaged?"

"No," Eric replied, "put him on," and with a smile of appreciation he heard her say, "I can put you through to Mr. Allenby now."

"Bill." Eric greeted him with warmth and confidence. Edna appeared at the door, mouthed, 'Coffee?' and Eric nodded, grateful for her tact. "Sorry Bill. Just finished a meeting."

"Did you know your wife was writing to me?"

Eric's hesitation was a mere instant. "She said she wanted to."

"Did you put her up to it?"

"No," Eric replied indignantly.

"So what have you been saying to her?"

"Well I... told her about my review."

"If you weren't happy with it why didn't you discuss it with me? That's what reviews are for. I thought I had a good relationship with my managers!"

"Well I... I think we have Bill. I hope we have."

Silence then Bill Ronson said, "Are you aware of the contents?"

"No Bill. She said she wanted to write to you because I was, well, disappointed." He sought to rebuild his bridges. "Particularly after the sales conference and what you said..."

"You didn't tell her what to write?"

"No. 'course not! She's her own person. She has her own views, her own opinions."

"Does she expect a reply?"

"I don't know. It would be a courtesy I suppose. You don't have to. I could tell her you've..."

"I'm not going to respond to its content. I'll put a suitable reply together." Bill Ronson grunted his displeasure. "I know we try to make wives feel involved socially. But if we're going to function as a company and work together as managers we can't be compromised by having our discussions subject to approval by employee's wives. I don't expect this kind of thing from senior men!"

Edna brought coffee and found Eric staring unhappily at the silent phone. "Problem?" she said.

Eric shook his head and put through a call to Sczelnick.

"You have to have a reason if you want to get rid of him," Sczelnick counselled. "You can't just sack him because you don't like him. And you should follow the laid down procedure; a first verbal warning..."

"I know, then a written then a final warning... It all takes time. And his figures aren't really that bad."

Sczelnick registered the exasperation in Eric's voice. "Then what's the rush Eric? What do you think these procedures are for? And by the way, don't forget your reasons for wanting to get rid of him have to be valid otherwise we could face a charge of constructive dismissal."

Eric sighed. He couldn't say it wasn't about the figures; the 'new account' record or 'calls per day'? Although none were outstanding neither were they in the 'unacceptable' league. No, it was the man's sheer arrogance coupled with the subtle non-co-operation that constantly threatened to undermine him. Eric pulled a draft set of statistics from his drawer, an analysis of Lambie's performance he'd been working on. His call rate was lower than that of his colleagues but on the other hand he was successfully handling a major slug of business. Eric asked Edna to bring in Lambie's file of call reports and began work, looking for a bone-fide justification...

Bill Ronson announced a training session. He was a great believer in training; it reinforced management skills and was an opportunity for the team to meet and build common goals and ideals. "Interviewing techniques," Knight said scathingly. "We spend half our bloody time interviewing. I should think we're pretty good at it by now."

Eric took his analysis down to show Bill and get his view. "I've been talking to Sczelnick and..."

Bill Ronson pushed Eric's figures back across the desk unread. "Why don't you just get on and do it Eric. I know all about their procedures. Just deal with the problem!" He checked his watch. "Was there anything else?"

"No Bill."

They were to be videoed by Sczelnick, carrying out a range of different interviews. Eric's case study was 'performance appraisal' and he was to conduct an interview with Paul Ridley, a development chemist. Eric had no fear of the camera but Paul might lack the confidence of the sales managers and Eric took Paul to one side. "You bothered about the camera?"

"A little bit," Ridley replied.

"Don't worry," Eric said reassuringly. "I won't try any tricky stuff with you."

They sat knee to knee with the camera trained on them and Eric teased out the underlying causes of a supposed dispute between Paul and a fictitious colleague when Paul suddenly said, "You're just trying to make this personal."

"I'm trying to solve a problem between members of my team," Eric replied.

"You're taking his side against mine! You're no different to any of the others," Paul snarled. "You're just trying to be smart with your half cocked ideas."

Eric heard sniggering amongst his watching colleagues and Bill Ronson, watching keenly from the back of the room raised a finger for silence. Eric turned to him. "We're off the plot, Bill," he protested.

Bill Ronson was unmoved. "Carry on, let's see where it leads us. Keep the camera running."

Eric fought to remain composed before his peers. Why didn't Bill intervene? Sczelnick remained impassive; he saw pity in Ritchie's eyes and unconcealed enjoyment in Knight's. He had promised Paul he wouldn't play any tricks and this was grossly unfair. "Look Paul," Eric said, "can we stick to the agenda?"

"I knew you'd got an agenda!" Paul cried with triumph and once more Eric was confounded.

At last Bill Ronson brought the interview to a close. "Very interesting," he said. "Thanks Eric. And you too Paul; you had me fooled for a minute." He turned to Sczelnick. "What do you say?"

"Very revealing." Sczelnick turned to Eric. "Thanks for that Eric. How did you find it?"

"It would have been better if I'd known it was coming," Eric said.

"We can't always know these things," was Sczelnick's enigmatic reply.

On the plane home Eric pondered on his ordeal. It must have been planned. There had been no reprimand administered to Paul for straying off the scripted agenda, nor had there been much debate about it afterwards, nowhere near as much time as they had given to the other case studies but he had seen Paul in close conversation with Bill Ronson just before the session broke up at the end. Eric sought consolation in reason. Perhaps they had wanted him to demonstrate the sort of quick thinking…? The hostess was offering more coffee; he gave a brief smile of thanks but she had already passed to the seats across the aisle and he turned back to the window but there was nothing to be seen, only the light on the wing, winking in the darkness. He examined the face reflected in the window. The distortions made him look tired and anxious. Too much travelling and rushing about; too much giving of himself. He needed to sleep, free from nagging anxiety. He wanted his confidence back again.

Home. There was silence in the room but not an absence of sound for they were watching 'The Street', savouring the dialect of northern England. But the companionable silence they had been accustomed to was becoming a gulf of solitude. Helen had started to tell Eric about Rita's letter but his replies were impatient monosyllables; he retreated into himself and Helen saw the marks of worry. "You alright Eric?" she asked gently.

Slumped in the chair, heavy with preoccupation he grunted in reply.

Helen tried again. "What's wrong love, what's worrying you?"

"Nothing." Eric shifted in his chair. "I'm just a bit tired that's all." His eyes were fixed on the screen but his mind was elsewhere. Unspoken, the words 'Leave me alone' hung in the silence between them.

In March the board announced Bill Ronson's appointment to Managing Director and there were spontaneous congratulations from the Sales Managers, delighted that 'one of theirs' had made it to the top. But the euphoria was tempered by the appointment of Reeder in Bill's place. Now they would all be reporting to him and at Reeder's first management meeting he announced what Knight called 'a royal progress' to each region. Eric listened to Knight's gleeful warnings, the dark hints about Reeder's cold parasitical nature and told himself this was his opportunity to rehabilitate himself and show Reeder a successful operation. Reeder's first evening in Scotland would be social, to facilitate a meeting of minds and establish a working relationship. He cautioned the team not to loiter in the office and asked Edna to book a table for three at the Hawes Inn at Ferrybridge.

"Very nice," Edna began, then, "Three! Och, you're no taking me out with you."

"No. Sorry Edna. But it won't do any harm for me and Helen to spend the evening looking after him."

The inn stood in the shadow of the Forth Road Bridge and they paused briefly at the rail by the water's edge to watch a flotilla of minesweepers passing in line beneath the central span towards the misty North Sea. On the northern shore the lights of the Royal Naval dockyard at Rosyth glowed in the failing light and the mighty structure of the railway bridge was already hazy in the deepening gloom. Unimpressed Reeder said shortly, "Shall we get inside."

Their table was by a window in an upstairs room and Eric murmured with satisfaction and secretly thanked Edna for arranging it to perfection. "Did you know Robert Louis Stevenson stayed here?" he said with the air of the knowledgeable host.

"Really." Helen spoke in support. "I didn't know he'd been here. You do mean the writer? The real one? You're not pulling my leg again Eric are you?"

"No," Eric replied, keeping the tail of his eye on Reeder. "He wrote part of Treasure Island here. That'll impress the kids Tony."

Reeder let the information pass. The irritation he had displayed since they collected him from his hotel remained as he picked his way through the menu. Eric brushed his knee against Helen's and sought inspiration in the menu but the silence was too inhibiting and he said, "What do you fancy Tony? I'm told the fish is good."

Reeder put the menu aside. "Steak I think. Is the meat alright here?"

"Should be," Eric replied boldly, then, because he'd hung himself on the fish, "Er, I think I might try the sole." In other circumstances he would have had steak too but this evening called for a display of independence.

They sat with Eric leading the conversation, Helen following and Reeder making desultory replies. Helen's smile became fixed and

Reeder began craning for the waiter. "Are they usually this slow?" he asked with scarcely disguised intolerance.

Eric searched anxiously; a waiter appeared in the distance and he raised his hand. "He's coming," he said. "We'll ask him to be quick." The waiter took their order and Reeder deferred to Eric's insistence on wine. "We must give you a proper Scottish welcome Tony. It's your first night here."

"A glass would have been enough," Reeder said and he turned to examine a sporting print on the wall beside the window. Eric exchanged a look with Helen and raised an eyebrow. He was running out of conversation. Short of talking shop, which would have excluded Helen, there were very few subjects left.

"It must be their busy night," Helen said with forced brightness.

Reeder turned to them and spoke with an expression devoid of any attempt at charm. "I don't regard Scotland as a success." A shock ran through Eric and before he could reply Reeder added, "And don't tell me about the salesman of the year awards. That's just for the salesforce. It doesn't reflect the overall strength of the business. Scotland's not doing as well as you seem to think it is." He snapped a breadstick, indifferent to the effect of his words.

Helen heard Eric listing the changes he had made, trying to justify himself. This was so unfair, so ungenerous, so lacking in courtesy. Reeder remained aloof. Uninterested in the food he refused a second glass of wine and picked sparingly at the cheese board leaving Helen feeling like a glutton with her pudding. She heard Eric say, "Coffee?" but to her relief Reeder said, "Take me back to my hotel. I've had a long day." A wintry smile in Helen's direction; she managed a smile of duty in return then he turned to Eric and said, "We've got a big day tomorrow."

For two days Eric endured Reeder's unrelenting criticism and when it was over he drove him to the airport and was summarily dismissed. "Don't bother parking. You've other things to be getting on with."

"Yes. Yes you're right," Eric said, relieved to be rid of the man. They shook hands and Eric drove away, the tension lifting from him like the sun rising after night.

"I'll get you a coffee," Edna said when he walked in. "You'll need one after that." Eric stood in the middle of his office now his oppressor was no longer there and breathed a heartfelt sigh of relief. "He's a hard one, that," Edna said. "How do you think...?"

"Don't ask Edna. I don't know what makes him tick. This morning he told me he doesn't have friends. He was proud of it. He didn't mean just at work either." Edna remained silent. "Well he can't be very happy. I feel sorry for his family!"

Mark Lambie walked in. His nose wrinkled at the smell of coffee and he said, "I'll have one of those Edna," then lounged against the door of Eric's office. "You're still here then."

There was knowledge in the smile playing at the corner of his mouth and insolence in his tone. Once again Eric found himself weighing the odds. He told himself Lambie's remark was innocent but it unnerved him to think that Lambie was so in tune with his own doubts. Edna rose to make the coffee and Eric read the message to Lambie in her eyes, 'Alright my lad, this time, but your turn will come'.

Eric replied disarmingly, "Oh I'll be here for another hour at least." But Eric knew exactly what Lambie meant. It was as if he had been at Reeder's shoulder.

Eric drove home unnerved from the exchange. He had promised himself he wouldn't be like the worst of the men he had worked for in the past; he had promised himself he would be different and even now he would be fair and honourable.

"You just don't understand," he protested to Helen. "It doesn't matter what Lambie thinks or what I think of him. My way is the right way Hel. I've got to give him a chance to save his job. If only for the sake of his family? Haven't I?"

"Oh my poor love. You will do it your way won't you." Helen shook her head at him. "I love you Eric. I love you for your kindness. And for your wisdom. They don't know what a good man they've got..."

411

At the June management meeting Ritchie announced that he was leaving. The news added to Eric's growing depression. Ritchie had been his mentor since he joined the company; he could laugh and relax with Ritchie but with the others Eric never let his guard down. "So where are you off to Ritchie?" Eric asked but Ritchie volunteered nothing beyond what was in the announcement of his resignation.

"Just felt it was time for a change," he said blandly. "I've been doing this for too long." But he gave Eric a fleeting, enigmatic look, unseen by the others, and raised a quizzical eyebrow as if to say, "Well...?" Had Eric registered it? Ritchie had no way of knowing and the moment passed as Reeder called the meeting to order. But if Eric was the man he thought he was, then Eric would understand.

"I have an announcement to add to Ritchie's," Reeder said when they resumed their seats. "I want you to join me in congratulating John James. He'll be taking over Ritchie's responsibilities in the North."

Chapter 47 - The tumbrel

Summer, and breakfast in the sunken patio with barley growing ripe in the field beyond the thicket. The patio was a suntrap, barely nine o'clock and already warm. Last night the afterglow had lingered until midnight and today the sun had been in the sky since four o'clock. Helen looked up from the letter she had received from Rita. "I'm so pleased she's happy Eric."

Eric poured more coffee and bent to examine a rosebud, swelled to the point of opening with deep red petals. "Beautiful," he murmured and returned to the table. "What else does she say? Has she got anybody else yet?"

"She says she's in no hurry. But she's still seeing the boys regularly."

Helen passed the letter across to Eric. He shook his head. "You know it's strange isn't it. Rita's made all the wrong moves, taken all the wrong decisions and now she's doing alright. Whereas I've always striven to be fair, do my best..." He rose and gazed out over the garden, trying to resolve the thoughts whirling in his mind. "It's not fair Helen. It's not bloody fair!"

Eric finished his coffee and began to prowl the border, silently ruminating. There was a cat in the thicket, moving with the utmost delicacy amongst the grasses. It paused, alert for something Eric couldn't see, the only thing marring its stillness the erratic flick of the tip of its tail. Eric remained as still as the cat, watching and admiring. The cat was black with a white chest and a white sock on its raised paw. It lacked camouflage but that didn't matter, its head went forward and the tail became still. How much longer could it hold its victim in the power of its stare? Helen called and as Eric raised his arm to her the cat jumped, impeded by the grass and slashed out with its white paw in a savage sweeping movement. But whatever was there had gone. With apparent unconcern the cat sat and began nibbling at its paw then gave two or three brisk shakes of its head. Eric stood in admiration of the cat's self-possession, its apparent lack of concern at failure. There would be other attempts and they would succeed.

Eric turned his attention back to the garden. He knew he had reached crisis point with Lambie. But perversely he decided he was going to stick to the course he'd set himself to turn the man round. He'd done it with Tom in defiance of the instruction he'd received on his promotion and he would do it again. That was the challenge and he knew the reward would be worth it. Eric closed his eyes and turned to face the sun, revelling in its warmth. He felt more clear-headed now than he had for weeks. It would mean more forbearance to achieve an improvement in his relationship with Lambie but he was convinced the breakthrough would come. And he had to show results in 'the rag trade' too but that was coming. He had appointments for the following week, a round trip taking in Leeds and Leicester. It meant additional nights away but there were ways of making it work; Helen would come with him; he would base himself in Sheffield and she could visit her mother. He wouldn't confide his decision to Reeder, he knew the reaction he would get; the main thing was to keep Reeder off his back long enough for his strategy to show results. Meanwhile weekends like this were precious! He turned to look for the cat but it had gone; the wild things of the thicket were safe until next time. At peace with himself Eric returned to the table and unexpectedly took Helen's hand and squeezed it. "It's alright," he said. "I was just thinking that's all." He stretched and smiled at her. "What a wonderful summer's day Hel."

"Were you watching that cat? I've seen it before. It keeps killing things. I've seen it with a bird in its mouth."

"Nature in the raw Hel. The jungle's on our doorstep. We should have a cat you know."

"Whatever for?" Helen cried.

"Well, living on the edge of the country like this. To catch the mice."

"We haven't got mice!"

"No, I know. You're right." Eric smiled. It was only whimsy.

"And anyway what would we do with it when we go down to Sheffield. I shouldn't be able to come with you next week."

Eric raised his hands in light-hearted protest. "Just a thought Hel. I'm not really serious."

"Or when we go on holiday," she added.

Eric smiled tolerantly, leaving Helen the last word and she turned to the sun and stretched out in the chair and closed her eyes. This was better. And the rest of the weekend to look forward to.

On Monday Reeder announced another visit to Scottish office. "OK Tony," Eric said as though it were the greatest pleasure in the world. "When are you coming?"

"Tomorrow. Meet me at the airport. Eight forty five, I'm getting the early shuttle."

Bloody hell! Eric's mouth went suddenly dry. "Well I'd... I've got some appointments lined up..."

"You'll have to re-schedule them."

"Yes... yes." Eric kept the uncertainty from his voice. "OK. Right, I'll see you in the morning." He turned to see Edna watching him and pursed his lips. "He's coming tomorrow."

"I heard. What does he want?"

Eric shrugged and tried to make light of it. "What does he ever want? Just a flying visit."

"Aye. Well," she said, "Is there anything outstanding? Anything you want specially?"

"Business as usual I think Edna. Close the door will you, I've got some telephoning to do."

His first call was to Helen. She would have some re-scheduling to do as well and she sighed in disappointment. "That blessed man," she said. "It's not just my mum, Rita's expecting me too. Can't you put him off?"

"Helen!" Eric replied with exasperation.

In the afternoon Reeder's secretary telephoned. "Tony says can you bring all your relevant business files to the airport with you? He wants to meet you at the airport hotel, he won't be coming into the office, he needs to get away on the earliest available flight after your meeting."

Edna saw the furrows on Eric's face deepen as he replaced the receiver. Christ, what's going on? Surely it's not… "The airport?" Edna kept her voice level and refused to speculate. "Och well, it saves me the pleasure of meeting him again."

"Thanks," Eric said ruefully. The sour ache in his stomach had returned.

"Tell me what you need," Edna said. "I'll get it ready for you."

The meeting went badly. Everything was a cause of dissatisfaction; sales to date, Eric's textiles project – "That's where I'd have been today if you hadn't suddenly made me change my plans!" Eric declared – and, inevitably, Lambie.

"What are you doing about him?"

"Tony listen. I can turn him round, I know I can but it takes time. Bill wanted me to get rid of Tom and look at him now. I did it with him and I can do it with Lambie."

"Tom had it in him. Lambie doesn't."

Eric was at a loss to understand Reeder's judgement. "I grant you he's difficult. But I'm his manager Tony. It's my decision to run my establishment as I see it. In the most appropriate way. As long as I get the figures…"

"I've seen your figures…"

"We're only half way through the year. There's some big contracts coming up."

"Jam tomorrow! It's always jam tomorrow isn't it!" There was malice in Reeder's thin, uncompromising voice. Eric hesitated and Reeder glanced at his watch. "Well I don't want to spend another four hours here. You can take me back to the terminal."

There were no parting graces and Reeder strode away with barely a word. It was all too late. Too late to change tactics, too late to redeem himself, too fucking late for anything! Even if he sacked Lambie tomorrow it was running away from him like water draining from sand. Eric's face creased into lines of regret and he slammed the car into gear. He couldn't face Edna and he couldn't risk Tom or any of the others seeing him the way he felt. He had to find space to repair his own tottering morale and keep the motivation of the team intact. At the weekend he had felt so good, bursting with confidence.

Oh God! Eric drew off the motorway at Linlithgow and parked in the lay-by in sight of home. He saw with shame that his hands were shaking and he wound the window down and felt the freshness of the summer air on his face. His breathing became easier; in a few minutes he would go to Helen. His mind wandered back to the weekend and the cat in the thicket. Then, he had been the cat; now he wasn't so sure.

He entered and slouched against the kitchen door shaking his head. "Everything I do is wrong! It's not wrong is it Hel? I just try to be fair that's all." He lifted his voice in a cry of exasperation. "We are successful up here! What the hell am I supposed to do?" He told her of Reeder's ultimatum regarding Lambie. "That's not even my decision any more! I've..." Words failed and he became incoherent, gesturing with hands raised like claws and went into the lounge and threw himself into his chair avoiding Helen in his shame.

"Eric," she pleaded, "Can't you go to somebody and tell them?"

He closed his eyes, shaking his head at her naivety. "Oh Helen," he breathed and she heard contempt in his voice.

"But... It's not six months since you had that wonderful evening at the conference Eric!"

Her words added to his distress. Nothing that Bill Ronson had said that night, that wonderful, triumphal night, was true anymore. Just words, cheap and false. "I was a hero when I joined the company," he mumbled. And in a voice rising with despair, "I would have done anything; I did do everything they ever asked of me!"

"But surely..."

"Oh stop it Hel. You don't know what's going on! You don't have to face it. You haven't had to sit and take it from the supercilious bastard!" Helen left him to his misery and there was silence in the house. Chastened, Eric went in search of her and found her in the kitchen with her head bowed over the sink, peeling potatoes. "Sorry Hel... I didn't mean to..."

She turned and threw her arms across his shoulders, careful not to let her wet hands touch his suit. "It's alright Eric. Hug me." There were tears in Helen's voice. "I need a hug. I can't stand it when you blame me for it."

Eric lowered his face against Helen's cheek. "I'm sorry Hel. I wasn't blaming you."

"As long as you still love me Eric. That's all that matters."

"Oh Hel, of course I love you. You know I do..."

But time was running out and with the quarterly business meeting only six weeks away Eric called Lambie into the office. He knew what it was going to be like and Lambie didn't fail him.

"Now what?" he said as he slouched into a chair in Eric's office.

Before another tirade began Eric said, "It can't go on Mark. If you're unhappy working for me then you should begin to look for another job."

"I should go and...?" Lambie began but Eric overrode him.

"Listen! Listen to me. All I want is for you to be successful. You're capable of so much more. You could be - you should be doing better than you are. I just wish you would understand!" Lambie sat impassive and Sczelnick's words echoed in Eric's head and he continued, "I'm giving you a First Written Warning..."

"Written warning..!"

"Your performance is below the standard I expect. We'll review it again in two months and if..."

Lambie's expression hardened into a challenge. "You think just because my face doesn't fit you can do this to me?" He rose abruptly and exited muttering, "Written warning...! We'll see."

Eric half rose to follow him but it wouldn't do and he sat back. Dammit, he was trying to be fair! Edna came to the door and raised an eyebrow hearing him murmur, "I wasted time, now doth time waste me." Conscious of Edna watching him Eric said, "Shakespeare, Richard the Second," and came back to the present with resignation in his voice. "Well – a Written Warning. Let's hope that pleases him. Coffee? Yes, thanks Edna that would be nice..."

Late summer and already the leaves were beginning to turn. "How long is it this time?" Helen asked as Eric prepared his overnight bag. "I thought the meeting wasn't until Wednesday?"

"Just for one night. Wouldn't even have been that but he wants me for a meeting tomorrow as well. You know what he's like; everything at the last minute. Something to do with strategy. We're discussing it before everybody else comes down for Wednesday's business meeting."

"Might be good news for a change," Helen said optimistically.

Eric smiled wryly. "Might." He zipped the bag closed and carried it down into the hall ready to pick up in the morning. "Anyway, I shall find out tomorrow shan't I?" He checked his shuttle tickets and placed them on the hall table. He turned to Helen and yawned, "You ready?"

Anxious to sleep, Eric spent a restless night with his thoughts. Perhaps Helen was right after all; perhaps he'd passed some test of Reeder's devising; perhaps his formal warning to Lambie had done the trick. He tried to convince himself with logic but logic was no match for the misgivings that constantly rose in his mind, pushing hopeful thoughts aside. And with the perversity that insomnia brings, the alarm clock woke him from sleep that had come too late.

"See you tomorrow Hel," he yawned. "I'll 'phone you tonight." He waved at the corner and was gone. Helen turned from the door clutching her dressing gown around her and refreshed the coffee in her cup. It was too early for breakfast.

At Heathrow it was Reeder who stepped forward to meet him at the arrivals hall. "I thought we could save a little time on the way," he said but as they drove from the terminal Reeder became silent.

"You mentioned something about strategy, Tony."

"All the documents are back at the office," Reeder replied.

Eric tried again, thinking hard. It could be his strategy, it could be the 'super task force'. It could be...? "Is it just Scotland or does it affect the others?"

"You'll have to wait 'till we get to the office."

Eric cast his useless optimism aside. He had tried to play the game; now he knew it was a ride in a tumbrel and a sour, churning sensation rose in his stomach as they drew into the carpark. "We'll go straight to my office." It was in Reeder's face and Eric's heart began to pound as they went through reception and up the stairs. Reeder's pace was brisk and as he hurried in Reeder's wake Eric saw the same knowledge in others' faces as they stood aside to let them pass, afraid of the contagion Eric was carrying.

"Would you like coffee?" Anna asked with exaggerated courtesy. "With sugar isn't it?" and suddenly Reeder was all courtesy too.

"You've had a difficult time in Scotland," he began. "Despite that everybody knows what a good job you've made of it up there."

Eric stared straight at him. I won't help you, I won't make it easy. If you're going to do it then you must do it; I won't do it for you.

Anna brought the coffee in and gave Reeder a discrete nod. There were three cups on the tray.

"I've asked Bill to join us," Reeder said.

Can't even do it yourself, you bastard!

Bill Ronson entered and bestowed a smile of greeting on Anna as she left. "Ah, coffee. I'll pour shall I? Coffee Eric?" Eric waited, sick to his heart by the charade. "Well I suppose…" Ronson began with a glance at Reeder. "You've…?"

Reeder shook his head. "I thought we'd wait for you Bill."

Bill Ronson stirred sugar into his cup. "We know how difficult it's been up there for you Eric…"

"Not difficult at all," Eric protested vehemently. "I've enjoyed it. It's a challenge. I am enjoying it. Well, you can see by what I've achieved."

Reeder leaned forward but Bill cut him short. "Man management isn't just about sales," he said with a deprecating smile and Eric squirmed at the condescension.

"I know that Bill. That's how I've managed to be so successful with Tom. And the others. I've given Lambie a written warning and he's beginning to respond. We've got a good team up there."

"Nobody's denying the work you've done Eric. And you've had your share of success. But…" Ronson raised his palms in the

420

practised gesture of a man caught helpless in circumstances beyond his control. "The business is changing Eric." He glanced over to Reeder and sat back. Now it's your turn, his expression said, I've set the scene.

"You've heard what Bill's said," Reeder began unnecessarily. "We need a new breed of manager." Eric kept his eyes on Reeder in an unwavering challenge. Go on you bastard, say it! "Things are changing Eric." Reeder took a breath, the reluctant bearer of bad tidings, and his eyes met Eric's. "I don't want you on my team. You don't fit."

But what about the others; Andrew Brock, James, Knight? None of them were better men than him. Ritchie had left Scotland an underperforming mess! Eric turned to Bill Ronson for support. "Why?" he cried. "Don't you want success?"

"I've told you my feelings," Reeder responded. "We've had a number of meetings about it. There's no depth in the business. It's..." he sought for a word, "superficial."

"What do you mean? Superficial?" Eric retorted, angry at the farce being played out before him. "What does that mean?"

"There's no point in our raising our voices," Bill Ronson put in quickly. "The decision has been made Eric. You're out I'm afraid."

"How d'you mean, 'out'?"

"Out of management. Out of Scotland."

"Fired?" he said incredulously.

Reeder exchanged a glance with Bill Ronson. "No," he answered carefully, "Not fired." His tone sounded almost surprised.

"We'll find something for you," Ronson added. "A company like ours needs talent..." Eric tried to get his mind in focus, to find reason in their bland phrases while his world fell about him. Bill Ronson raised the coffee pot. "Would you like some more...?"

"I don't want bloody coffee!"

Bill Ronson turned to Reeder, all pretence at courtesy gone. "Well that's it Tony. I'll leave you and Eric to sort the rest out. I've got a meeting..." He turned to Eric. "I'm sorry it hasn't worked out for you Eric." And to Reeder, "I'll see you in my office when you've finished."

"Thanks Bill." So cosy. So complacent. Reeder gestured toward the coffee pot. "Are you sure…?"

Breathing hard and silently Eric clutched the edge of the table, his knuckles white. He looked at Reeder, tension rising in him. Reeder moved away to the bookcase keeping the desk between them, watching Eric. It would be so easy to spring across the desk and choke the life out of him before anyone could intervene. And the salesforce would cheer him! And then what? Reason asserted itself and the tension began to ebb away. There was the job, the pension, the assault charge that would follow. And Helen. She knew nothing of this and while his heart cried out within him, 'Do it! Do it now. At least give yourself that satisfaction,' Eric capitulated. "You said you'd got something sorted out for me."

"Not yet," Reeder said. "We can do…" His voice didn't carry Bill Ronson's conviction and he gave a shrug. "Unless you'd rather…"

"Rather what?"

"Well. You have skills. In sales management. They are very saleable. You might want to pursue your career elsewhe…"

"Sales management!" Eric shouted. "You've just told me my bloody skills are no good!"

Reeder's gaze remained impassive. "You need to think about it. Consider your options."

"I've no fucking options to consider have I?"

"You heard Bill. Meanwhile I think you need to talk it over with your wife first."

"But I've done nothing wrong!" Eric repeated.

"I've nothing else to add. That's it."

"When?"

"Well," a moment's hesitation, "when you've decided what you want to do. You'll caretake in Scotland pro-tem. But it's not negotiable."

Eric gave a gasp of exasperation. "But I don't know what bloody options I've got yet."

"I've told you, I'll see what I can do."

It was becoming bewildering. "Does anybody else know yet?"

"Not yet. We'll make an announcement later. When you've…" Reeder hesitated. "You'll be staying on for tomorrow's meeting?"

"I don't think so," Eric replied heavily. "Tell 'em I'm ill. Get Anna to get me a seat on the next Edinburgh shuttle."

"What about the Scottish salesforce?"

"No! I'd like to tell them myself," Eric replied.

Eric returned to find the house deserted. He threw his overnight bag onto the stairs and wandered from room to room. He wanted to be able to think clearly, but the pounding of failure in his brain drove coherent thought away. He couldn't understand; he wanted to understand but the only thing in his mind was, 'I've done nothing wrong! I've done nothing wrong!' the rest was incoherent turmoil. He put the kettle on and went outside to escape the oppressing silence. He'd never intended staying here forever but now Scotland was being taken from him he wanted it desperately. Here he had briefly tasted success. He wandered out along the drive and stood by his car, gazing at the tree, the landmark from the day when their home had been a bare plot. What have I done wrong?' he cried in silent desperation and turning to the gate between the garage and the house he went through into the back garden and stood by the fence overlooking the thicket. It all looked so established but there was no permanence for him. The summer barley had gone, now the field was bare rows of stubble. His brain was dark, he couldn't think. When Helen asked, as she would surely ask, 'What are we going to do?' he had no answer for her. He tried to weep but no tears came; only torment showed in his eyes. Then his words to Reeder came back with a start, 'I'd like to tell them myself.' He went inside and telephoned Edna. "I want you to call Tom and Denis and the rest of the boys," he said, keeping his voice as even as he could. "I want to see them all individually tomorrow. Each man for half-an-hour alone. Starting with Tom. Tomorrow morning. Ten o'clock."

"Some of the boys will have appointments…"

"Tell them to cancel. Make a schedule for them to come in and tell them I expect to see them when you say. No excuses."

"Sounds like something exciting going on," Edna said with disingenuous loyalty. "What about tomorrow's management meeting?"

"I'll tell you in the morning Edna. You and me first."

Edna probed gently. "You're not saying anything now then?"

"Not now. In the morning Edna. Face to face. Alone." He sensed her evaluating his words, his tone. "Me and you; nine o'clock," he said. "I don't want anybody in the office until you and I have spoken."

He replaced the telephone with relief. The kettle had gone off the boil and he put it on again and sought a biscuit. He had missed lunch and he was getting hungry. The desolation of the house began to overwhelm him and he carried his tea out into the garden, pacing the lawn restlessly. He began to feel lightheaded and once again he stood looking over the thicket. There was an image that troubled him, dark and violent but it wouldn't come clear. And where the hell was Helen! He had sat in the lounge at Heathrow amongst busy, confident businessmen. Gazing down through the aircraft window he'd felt like an outcast and declined refreshment from the stewardess with a brusque wave of his hand. At Edinburgh he had watched them as they disembarked bustling off through the terminal to meet colleagues, being welcomed and whisked into waiting cars while he walked like a ghost to the remoteness of the carpark. Now, waiting for Helen, he began to seethe. 'Where the hell are you Helen! Why aren't you here!'

Chapter 48 – With murder in mind

Helen had spent the afternoon in Edinburgh with Janet. They shared tea and scones in their favourite little café in Rose Street and then caught the train in time for Janet to be home for Mitch. Helen had seen a nice coat in House of Fraser and at the weekend she planned to take Eric along and buy it. But her surprise at finding the car on the drive and her unexpected delight was replaced by vague misgivings. Eric's overnight bag was in the hall but the house was silent; there was no music and no response when she called his name. She hung her coat in the cloakroom and went upstairs to search for him but the bedrooms were as silent as the rest of the house. From the back bedroom window her eye caught a movement in the garden below and she relaxed, unaccountably relieved. Of course, where else would he be? A smile of pleasure twitched the corner of Helen's mouth and she hurried down but as she approached him the playfulness vanished. The stoniness in his stare was matched by the scowl on his face.

"Where've you been Hel!"

Taken aback Helen said, "I've been into Edinburgh with Janet." He turned from her, moving along the fence in a dejected shuffle. "Eric. They haven't…? They've not…?"

He stopped and muttered, "Come inside. Don't want everybody looking." Helen glanced across the garden at the adjacent houses; their faceless windows reflected the pattern of the sky and she followed, closing the kitchen door behind them. Eric leaned against the sink and his shoulders began to heave. "It's over," he said. "It's bloody finished. I've been…"

"They've not sacked you!"

"No they bloody haven't!" he cried. "I don't know what they've bloody done!"

"What then Eric? What's happened? I don't understand."

He told her and it seemed there was nothing to justify what he had to tell…

Edna opened the office early and had fresh coffee waiting when Eric arrived. "My you look worn out," she said.

"Just give me a second Edna." His voice was croaking.

"You need something for that throat. I'll away and get you something."

"Edna!" Eric rasped urgently. He hadn't wanted to speak sharply but he didn't have time.

"I'll put the 'phone on message," she said.

Eric nodded. "Yes do that Edna. Then you'd better come in. Bring the pot with you."

Edna settled herself in front of Eric's desk and heard the carefully chosen phrases in silence.

"You're going to be here after I've left, Edna."

"Och no. I'll be away too."

"Edna," Eric insisted quietly, struggling with his damaged larynx, "you have a good job here. You're well respected. Hang on to it. The boys need you. Scotland needs you."

"Aye," she demurred, "some of them do. Others I can do without." Eric was silent. "I know you're trying to be loyal and fair Eric. But they're bloody fools. Aye, I know you don't often hear me swear but they deserve it. They don't know what they've done. They're losing a good man. I mean it."

"Thanks Edna." He spread his hands and sighed. "Anyway... You'd better get the telephone active again."

"I want you to know Eric, I'm really, really sorry. Tom'll be here soon. He's the first, like you said. Would you like me to make fresh coffee?"

"Yes," Eric croaked, then because he didn't think his weakened voice had carried the first time. "You'd better make a fresh pot for each of them when they arrive."

"Aye, I will," she said. "And I'll away and fetch you some lozenges too."

Tom arrived.

"What's the matter with your voice?" he asked, settling into his seat across the desk.

"Laryngitis," Eric replied shortly. Let Tom draw his own conclusions, he wasn't going into explanations. Dignity was even more precious now and they wouldn't understand. Even Edna wouldn't understand the screaming, screaming, as he tried to dissipate the anger boiling inside him. On the way to the office his rage, fuelled by the anxiety of meeting his people had become a physical pain. His chest felt as though it would burst and with a single image fixed in his mind Eric had pressed the accelerator to the floor and screamed, "You bastard! You bastard! You bastard! Reeder you bastaaaard...!" screaming blindly to drown the rising whine of the engine in the sounds of rage until the car would go no faster and glancing beyond his knuckles, white and steady on the wheel, he saw a curve ahead in the motorway racing toward him. He took control of his breathing and shifted his foot from accelerator to brake. A hundred and eighteen; a hundred and fifteen; Christ he was too late! A hundred and ten; ninety... He swept wildly into the curve and swallowed, relieved that normality had returned and he was still alive. But his voice had gone.

"We'll stop working until they reinstate you," Tom said. "I'll talk to the rest of the boys. They'll feel the same. They can't do this."

"Lambie won't," Eric said quietly. He leaned across and opened a filing cabinet drawer. "Your personnel file Tom. I want to give you these." He extracted a series of letters and reports. "They're your written warnings from..." Eric's chin began to quiver and he quickly tore the reports in two and pushed them across the desk. "I don't want... whoever comes after me... to see these and... well... you know."

Tom's eyes moistened in gratitude. "Thanks Eric. Is there anything...?"

"Just look after yourself Tom. Keep being successful." Eric paused and added, "The king is dead. Long live the king." It sounded forced and melodramatic but Eric knew that Tom understood.

With Lambie it was different. Eric told him the news briefly and without malice. Lambie merely shrugged and walked away but as he left the office Eric heard Edna say, "This is all your fault and I hope you know what you've done!" Vainly Lambie turned to protest but Edna continued, "And you needn't think it'll do you any good Mark Lambie because they've got the measure of you as well."

Eric waited until late in the afternoon when his voice had recovered to something like normal then he closed the office door and telephoned Reeder.

"I've decided. I'm not leaving. You said you had something for me."

Reeder sighed. "Bill said we'd try and find something for you. He didn't say there was…"

"He said the company needed my talents!"

"It might not be in Scotland. Almost certainly it wouldn't be in Scotland."

The insensitive fool! "I don't want to stay in Scotland!"

"There's nothing arranged for you. You must understand. It will have to be… We can't do anything. Not until we know your decision." Christ! I've just given you my decision! Hearing the reluctance in Reeder's voice Eric remained silent, waiting to see what would come next. "You're sure? You want to stay? There's hardly been time…"

"You've had my decision. I'm staying," Eric insisted doggedly.

"Well perhaps… There might be… Possibly in the midlands. Or the north. You used to live in the north didn't you?"

"Sheffield."

"I'll see what I can do… I can't promise anything mind…"

Eric clung to Bill Ronson's words. "Bill said the company would use me! 'We need talent,' he said. Those were his words."

"It'll take some arranging. I'm going to be on holiday for a couple of weeks. When I get back… If you're sure that's what you want…?"

Like a man condemned to a padded cell, Eric threw himself in desperation against the walls of his misfortune. He could see no direction except trying to preserve their life and standard of living but there was no way ahead for them, no certainty.

"But what are we going to do Eric?" Helen asked for the umpteenth time.

Deep in his armchair consumed in icy concentration Eric heard her with sullen resentment. Why keep asking? "Well I'm not going to be marooned up here without a job!" he muttered at last.

"Why don't you leave Eric?"

"Why should I? Why should I leave? I've done nothing wrong! Ronson's promised me... It's Reeder; it's him! He's the bloody problem." Anger gave way to self-pity. "He doesn't want me. Not on his team. Not in the company! Anywhere! He wants me out!" He raised his eyes and snarled, "Well I bloody well won't go. I won't! I won't!"

Helen sighed. It was beginning to happen again, the descent into rage and self-recrimination, lashing out at anything, anyone within range, and she protested gently, "You'll make yourself ill Eric..."

"I'm not being bloody pushed aside!"

"You could get another job Eric. You're only half way through your career."

"They've no right to Helen. I've been successful up here; more successful than he's ever been! Eastern Region were throwing their hats in the air when Reeder left; my people are wanting to mount a protest on my behalf. And more successful then Ritchie ever was. The problems he left behind him."

"Well I don't know... I don't understand it..."

"I bloody don't either!"

Helen left him to his introspection. Presently she sensed him standing in the doorway; she looked up from the letter she was struggling to write and laid down her pen, waiting, yearning to bestow her forgiveness for the wrong done to him and the wrong he was doing to her. "I'm not your enemy Eric," she said. "All I want is for you to be happy."

"But that's why I did all those things, for us to be happy together. Why I brought us here. I'm sorry... I'm sorry..."

"I'm just sorry they've treated you this way."

"Well that's alright then; we're all bloody sorry aren't we!"

"Eric!"

She saw his face soften into regret.

"I can't be your batting board Eric. I don't deserve it. It's no good for us, all this. You've got to try and get it sorted out."

"I'm trying to Hel!" he cried desperately. "What d'you think I'm doing?"

"I might go and see my mother for a few days…"

Eric beat his fists against the air. "Why Hel? Why? Don't leave me Hel."

"I'm not leaving you Eric. But I need a bit of space, a bit of calm. You're so angry it frightens me Eric."

"I won't hurt you Hel, I won't hurt you," he pleaded.

"I don't mean you'd hit me or anything. But your anger… It's frightening. I sometimes think you don't know what you're doing when you lash out."

"I've never hit you Hel." Eric's hands went to his brow in desperation. "When I slam the door… It's just things Hel. Just… I need to let off steam! There's such anger boiling inside!"

"You shouldn't be angry with me Eric."

He pulled Helen to her feet and threw his arms round her. "I'm not, I'm not," he protested. To his relief he felt Helen's arms rise from her side to hug him.

"I won't go," she said and crumpled the letter on the table and tossed it aside. "It was just…"

"I'm sorry Hel." There were tears in Eric's eyes. "Don't know what to say."

"Try not to be so angry Eric. It frightens me."

It became a question of escape before Reeder returned from holiday and closed the bolthole that Bill Ronson had so tenuously provided. Eric spoke to Sczelnick and pulled out all the stops. "It's been agreed with Bill and Reeder's lining up a position for me in the north. It's his idea actually. And Helen and I can rejoin our family and old friends again. Marketing. Well, that's where I have a lot of experience. And Bill agrees."

Sczelnick put the relocation procedure into motion and Eric reported the news to Helen with relief.

"So quickly?" she said.

"We've got to do it Hel. There's no point in hanging about. My career's finished here. I'm a spare part."

"But what will you be doing?"

"I'll be discussing that with Reeder when he gets back. He's got something, he said... Well anyway we can't just sit around waiting for him to tell us what to do. Well can we!"

Helen understood. Eric didn't trust Reeder to keep his word and neither did she but regret clouded her eyes when she looked round. They had made the house a lovely home and now, to find security they were being forced to leave it. "We'd better put it on the market then," she said with resignation.

There was immediate interest and they listened to the estate agents' feedback with mixed feelings. "You're right," he said, "it's a lovely home. We're expecting a lot of bids. I shouldnae be surprised to see the house go for well in excess of asking price." A lovely home... Helen shut off that line of thought. It only added to her unhappiness and she prepared the house in readiness for each viewing with the smell of baking and fresh brewed coffee. And meanwhile their uncertainty and tension increased.

Helen brought a tray of scones and jam in for their supper. "We've got to eat them Eric. We can't just throw them away." Eric looked for a smile but Helen handed him a plate in silence.

"I'm sorry Hel," Eric pleaded, "but what else can I do?"

"I'm not saying you can do anything," she retorted.

"Well what...?"

"It's not you Eric. It's not you I'm angry with."

"Well it feels like me!"

"It's that..." She could hardly bring herself to have his name on her lips. "...Reeder!"

"Well," he sought to mollify her. "We don't have to sell..."

"Of course we do! We've no option. He's left us no option! Unless you want to be out of work!"

"I've told you – they're getting something lined up."

"What?"

Eric raised his hands in exasperation. "How many times..."

431

"You don't know do you!" Helen cried. "And we're uprooting ourselves again. For what Eric. For what?"

"Oh for God's sake Helen!"

"I was always happy to move with you before..."

"But what then? What are you saying Hel? Eh?" He put the scone aside and his voice began to rise. "What point are you trying to make?"

Helen closed her eyes in an expression of pain. 'Not again,' pleading with her cup poised before her lips. It was the same routine every day; the same argument, the same accusations, round and round in circles, getting nowhere until they sat opposed in silence. Finally Helen opened her eyes and rose wearily. "I've got a headache, I'm going to bed. Have you finished with your cup?"

"In a minute," Eric snapped, instantly regretting it but too late as Helen slipped quietly through the door...

Eric had intended presenting Reeder with a fait accompli but he was forestalled by a telephone call. "What's this about you moving?"

"I've sold the house."

"Already! Who told you to?"

"You did."

"I did no such thing! We haven't got anything sorted out for you yet! You had no right to..."

"You said you were getting something lined up for me in the north of England. Or the midlands. So that we could move back to Sheffield!"

"I said I would try to see what I could do. When I got back from holiday! You had no right to jump the gun!"

"Well we've got bids in."

"So it's not actually sold then?"

You bastard! "Well of course it's sold. We're committed to accept one of the offers. It's not like selling a house in England!"

Reeder was unconvinced. "You've made it very awkward for me. I'm doing my best to try and help you..." Eric scowled as he listened to the reprimand delivered in the voice of self-justification. Doing your best? You've never done anything but your best to ruin things for me! "Well you've done it," Reeder concluded. "You should have waited for me but… It limits my freedom of movement to help you. I'm not sure… I'll have to see what I can do."

Eric took a deep breath. Dammit, he still needed the man's goodwill, such as it was, and his voice was as unemotional as Reeder's. "You know what Bill said…"

"I'm perfectly aware of what Bill said," Reeder replied icily. "You've compromised yourself, going off half cocked like this."

"Well we're going to Sheffield at the weekend to see some houses."

There was a grunt of displeasure at the other end and Reeder hung up.

Driving home in the rain from the office Eric is preoccupied. Once more the internal conversation rages inside his head. Why shouldn't I take decisions on behalf of myself? I'm still a manager, making decisions! Well this is another decision. You wouldn't look after our interests you swine, you'd just as soon abandon us as look at us. How did you get where you are? This was a good company until you came along… The drizzle reflects Eric's misery; the day is grey, lifeless, devoid of colour. Headlights are on approaching cars and the wipers make intermittent sweeps, Whap! Whap! Whap! Whap! The red tail lights ahead vanish into the mist, Whap! Whap! Wha… God! – brake lights! They've stopped! Arms rigid, braced back against the seat, off the brake, turn into the skid, the wheels grip, got it back again and stop! Oh Christ! Oh God! The traffic begins to move and Eric completes his journey home driving with exaggerated care…

Helen studies him with concern. "You alright Eric?"

"I'm OK," he mutters, clearly far from it.

"What's happened? Is he back? Has he said…?"

"Nothing! I'm alright. Leave me alone."

Eric went into the lounge without a further word. When the pressure of the day had worn off Helen knew he would come-to and she would say, "Would you like a cup of tea?" and the evening would be theirs. But Eric didn't come and stand behind her and put his arms about her and beyond the news on the kitchen radio there was silence. Helen checked the pans on the cooker and poured tea into a mug and sugared it, and put just the right amount of milk in, just the way Eric liked it, and took it through to him. "Tea won't be long," she said, placing the mug on the small table beside his chair but Eric couldn't reply. He was crying...

In the barren darkness of night, deep in the recesses of his mind Eric lays and plots while beside him Helen sleeps sorrowful and alone. Self-pity is absent in Eric's plotting. He is become a terrible thing, revelling in the anticipation of pain and the bloody violence engulfing him. For the extent of Eric's isolation has been finally revealed.

A telephone call to Knight, Eastern Region. "Hi." Eric's bright greeting is calculated to re-ignite comradeship. "Looks like I might be coming to join you. Has Reeder spoken to you yet?"

"Not me tosh. I'm up to speed. I'm doing no more reorganising." Confident words close the door to further speculation and Knight will not reveal that he has refused to consider Reeder's suggestion. He closes the conversation. "Was there something specific you wanted? Only I'm..."

"No, no," Eric replies. "It was just something..." The lame words are allowed to hang between them and Eric hangs up.

And Brock. "He didn't say he was shifting you down here did he? He's not discussed it with me. Just hang on there, I'd better give him a ring..."

"No, no Andrew. It was just something he said. In passing really. I thought I'd give you a call; I didn't know if I'd heard him right. No don't call him. It doesn't matter."

"How are you keeping anyway my old son?" Again the forced bonhomie.

"I'm fine. Really," Eric protests, a shade too eagerly.

"Thought you'd have got something lined up by now."

"What?"

"I should have thought you'd be on your way." And Brock adds, inviting indiscretion, "I shan't say anything."

"On my way? Whatever for?"

"Oh well, if they've got something in mind for you. Anyway, listen, got to go, I've got somebody waiting."

"Yes. Cheers."

You bastard! Eric will not demean himself to make more calls. Already in his mind he hears the result of the two futile calls. 'Poor bugger's looking for a lifeboat. Don't know what Reeder's said to him...' And the murmur of incredulous laughter, 'You'd think he'd see the light wouldn't you...' The isolation gives rise to secret, inaudible words delivered into the darkness, "You Bloody Bastard Reeder. I will not leave! I will not be driven out. I've done nothing wrong!!"

The cold light of approaching dawn reveals a face of impotent sadness as Eric turns fitfully and dreams of inconsequential things... He would have liked a cat. As a child he never had a cat. The goldfish Timothy wasn't a pet. Timothy was a chore, a mere distraction in the corner of the room on the shelf where he kept his moneybox. Until it died unloved, bloated, hanging lopsided in the water with excrement dangling from its belly and they threw it in the bin. But a cat! Eric's mind creates memories. He would have liked a cat for its independence and self-sufficiency. He might have learned from a cat, for while he stroked it... 'Bloody cat! It's scratched me!' There is blood on the back of his hand and he flings the cat away. Beyond the French window of his dream snow is falling in the silent garden, building a deep layer of white purity, making beauty of neglect. Time winds on in silence and in the garden the cat sits enigmatic and serene, watching him through the window, untroubled by the whiteness falling all around it. And the weary staircase is waiting to lead him to rest and Eric is strangely hopeful and unhurried. No sense of departure, no decision remaining, only a journey to be undertaken... There are fragments of real memory in the air, intangible remains that float about him like the miasma of dust in sunlight; like the intangible, dancing etherea of light that he watches in solitary darkness. Outside it is growing colder but he cannot disturb the memories hovering about him. The cold is raw, the cold is damp, there is no satisfaction in cold like this. 'Why am I here?' Eric's face crumples briefly in pity but he will not have tears! Memories. Music enriching shared occasions, adding greater significance to the stolen hours of friendship. Other sounds are sweeter, melodies of life, binding memories to the mind; a child knee high in grass; lovers on a hillside elbow deep in Tosca, the perfume mingling and rising from her with the scent of body-sweat and passion. Distant sounds; a cuckoo in the valley, the hum of insects in the grass, a minute world in tumult. Happiness fading into the past, always in the past. Stolen pleasures... "You have stolen all my pleasures!" Eric's voice within the bedroom is unreal, loud and beside him Helen briefly stirs. The illusion of happiness; daddy's hand, Helen's hand; children that might have been; cliffs, the sea, surging and pressing and rising against the land; the beach sunlit and golden; children screaming! - it's alright, just children screaming and running on the beach. At play. The garden sleeps beneath the snow, the house is cold and the cat gazes at him, unmoved, unperturbed... Dawn breaks into day. The dream is gone, Eric wakes and tiredness hangs about him like a shroud... He turns into the pillow and draws the covers over him and seeks sleep again cocooned in warmth before another wakefulness...

Time is not the healer; it never was. Time is the catalyst by which hate becomes obsessive and although it may be masked by the diversion of laughter and the carefully fostered illusion of success, hate is never eradicated. Eric sits in a lay-by on the high Derbyshire moors overlooking a distant vista of the city to which they have returned. It is Friday afternoon in grey November with a weak, miserable rain shrouding the landscape. He has been more than an hour alone with the thoughts seething through his mind, busy with a pad of paper and the small book of poetry - a gift Helen had bought him on an impulse - open on the passenger seat alongside his pen. But his inadequate first draft of verse lies crumpled on the floor; for it could never replace a look, a touch, a smile. Eric raises his face to the mirror and sees? Not a smile, for Eric's smile is a ghastly thing, a grimace of triumph acknowledging hate. The gentle smile in Eric's heart is hidden for his heart is troubled and there is not the will to gentleness. And so he sits hidden in the gathering mist, wasting the afternoon until it is time to go home, with a sheet of fresh paper in his hand and the discarded letter with the book of poems on the seat beside him. The letter is a protest of worth and value and innocence, an apologia of sorrow for hurts received and hurts to be inflicted. But not a justification, for no justification is needed; it is in Eric's mind to do it and his mind is conceiving other pictures, passing time.

Reeder – the name conjures another surge of hatred. "Reeder you Bastard!"

The sound of his voice spoken in the solitude of the car startles Eric but it clears his mind briefly; another small piece of hate chipped away. Eric shivers, sighs and turns on the engine for warmth and taking up the small book of verse, seeks for words to write but flicking the pages he cannot find it, only something unsatisfactory, something... 'Oh God - I long for peace in a place where man has never trod...' No, no, he chides himself, that's not...

He wakes with a start from his reverie. The pad has slipped off his knee and the pen is loose in his fingers. He retrieves the pad from the floor. God what is this?

'Dear Helen, this is something I ought not to do. Write to you I mean. We should talk properly and I'd try to tell you what I really feel. And you would take my hand and hold me close and comfort me, just as you always have. And I would love you in return. That's what we always had – what we still have. And really that's why I find I have to write and tell you these things. Because I love you so much. Only even now it's so difficult to say and I ask you to forgive me but I fear you never will....'

Helen's first tear drops on the page; his tie is beside her, his coat nonchalantly thrown across the chair.

'.... but I do love you, dearly, with all my heart. But you see, with all my heart I cannot do what I would want to do for you. With you. We had so many hopes and dreams. We seemed to be achieving so much. And I've made you so unhappy. I used to feel the world was ours to make our way in but now I see I can't....'

Unable to read more she will take the crumpled letter she cannot read up to the silent room. Too late, the door is closing, shutting out the day, leaving her alone in silence. But it isn't Helen who has crumpled the letter, it is Eric and now it lies discarded with the other on the seat beside him. The letter will not do, it does not have the eloquence of retribution...

Commit nothing to writing, leave no evidence. This is far more satisfactory. Two hours from Sheffield to Hemel Hempstead then two hours back again. That is all it will take.

"You bloody bastard, I'm going to do it!"

The pool of dim yellow sodium light from the street lamp reflects on the wet pavement, its effectiveness reduced by the icy drizzle and the overhanging branches of the trees lining the avenue. Standing in shadow beneath the plane tree Eric draws the collar of his raincoat closer against the drips falling from the leafless branches and stamps his feet. The cold is beginning to bite and he checks his watch; 7-15. Christ! His feet have been in this slush of leaves for almost an hour. Never mind. On this miserable night there have been few passers-by and no matter how cold it becomes he is determined to wait and remains standing in the shadows. He draws comfort from the feel of the baseball bat under his raincoat with the handle snug beneath his left armpit, the other end gripped tight against his thigh. It is a good bat; not one of those sporty alloy jobs but a smooth, solid, heavy shaft of hickory, beautifully turned and polished to display the grain. And endlessly in his mind the metronomic reaffirmation of purpose, of his cold intent, "Tonight you bastard; tonight you bastard; tonight..."

A car approaches. Eric knows it is Reeder's almost before he can see it clearly. BMW! Yes, that's him the bastard. And as the car turns into the drive the pounding of Eric's heart begins. Emerging from the shadows beneath the tree he begins walking steadily towards the house. The car is on the drive; the engine is switched off and the driver's door opens. Reeder emerges and turns to reach back inside for the dark overcoat folded neatly on the passenger seat beside him. But he turns with a start as he hears his name, "Reeder!" spoken in a harsh whisper from the gloom, and peers at the figure silhouetted in the misty glow of a streetlight as recognition begins to dawn coupled with instant indignation. He begins to speak, not words of welcome but, "You! What are you doing here! At my ho…?" But the words are unfinished as the baseball bat crashes onto his head. It connects with a curious knocking sound, reducing Reeder to insensibility and he slithers against the car onto the wet ground, mercifully oblivious to the blows which follow; one against his upper arm, unsatisfactory and ineffective then two more in quick succession to the head. The first draws blood, the second one splits the cranium. And then a final triumphant blow pulverises the broken skull…

Eric leans on the bloody bat and watches the dark stain flowing from Reeder's head, running across the asphalt. He is breathing hard and a half smile flickers briefly but it is not a smile of triumph. No, not that, it is a smile of sorrow for himself, and a silly, trite phrase comes into his mind and is gone again. No matter. He listens but there is no sound. The only sound in his memory is the first unexpected 'knock' of wood on bone. He looks around quickly. Reeder is slumped against the open door of the car and the courtesy light is spilling on the body but it is shielded from the house and no-one is in the street. Right! Close the door normally as though the car is yours and Reeder's body sags and comes to rest in the blood. Now the plastic bag, a bin liner drawn from his raincoat pocket. Nothing to hide, just put the hickory bat inside it - a child's present - and walk away, a businessman going to the local for a swift half before supper. Past the pub to the car instead, parked innocently in the precinct with so many others. The baseball bat will burn. The plastic bag will burn. Follow the signs out of town, 'M1 North' and drive into the gathering sleet...

As Reeder lays unseen against his pride and joy, Reeder's wife wonders why he hasn't come straight in as he usually does when he returns from work. Hearing the car she has pulled the curtains aside and seeing the headlights swinging into the drive she has gone to turn on the microwave. Now she peers out again, wiping the steam from the kitchen window and five minutes after that irritation gets the better of her and she goes outside and finds him in the darkness lying by the car.

'Oh my God!' She clutches at her throat, looking at the body in the shadows. 'A heart attack!' and she turns and runs inside and telephones for an ambulance then she runs outside again and kneels to him and looks aghast in the gloom at the shattered head in her hands and feels the stickiness of his blood and screams and screams and screams and...'

Chapter 49 - Island in the sun

Eric emerges from his reverie, his dream of revenge evaporates and he leaves the lay-by on the moor to drive home leaving the misery of the day behind. Home is a detached house on a corner of the avenue with lawns on three sides, a view of Beauchief to the west and woods descending to the railway line and the park. The windows reveal comfortable rooms glowing with warmth. "That you love?" Helen's voice is wafted by the smell of casseroled lamb, delicately spiced with herbs and Eric picks up the day's post from the hall table and glances at the phone to see if there are messages. "John James phoned. Says will you call him back." All is normal and well.

Helen appeared from the kitchen with their neighbour Jill, brown eyed with auburn hair curling to her shoulders. "You'll think I'm always here," Jill said, smiling at Eric and the last vestiges of his mood evaporated. "Anyway," she turned to Helen, "I'll go now Eric's back. Peter's sure to be close behind and I haven't even begun his tea yet. I'm not sure what we're going to have. Perhaps he'll take me out instead as its Friday." And as Eric stood aside for her to pass, "I'll let Helen tell you."

"Tell me what?"

"It's Peter's birthday the week after next," Helen said. "Jill's asked us round for a meal."

"Nothing very grand," Jill said modestly. "I'm not half as good a cook as Helen. Anyway, must go." She waved and was gone.

"Oh well," Eric said. "Peter's birthday eh? That'll be nice."

"Yes. I like Jill. Tea's nearly ready. Are you phoning John James first? Don't be long if you are."

Eric's stomach tightened. He should have gone to Macclesfield but he'd spent the afternoon dreaming. "I'll phone him in a bit," he said.

"Oh - and Rita's invited us round tomorrow night. She wants us to meet Alec. The boys might be there too."

The boys? Tearaways! Raymond certainly was; Antony wasn't too bad, but intense and insecure. Hardly surprising considering...

Eric went up to the study with waning interest. To meet Alec? It would be more accurate to say the boys were being introduced to Alec and Rita wanted him and Helen there as referees! It was all so bloody unsatisfactory! They had returned from Scotland with carefully nurtured stories of triumph. How Eric had built his division to be the most successful in the company, how his unique marketing skills had led to his new appointment and the reward of returning to Sheffield to manage his new responsibilities from home. On such images Eric sought to rebuild their lives, hoping for a return to life without complications. But it wasn't that simple. Alice accepted their return without question, but when he took his father for a reunion drink he regarded Eric knowingly.

"Not management then."

"Done that dad," Eric replied with careful nonchalance. "Been there and done it. We might have stayed on a bit longer but I'd achieved what I'd set out to do. Time for a bit more personal success instead of making it happen for others."

And now they were going to meet this Alec. Eric sat gazing at the day's unopened post. More questions, more explanations, more concealment. Helen called, "Dinner's ready. I'm putting it out..."

In the event 'the boys' weren't there. "You know what they're like at that age," Rita said. "They'd have liked to see you again but what can you do?" She hung their coats in the confines of the entrance hall. "Come and say 'hello' to Alec." Eric exchanged a look with Helen. He hoped it wasn't going to be like it had been with Gerry. "It's a bit small," Rita said, "you'll have to sit where you can. Anyway, this is him." Alec rose to greet them. "Alec, this is my best friend, Helen. And Eric. Helen and I have been friends forever, haven't we Hel." They arranged themselves in comfortable informality and Rita hovered about them. "I'll get us some drinks. What would you all like? Another lager Alec?"

Susan jumped up from the pouffe beside Rita's chair. "I'll get them mummy." She took their orders carefully and departed to the kitchen.

"So what do you do to earn your crust?" Alec's voice was clear and confident, as strong as the hand that gripped Eric's, and Eric regarded him closely. Alec was relaxed and easy; his clothes were good; the sweater over the sharply creased trousers looked like cashmere.

"Marketing," Eric replied evenly. "Industrial resins."

"We're just back from Scotland," Helen added.

"Oh, holiday?"

"No, they've been working up there haven't you?" Rita said.

Helen nodded vigorously. "Just over three years," she said. "Eric was the manager."

"So what's brought you back here then?"

Jesus Christ, this was moving at a pace! Eric's reply came quickly, carefully. "You know what it's like." He tried to be offhand and put on a casual air. "Big company. Things change…" No, that wasn't the gambit he'd wanted to use. Eric tried again. "We're erm… we're looking at a new marketing opportunity…"

"Eric's been put in charge."

Eric shot a glance at Helen and added a smile. Too much protestation! Relax, slow down, let the conversation evolve. Shift the focus onto him. "So what about you… er, Alec?" God, he was so uptight he nearly called the man Gerry! "Who are you with?"

"I'm with meself." The reply was friendly enough.

"Oh, what do you do?"

"Alec has his own business," Rita said, and added. "That's his car outside."

"Oh, nice." Helen had been admiring a nice looking car outside.

Eric sought another opening while Alec said casually, "… due for changing next month but I might keep it a bit longer. Just to spite my accountant." He gave a self-satisfied smile. "It's still going pretty well." Eric grinned back to show he was happy to share the joke. Bloody Hell! Going well! Did he mean the business or the car? It made it sound as though being on the payroll of an industrial company with a company car was inferior in some way.

Susan returned with the drinks and Rita said, "Lasagne? I thought I'd be safe with that. Susan's done the salad." Susan blushed with pleasure and Rita said, "We can eat as soon as you're ready…"

In the event it was alright. Alec didn't give himself airs and they promised to meet again soon and Rita stood framed at the door with Alec's arm casually draped over her shoulder to wave them off.

"I enjoyed that," Helen said. "He seems nice doesn't he?"

"He's alright," Eric replied.

"There's nothing wrong with him is there?" Helen asked.

"He's better than the other one anyway."

"That's what I thought," Helen said.

"Did you see his car?"

"Yes, nice."

"Alfa Romeo."

"Gosh. Very nice."

They drove on in silence.

"You know, he's only a tally man Hel."

"Tally man?"

"Sells carpets door-to-door on tick. Market stalls. That kind of thing."

"Well whatever he is he's doing well for himself. And he's got a nice car. And Rita's happy. She deserves it after all…"

"Nobody 'deserves' anything!" Eric muttered. "I deserved…" He paused, then, "I didn't deserve this anyway."

Helen sensed another mood gathering and fell into a dismayed silence. Eric changed gear and slowed for a junction with his lips tight pursed then the lights changed and he pulled away in silence.

"What are you thinking about?" Helen finally ventured.

Eric grimaced and made no reply, filled with nostalgia for the world of his youth. Alfred with his frayed cuffs and nicotine stained fingers; the camaraderie in the van; Monty's office on the landing at the top of the dingy staircase. That was Alec's world, only Alec wasn't Alfred or even the bully Len. '…and I'll bet he hasn't got half the hassle we've got! Might not have been such a bad life after all…' Helen's voice broke into his thoughts. "Did you hear me Eric?"

"Oh I was just thinking what would have happened if I'd stayed on the road selling vacuum cleaners? I might have had an Alfa now."

The public face hid private misery. Once again Helen found Eric deep in the chair, shrouded in solitude.

"Cup of tea?" she asked.

"Not bothered."

"I'll make one if you want one. I'm having a cup of coffee."

"Oh leave me alone!"

She sighed and turned away. A few moments later she returned and placed her coffee on the small table beside her chair. Eric looked across. "Well you said you didn't want one," Helen protested. "I'll make you one if... You only had to say..."

"Oh don't bloody bother!"

He rose and left the room; she heard the kitchen door slam and Helen's eyes creased in despair. 'Oh no,' her heart cried, 'Not again. I can't stand it...'

She found Eric gripping the edge of the sink, unaware of her presence, speaking to himself before he registered her presence and turned to her. "Why?" he cried, "Why? It's not bloody fair! It's him! Him! Him!"

"Eric. Come on, come back in here where it's warm." She stepped toward him but Eric pushed past her and the lounge door slammed. She followed him sobbing, "Eric..."

He was standing by the window, staring at the curtains drawn close against the darkness, seeing nothing.

"Eric." She knew he had heard her. "Eric. You can't go on like this. It's going to make you poorly. Eric. Look at me." She took a step closer, her eyes brimming. "Please Eric. We can't carry on like this. It'll make us both poorly." She brushed the back of her hand over her cheek and Eric turned shamefaced.

"I'm sorry Hel." His voice was choked. "I... I don't know what to say."

Helen's overwhelming desire was to fold her arms about him and stroke him and give him comfort but instead she braced herself to say, "You've got to see a doctor Eric."

He raised his eyes, casting about the room. "I don't want a bloody doctor Helen! I want my bloody job back!"

"But Eric you…"

"I don't want bloody pills! What do I want with a sodding doctor?" He began to pace, muttering and railing against the world. "It's not bloody sedation! I want my life! My Life!" he cried. "My self respect! My job, my career," and his fingers began tearing at his hair, "I want my fucking life back!!"

"Please Eric, please. Stop it! I can't stand it when you…"

"Well you know what you can do then!"

"Eric I can't…"

"D'you think I can stand it?" he shouted. "Eh?"

"Eric…"

"Oh - leave - me - alone!" he snarled, punctuating each word with his forefinger. "If you don't fu…" In the midst of his outburst he checked himself, "- like it…!" He stormed from the room and another door slammed leaving Helen with her head aching with incoherent thoughts. Presently the door opened softly and Eric placed a mug of coffee at Helen's side. "I'm sorry Hel. I don't know what to say…"

"We've got to seriously think about it Eric."

"I know. I know."

He knelt and buried his face in her lap and Helen nursed him in the stillness, caressing his hair. "It's not your fault love," she said, relief mixed with sorrow. "But if you carry on like this you'll be ill. You've got to do something."

"What can I do?" he wailed softly.

"Why don't you try and get another job?"

She felt his head shaking against her thighs. "Who'd want me…"

"Why not? You're only half way through your working life Eric." He didn't answer, afraid to disturb the calm that now surrounded them. "Didn't you make yourself a drink?" Helen said at last, lifting her hand from Eric's head. "Come on, I'll make some fresh and then we'll go to bed shall we?"

To sleep and dream contented dreams. They pulled covers over themselves and lay in the darkness, perfectly matched with Helen curled in Eric's knees. "Like spoons," he murmured.

"Like spoons," she echoed softly and snuggled against him as though she would fuse the two of them together into one.

"Sleep tight love."

"Sleep tight."

November was drawing to a close. The onset of winter. With clouds of depression still hovering about him Eric started replying to adverts.

"Eric," Helen said carefully over tea, "I hope you don't mind, I've found us a holiday."

"A holiday! When?"

"A late offer. A week in Majorca. Winter sun."

"Majorca? I can't go to bloody Majorca!"

"Eric I…"

"For Christ's sake Helen! Show some bloody sense will you!"

They ate in silence and with the meal over Helen gathered the plates and carried them to the kitchen. Eric remained silent and she began to make drinks, tea for Eric and coffee for herself. She sensed him standing quietly in the doorway. "I'm sorry Hel. I shouldn't have gone off at you like that. When did you say?"

"It's for the end of the month. I thought… You've still got some holiday owing…"

Eric hesitated then said, "Alright. Yes, why not."

He went off to phone John James.

"You've only just joined the division," James said. "You've a lot of work to do if you're going to make your target."

"If I don't take some holiday now I'll lose it altogether," Eric countered stubbornly. Christ! He'd never given his people in Scotland this amount of grief over holidays. He'd sometimes had to force Tom to take his. Eric put the phone down and went in to Helen.

"What did he say?"

Eric shrugged. "What can he say? It's my entitlement. I'm going to take it!"

"I can book it then?"

Eric nodded and a wave of relief flooded through her. Eric needed a holiday. They both did.

Their hotel was far removed from the high-rise Costas of the south. Built in traditional Spanish style on the promenade that lined the bay of Puerto Pollensa it was dark inside with panelled walls and a heavy wooden staircase leading to a balcony overlooking the entrance hall. But from their room at the corner of the building they could see palm trees, the sea, and low hills at the southern end of the bay curving into the distance. It was perfect and they walked the deserted promenade into town and sat in the square, watching the quiet activity round the marina. The sun shone, the nights were cool and life was free. They hired a car and drove up through wooded hills to the monastery of Valdemosa and visited the shrine to Chopin in the quiet cell off the long stone corridor. The small veranda above the monastery garden overlooked the island down to distant Palma. They had lunch in the square but despite the sunshine a wind blowing from the orchards in the valley chilled them. Eric shivered. "God!" he said, "If it was like this no wonder it killed him."

"We'll go back to the coast, shall we?" Helen suggested, drawing her jacket over her shoulders. "It's a shame; it's actually quite beautiful here."

Memories of Chopin's cell lingered; the piano on which Chopin had composed with a red rose on the keys and the red and white standard of Poland draped behind; the original manuscript of the Raindrop Prelude scored in Chopin's own hand, so apt for such a cold place of recuperation. Feelings Eric had been trying to hide rose again; rejection, unrecognised talent, a job reluctantly granted. He walked to a wall overlooking another garden. Here it was warmer with a profusion of flowers and olive trees on the hillside and he searched for elusive fragrances coming from below, trying to escape the persistent memory lodged deep in the recesses of his mind. 'I don't want you on my team...' The words jangled and tormented with deadly insistence. "I'm trying to persuade Automotive to take you on," Reeder had said, followed by, "They can't use you. They're too small and too specialised..."

Others followed; 'I don't want you on my team...'

And then, in the middle of September, steadfastly refusing to compromise he had received the unexpected summons to Uxbridge.

"Textiles."

"What?" Eric was incredulous. Textiles was the last thing...

"And you can thank someone else's influence."

"What do you mean...?"

"It was one of your key responsibilities after all." The voice was mocking. "Not that we saw much come of it!" Reeder paused; the decision hovering between them. It was Eric's only option.

"Right." Then, cautiously, "And er, I report direct to you?"

"You'll report to John James. I don't have the time. You'll have UK wide responsibility but you'll be on his team. But it will be up to you to justify your place. They're an elite team."

"I know they're an elite team!" Eric cried. "I used to be a member of that team! In the North! With Ritchie! Before..."

Reeder flicked his hand impatiently. "Your salary will be reviewed in December." Eric's heart briefly lifted, then Reeder continued, "Off management grade of course. You won't expect to be placed on the top scale when you've done nothing to justify it? You'll be working to agreed targets. It gives you an opportunity to improve your earnings..." Echoes from the past. "And your car..." Anger began to froth and seethe. Not simply demotion. Reduced wage. Lower status. Like some wet-behind-the-ears rookie set up to fail! Eric accepted.

Another, softer memory, the farewell dinner with Tom and Margaret. Towards the end of the evening Tom had become unexpectedly bashful. "A little souvenir," Tom said, offering a carefully wrapped parcel.

"To remember us by." Margaret smiled gratefully. "And to say thank-you."

Eric peeled the paper away and lifted the unexpectedly heavy vase from its box.

"Caithness crystal," Tom said. Once more there was moisture in the eyes of the craggy face across the table.

"You shouldn't have Tom. I don't know what to say. We'll treasure it." Eric smiled wistfully at the memory. The little vase now had pride of place in the dining room alongside the cut glass decanter presented to him by Edna...

"You alright Eric?" Helen appeared alongside him at the garden wall overlooking the distant sparkling sea. She was looking at him with a hopeful expression.

"Yes," he said, "I'm fine." He gestured at the garden below the wall. "It's so pretty. And you can catch the scent from the flowers. It must be beautiful in summer."

But the last day, so far away a few days ago, now loomed perilously close. They went to the café at the corner overlooking the marina and sat at an aluminium table with coffee and liqueurs. The promenade and beach were deserted; no 'beautiful people' displaying their tans in bikinis and vying for attention. No middle-aged competing round the hotel pools, layered with the veneer of glamour, yearning for elusive youth and status in the sun, laced with money, brashness and envy. Eric sipped his brandy and said, "I think I like it better at this time of year Hel."

An elderly matron and her spindly husband ambling toward the marina introduced a jarring note to Eric's contemplations. He regarded them with unjustified disapproval. Their youth was behind them, the sweat, toil and passion of their lives beyond their memory. Shapeless baggy shorts flapped about her pasty thighs as they wandered past, lips compressed, afraid of a world defined by their complaints. They receded into the distance, a metaphor of lost youth. Eric swore he would never allow himself to descend to such a narrow, sterile existence. Life still held other pleasures, the touch of naked flesh and tingling anticipation. 'All you need is love.' It had all seemed so simple, back in the days when the Beatles had sung their anthem. All you need is love! He was suddenly aware of Helen's scent and he gazed approvingly across the table. Whatever else, there were still pleasures to give and to receive in their own private, sensual world. Helen's eyes met Eric's and she blushed. Under his gaze she was sixteen again with the golden thread of youth as taut as the first pulse of desire that had passed between them.

"Don't," Helen said, her blushes receding. "You'll have people looking."

"Doesn't matter," Eric replied, contented. "We'll have lunch here shall we Hel?"

"Yes, if you like."

The meal finished they left the cafe and retraced their steps to the hotel and spoke of inconsequential things.

"You were right Hel."

"Right about what?"

"This holiday. It's been so good hasn't it."

"You see," Helen said, "I know what's good for you."

They went up to their room and closed the shutters and undressed and made love in the shaded room and afterwards they lay thinking this was their last afternoon and it was a shame not to be outside, making the most of the sun. But they kissed instead and put other thoughts away, for this was a day of indulgence without the guilt of having to replace stolen time.

After dinner, the packing done they joined other guests in the hotel lounge and found seats in a corner and nodded greetings but the responses were guarded. This was only their second time in the lounge and they were considered 'stand-offish'. The little three-piece band struck up and a solitary couple tried a self-conscious quickstep and sat down, smiling in embarrassment. Eric reached for Helen's hand. "Come on, before they finish." They began to dance, improvising steps together, oblivious to others in the room and the band's air of boredom vanished and they played on. "What the hell," Eric said when they returned briefly to their table for a drink, "what does it matter what they think? We're never going to see any of them again." What if it was lovemaking in dance, an exhibition of temptation and pursuit? They were lovers and the band played for them and they danced unmindful of the rest. And when the evening was over they left and climbed happily to their room and consummated the dance with the curtains open and the shutters thrown wide, with the moon shining in on them and the moonlit sea lapping quietly on the beach below...

The memories of Majorca began to fade. Eric grunted, reading the memo again and the attachments that came with it.

"What are you doing?" Helen asked incredulously. It was Sunday; their return the previous night had been late and they were indulging in a lazy breakfast. "Can't that wait 'till Monday?"

"Annual Review time," Eric replied.

"Put it away until tomorrow. You're still on holiday." She raised the percolator. "More coffee?"

Eric made a note in his diary and rubbed his hands. "You're right. Its holiday time and I love you. What would you like to do today?"

"I ought to go and see my mother." But her words didn't diminish Eric's smile...

Eric returned to work refreshed and optimistic. He had secured a letter of intent from a new customer with the promise of major business in the New Year and went to his Annual Review with all his flags flying. He returned with a seething sense of unfairness.

"Says I've got a lot to do to prove myself! I can't just expect to walk in and expect special favours just because..." He couldn't finish the sentence and gave a gasp of frustration. "I'm not asking for special bloody favours Hel!" To her dismay he began pacing the room again.

"Well what about that new customer?" she asked. "Didn't you tell...?"

"Of course I bloody told him! That doesn't count!"

"Doesn't count! Why...?"

"Not 'One Of Our Objectives'!" Eric spoke with heavy irony. "Whatever that means! It's not New Business!" Eric explained with exaggerated emphasis. "Because it's 'one I was already working on' in Scotland. Because it's 'not one that has been newly identified' since I joined the North! It's 'only a promise' and doesn't count as 'actual' business! He's got a hatful of excuses! He says it's…"

"But you've got a letter of intent…!"

"Oh for God's sake Hel." Eric ran his fingers through his hair remembering John James' actual words. "…it's a piece of opportunistic luck…"

"But you've been working on that account forever," Helen cried and Eric turned on her.

"You're telling me what I already know!" Startled, Helen took a step back and Eric was immediately contrite. "Sorry Hel. I didn't mean to yell at you."

"Come on love, come and sit down. What else did he say? What about salary?"

"Nothing until next year. It will depend on my performance." There was something else. Helen braced herself. "He wants the car," Eric added bitterly. "It's got to be given to… I don't know… somebody at Uxbridge."

"They're taking your car?"

"Yes, they're taking the bloody car!" He wandered across the room. "I'm getting a used one from one of the other regions. A bloody reps car!"

There was nothing she could say. Majorca seemed so far away.

Chapter 50 - Songs of life

Eric did the final run up to Christmas delivering obligatory bottles of good cheer and appreciation to the few deserving customers on his list. Just another day and then a week off, he told himself; three more bottles, one more day then a week to forget about Reeder and John James and the rest. Helen was leafing through a shoal of Christmas cards when he walked in. "There's one here for you," she said, passing the envelope across to him. "Oh, and a letter."

Eric took the card and opened it. "Merry Christmas to you and Helen," he read. His face darkened and he flung the card down. "John James! Bloody hypocrite!"

"There's one from Reeder as well. I opened it because it was addressed to us both."

"Chuck 'em on the fire," Eric mumbled.

"Eric…!"

"I mean it!" he ordered tersely. "Bloody hypocrites! Chuck 'em on the fire! Both of them Hel. And I hope they burn with them!"

"Eric don't. Not at Christmas."

Eric was busy with the letter; it wouldn't peel neatly and he swore in frustration and ripped the envelope open. Reading it the rage evaporated as suddenly as it had risen. "You'll never guess Hel!" Before she could reply he said, "I've got an interview." He sounded incredulous.

"Who with?"

"That agency." He checked the letterhead. "I'd given them up. Bloody hell, Helen. You remember, before we went to Majorca. They want to see me. In the New Year. Twelfth of January." He gave a gasp of joy. "It's a sales manager's job Hel." He grinned and passed the letter to her and Helen saw the spark of real delight in Eric's eyes. "I'll bloody show 'em Hel. Just you wait. I'll bloody show 'em!"

Christmas came and all Eric's cares were put aside. They spent Christmas Eve with Rita and Alec and found Alec fun to be with; he didn't care about status or position and when work was over it was over. He enjoyed the fruits of his endeavours and what was wrong with that? And, Eric said to Helen, that's the way it should be. Isn't it?

New Year's Eve was at Malcolm and Jenny's. Frost sparkled on the roofs and the gardens twinkled with a frost so deep it looked like fallen snow. But warmth and laughter cemented renewed friendships, as though they had never been away, as though the years had vanished and they were young and just married. For one evening at least it felt the way they used to be and even Alec was able to share the laughter their memories brought them. Rita and Helen paused for a brief respite beside the staircase in the hall. "Is it for real Reet?" Helen asked with grave alcoholic sincerity.

Rita smiled. The cares of recent years had fallen from her and she said, "Do you like him Hel? Do you really?" She fixed Helen with a look of entreaty. "Susan likes him. She idolises him. He's so good with her."

Helen raised her glass of Martini Rosso. "Well I'll tell you what I think Reet. You've got a good man there and I'll drink to that!" She sipped and regarded the empty glass with surprise.

Rita scrutinised her own glass and said, "I think we'd better get another. It's nearly time." She drained the remnants and giggled. "I'm glad you like him Hel. He's a... a lovely man. And I'm a very lucky woman. In every way." This time there was nothing forced. "In every way..."

A shout came from the lounge; it was Malcolm calling over the din, "Come on everybody, make sure you've all got a drink, it's nearly midnight."

They refilled their glasses and pushed their way into the gloom of the sitting room. Eric and Alec were with Jenny, looking round for them and Malcolm turned the radio up and the sound of Big Ben rose above the hubbub and everyone shouted the countdown to midnight. Eric seized Helen's hand, she linked hands with Alec and as the ponderous chimes ushered it in they joined in a great cry of 'Happy New Year'. Helen hugged Eric, they kissed and all around them friends were milling in an ecstasy of kissing and goodwill. "A better year this year love," Eric whispered.

"I know." Helen smiled happily. "I can feel it." They linked hands again and joined in the boisterous tradition of 'Auld lang syne'.

The interview was in Leeds. "Now don't undersell yourself Eric." Helen examined him as he stood at the hall mirror, fastening his overcoat against the thin sleet outside. "You look every inch the businessman. I should have said the successful businessman."

He turned to her nervously. "If it was only about looks Hel."

"Remember all the good things you've done Eric. Remember Tom. Even Ireland was a success. You wouldn't have got Scotland without Ireland. You deserve it Eric after the way they've treated you."

"I wish I felt it."

Helen placed her hands on Eric's shoulders and looked deep into his eyes. "You're a good man Eric, and lots of people think so. Go and let them see what a good man you are." She kissed him then brushed her fingertips across his cheek in case her lipstick had marked him. "Remember Gilbert and Sullivan," she said. "You must blow your own trumpet. Don't be modest Eric. You've nothing to be modest about." He kissed her then turned at the door and to her relief Helen saw determination in his eyes. "Love you," she said, suppressing shivers as the cold swirled about her. At the end of the drive he lowered the window and leaned across the passenger seat. She saw him wave and blew him another kiss and mouthed 'good luck' and then he was gone.

Helen filled the hours with speculation but her faith in him was absolute. How could it be any other? She alone knew the dedication Eric applied and the degree of personal loyalty he was capable of commanding. She willed him to phone but she was held back by nagging, superstitious doubt. Would it prejudice the outcome if she prepared to celebrate? Or would Eric want to take her out instead? Would there have to be a second interview. She bit her lip in nervous anticipation and checked the time again. She kept telling herself it was wrong to pin too much on one interview but she didn't care. This was the one. It was fate, she knew it. She hoped it was. She looked out into the sullen darkness of late afternoon. "I hope he's alright," she said and checked her reflection in the mirror.

Eric entered the house quietly.

"How did it go?" Helen asked.

"Alright." His voice was flat and his face expressionless as he draped his overcoat across the banister. "Any tea?"

"Yes... I'll put the kettle on."

He followed her into the kitchen. "I'm not going to get it."

"Why? What did they say?"

"Oh it's... it's not me Hel."

"Have they said you're not going to get it?"

He paused, ruminating. "They've got other candidates better suited."

"But you don't know for sure yet?"

"They'll be inviting people back for a second interview. I... I won't be on the list."

Helen fell silent, arranging tea-cups and saucers on the table. What to say? The kettle began to boil and Eric lifted the kettle from the stand and began making a pot of tea. He gave her a wan smile of acceptance.

"What do you want to eat?" Helen said. "I wasn't sure what to... I could get us something quick. Unless you'd rather go out," she added hopefully.

"Don't mind," he said, and wandered off into the lounge carrying his cup. He could have made the job his. Beyond any shadow of doubt he could have done it. Helen joined him and sat waiting, watching Eric with his tea, brooding on the afternoon's events. All had been going well until that fateful question! God! How could it have...? He didn't even know he was doing it! And then to have to sit like some deserving case and be told...

"You're a good man Mr. Allenby. You've got all the qualifications and experience my client is looking for and I would have no reservations about putting you forward, but..." leaning forward. "Do you mind if I give you a little advice?" Eric had

457

shaken his head dumbly, wondering if this was some kind of new fangled psychological trick. "You've got to control your mouth." It wasn't said unkindly, there was nothing in the man's manner he could take exception to. "You've had a bad experience and I sympathise with you. But my client won't be interested in that. What we need to hear is positive ideas for dealing with the challenges my client is offering."

"But it's all part of the experience that equips you to deal with different issues."

"I dare not risk it. To be brutally frank all I've heard from you is your inability to get along with your colleagues." He held his hand up against Eric's protest. "There's no denying the considerable success you've achieved. And, in different circumstances I've no doubt you could do the same for my client. But you must get over the anger and the resentment you feel. I'm sorry. I hope you don't mind my talking to you like this. I like you Mr. Allenby and I wish you success." He looked at his watch. "There's coffee outside in the waiting room if you'd like one before you leave."

One little question. That was all it had taken. Eric sat nursing his tea in silent disillusion. The resolution of all his problems, the start of a new life had turned on the way he had replied to the words, 'Why do you want to leave your present position Mr. Allenby...?'

The memory of the interview hung round Eric's neck like an albatross. He knew his reputation was compromised and he took refuge in 'working from home' as much as he could, 'thinking' and 'planning strategy'. And meanwhile John James was unrelenting in his pressure for reports and analyses and... 'Swapped one bastard for another. I could do his job standing on my head!' Now it was eleven o'clock in the morning and he was working on a technical report for a customer. Helen interrupted him carefully, "I've made a pot of coffee. You're looking so tired Eric."

"Well of course I'm bloody tired. I'm tired of the job, I'm tired of the company and the people I've got to work with!"

"If only you could get another job."

"I've got a job!" he shouted. "That's the bloody problem, and I'm trapped in it! There's no escape Helen. I wish there were…"

Memories of their courting days when Eric's teenage angst and moods of black despair rising from nowhere engulfed them in misery. Only this was worse. And the crying, that was worse too. But he wouldn't let her get him to a doctor, instead recoiling and glaring at her, rage overtaking his tears. "No! I won't, I won't, there's nothing wrong with me! They'll just give me bloody pills. It's not what I want!"

"Eric, please, you can't carry on like this."

"Oh can't I? I'll show you whether I can carry on or not. Who says I can't?"

"Please Eric."

"Please Eric," he mimicked her cruelly. "It's easy to bloody cry. Oh go on, cry. What have you got to cry about?"

"I can't go on like this either Eric, I can't. It's not just you suffering, it's me too. You've got to do something."

"Oh! Do something? What do you think I'm doing? I'm fighting for my bloody job here and you don't seem to understand what I'm going through."

"I know what I'm going through Eric!"

"Oh for Christ's sake Helen don't start on me again!"

"I'm not starting on you Eric."

The darkness of Eric's mood passed. Helen offered no recrimination for she knew that wasn't the real Eric. But the mindset was becoming more fixed and if this was going to become a permanent way of life she couldn't face it. She tried to tell herself the abuse wasn't about her and she would continue to give him all the love he needed, but she knew that even her love, that transcended everything else, was being eroded and it was breaking her heart…

Snow came on the second Friday in February. In the city it was no more than a dusting, just enough to cause an evening of rush hour chaos, but on the skyline, clearly visible from the suburbs, the high moors remained white.

"Rita's been on," Helen said when Eric finally arrived home. "If it stays snowy on Sunday she says would we like to take Susan sledging in Derbyshire?"

"Yes. Why not?" he replied. The weekend was upon them and no more work.

"I'll call and tell her," Helen said.

"It'll make up for tonight," Eric called.

"Why? What's happening tonight?"

"I had thought we'd go out to dinner. We'll stay in by the fire instead shall we?"

"Sounds nice," Helen said...

On the slopes of Mam Tor above the Blue John mines of Castleton they took it in turns on the sledge with Susan and pretended it was the Cresta Run. Eric and Alec vied for the fastest time and the best line out of the gulley. It was exhilarating fun and after a couple of hours they returned to their cars to shed their waterproofs glowing with exhaustion. "You are coming back for tea, aren't you Hel?" Rita called through the open windows between the cars. "It's all made."

"If you're sure."

"We're expecting you."

They spent a lazy evening together nursing the aches that unexpectedly materialised.

"That was a good day," Alec said with a yawn.

"Be nice if we could go sledging again," Eric said, stifling another yawn.

Rita turned to Alec. "I wish you'd stop yawning. You're making us all feel tired!"

"If the snow stays we could do it next weekend," Helen said, with a smile at Susan.

Alec yawned again. "Snow'll have gone by Tuesday I reckon."

"Can't understand why it's my ribs that are hurting," Eric said, probing his ribcage gingerly.

"It's not that," Rita said, "It's my bum. Just here…" Alec looked on appreciatively and offered to rub it for her. "You'll get more than you bargained for if you start that," Rita laughed.

"Mother!" Susan exclaimed and they all exchanged looks and smiled at her embarrassment.

The evening passed and Eric began to stir from where he was dozing on the settee. Alec got up with him. "A nightcap before you go?" Alec offered, en route to the drinks cupboard.

"I'm going to make us some coffee," Rita said.

"Go on then," Helen replied gratefully. "Then we really must go."

On Tuesday evening Eric received a call. He put the handset down thoughtfully and went into the lounge where Helen was watching television. "Another bloody meeting," he said.

"Who was it?"

"Who d'you think. Bloody James."

"Oh." She returned to her programme.

"He wants to make it an overnight do," Eric said carefully.

"When?"

"Next Monday."

"Oh. You'll be away Monday night then."

Eric watched the programme with Helen for a few minutes then said, "I'll be home Monday night. It's just a one day meeting. It should be finished by then."

"Oh that's alright," Helen answered absently. The programme was drawing to its close and Eric waited until it had finished. "I thought that was going to be better than it was," Helen sighed. "Anyway it's the nine o'clock news next if you want it. Or there's…" She reached for the Radio Times.

"Going to be away Sunday night I'm afraid Hel," Eric said gently.

"What! Sunday as well!" Helen protested.

"He wants us all meet up Sunday evening for dinner then we have this meeting on Monday."

"Where's it being held, this meeting?"

461

"Northern office."

"Well if it's only there why have you got to go overnight? Why Sunday? You don't usually stay overnight when you go there." Helen's voice was filled with resentment. There had been a time when she would have put up with any inconvenience the company imposed: Eric's week long absences to Ireland, meetings in the south, days away in Scotland, the upheaval, last minute changes and the interruptions to their marriage. Not any more! She listened as Eric used the words John James had blithely spoken about team building, bonding, esprit de corps, and the words sounded hollow. "It's not on Eric. You work for them during the week. They can't have you at the weekend as well!"

"Well what can I do?" Eric protested.

"Well you'll have to go I suppose."

"Yes!" Eric exploded, "I suppose I bloody well will. I will go. I can't not go Helen! Can't you see that?"

"It's not fair," Helen replied sullenly, "I know that!"

She got up and left the room.

There were four days of truce. Eric planned on leaving at around four o'clock and they determined Sunday would not be marred by the intrusion of the company. The snow didn't return but freezing winds came and to Eric's relief there was no question of sledging; there wouldn't have been time. He thought about taking Helen for Sunday lunch but abandoned the idea. Two full sized meals in one day would be too much. Perhaps a Sunday morning run into Derbyshire? But nothing came of it and they spent an idle morning trying to pretend it was a normal Sunday instead. Helen warmed croissants for breakfast and they lounged around trying to behave as if time was of no consequence but by lunchtime both he and Helen were aware of his looming departure.

"I'm sorry Hel," he said. "I know what it's like."

"Oh do you? Do you really Eric. What am I going to do this evening while you're away?"

"Oh come on love," he pleaded. "You know I've got no choice."

"Well I just wish you'd tell them how we company wives feel! There must be more than me who feels it's unfair, the demands they make!"

Why did she have to be like this? "It's only one night," Eric pleaded.

"Yes. Well! As far as I'm concerned it's one night too many!"

Eric sighed. She wouldn't be placated and it was going to spoil the rest of the day. He looked at the clock then turned to the window, looking at the clear bright day outside. It was a shame; they should have gone on that run into Derbyshire. The sky was clear and blue and it would have been exhilarating to wrap themselves up against the cold and walk along the banks of the Derwent at Bakewell or Chatsworth Park then come home and spend the afternoon before the warmth of the fire together. But it was too late now, by the time they got changed and ready it would be time to come back. Eric resigned himself to waiting, filling in time until it was time to go. "Would you like a coffee?" he said. "I'll go and put the kettle on."

"I'm going to make lunch in a minute. You won't want anything at teatime I suppose."

"Don't do anything special. Just a sandwich or something…"

"Bacon and egg? I was going to do it for about two o'clock."

"Yes. Fine. I'll…" He drifted over to the door. "Do you want a cup of coffee now? Or later?"

"I'll have one now - if you're going to make it," Helen replied shortly.

Anything to please! Anything to escape Helen's disapproval. He went to the kitchen and put the kettle on and stood waiting for it to boil. It was such a shame to waste the day like this. Perhaps if they had lingered in bed and made love. But somehow it hadn't happened. Although he had sensed Helen wanted to and he wanted her, their minds played cruel jokes. 'It's only a sense of duty to try and please me,' the voice in Helen's head whispered as she lay against the pillows with the morning coffee Eric brought her. And although Eric had been more than usually conscious of her lying by his side the doubts arose. 'She'll think I just want satisfaction; she'll do it from a sense of duty and there won't be any real pleasure for her but she'll try, but trying won't make her orgasm come and it'll be no good and…' And so they had lain, trying to please each other and failing, listening to the clock ticking the time away.

He made a large pot of coffee and took it through to the lounge.

"I'm sorry," Helen said.

"It's alright love. I'm going to start writing for jobs again next week."

"I've got some mushrooms if you'd like them. And fried bread. How does that sound?"

"Yes, nice," he smiled with a nod.

At quarter past three Eric disappeared to begin packing his overnight bag. Helen followed him to the bedroom. "You going already?"

"Well I've…"

"I thought you weren't needed until dinner time!"

"I've got to get there Hel. Anyway I'm not going this minute. But I want to give myself time. In case there's frost, ice on the road…"

"You ought to stay at home if it's that bad!"

"Helen!" he protested wearily.

"I suppose you'll do what you want to do. You usually do."

"Helen! That's not fair. I've got no choice. You know that."

"But you're glad enough to be going!" Helen heard herself utter the unreasonable accusations and wished that she could stop. But it wasn't fair! She was going to spend an evening alone with just the television for company and he would be living it up. No matter what he said, that's what this little trip amounted to, a jolly in a nice hotel and dinner all paid for! "Well I didn't think you'd be going this early!"

Eric tried to cajole her. "Helen, look outside. It's freezing cold. I just want to get the journey over before… I just don't want to have to rush that's all."

"Oh go on then. If you must! If you have to!" She turned from him and left him to zip the bag closed.

Oh what was the point! It was no good. They couldn't carry on like this. Bloody good job he was going. Well out of it! This job wasn't going to bloody work and he was determined about what he'd said earlier, he was going to get another one, come what may. Meanwhile... Eric carried the bag downstairs and took his briefcase out to the car. Helen remained in the lounge as he put the overnight bag in the boot.

"I'm going then Hel." Eric's voice, speaking from the doorway.

Silence.

"I'll have to go Hel," he murmured hesitantly.

"If you've got to go then you'll have to go won't you." Still her voice carried uncompromising resentment.

"Hel, come on..."

"No you go!" she said. "You've got more important..."

"Oh for God's sake!" Eric muttered angrily and strode into the room and bent to kiss her but Helen was determined not to yield and he planted the kiss of duty on her forehead. "I'll call you later," and trying to smother the rising feeling of rage Eric strode out.

She heard the car door slam; before she could reach the front door he was already backing onto the avenue. 'He'll stop and come back' Helen assured herself, but the car swung into the road, turned and he began to drive away. Helen called and waved; she saw his hand rise in a perfunctory, angry farewell and suddenly she wanted to cry for foolishly wasting the day. Just before it vanished from sight at the corner she saw the rear lights of the car come on, two red points of light receding along the road then she returned into the comfort of the house and in the west the late afternoon sky was turning from blue to green, heralding the approaching end of day and the freezing night to come...

EPILOGUE - 1984

i - THE UNACCEPTABLE FACE

It was such an act of betrayal; a betrayal of everything which Helen had held to be sacrosanct. Where was the trust and confidence, where their years of love? Where was the confiding and the sharing of hearts? It was crystallised into the unlovely frozen shape they carried as they came stumbling from the hillside. An unrecognised weeping bundle that thawed and dripped onto the floor of the van as they brought him from the high moorland and down the Snake. Helen's need for tears was as much for herself as for Eric, for there was no 'goodbye' to this form they returned to her. How could she have loved the waxen stranger that lay before her in folds of silk? The features of life were gone and only a pale imitation of what used to be remained. He had gone with no farewell and not returned to her, and she stood and stared and wondered how long she had been alone before this and hadn't known it.

'Not this! Not this!' Helen's heart within her cried but her mind wouldn't clear and her eyes remained dry. She sought the relief of tears but they would not come and now she stood with detachment gazing into the coffin, seeking memories of comfort but the memories wouldn't come either. Only solitude; profound, silent and intense in the scented bareness of the room. Despite herself, Helen's mind shifted to a different, totally inappropriate scene and she willed herself back to the present, watching the body and seeking recognition but she could not feel what she wanted to feel and the unbidden scene rose in her mind again, sunlit and warm, filled with the sounds of children. Waves gently lapping on the sand beneath a summer sky; the weekend that had become an unspoken pilgrimage to Trearddur Bay where so many happy holidays with friends had been spent.

In recent years they had discovered Shirley's guesthouse and always there was the fulfilment of expectation when they entered the room and threw their luggage by the window to gaze at the wide expanse of the unspoiled bay. And Helen's father had loved it too, sharing the childish pursuits among the rockpools, scrambling about at the sea's edge with a bucket and line with a limpet impaled on the

467

hook. The moment of triumph as a crab scuttled unwarily from the cover of the weed for the limpet, to be hoisted from the sea and dropped into the bucket. And she saw herself and Eric lingering in silence by the shore where broken rocks tumbled below the cliff, watching the softly encroaching waves and the letters inscribed in the sand awaiting the first kiss of the sea.

They had returned to the bay, listening with pleasure to the sounds of children and families on the beach, the sounds of childhood, the sounds of their own past. And Helen had brought precious memories and her father with her; not to Trearddur Bay itself but to the intimacy of the bay they loved the most; Porth Dafarch, safe between the arms of the headlands with the derelict chapel in the lee of the cliff, protected from the direct surge of the tide. They had walked in silence on the ledge high above the bay and the sounds of laughter below them mingled with the soft wind and the breaking of small waves on the beach.

"Just here I think," Helen said.

She drew the cork and her gaze wandered from the scene on the beach below the ledge to the flask of ashes in her hand. She turned it slowly and murmured, "I want you to be free dad."

The coarse grey dust poured into Helen's hand and the breeze took a delicate cloud and swept it away over the cliff amongst the June flowers cascading down the cliff face. Helen raised her hand and turned it with a small giving gesture to the air and again the breeze took the ashes and carried them down the cliff, dispersing them amongst the rocks below. Eric stood silently as Helen spoke silent words to herself, watching the cloud of ash vanish. There were tears in Helen's eyes and she turned her face to Eric's shoulder.

"I'm sorry," she murmured, "I know it's daft."

"No it isn't," Eric replied.

"It's just something I felt I had to do."

"I know."

Helen gazed briefly down again then turned away and said, "I want to go down there."

They walked slowly back along the ledge, pausing to smell the scent of flowers growing along the path.

"Thanks Eric." Helen stooped and pulled a knot of small blue flowers from among the grasses.

"It's alright," Eric replied. "It had to be done."

They descended to the beach and walked hand in hand to the rocks at the base of the cliff, close to the water's edge.

"I need a stick."

"Don't worry," Eric replied, "we'll find one."

"Do you think the tide's coming in?"

"It's just turning," Eric said.

They found a thick stem of bladder wrack amongst the rocks and Helen took it and wrote her father's name in the sand and placed the flowers upon it. They stood for a moment then sat in silent contemplation, listening to the sounds around them within the bay, the unchanging memories from the past as the sea gradually crept towards them as though loath to approach, feeling its way toward the small memorial. A group of divers arrived but Eric and Helen remained undisturbed by the divers' banter as they donned their flippers and adjusted the tanks upon their backs. This was the way it had always been, filled with leisure and happiness. And then the divers were gone, stepping backward into the waves, leaning back and rolling from sight under the sea.

Now the lapping water touched the first letter of her father's name, dissolved it and receded, taking that part of her father with it, then another wave reached the name and took that part of it too and as she watched Helen saw the water taking her father from them. But loath to take Helen's tribute yet, the sea pushed the small blue flowers up the beach towards them until the name was almost gone.

Helen rose and watched the sea sparkling in the sun. "I'll always be able to come here and feel that my father is here." She turned to Eric and said again, "Thank you."

"It's alright," he said. "You needed to do it. To say... well... you know."

In the vaguely scented room Helen emerged from her reverie and looked again at the blank face in the coffin. That was the meaning of the betrayal. Everything had been taken, happiness, love, all they had ever meant to one another, all the love that had sustained them. Desperately Helen searched her memory but the pictures were blank and she wept for herself in her loneliness. With her father she'd had a place to return to but with Eric there was only a cold hillside, inaccessible, forbidding and remote. Helen's memories of the places they had loved were barren, for the high moor which had taken Eric had left her with unfulfilled images of his final loneliness. Eric's rejection of her was a final act of cruelty of which Helen had known nothing until... And the secret remained locked within him and through her tears Helen stared at the enigmatic face of Eric and there was nothing. No memories and no past. And the future? She asked the question and the answer was reflected in the bland indifference of that unacceptable face before her. There was nothing beyond the emptiness of the vacant door where she had stood, the car lights disappearing into darkness and a future of unrequited sorrow and unfulfilled expectations robbed of memory. Not a word, not even...

ii - THE CATHEDRAL

The secret Helen sought but could not find remained hidden, just as it had been hidden from Eric for there was no premeditation, no last minute intent; but beauty and peace had unexpectedly presented itself and Eric had followed to where it beckoned...

Across the ravine below the high moors the pine plantation lay gleaming and ghostlike, soft in the deepening shadow of the hillside and the icy green sky was flushed with pale orange sunset. The road climbing along the edge of the ravine was still illuminated by the dying sun and the spikes of ice on the trees and hedgerows glistened like crystal. A strange tranquillity overcame Eric as he drove and the anger with which he had set out on the journey began to dissipate. Oh! That this feeling of calm could be captured. Oh! That he could step into that tranquil, clean and freezing air and be cleansed and purged of all the confusions, the rage and distress oppressing him. His eyes began to mist with regret and he slowed, driving as if in a reverie, unchallenged by any other traffic, alone as far as he could see.

Alone in all the world, Eric moved slowly through the landscape, awed by the frail beauty of the day. And climbing the Snake into the sun he began speaking, softly: 'Helen I'm so sorry. I didn't mean to... But I wish you were here with me to see and feel this magical world. I love you so. But life in the other world awaits with all its traps and betrayals and the struggle is killing me. Joy and spontaneity is replaced by care and desperation and the innocence, all our shared innocence in which we could gaze with wonder and delight at such a scene as this is clouded over. Our happy life, the happiness we created together belongs to yesterday in our hearts and memories... Oh Helen I don't want you to grow to dislike and hate me. I don't want you to talk about me with disparagement as fearful insecurity encroaches with age. But what else am I to do except to go and do their bidding? I want to be with you but I don't have the courage to stay and leave them and the whole beating world locked outside our lives forever...'

The sun was dropping rapidly from the sky and as the shadows began climbing up the sides of the ravine Eric slowed, not driving now but drifting reluctantly along the road. He could not go on. Ahead of him in a hotel they were waiting for him, John James and the rest, waiting for an evening of jollity and chatter. And Eric saw himself with unnerving clarity wearing that mask again, the pathetic face he had to wear, peering with resentment through the eye-slits of the mask, trying to conform to their world, the world in which he knew he was no longer welcome, an outsider carrying the taint of failure. And they were deceived too, for they could no longer tell what was real and what was not. Just so long as he conformed and did their bidding and the real Eric would be hidden from them for he would not allow them to see the hurt they had inflicted, and the weakness he tried to hide as he donned again the unacceptable face...

And with that knowledge Eric knew he could not continue and he cried out to her. 'Oh Helen, Helen I only want to be with you. Not here on this journey but home, back home where I belong...'

471

There was a bend in the road ahead where a gully formed a cleft in the hillside and a small bridge beneath which the frozen stream cascaded into the ravine. And Eric had a sudden overwhelming, irrational desire to savour the texture of the frozen landscape before it was too late. He steered the car onto the verge of rough ground adjacent to the low stone parapet and turned the engine off. No radio, no heater, no fan roaring through the vents. Just profound silence and an intense feeling of solitude in knowing he was the only living being in this pure and frozen world. And as Eric sat there the wind, the small wind that had blown all day died away, and now the landscape had him it held its breath and waited.

He wanted to share it, to belong to this, to experience in full the mystic purity of it all and as he sat the final remnants of light began to die. Suddenly there was so little time. Gingerly, Eric stepped from the car and carefully he placed his hand on the frosted parapet of the bridge. It responded to his touch and when he took his hand away the impression of his fingers was left upon the hoarfrost, his mark, his presence made known, a symbol of acceptance. Beneath Eric's feet the imprint of his foot lay in the brittle grass, the frozen blades broken like a filigree of crystal. He wanted more; to feel it on his face and wash away all the grubbiness of his life in the clear pristine cold of implacable nature and then return as though from vigil, purified and with renewed energy and purpose. Away with the world! Here there are no more compromises, only knowledge. Here was the solitude to commune, free from every symbol of that other hated world. Eric took his overcoat and pulled it close about him for comfort, locking the car safely against intrusion upon this desolate road and walked into the gully, into the hillside and began to climb.

The exertion was great and Eric was out of condition and he began to pant as he climbed, his breath hanging in great clouds about him, grasping clumps of coarse grass and bracken until his glistening wet hands were red and he was glowing with the effort. Until at last, at last Eric was on the summit of the high moor and he stood triumphant, gazing on the frozen landscape gleaming endless and white around him beneath the darkening sky. Oh, he could have shouted with exultation! But all about him was the sky and beneath it the summit of the moors gleaming with soft iridescence stretching away into the distance. And the vast solitude inhibited him.

And standing in seeming endless irresolution Eric became aware of numbness in his feet and the cold penetrating through the layers of his clothes and turning he drank the dew from his lips but he was rooted, unable to leave the spot he occupied beneath the vast, dark cathedral of the sky where the moon now shone, casting a halo of light in heaven and on the earth below. And now the world that Eric knew was beyond him. No tomorrow looming with retribution for his sins; only yesterdays with memories of happiness; people, love, all the love he had ever known stretching endlessly back along the road, down the hill to the house where Helen waited and beyond. Day upon day, month upon month, year upon year along eddying currents of hopes and dreams, an endless river of time. Recklessly Eric crouched then sat waist high in the brittle heather and a wave of cold rising from the ground rushed through him. And with it came a kaleidoscope of images rising from the memory of his childhood where every day was suffused with love and carefree happiness. Throwing stones and fishing; going for a ride, cycling along the country lanes of summer. Christmas; the magic and excitement leading up to Christmas morning... Words came to him from God knows where, half-remembered, sad, disjointed and inaccurate; 'Oh to sleep untroubled as a child...'

Eric shook the memories away and began to panic; he staggered to his knees, rising to his feet but his legs were numb and cramped so that attempting to retrace his steps he stumbled and fell down amongst the heather. And rolling over he searched the sky for comfort but the sky made no response; only the earth sending the cold to purge him of all the anguish that had brought him here and a tear of sadness welled for he should have... But he hadn't known - How could he know where the river of time would lead? Eric looked for meaning up to the stars but there was none, only the implacable intensity of the cold sky, intensely dark beyond the halo of the moon. More half-remembered words; he wished he had brought Helen's little book up here with him, to help him go where women neither smile or weep... Where had he heard that? And he lived again through all the precious moments of his life and felt no anger at the betrayals that had brought it to this; except... he wished...

Now the images were becoming blurred, overlapping as if in a dream. From the void, indistinct at first, then taking form came a sound. Eric closed his eyes and peered into the darkness of his mind. But all that he was conscious of now was music – a sound that he had loved – and Helen, fleetingly glimpsed before the cold enfolded him and began to shut down all his senses save the insistent pulse of music. Oh how he had loved... and been loved. Eric fought to stem the penetrating tide of cold while he searched, just long enough to recognise...? Ah yes, of course... of course... Mozart... the rise and fall of a clarinet, as lonely as the moor on which he lay... the beloved Adagio... And he opened his eyes, searching for Helen's face and saw, instead, the bright moon hanging high above him. He saw her face as large as all the world, holding back the darkness, bathing him in light. Would it be the same for Helen too? Would she see the moon, the beauty of her as he saw her now?

'She is coming for me. Helen... coming for me... nothing but the moon... waiting... waiting for me.'

And as he lay listening to the sounds within his mind Eric ceased to struggle, only gazing until his features relaxed as he gave himself. Only... he wished... he wished... oh how he wished... and his face briefly creased in frustration as more fleeting lines rose into his darkening mind, tumbling, wrong, incoherent and fading. "Helen..." He breathed her name and saw it carried away on the faint eddies of his breath. "Helen..." and saw her face, her lovely smile, and the final jumbled words would not be denied... 'Troubled here I lie, the grass my bed beneath the vaulted sky...'

Silence now and peace.

Silence...

Peace... beneath the fading halo of the moon...

Only... He wished...   He wished...

He wished he could have said...

'Goodbye...'

More great books from the pen of

BRIAN JACKSON

'The Unacceptable Face' is the third in a trio of powerful novels comprising

THE TEARS of AUTUMN

&

SLEEPERS AWAKE

Each dealing with a range of human emotions:
love, guilt, infatuation, insanity and abuse.

'The Tears of Autumn'

Set in the immediate post-war years David's world is torn apart by the loss of his mother and he is sent away to an aunt. Until his father, Bill falls in love with Dorothy. But Bill's failure to comprehend David's needs as he struggles with Dorothy's insanity is the prelude to the story's tragic climax.

'A doomed relationship played out against a backdrop of wartime Britain...'
('The Ross Gazette')

'...far more accomplished than your average romantic fiction...'
('The Gloucester Citizen')

'...a 500 page epic - all the big issues; love, lust, loss and loyalty'
('Herefordshire & Worcestershire Life')

'Powerful... a moving story of heartbreak and love...'
('Country Quest')

'...classic elements of the family saga... tragedy, romance, betrayal.'
('Sheffield Telegraph')

Reader's appreciation:

'A wonderful story... but make sure you have a box of tissues...'
S. Dolby (Ms.)

'The best work published in the last four years that I have read.'
G. Amner (Mr.)

'I wonder if you realise the emotions you arouse in your readers.'
R. Smith (Mr.)

'A brilliant read... desperate to read on'
Penelope Binder

'Beautifully written... one of the best reads I've enjoyed for some time!'
Sally Mottershead

'Compelling from page one to last page'
K.C. Holland

'A wonderful book...reading the last pages I cried.'
Ellie Young (Ms.)

'Sleepers Awake'

Was it suppressed guilt over the death of his son that drove Michael to betray his best friend? As Michael seeks to forget the events of the past in a new life in Africa, awakened memories of a terrible event drive him to commit a final tragic act.

Readers Appreciation:

'A very good read; I would recommend it.'   Matt Hawkes

'Excellent… I was there… it's like he's building a house, building rooms… Why haven't we heard of him before?'   Joan Mason (Ms.)

Also available on AMAZON KINDLE

Boy's Tales
The Chronicles of David

A volume of short stories set in the streets of post-war Sheffield. More than an idyll of childhood, here are the adventures, the bullying and the scares and the awakening emotions as David and 'the gang' grow toward adolescence.

Available on AMAZON KINDLE

…and for Children

The Butterfly Princess
A fantasy for children

When the Land of Faerie becomes threatened by the witch Yaga-Bella and the dragon Gringomel, Julia is kidnapped and transported to the aid of the fairies. How she and her best friend Nickola set out to frustrate the witch's plan aided by the Wizard's cat and Lachnith the fairy is the story of:

'The Butterfly Princess'

With illustrations by
Samuel Callan.

'…fantastic book. Abbi absolutely loved it. Your books are fabulous.'

D. Hughes (Ms.)

ABOUT THE AUTHOR

Brian Jackson is a Yorkshireman, born in Sheffield, England. An avid reader of history and biography he has travelled extensively in Europe and the USA. He and his wife share a love of theatre, in which Brian has won awards both as actor and Director. He now lives in Herefordshire.

47039952R00271

Printed in Poland
by Amazon Fulfillment
Poland Sp. z o.o., Wrocław